ROGER'S

W9-BEG-062

"As ROGER'S VERSION unfolds, adultery—as well as the attendant emotions of jealousy, guilt, and resentment—begins to push the question of religion off center stage, giving Mr. Updike plenty of room to examine, with his usual skill, the patternings and shadows of domestic life in the middle class.... his command of narrative techniques—his orchestration of emotional and physical details, his modulation of voice, his quick, lyric facility with language—is so assured in this novel, so fluent...the reader is soon drawn irresistibly into Roger's fictional world...another eloquent chapter in Mr. Updike's continuing effort to memorialize the way we live today."

The New York Times

"Wonderfully tricky and nakedly sharp-minded...it is one of the pleasures of the novel to watch the author both outmaneuver avalanches of theories by other folk...and also outfox chatty, raunchy Roger.... Updike's Roger Lambert is a perfectly 20th-century beast—boastfully wicked in all directions."

The Washington Post Book World

JOHN UPDIKE

"One of the most intelligent and resourceful of contemporary novelists."

The New York Times Book Review

"A superior novel. The aggressiveness of Updike's imagination is often a marvel, and he still has few peers in his use of language."

"John Updike is a straight-A student who just happens to write the most vivid prose in America. . . . Updike's world is so distinctive, so utterly his own, that he's coined a word to describe its quality: *Updikeness*. It's a world that encompasses adulterous dentists, suburban wives, used-car dealers, and golf-obsessed priests—a world so recognizably American that it's impossible not to come across ourselves in some corner of Updike's popular *oeuvre*."

ROGER'S VERSION

"Churns with Updike's brilliance . . . one feeds on the sheer wizardry of Updike's syntax, his intellectual agility, his consummate drollery. Like every Updike novel ROGER'S VERSION contains as many main events as you care to spotlight . . . Updike, Protestant novelist extraordinaire."

"Updike has provided fascinating argument, elegant prose, and plenty of the sex he is famous for."

Fawcett Crest Books
by John Updike

BECH IS BACK

THE CENTAUR

THE COUP

COUPLES

MARRY ME

A MONTH OF SUNDAYS

OF THE FARM

PICKED UP PIECES

PIGEON FEATHERS

THE POORHOUSE FAIR

PROBLEMS

RABBIT IS RICH

RABBIT REDUX

RABBIT, RUN

ROGER'S VERSION

TOO FAR TO GO

John Updike

ROGER'S VERSION

FAWCETT CREST • NEW YORK

A Fawcett Crest Book
Published by Ballantine Books
Copyright © 1986 by John Updike

*Heartfelt thanks to Michael L. Dertouzos, Jerome Kanter, and
David Hawkes for generously sharing their knowledge of
computers. And to Jacob Neusner for helping with the Hebrew.
Ideas in this novel derived, in part, from books and articles by
Paul Davies, Robert Jastrow, George Gale, Ann Finkbeiner, Sir
John Eccles, Fred Hoyle, Chandra Wickramasinghe, Martin
Gardner, P. W. Atkins, James S. Trefil, Alan H. Guth and Paul J.
Steinhardt, Gerald Feinberg and Robert Shapiro, Alan
MacRobert, Norman Macbeth, A. G. Cairns-Smith, Francis
Hitching, and Gordon Rattray Taylor.*

Grateful acknowledgment is made to the following for permission
to reprint previously published material: Heroic Music: excerpt
from "Girls Just Want to Have Fun" by Robert Hazard. © Heroic
Music 1979. Permission to use lyric granted by Heroic Music
(ASCAP), for songwriter, Robert Hazard. 65 West Entertainment
Company, Inc.: Excerpt from "She Bop" by C. Lauper, S. B.
Lunt, G. Corbett, and R. Chertoff. © 1983 by Rellla Music
Corp., Noyb Music Co., Perfect Punch Music (BMI), Hobbler
Music (ASCAP), C. Lauper, S. B. Lunt, G. Corbett, and R.
Chertoff. Used by permission.

Library of Congress Catalog Card Number: 86-45298

ISBN 0-449-21288-2

First International Edition: April 1987
First U.S. Edition: September 1987

To what purpose is this waste?
        —Matthew 26:8

O infinite majesty, even if you were not love, even if you were cold in your infinite majesty I could not cease to love you, I need something majestic to love.
        —Kierkegaard, *Journals* XI²A 154

What if the result of the new hymn to the majesty of God should be a new confirmation of the hopelessness of all human activity?
        —Karl Barth, "The Humanity of God"

god the wind as windless as the world behind a computer screen
        —Jane Miller, "High Holy Days"

I

i

I have been happy at the Divinity School. The hours are bearable, the surroundings handsome, my colleagues harmless and witty, habituated as they are to the shadows. To master a few dead languages, to parade sequential moments of the obdurately enigmatic early history of Christianity before classrooms of the hopeful, the deluded, and the docile—there are more fraudulent ways to earn a living. I consider my years spent in the active ministry, before meeting and marrying Esther fourteen years ago, if not exactly wasted, as a kind of pre-existence, the thought of which depresses me.

Yet when this young man called me at the school and, requesting an appointment, named my half-sister Edna's daughter Verna as a friend of his, and he explained that he, like me, came from the Cleveland area, my wish to hang up was less strong than my curiosity. I named an afternoon and an hour, and so he came. The time was late October, a time in New England of golden leaves and tumultuous, luminous skies.

He was, I saw as he came in the door, the type of young

man I like least: tall, much taller than I, and pale with an indoors passion. His waxy pallor was touched along the underside of his jaw with acne, like two brush burns, and his eyes in their deep bony sockets were an uncanny, sheepish, unutterably cold pale blue, pale almost to colorlessness. He had been wearing a wool knit navy-blue watch cap, which he stuffed into the pocket of his army-surplus camouflage jacket as he stood there awkwardly, taking up too much space and in his embarrassment blinking and looking around, at my bookshelves and through the lancet window beyond my head. His dirty-looking, somewhat curly brown hair, I could see at his temples, was already beginning to thin.

"These are lovely buildings," he said. "I've never been to this part of the university before."

"It's a bit out of the way," I told him, wishing it were even more so. "Where do you normally, uh, hang out?"

"Computer labs, sir; I'm a research assistant for a special graphics project the Cube has taken on on a combined government and private-sector grant. Artificial intelligence is what the higher-ups down there really care about—you know, yoking hundreds of minis together to modulize the problem, trying to develop rules that keep the search tree from expanding exponentially, using heuristics to generate new heuristics, and so on. But in the meantime it's data processing and bionics and now graphics that keep the wheels greased, or the bread buttered, or whatever."

I am a depressive. It is very important for my mental well-being that I keep my thoughts directed away from areas of contemplation that might entangle me and pull me down. The young man had, with his computer-talk, conjured up just such an area. The Cube is the jocular local name for the University Computer Research Center, which is housed in a new building whose edges are all equal in length. I have never entered it, nor do I hope to. I smiled, and told him, "We haven't yet introduced ourselves. I, of course, am Roger Lambert."

"Dale Kohler, sir. I really appreciate your seeing me." His handshake was just as I expected: bony, cool as wax, and too earnestly firm in its grip. He did not seem to want to let go.

"Let's sit down. You said you know my sister's daughter, Verna. I'm very curious to know how she's doing. Very. That was a set of shocking developments."

In sitting opposite me in the official wooden armchair the university provides to hundreds of its offices and rooms (each element, an accompanying brochure boasts, carved of a different wood—the seat of adamant oak, the spindles of fine-grained maple, the curved arms of ruddy cherry, and so on), the boy somehow got a pocket of his camouflage jacket caught, and there was a certain amount of apologetic heaving and writhing before he was settled. His knuckles and wrists looked huge, morbidly enlarged. I judged his age to be in the late twenties; he was no fledgling student. You see many of them in a university town, these people who settle into the casual uniform and cunning ingenuousness of the youthful learner as though it is a permanent, and paying, profession. Some grow gray hair and great bushy tails of ill-fed progeny while still innocently pursuing knowledge.

"Which do you mean was shocking?" asked the young man, who, awkward as he seemed, had something challenging, something of impudence and insinuation, about him. He offered me a choice: "The race of the father, the fact that the father has copped out, or the crummy way her parents have treated her?"

3

I took offense. All of us at the university are racially liberal. "The race, of course, was and is dandy, other things being equal. But since they so clearly weren't, I *was* surprised that the child went ahead and had the baby."

My visitor shifted weight, like a man with too full a wallet in his hip pocket, and I was reminded to reach for my pipe. "Well . . ." he began.

The pleasures of a pipe. The tapping, the poking, the twisting, the cleaning, the stuffing, the lighting: those first cheek-hollowing puffs, and the dramatic way the match flame is sucked deep into the tobacco, leaps high in release, and is sucked deep again. And then the mouth-filling perfume, the commanding clouds of smoke. Oddly, I find the facial expressions and mannerisms of other men who smoke pipes stagy, prissy, preening, and offensive. But ever since I, as an unheeded admonition to Esther some years ago, gave up cigarettes, the pipe has been my comfort, my steeplejack's grab, my handhold on the precipitous cliff of life.

"Once she was pregnant," he confided to me out of his lopsided slouch, "it was a religious decision." His face—his uncanny long face with its swipes of acne and a curious unshaven fuzz high on the same jaws, an incipient fur vivid in the light from the tall window behind my head—expressed displeasure at my smoke. This generation, which by and large has lost all inculturated instinct for the Judaeo-Christian sacral, has displaced much of its religiosity onto anti-pollution, ranging from the demand for smoke-free zones in restaurants to violent demonstrations in front of nuclear-power plants.

"Religious?" I framed the word between aggressive moist puffs on my pipe.

"Sure. Not to kill it."

4

"You're of the same school of thought, then, as our President?"

"I'm not saying I am, I'm just saying Verna's not getting an abortion had some reasoning and feeling behind it, but now . . ."

"Now?" The tobacco was still burning on only one side of the bowl. I began to feel cross-eyed—another of those habitual expressions that irritate me in my fellow pipe-smokers.

"Now it's not so good, sir. The little girl's about one and a half, and I guess that's a demanding age, at least Verna says the kid is driving her crazy, babbling and getting into things all the time. She says it *clings* to her and I say to her, What else do you expect it to do, go out and get a job? I try to swing by once or twice a week at least; but this project she's living in . . . I don't want to sound racist—"

"Yes?"

"It's not a good place. She has no real friends."

"Odd," I offered (the pipe smoothly functioning at last), "her decision to come *here* to live."

"Well . . . I don't know how much you know."

"Very little. My father divorced and remarried when I was very small—the precipitating affair had evidently been progressing while my mother was pregnant with me—and with his new wife, he had this little girl, this other child, scarcely a year after I was born. I used to see her, my sister, or half-sister I should say, only when visiting *him*—sometimes, I admit, for as much as a month during summer vacations. So Edna and I didn't grow up together at all in the ordinary sense; and I scarcely knew her own family, once *she* married, living as they all did in Cleveland Heights. Her husband and Verna's father, as she may have already described to you, is this quite rigidly philistine, cold-blooded

brute of Norwegian descent called Paul Ekelof who works as
an engineer and now is some sort of executive at one of the
Republic steel plants down in the Flats, along the river—
why am I telling you all this?"

"Because I'm interested," Dale Kohler said. His pious
smile was insufferable.

"I'm almost done. Edna had Verna rather late in life—
she was well past thirty—and I was long gone, first as a
minister, and then as a professor. So, yes, I saw the child
very little, and didn't know what was expected of me when
my sister, my half-sister, wrote me over a year ago to say
how upset they had been with Verna, and that she had
moved to *here,* of all places."

"Well," Dale said, yet again, "it's East, and I think she
thought, with the half-black child, it might be more toler-
ant, being a university town, and also I think Verna thought
there would be a lot to do—art films, free lectures. She and
I met, for instance, at this symposium on Nicaragua at a
Congregational church. We got to talking over the Kool-
Aid and discovered we were fellow Buckeyes! Also, I think
she wanted to put distance between herself and her parents,
she was so angry with them. Not that Cleveland is that far
away any more; they have these nonstop flights, you used
to have to come down in Pittsburgh, and if you go standby
it's almost as cheap as the bus."

One's time is hard to put a value on: much of it, clearly
and inevitably, is spent to no immediate profit, and one of
the Christian consolations, as I construe them, is that the
Lord's unsleeping witness and strict accountancy redeems
all moments from pointlessness, just as His Son's sacrifice
redeemed Time in the larger sense. But *my* time, surely, was
ill-spent in sitting and listening to the praises of the sched-
uled air service to Cleveland, that most dismal and forsaken

of rust-belt metropolises, to which nothing but funerals has induced me, for thirty years, to return. Why was this young man seeming to suggest that I should fly back there, back to that muggy, suffocating heartland? Why was he here at all? How had we become entangled, in this sudden stilted intimacy?

"How is she," I asked him, "as a mother? Verna, not Edna." Of Edna's mothering I had seen, at wide intervals, something: like most of what she did, from playing tennis to driving that Studebaker convertible my deplorable father had bought for her when she turned eighteen, it was impulsive and slovenly, characterized by an absent-minded and serenely selfish carelessness she expected the world to forgive and overlook for the sake of her "warmth," her fleshly charm. From infancy on, Edna had had a peculiar carnal pungence, a scented sponginess to her flesh; when, she a bumptious thirteen and I a recessive fourteen and condemned to spend all of August with my father and my vapid stepmother (whose name, Veronica, seemed as faded and prissy as she, the vampishness that had pre-natally wrecked my life collapsed into the dreariest sort of domestic respectability) in Chagrin Falls—when, I say, Edna began to menstruate, I had the powerful impression that the days of her "period" flooded the house with her sticky, triumphantly wounded animal aroma, even to the corners of my room with its boyish stink of athletic socks and airplane glue. Edna had had naturally curly hair and an obstinate, pudgy face that sprouted a dimple when she chose to smile.

"Well," the boy allowed, "I don't know how good anybody would be, only nineteen and figuring the world is passing you by, with just this baby and the welfare check for company. She says what she really minds is not having graduated from high school, but when I tell her there are these courses you can take, and equivalency tests and so on, she tunes me right out."

"If she were good at tuning in, she perhaps wouldn't have got so involved with this young black man and had his baby."

"You'll pardon my saying this, sir, but you sound a lot like her mother when you say that."

A rebuke in this, and an aggression in his repeated sirring of me. I resented it. *Ressentiment:* according to Nietzsche, the kernel of Christian morality. I have a dark side, I know, a sullen temper, an uprising of bile that clouds my vision and turns my tongue heavy and ugly; it is the outward manifestation of my tendency to be depressed. In the professor's role, I have found it easier to control (perhaps because less often stimulated) than in the clergyman's. I generated some more smoke as pesticide against my visitor and, ignoring his coupling of me with that brainless Edna, asked him from behind my armor of amiable tweed, "Is there anything, you think, I could do for Verna?"

"Do what I do, sir. Remember her in your prayers."

My inner cloud darkened. The present generation of Jesus addicts, though not, like their Sixties predecessors, wildly intoxicated on such heady blends as LSD and the NLF, have a boneless, spaced-out benignity and an invincible historical innocence that tend to madden me. I smiled. "That is certainly the least I can do," I told him. "Do give her my love when you see her next."

"Also, if I may say, you could visit her yourself. Here she has been in your neck of the woods for over a year, and—"

"And she has not once sought to reach me. Surely there is a message there. Now, was there anything else you wanted to talk to me about?"

"Yes." He leaned melodramatically forward. His corneas had a fishy shine, vertically speared by the reflected shape of the tall pointed window at my back. "God."

"Oh, really?"

"Sir, have you been following any of the recent developments in physics and astronomy?"

"Only in the vaguest way. The moon shots, and the rather marvellous photographs of Jupiter and Saturn."

"Begging your pardon, but that stuff is utterly trivial. Even our whole galaxy, relatively, is a trivial case, though symptomatic, you could say. Professor Lambert . . ."

A long pause while his pale eyes lovingly glittered at me. "Yes?" I seemed compelled to answer, like Lazarus awakened.

"The most miraculous thing is happening," my visitor proclaimed with a painful sincerity, probably overrehearsed. "The physicists are getting down to the nitty-gritty, they've really just about pared things down to the ultimate details, and the last thing they ever expected to happen is happening. God is showing through. They hate it, but they can't do anything about it. Facts are facts. And I don't think people in the religion business, so to speak, are really aware of this—aware, that is, that their case, far-out as it's always seemed, at last is being *proven*."

"That sounds charming, Mr.—"

"Kohler. Like the plumbing."

"Kohler. What kind of God is showing through, exactly?"

The boy seemed shocked. His tufty, rather nibbled-looking eyebrows lifted. "*You* know," he told me. "There's only one kind of God. God the Creator, Maker of Heaven and Earth. He made it, we now can see, in that first instant with such incredible precision that a Swiss watch is just a bunch of little rocks by comparison."

While tapping out my pipe on my square-edged glass ashtray with its chipped corners, I took the opportunity to glance behind me out the window; its neo-Gothic panel of ornamentally leaded transparency contained, from bottom to top, the lank grass and reddening oaks of the quad, and then a construction site throwing up dust behind a chain-link fence (our neighbor the University Chemical Research Annex expanding), and then an autumnal sky loaded with radiant, baroque clouds. Clouds are strange: at times they seem gigantic sculptures, bulging with three-dimensional form like those musclebound marble Berninis gesturing halfway up Saint Peter's walls, and at other times, the exact copies of these same clouds, mere smudges of vapor, virtually nonexistent. They are with us, and yet not with us.

My visitor waited for my gaze to return to him before he asked me, "How much do you know about the Big Bang theory?"

"Very little," I told him, with I suppose some agnostic smugness, "except that it is evidently correct."

He affected pleasure at my answer, using that hoary teacher's trick, positive reinforcement for the sluggish student. "Right! And believe me, sir, the scientists have had a hard time with it: they've been betting on eternal, unchanging matter ever since Lucretius. But they've had to swallow the pill, and now they're finding out it's even bitterer than they thought."

How had I become captive, I kept asking myself, to the milky effrontery, the assaultive verbalizing earnestness, of this youth? Verna, I remembered, and behind her, a cloud of odorous memory, Edna, my semi-sister, my shadow in blood.

"There are three main problems with the Big Bang theory," my visitor informed me, sketching with his oversize hands as if with blackboard chalk. "The horizon problem, the smoothness problem, and the flatness problem. Uniformity: the background microwave radiation of three K discovered in 1964 has been observed to be uniform within one part in ten thousand, but we're dealing here with sections of the sky separated by more than ninety times the horizon distance, the distance that light could have travelled at the time the radiation was emitted. So how could these regions have communicated with one another to achieve the uniformity? It seems impossible. Smoothness: to have galaxies now, you had to have had inhomogeneities in the primal fireball, but just short of absolute smoothness—absolutely smooth, you'd have no clumping; a little bit too much, you'd have much too much. There are figures for all this, but I don't want to bore you. The fact is, for galaxies lasting billions of years to exist at all is statistically very strange. Flatness: the total energy, that is, everything in the universe, and the expansion rate of the Big Bang had to be initially in precise balance, virtually, for the ratio to be what they observe it to be today, between point one and two point oh. This may seem like a spread, between a tenth and two, but in fact it means that, for the ratio to be this close today, energy density at the time of the Big Bang had to equal the expansion rate to one part in ten to the fifty-fifth power: that's ten followed by fifty-five zeros. Now, if that's not a miracle, what is? A little, *really* little, bit less outward push, and the universe would have collapsed back onto itself in a couple million years—that's nothing, in cosmic terms. I mean, the human species has been around that long. A little bit *more*, and the stars and galaxies never could have formed; matter would be blowing away too fast, out the window, so to speak. The odds of its working out the way it did are just about as long as you taking some kind of a supergun and hitting an inch-high target on the other side of the universe, twenty billion light-years away." The young man held his fingers up to indicate the dimension of an inch. The gap seemed a gunsight between our pairs of eyes.

I hazily asked, "Isn't this the same thing as an open versus a closed universe? Didn't I read a while back that they settled it was open?"

"They tend to say that; but nobody knows how much dark matter there is in the galaxies, or if the neutrino has mass. The point is, it's debatable, it's that close. For it to be that close now, it had to be terrifically close then, at the outset. Why? Why so? These amounts are arbitrary, they could have been *any*thing. And there's dozens of amounts like them that have to be *just* what they are in order to give life time to evolve. Take the strong force, which binds the atomic nuclei together. Make it five percent weaker, and the deuteron couldn't form and there would be no deuterium, which means the main nuclear reaction chain used by the sun couldn't function; if it were two percent *stronger,* two protons could stick together and the existence of the di-protons would make hydrogen so explosive the present universe would consist entirely of helium. In either case, we wouldn't be here, would we? There wouldn't even be a here to be here *in.*"

"But if this God of yours—"

"Or take the weak force. You know what the weak force is, don't you, sir?" In his expository excitement he had been forgetting the "sir."

"It causes decay in atoms?" I guessed.

"That's close enough. It's about ten-to-the-tenth times weaker than the strong, which is mighty weak; but if it were any weaker, neutrinos couldn't exert enough pressure on the outer shell of a dying star to bring about a supernova, and without supernova explosions there would be no heavy elements scattered in space, and planets like the Earth wouldn't exist, and structures like you and me with the carbon and calcium and iron our bodies have to have wouldn't exist either. Or take the mass of the neutron: if it were only point nine nine eight of its actual value, that's point oh oh two less, less than *that* much"—his fingers now measured a gap so small that only a hairline of his eyes' uncanny blue showed through—"free protons would decay into neutrons via positron emission and there would be no atoms at all!"

His bony bright hands moved with such rapidity through this last revelation that it seemed, in the leaden but radiant filtered afternoon light of my office, he had indeed pulled the divine rabbit from the cosmic hat. I took in breath to make some obvious objections.

He leaned forward, closer, so that I saw photons bounce from the bubbles of saliva in the corners of his mouth. He insisted, "The sun. Yellow stars like the sun, to give off so much steady heat for ten billion years or so, are balanced like on a knife edge between the inward pull of gravity and the outward push of thermonuclear reaction. If the gravitational coupling constant were any smaller, they'd balloon and all be blue giants; any smaller, they'd shrivel and be red dwarves. A blue giant doesn't last long enough for life to evolve, and the red dwarf radiates too weakly to ever get it started. Everywhere you look," he instructed me, "there are these terrifically finely adjusted constants that have to be just what they are, or there wouldn't be a world we could recognize, and there's no intrinsic reason for those constants to be what they are except to say *God made them that way.* God made Heaven and Earth. It's what science has come to. Believe me."

"It's not my business to doubt you, Mr. Kohler," I said, seeing that he had momentarily finished. As he settled back into his chair, it seemed to me that even at this pitch of eloquence, which had reddened his unhealthy cheeks (his face was simultaneously bony and doughy, a face fed on junk food) and which made his acne flare, his eyes somehow floated above his passionate facts. There was a happiness to their pallor but also a coolness, a withdrawal. It would take more of an attack than I could mount to shake him. I set down my pipe and picked up from my desktop a pencil—hexagonal, green, stamped with the name of the private school, PILGRIM DAY, that my twelve-year-old son attends; I had evidently stolen this from him—and focused upon its point, saying, "I do worry a bit about this concept of probability. In a sense, every set of circumstances is highly improbable. It is highly improbable, for instance, that a particular spermatozoon out of the millions my father ejaculated that particular day" (my father, who deserted my mother and me and skedaddled from job to job in the middle echelons of the Midwestern insurance business, whose idea of pleasant conversation was to relate an off-color joke he had heard that morning in the barbershop, who wore cologne and cuff links and an ex-athlete's fragile false heartiness to the day of his death, of a cerebral embolism; where had he come from, spurting into these immense matters?) "would make its way to my mother's egg and achieve my particular combination of genes; but *some* such combination, given their youth, attitude toward birth control, et cetera, was likely, and mine *as* probable as any other. No?"

"That's good," my visitor had the gall to tell me, "except that, as you say, babies are born all the time, and there's only one universe, that we know of. That's what the scientists, to keep their old atheist materialism, are trying to get around. Rather than admit the obvious, that some purposeful Intelligence fine-tuned the physical constants and the initial conditions, they're proposing a crazy many-universes theory, in which ours is just the one that happens to have the right conditions for intelligent life eventually to emerge. Some of them don't actually *say* there are all these other universes out there, or back there, somewhere, collapsing or dispersing or churning around unobserved; they just say that because we are here observing, the universe has to be such-and-such, which they think takes the sting out of it, much as if you said, 'Of course the planet Earth has water and oxygen, because we're here.' That's the anthropic principle, which, in its weak form at least, is simply a way of begging the issue. Another theory claims that there's a kind of infinite branching out of quantum-theory indeterminacy. You know, when an electron hits a proton, the wave scatters both left and right; if measurement indicates that the particle in fact went right, then the lefthand part of the wave collapses. Where did it go? It went, according to this theory, into another universe, and so did the observer, a duplicate of him with this small difference, and his instruments, and the room he was in, and the building, and on and on. Furthermore—like I said, it's crazy—you don't need an observer for the splitting, it happens whenever a quantum transaction takes place anywhere, on any star: the universe splits into two, over and over, all the time. No way to check it, but they're there, all these other universes, a million million every microsecond. I mean, *really*. Another guy lately, to get around these really severe embarrassments— severe unless you simply say God is the Creator—proposes that in some ridiculously short fraction of the first second of the Big Bang the universe, because of some theoretical anti-gravitational force that nobody has ever seen in action, expanded exponentially, doubling every ten-to-the-minus-thirty-fourth second or so, increasing the diameter of the universe, which was smaller than that pencil point to begin with, by a factor of ten to the fiftieth before cooling back to normal expansion; so instead of the many universes we have the one big *fat* universe, so to speak, of which the universe we see, right out there to the quasars at ten billion light-years and beyond, is a tiny, and I mean tiny, fraction, like a Ping-Pong ball in Shea Stadium. And they think religious people stretch the facts. These guys are *des*perate, the ones aware of the problem. They are *squirm*ing."

He seemed too happy about this—un-Christian, even. "I suppose a fundamental question," I ventured, "about any modern attempts to relate the observed cosmos to traditional religion becomes the sheer, sickening extravagance of it. If God wished, as Genesis and now you tell us, to make the world as a theatre for Man, why make it so unusably vast, so horribly turbulent and, ah, crushing to contemplate? The solar system, with an attractive background spatter of stars, would have been quite enough, surely. To have the galaxy on top of that, and then all those other galaxies . . ." My pencil point minutely gleamed, magnitudes bigger than the original universe. With enough scrutiny the faceted sides of graphite left by the sharpening could be seen in the gray light, and flecks of carbon granule. Since the age of eight, when I was praised by the family ophthalmologist for prattling off even the bottom line of his chart, I have taken an innocent pride in the keenness of my eyesight, which reading glasses, acquired seven years ago when I was forty-five, amplify but otherwise leave uncorrected.

"I know. It's a stunner," the boy agreed, in one of his irksome glissandos of unexpected serenity and amiable yielding. "Maybe it's like a demonstration. Of what infinity is. So we won't say glibly, 'God is infinite.' But it's all just figures, isn't it? Measure. And there are things we can't measure. We can't measure our selves, for example—"

"Or love, you're going to say."

"I was?"

"I think you were. Mr. Kohler, I've been dealing with your age group ever since I retired from the ministry, took my Th.D. at Union, and found an assistant-professorship up here. You're all wild about love, the word if not the actuality. The actuality, my impression is, is somewhat thorny."

"Sir, I think I may be older than the age group you usually deal with. I'm twenty-eight. From Akron, originally. I got my B.S. in computer science at Case Western Reserve and then spent a year pulling my head together being a fire watcher in the Salmon River Mountains in Idaho. Then I came east, and I've been taking grad courses and involved in various computer research projects ever since."

"You're not, then, a physicist?"

"Nawp: I sort of backed into cosmology in connection with my personal philosophy. The physicists, they just want to deal with the numbers, they don't want this stuff to get out, you have to dig it out. The best brains working on the real implications—Carter and Hawking and I suppose you'd have to include Hoyle—are over in England; all the Americans care about is GUT, for Grand Unified Theory, and that's just numbers. Numbers about hot air, really. I mean really *hot*, like ten-to-the-twenty-sixth degrees Kelvin, and you have the strong and electroweak forces theoretically combined, and symmetry domains coming out of the freezing, and one-dimensional string defects that would weigh a million tons if they were long enough to go across an atom, and I can't begin to tell you what-all other stuff, none of which they can prove for beans. According to GUT, protons have to decay, but nobody's found a decaying proton yet, and if proton life were any less than a million times the age of the universe, you and I would be as radioactive right this minute as the core of a nuclear reactor. Like I say, hot air. Don't get me off on it; I try not to get spiteful. It's just that these atheists are so *smug;* they don't even think there's an *ar*gument." He was relaxing, his legs growing so long that his feet in their scuffed Hush Puppies were underneath my desk.

"Twenty-eight is a very common age, actually," I said, "for people to turn back to religion."

"I never turned away," this young man said. The pious often, I have noticed, have a definiteness that in others they would judge rude. "I've stayed the way I was raised. My mom and dad had so little to give me intellectually I couldn't afford to give up anything. The walls in the house were so thin I used to hear them praying together sometimes." *Why am I telling him this?* I could see him asking himself. His hands began to move, on the defensive attack. "Anyway, what you call religion around here is what other people would call sociology. That's how you teach it, right? Everything from the Gospels to *The Golden Bough,* Martin Luther to Martin Luther· King, it all happened, it's historical fact, it's anthropology, it's ancient texts, it's humanly *interesting,* right? But that's so safe. How can you go wrong? Not even the worst atheist in the world denies that people have been religious. They built these temples, followed these taboos, created these traditions, et cetera. So what? Your average normal cheerful nonbeliever says it was all poetic, pathetic foolishness, like a lot of other aspects of human history, like *all* its aspects, really, considering that everybody dies and until he does spends most of his energy trying to feed himself, stay dry and warm, and, what's the word—?"

"Propagate?" I offered.

"Sure," he said, slouching lower. "I looked over your catalogue before I came, and studying all that stuff doesn't say *any*thing, doesn't com*mit* you to anything, except some perfectly harmless, humane cultural history. What I'm coming to talk to you about is God as a *fact,* a fact about to burst upon us, right up out of Nature."

"So you've said," I said, setting down my son's sharp pencil and discreetly glancing at my watch; my two-hour seminar in ante-Nicene heresy met at three. Today we were to take up Marcion, the first great heresiarch. He plausibly argued that the God of the Old Testament and that of the New were two different Gods—a ditheism that blended into Gnosticism and anticipated Manichaeism. He poured scorn upon the Hebraic Creator-God, who created evil, made pets of licentious and treacherous rascals like King David, and was responsible, this ignorant, vacillating God, for the humiliating and painful processes of copulation, pregnancy, and childbirth, the contemplation of all of which filled Marcion with nausea. He had a case. "Be all this as it may," I said with deliberation, "what exactly can I do for you, Mr. Kohler?"

A certain pinkness of agitation again suffused my visitor's unhealthy skin, and his voice dropped so that I had to strain to hear. "I was wondering, sir, about a grant. Whether the Divinity School would like me to pursue, you know, what we've been talking about. This evidence that proves that God exists."

"Well. Worth proving, let us assume. But, as you've so shrewdly described our curriculum here, I doubt we could spare a dime. We're very comfortable, according to you, in asserting that so-called religions once did exist and in teaching Geez and Aramaic to the fanatically interested."

"Sir, don't get so huffy, please. I don't know what you personally believe."

"I believe quite enough, I think. Though it's been fourteen years since I served my last parish, I still am an ordained Methodist minister in what they call good standing. Also, let me tell you, I have a class to teach in seventeen minutes."

"Dr. Lambert, aren't you excited by what I've been trying to describe? God is *breaking through*. They've been scraping away at physical reality all these centuries, and now the layer of the little left we don't understand is so fine God's face is staring right out at us."

"Sounds rather grisly, frankly. Like a face through a frosted bathroom door. Or like," I offered, plucking from my subconscious an image that had been troubling me for months, "that poor young sailor from the Franklin expedition they found this past summer up in Canada, nicely preserved by the ice. He was staring right out at us, too."

Kohler leaned toward me alarmingly, his speckled jaw bent to one side by the pressure of his conviction. "If God," he said, "in fact created the universe, then as a fact it *has* to show, eventually. Let me put it another way: God can't hide any more."

"If He is omnipotent, I would think it within His powers to keep hiding. And I'm not sure it isn't a bit heretical of you to toss the fact of God in with a lot of other facts. Even

Aquinas, I think, didn't postulate a God Who could be hauled kicking and screaming out from some laboratory closet, over behind the blackboard."

The young man said, "You're being satirical. But do you know why you're being satirical?"

"A, I am? And B, No."

"Because you're afraid. You don't *want* God to break through. People in general don't want that. They just want to grub along being human, and dirty, and sly, and amusing, and having their weekends with Michelob, and God to stay put in the churches if they ever decide to drop by, and maybe to pull them out in the end, down that tunnel of light all these NDEs talk about. That's another place He's breaking through—all these near deaths, and all these blissful people reporting back. Until they had this modern medical equipment they couldn't keep pulling people back from the grave. But I don't want to use up my seventeen minutes."

"Twelve. Let's say ten. I have to glance over my notes." They were on my desk; I pulled them toward me and glanced at them. *Marcion excomm. Rome 144,* I read to myself. *Tertullian wr. Adversus Marcionem c. 207.* The boy was making me rude.

He persisted. "Aren't I right, though, sir? You're horrified to think that God can be proven."

"I'm horrified, if I am, to hear so much blasphemy coming out of you so serenely."

"Why is it blasphemy? Why is it blasphemy in this day and age always to raise the possibility that God might be a fact?"

"A fact in our lives, yes, a spiritual fact—"

"That's like a virtual particle. A piece of hot air."

I sighed, and sincerely wished the boy dead. This tangle of suppositions about the absolute and unknowable which he had agitatedly sketched reminded me of my dead, the dead who give me my living, those murky early centuries of passionate anchorites and condemnatory prelates whose storms of fine distinction swept back and forth from Athens to Spain, from Hippo to Edessa. *Homoousios* versus *homoiousios*, the *logikoi* versus the *alogoi*. Montanism and modalism and monarchianism, hypostasis and Patripassianism. Blood-soaked discriminations now dust like their bones, those grandiose and prayerful efforts to flay, cleave, and anatomize the divine substance. "The Christian Church," I began, then halted myself to ask the boy, "You do consider yourself a Christian?"

"Absolutely. Christ is my Saviour."

I loathed the icy-eyed fervent way he said it. Back home such flat statements were painted on barns and needlepointed on pillows. I said to him, "The church preaches, I believe, and the Old Testament describes, a God Who acts, Who *comes to us*, in Revelation and Redemption, and not one Who set the universe going and then hid. The God we care about in this divinity school is the living God, Who moves toward us out of His will and love, and Who laughs at all the towers of Babel we build to Him." I heard myself echoing Barth and the exact quotation flickered at the edge of my mind. Where? I was wearing beneath my coat a cashmere V-necked sweater ("camel" was the name of the shade on the label, amusing Esther, who thinks of my academic specialty as the Desert Fathers, when she bought it last Christmas, in Bermuda, at Trimingham's), and abruptly I felt too warm, and began to sweat. I was trying too hard. I was dredging up beliefs I had once arrived at and long ago buried, to keep them safe.

"I know, I know, that's great," my inquisitor said, alert and interested but not shaken by my promulgation. "Still, if He acts as you say, if He is dynamic, then He exists in some way that a complete physical description of the basic universe, which is what we're at most a decade short of in science, can't avoid detecting. That's all I'm saying. We're almost home, Professor Lambert, and science, because it's been atheist so long, doesn't want to admit it; you need somebody like me, who's willing to make the announcement—to pull all the evidence together and run it through a computer. A computer, see, is a basically simple device, but it can do its simple things over and over very rapidly—"

I interrupted, "It's surely *too* simple, by the way, to say that all scientists have been atheists. Eddington wasn't, and Newton, as I remember, was quite a zealot. Pascal, Leibniz. Einstein talked about God not rolling dice."

"Oh, there's been a few, sure. But by and large—you don't deal with these guys the way I do, every day. To them the idea of anything that isn't chance or matter is absolutely out of bounds. They *hate* it. Do you have a minute for just one more thing? I can see you're getting edgy. About fifty years ago, a physicist called Paul Dirac asked himself why the number ten to the fortieth power keeps occurring. The square of the number, ten to the eightieth, is the mass of the visible universe measured in terms of the mass of a proton. The number itself, ten to the fortieth, is the present age of the universe, expressed in the units of time it takes light to travel across a proton. And, get this, the constant that measures the strength of gravity in terms of the electrical force between two protons shows that gravity is ten-to-the-fortieth times weaker! Also, ten to the fortieth to the one-fourth, or ten to the tenth, just about equals the number of stars in a galaxy, the number of galaxies in the universe, and the inverse of the weak fine-structure constant! If you—"

"Perhaps you should save all this for your computer."

"Then you're giving me the green light on my project?"

"Not at all. It's not for me to give you a light of any color. If you want to apply for a special research grant from this school—which is very poorly endowed, I should state, the clergy not being a wealthy class of alumni and already having many claims on their charity—if you want to apply, I repeat, they have all the appropriate forms in the front offices downstairs. The head of the Grants Committee is a very nice bland man, I can tell you, called Jesse Closson. For myself, I must confess I find your whole idea aesthetically and ethically repulsive. Aesthetically because it describes a God Who lets Himself be intellectually trapped, and ethically because it eliminates faith from religion, it takes away our freedom to believe or doubt. A God you could prove makes the whole thing immensely, oh, un*in*teresting. Pat. Whatever else God may be, He shouldn't be pat."

"But sir, think of the comfort to all those who want to believe but don't dare, because they've been intellectually intimidated. Think of the reassurance to all those in trouble or in pain and wanting to pray."

I said, "I doubt that reason ever kept anybody desperate enough from doing just what he wanted along those lines."

This startled him. His brows and lids lifted and his eyes lightened like tiny rooms where the shades have been rattlingly raised. "Begging your pardon, but I'm not sure that's true. I think people are very conscientious about trying to be up-to-date—look at all the science news in the papers, for instance, and these shows about mimetic insects on public television. You mentioned faith, and removing it and so on, but remember we're not trying to prove anything about the Incarnation, or the Trinity—a Hindu could be just as happy with this news as a Christian; in fact, Fred Hoyle's right-hand man is a Hindu, Chandra Wickramasinghe. There'd still be lots of room for faith and different modes of worship. I mean, all we've got here is the absolute basics—the bottom line, as it were. The individual still has to fill in the specifics. There would still have to be all these matters of faith. But you've got to remember that faith wasn't meant to be an everlasting virtue, just a kind of holding action until Christ came back and declared the Kingdom and everything came clear. Paul and those others didn't expect the world to last past their lifetimes."

"There has been, of course, some question on that, on exactly what the disciples expected. As well as on exactly what they saw. But I really must go to my class, Mr. Kohler. I *will* say . . ."

He jumped at the gap, the glimmer of light. "Yessir?"

"I probably shouldn't say anything," I allowed, and wondered, indeed, why I was seeking collusion, adopting a toadying, seductive tone with this pale and presuming young man, "but it *would* be a relief, as far as I'm concerned, to underwrite something around here other than black or feminist studies. Or these pathetic papers on 'street religion,' which amounts to gypsy fortunetelling and superstitions about numbers on license plates and subway cars. If you do go ahead with the application, you can say on it you talked with me and I found your ideas and facts . . . what shall we say—?"

"Compelling?"

"Amusing."

I pulled my notes toward me and stood, looking down at them. *Marcion a more radical Paul. Galatians. Circumcision. Judaism legalistic, exclusivist. Marcion's Christology Docetic: dokein, decent.* What did they mean? I had a dizzying, dreamlike sensation of total ignorance, like a foreign traveller who has forgotten the local language.

"All I'd ask for would be something to cover my time." The young man was rising and hurrying the words. "I'd use the computers over at the science buildings, on the sly. How can I phrase that in the application?"

"Just say you're robbing the power-rich to give to the power-poor. Do give my regards to Verna. Ask her if there's anything she thinks her uncle should be doing."

"Oh, she doesn't expect you to do anything. From her description I thought you'd be much tougher than you were."

"Tough? Is that how she sees me? Then I think I really should seek her out. We can't have her imagining she has a wicked uncle."

We parted without shaking hands, the boy holding his upper body at an awkward, tense angle so that his hand could have shot out quickly if mine had made a corresponding move. Since it did not (altogether too much handshaking has been introduced into American life, along with that inane wishing virtual strangers a good day, a great weekend, a pleasant holiday, a nice night), his eyes wandered to my walls of books—sensible-spined university-press treatments of all corners of church history, yellowing pastel journals of medieval and ecclesiastical studies, sturdily bound fat German tomes and debonair Gallic paperbacks, uniform theological sets like rows of stubby organ pipes, all flecked with torn bits of paper, page markers, giving a frothy look to the massive compacted rows, rather like those Japanese bushes at Shinto shrines to which prayer strips have been thickly tied, or those smaller paper petitions tucked into the crevices of the Wailing Wall. Amid these books and their prayerful frayed markers, in this tall office riddled with gray autumnal light, while the skies beyond the lancet windows roiled, Dale and I seemed souls as understood by the Gnostics, shards of shattered Godhead captive in the darks of matter, bewildered amid these shelves as if newly released among the ladders of angels, the impalpable hierarchies, with which popular Gnosticism unaccountably cluttered its common-sense dualism twenty centuries ago. (What is stranger in the religious impulse than its passion for complication, the love of clutter that renders most churches hideous and every living creed grotesque?) We seemed to float, Dale and I, in lightly etched immensities of space.

"Good luck," I said.

"We'll be in touch."

It seemed unlikely and not to be hoped for. My mind darted ahead to my lecture, its invariable close. In the history of the early church, Marcion is a giant negative. His image must be developed from the works of others: Tertullian, Irenaeus, and Epiphanius in their anti-Marcionian tracts. Marcionite churches flourished alarmingly, and some were still extant in seventh-century Syria. Marcion's appeal not easy to fathom. Forbade marriage. Denied the physical resurrection. He did offer his followers, interestingly, the first fixed scripture, consisting of ten sharply edited Pauline epistles and a Gospel close to Luke. This compilation goaded Valentinus and Justin Martyr and Tatian into assembling the orthodox New Testament canon with its blithe jumble of contradictions. *Main point:* In opposition to Marcion, Rome armored itself ever more thickly in authority and dogma. Though not a word from his hand survives, he continues to fascinate: *e.g.,* Harnack's two impassioned volumes. And Paul Tillich detects Marcionism in the revelationist severity of Karl Barth, my own, I must confess, rascally pet.

The seminar would titter. Barth, in this liberal seminary dominated by gracefully lapsed Unitarians and Quakers, was like sex in junior high school: any mention titillated. In the fall, the students are still open and anxious enough to be grateful for any flirtation from on high: grim gray teacher lifting his hairshirt to bare a patch of cuddly belly.

Thus foreseeing my future, I was disconcerted by a strange unwilled vision: I foresaw Dale's as well. In one of those small, undesired miracles that infest life, like the numb sensation of hugeness that afflicts us when we stand after long sitting or the nonsensical, technicolor short subjects the mind runs preliminary to falling into sleep, my disembodied mind empathetically followed Dale Kohler down the hall, the long Divinity School hall lined with frosted classroom doors and floored with a strip of chocolate-brown linoleum. He reaches the broad stairs of carved oak, turns on the landing underneath the tall arched window, almost a slit, of bevelled granite and gray lozenge glass, and walks, in his rustling camouflage jacket, along the main hall downstairs. From behind the classroom doors arises, in binary fashion, laughter or silence. The walls are dotted with the tacky residue of old posters, with bits of Scotch tape and tinted Xeroxed paper. New, competing posters overflow the appointed display boards, advertising rallies to protest pollution in Maine and interference in Central America, and discussion groups concerning "hunger awareness" and "goddess thealogy." Lightheaded with momentary relief that his encounter with me—me, the monster—is over, Dale proceeds back to the front offices, that warren of desks and low partitions where he has already inquired as to the whereabouts of my lair. He talks again to the receptionist; she is petite and black, with hair done up in corn rows as regular and tightly shiny as small

magnetic coils. Her name is Noreen Davis, but I and not he
know this. Her broadly smiling lips have been painted an
electric red unexpected and lurid against the mat purplish
brown of her skin. For make-up she also wears eye-shadow
and blusher of a dragonfly violet. He is stirred. (I do not
envision him as gay.) Regretfully he perceives that her smile
has nothing to do with him but instead with some joke still
hanging in the air of this large room, where everyone—a
bald man by the wall, a frizzy-haired woman sorting a tray
of folders—is smiling, waiting for him to leave so their
nameless fun can resume. Someday, Dale thinks, this black
girl will marvel at this moment, remembering his shyness
and shabbiness and acne and air of confusion. For in the
years to come she will live within a world he has discovered
and proclaimed, the world of the evident God, Whose elusive surfaces will have been relaxed into their rightful, right-
angled obviousness. Standing above her, accepting the applications she offers with so mocking and yet inviting a
diffident mortal smile, he sees them both enclosed in this
future perspective, in the transparency of the revelation he
will bring, like two tiny plaster figures within a ball of glass.

My mind reversed current: I saw him in swift replay
retrace his steps down the hall, up the stairs, toward my
office, and as he opens the door I see myself as he must have
seen me, my gray hair and gray jacket, my half-moon reading glasses flashing double-barrelled light and the sky behind me crammed with blinding clouds, silver dissolved in
silver, I the obscure portal to money and, if his ideas prove
true, immortality.

ii

And, walking home in the dusk, my seminar and a conference with a troublesome student behind me, I had the sensation of following in his steps. Leaving Hooker Hall (the often joked-about name of our main building—Thomas Hooker being, of course, a distinguished Puritan divine whose relatively liberal views upon baptismal efficacy and inward preparation for grace caused him to be exiled from Massachusetts into the wilderness of Connecticut), Dale would have walked the same streets as I, the streets of my own neighborhood. I live three shady blocks from my place of work, on a relatively secluded and increasingly expensive small residential street called Malvin Lane. The sidewalks are brick and, in a few stretches, slate, slabs pleasantly heaved by the swelling roots of trees that, at this early-evening hour, existed overhead as fanning depths rendered alternately brilliant and cavernous by the rays of the streetlamps —islands of light in a jagged arboreal ocean. The neighborhood consists of large wooden houses, many of them behind eight-foot wooden fences, none of them sitting on more than a fraction of the acreage that, in a suburb, would have accompanied their pretensions and scale, their dormers and chimneys, their pillared porticos and round-arched windows and gingerbreaded eaves. Aged domesticated trees— beeches and maples and locusts and oaks—fill the narrow yards to overflowing, their branches impinging on telephone wires and upstairs porch rails. At this time of year, late October, damp flattened leaves covered the sidewalk with a brocaded richness. My student conference, squeezed in at her importunity, had been with an exceptionally earnest, exceptionally unattractive female Master of Divinity candidate who has brought to her dissertation ("Helen and Monica: Two Women of the Early Church") a complicated, challenging sexual politics it wearies me to thread my tactful way through. This would-be mistress of divinity's face—squarish, mulish, with a distracting colorless wart near one nostril, and shy yet adamant words of protest perpetually trembling on her also colorless lips—hung depressingly in my mind as I scuffed along beneath the gold of the beeches, the rust of the oaks. I noticed at my feet, in a bright rag of light fallen between the shadows of two trees, a pink sugar-maple leaf like a small splayed hand clutching at the spilled wealth of beech leaves; and I knew that he, that tall waxy-pale intruder, had noticed this same strange emblematic leaf three hours earlier, on his way through my neighborhood to his dismal, distant own.

These houses are occupied by university faculty members in the main, or else the spinster daughters of late classics professors, or sickly offshoots of families whose fortunes had been made so long ago the money has become abstract, a mere matter of numbers and paper. There is a shady narcotic gentility to these blocks that becalms lives, instilling the notion that there is nowhere better to go, and my young man would be attracted and lulled by this quality, trying to imagine, as he walks along, from the glimpses of books and lamps and knickknacks that the curtained windows allow, the shape and taste of our lives, coveting our possessions before he passes out of the neighborhood. Perhaps Dale is not heading home but is going to visit my disreputable niece, Verna, in the prisonlike project where she and her eighteen-month-old daughter live. Grates on the lower windows. Graffiti in the entranceways and up the metallic, shuddering stairwell. Verna opens her door and greets Dale without enthusiasm. She knows him and knows what he can and cannot do (perhaps he *is* gay). But she acts pleased to see him. They talk, about me and my reaction to his plan to prove God by computer. I hear her say something like "Uncle Roger always was a prick. You should hear my mother talk about him." She has a scratchy, wised-up voice almost still a child's. Also Edna's soft semi-fluid dull flesh, flesh with the pungent, sullen capacity to change the atmosphere throughout an entire house. Verna's female tot, light brown in color, wobbles forward on darling little knobby-kneed legs and points at Dale, repeating the syllable "Da." She does this until Verna screams, "That's not Da, damn you!" and reaches down and with matter-of-fact brutality swats the child. Dale hangs there awkwardly, witnessing, planning his escape, into another part of the city, into his research.

Really, what a preposterous glib hope, his of extracting God from the statistics of high-energy physics and Big Bang cosmology. Whenever theology touches science, it gets burned. In the sixteenth century astronomy, in the seventeenth microbiology, in the eighteenth geology and paleontology, in the nineteenth Darwin's biology all grotesquely extended the world-frame and sent churchmen scurrying for cover in ever smaller, more shadowy nooks, little gloomy ambiguous caves in the psyche where even now neurology is cruelly harrying them, gouging them out from the multifolded brain like wood lice from under the lumber pile. Barth had been right: *totaliter aliter.* Only by placing God totally on the other side of the humanly understandable can any final safety for Him be secured. The positivism of revelation, as Bonhoeffer described it. All else is mere philosophy, churning the void in the hope of making butter, as it was put by the junior Oliver Wendell Holmes, the

Supreme Court justice, he who left all of his worldly goods to the United States government: one of the saddest wills a sane man ever made.

My neighbor Mrs. Ellicott was tottering toward me in the gloom, her little Lhasa apso on a long red leash. With its flaxen hair falling into its eyes and down its sides so that its legs were entirely covered, the animal seemed to be moving along on tiny rapid wheels as it fussily sniffed at the bases of trees and fence pickets for a spot worthy of its urine. "Good evening, Professor," the old dame croaked. In her prime she had had a peculiar knack of driving her husbands to suicide; at least two had done away with themselves, leaving her their real estate and furniture, so that her present holdings were like layers of sedimentary rock compacted by the pressure of the years, the shifts of the economy over the last decades all traceable in the composition of her portfolio. "Doesn't look so good for our side, does it?" she added.

I slowly deduced she meant the coming election. I had expected a question about the weather. "Not so hot," I said, still weather-minded. Like most of the neighborhood, she was a fighting liberal, fighting to have her money taken from her. For all her exertions, it never was.

"Isn't it terrible?" she called after me, pinned to her spot on the crumpling sidewalk by her pet's sudden decision to confer its golden tinkle on a certain, already thoroughly browned bit of privet.

I hoped she would mistake my failure to answer for her own hardness of hearing. But, then, these Brahmins are so thickly armored in their own rudeness as to feel hardly any rudeness produced by others.

My high house and its warm lights loomed. I turned in at my yew hedge and with a householder's satisfied grunt stooped and picked up several sales fliers scattered upon my brick walk and semicircular porch, with its four Ionic pillars and the charmingly carved curved fascia just under its copper roof. I loved this house, built early in our elderly century, when the working classes and the work ethic were still hand in hand and skilled labor was cheap, as shown by a quiet outpouring of refined details—the graceful tall many-paned side windows, for instance, through which, bending over to gain light with which to sort my front-door key out of the pound of metal one must carry these crooked days, I glimpsed my wife, her thin petite figure and fluffy upswept head of gingery red hair, moving with a preoccupied slouch, holding a tilting glass of what looked like blood or burgundy, from the living room across the hall to the dining room.

Secret glimpses, even as innocuous as this, of life proceeding unaware of my watching have always excited me. Of the days of my ministry I remember keenly the lit windows of my unsuspecting parishioners as I stealthily, in my burglarous black garb, approached up their front walks for an unannounced call, pouncing upon them in their evening disarray with the demands of the Absolute. Like eyes the windows seemed—defenseless, soft, and bright—and like the wadded curves of interior flesh the arcs of sofa back and armchair and lamp base within. Esther, spied upon unawares, looked like prey—someone to sneak up on and rape, another man's precious wife to defile, as a kind of message to him, scrawled in semen. Her mouth moved indolently, forming words I could not hear but presumed to be addressed to our son, who must be in the kitchen, beyond the dining room, doing his homework at the table where we would later eat. Why, with a living room, a library, and his own good-size bedroom at his disposal, Richie insisted on doing his homework on the very surface where his mother was trying to arrange place mats and dinner plates, while a ten-inch Sony crackled and chattered not a foot from his face, I couldn't imagine. Or so I said, in repeated admonition. Of course I secretly understood: the primitive appeal of the hearth. Television is—its irresistible charm—a fire. Entering an empty room, we turn it on, and a talking face flares into being: better than the burning bush. Compared to the warmth and bustle of the kitchen, the rest of the house would seem a wilderness to a twelve-year-old, and possibly haunted, if not by half-piously believed-in ghosts as in my benighted childhood then by those real-enough burglars, assailants, and doped-up home invaders against whom everyone in this respectable, inviting neighborhood carried a leather booklet of keys, crucial as a priest's missal. For no part of the city was more than an hour's bus or subway ride from any other, and the ideals of a democracy, and an actual, pragmatic democracy of costume, made access impossible to limit. In this era a preppy and a criminal dress very much alike, and on these tree-shaded streets a polyglot and idealistic African exchange student and a crazed avenger from the ghetto were cats of the very same shade. The thirty-year-old daughter, indeed, of Mrs. Ellicott had ten years ago been dragged from the sidewalk into a small and pretty park not two blocks away, where the rhododendrons were prodigiously in bloom, and had been raped and strangled while the neighbors confused her cries with traffic noise, or screams on television. Though the park has been renamed after her, her attacker has never been found.

I let myself into a hall foyer. The built-in benches meant to receive wraps and packages were laden with magazines and books. Since the commercial success of some rabbi's recent querying of why good things happen to bad people (or was it the other way around?), clergymen seem to be cranking out books as rapidly as Southerners, and many are sent to me, as well as the latest gilt-edged, grant-underwritten treatise on Athanasius and the Cappadocian Fathers. I hung my scarf and bog hat (looks pompous, I know, but has saved me many a head cold since I impulsively snapped it up at the Shannon airport, a day after a disappointing squint at the Book of Kells) on a swarthy oaken coat rack and carried my pipe in my teeth and my briefcase in my hand into my library, on my left. I have been happy in my library.

As I had known she would, Esther heard the door slam and came down the hall looking for me. Why do women's footsteps always sound more aggressive than men's? It can't be just the high heels; it must be an energy, a pouncingness, in the gender. She came in to me, a hundred pounds of well-known woman, and all sense of her being another man's precious wife instantly dissipated. Boredom wafted from her like the scent of stale sweat, boredom so intense as to be the cause of boredom in others; the hinges of my jaws ached as I sought to suppress a yawn of sympathy.

Esther, thirty-eight, is fourteen years younger than I—an age difference that has grown, not shrunk, in the fourteen years since we met and coupled and, after my divorce, wed. Though I was a parish minister at the time, she was not among my parishioners; indeed, one of her charms for me was her tranquil indifference, an indifference beyond scorn, to the things of religion. Being with her in her crisp disbelief was like a long drink of pure tonic water after too much sour wine. A friend of her aunt's had brought her along to swell our Christmas choir. Esther, then a mere twenty-four and secretary to a tax lawyer, loved song, that opening of

oneself to wind, that unnatural transformation of the body
into a hollow pipe, a mechanism with muscular valves. Her
own voice was a startlingly strong mezzo-soprano, a voice
bigger than her tiny body and warmer than the expression
on her face. Her mouth in repose looked pursed and wry
and yet when she sang became a great, joyous hole. She had
been filling the house, in my absence, with the sound of
Luciano Pavarotti mooing and sobbing his way through
some unintelligible chestnut of an aria. I pictured his tuxedo, his floppy white handkerchief, his loathsome little
beard flecking the immensity of his trembling jowls. My
parents, back in South Euclid, had every Saturday afternoon tuned in, on station WHK, the broadcast from the
Metropolitan Opera House in New York City, and I had
found this depressing. The voices had filled the big house
with their pleading and protesting and even pursued me
upstairs into my mystery novel, or down into the cellar,
where my model airplane waited to be delicately assembled;
the third-act climax shook the floor and pipes overhead so
that dust drifted down into the wet airplane glue as, emit-
ting that unforgettable ethereal smell, it tried to harden at
the join of two balsa-wood ribs. My own musical taste runs
toward muted string quartets, dainty Renaissance ensem-
bles, almost inaudible oboe concertos, and small Mozartian
orchestras with the old, brittle instruments. *"A te, O cara,"*
Pavarotti bellowed, so the panes in my glass-fronted book-
cases vibrated.

"Darling," said Esther dryly, offering her face for a kiss.
Though I am far from tall, she is shorter. This was not true
of my first wife, though Lillian always wore flat shoes and
even developed a little stoop for my sake. My sense of
towering above Esther, in the dizzying days when we illic-
itly courted, had been reinforced by the shape of her face

—her broad pure forehead and large green eyes dwindling to a short freckled bump of a nose, wryly pursed mouth, and small underslung jaw, so she seems to be, even when seen level, foreshortened. She is intelligent; a pressure of acuity bulges her eyes outward, with a look almost of alarm, which her sardonic mouth seeks to disown. Her upper lip looks puffy; her lower recedes beneath it. Her mouth is complex beyond words; at times a blur passes across it, a pressure of gladness or grief like mist on a mirror, and I feel, even now, late in our marriage as it is, that she is about to express something quite wonderful. "You're so late." The burgundy was a bit sour on her breath, mixed with cigarette smoke; I wondered how many glasses she had had, she and Pava-rotti and his *cara.*

"A conference," I told her. "*Damn* Corliss Henderson and her heroinic saints! She was trying to tell me today that Monica would be famous even if she hadn't been Augus-tine's mother. Now that she's too deep into this thesis to back out it's hit her, both these women's claim to fame is that they had these sons and otherwise there isn't much to know about them."

" 'Tis ever the way," said the mother of my son.

"How's Richie's cold?"

"He thinks it's settling into his chest. I don't wonder, the way they make them run around after school on the soccer field."

"Couldn't he be excused?"

"He doesn't want to be excused. He'd rather be sick. I think," she went on, on a mocking, singing note, "he thinks he's rather good at soccer."

"And you're saying he's not?" Her distrust of men was extending to her son, now that he was nearing manhood.

She looked up at me, my dear feminist manqué, and there

was a glaze; a big-eyed white fish had swum up close to the green aquarium glass and let escape a flash of her furious tedium at going around and around in this tank every day. "No, my dear Roger, I'm not saying that," she pronounced in her lovely, lustrous woman's voice, only slightly roughened by time and cigarettes. "I hope he *is* good at soccer. But I don't know why he would be. I was always awful at games and I haven't heard, my darling, that you were such great shakes either."

"They didn't have soccer when I was in school," I said. "All they had was football, for the brutes. My father despised me for not playing, even though they would have killed me. If I had played soccer, I might have been good. Who knows?"

"Who knows anything?" Esther said.

"You seem depressed."

"Fall," she admitted. "I was out there today thinking we need some pine boughs to keep the oak leaves in place over the beds along the fence for the winter. Where in this city can you buy pine boughs? We go through this every year."

"If you could wait until after Christmas we could chop up the tree."

"You say that every year. And then what do I say?"

I pondered, and looked at my shelves, and remembered that I had wanted to look up something in Barth. "You say that'd be too late. The leaves will have blown all around the yard again."

"That's right. That's very good, Rog."

"And what *do* we do about the pine boughs every year? That I *have* forgotten."

"We drive out into the country, and steal them from the evergreens in the woods around a truck stop. Except every year more and more of the lower ones are gone; we ought to take that long-handled pruning saw that sits gathering rust up above the garage rafters."

"I think Richie broke it, trying to make a tree house."

"You're always blaming Richie."

But in truth I blamed Richie for nothing; it was clear to me that without the boy Esther and I would have almost nothing to talk about, and the coldness between us would increase. I sought for something to mention, some sop to toss her as she looked up at me out of her bestial boredom. "I had another conference," I told her. "Earlier. A really crazy kid, quite repulsive somehow, though he looked more or less normal physically, one of these computer types from the science end of the university. God only knows what brought him over to the Divinity School. I do know, actually. Apparently he's good friends with awful Edna's awful daughter Verna, remember, who had the illegitimate black child and lives over in some project in the slums—"

"Keep talking," Esther said. "I have to run see if the broccoli's boiling over."

She darted down the hall, angling right through the dining-room arch, then on into the kitchen, and I watched, enjoying my favorite view of her, the rear view: erect small head, taut round butt, flicking ankles. It had not changed since I would longingly observe her swishing away from me down the church aisle after choir practice, shaking the dust of my church from her feet. In those days, the days of miniskirts and flower power, she wore her vivacious pale-red hair long and bouncing loose down her back; it seemed to equal the mass of her entire body. In the years since, some white strands have appeared, most thickly at the temples, and she twists and clips and pins her skull's frizzy adornment in an illimitable variety of buns and tucked wings and more or less strict, prim, Frau-Professorish coils.

At night, her hair let down is an even bolder sight than her still-effective nudity. Esther keeps her figure trim by a very simple procedure: she weighs herself on the scales every morning, and if she weighs more than a hundred pounds she eats only carrots and celery and water until the scales are brought into line with ideality. She is good at mathematics. She used to help that tax lawyer rig his figures.

Rather than follow her, I seized the moment to look up the Barth quote. It involved, I remembered, a series of *vias*, each discounted as a path to God. It was almost certainly from *The Word of God and the Word of Man;* I took down my old copy, a paperbound Torchbook read almost to pieces, its binding glue dried out and its margins marked again and again by the pencil of a young man who thought that here, definitively and forever, he had found the path, the voice, the style, and the method to save within himself and to present to others the Christian faith. Just glancing through the pages, I felt the superb iron of Barth's paragraphs, his magnificent seamless integrity and energy in this realm of prose—the specifically Christian—usually conspicuous for intellectual limpness and dishonesty. "Man is a riddle and nothing else, and his universe, be it ever so vividly seen and felt, is a question. . . . The solution of the riddle, the answer to the question, the satisfaction of our need is the absolutely *new* event. . . . There is *no* way which leads to this event": here I thought I had it, in "The Task of the Ministry," but no, the passage, though ringing, did not have quite the ring impressed, three decades earlier, upon my agitated inner ear. Farther into the essay, I stumbled on a sentence, starred in the margin, that seemed to give Dale Kohler's line of argument some justification: "In relation to the kingdom of God any pedagogy may be good and any may be bad; a stool may be high enough and the longest ladder too short to take the kingdom of heaven by force." *By force,* of course: that was his blasphemy, as I had called it. The boy would treat God as an object, Who had no voice in His own revelation. I searched impatiently, at random; I could feel Esther's boredom pulling at me, sucking at me, wanting me there with her in the kitchen, so we could be bored together. And at last, just as I had abandoned hope, the loose, scribbled pages opened to the page where, in triple pencil lines whose gouging depth indicated a strenuous spiritual clutching, my youthful self had marginally scored, in "The Problem of Ethics Today," where one would least think to find it:

> There is no way from us to God—not even a *via negativa* —not even a *via dialectica* nor *paradoxa.* The god who stood at the end of some human way—even of this way —would not be God.

Yes. I closed the book and put it back. *The god who stood at the end of some human way would not be God.* I have a secret shame: I always feel better—cleaner, revitalized— after reading theology, even poor theology, as it caresses and probes every crevice of the unknowable. Lest you take me for a goody-goody, I find kindred comfort and inspiration in pornography, the much-deplored detailed depiction of impossibly long and deep, rigid and stretchable human parts interlocking, pumping, oozing. Even the late Henry's *Opus Pistorum,* so vile it was posthumous, proved not too much for me, for me had its redeeming qualities, exalting as it did and as such works do our underside, the damp underside of our ordained insomnia, crawling with many-legged demons. Lo! the rock is lifted. And what eventuates from these sighing cesspools of our being, our unconscionable sincere wishes? Cathedrals and children.

Richie was crouching blurry-eyed over his homework while trying to keep a rerun of "Gilligan's Island" in focus. I ruffled the back of the boy's hair, dark brown like my own before gray infiltrated everything but my eyebrows, which remain solid, dark, long, and stern. "How'd school go?"

"O.K."

"How's your cold?"

"*O.K.*"

"Your mother says it's getting worse."

"Dad. I'm doing homework. What's twenty-seven to base six?"

"I have no idea. They didn't have bases when I was in school."

Actually, I had tried to understand them with him, and by following his textbook closely had seemed to succeed; but the slidingness of exponentiality repelled me, and the revelation that base ten was in no way sacred opened an unnecessary hole in my universe. Thinking of mathematics, I see curves moving in space according to certain aloof and inevitable laws, generating the beauty of trajectories, expanding, carrying truth upon the backs of their arches, like cherubs on dolphinback, farther and farther out, plunging and rising. The Gnostics' hierarchies of angels and of human degrees of susceptibility to the pleroma, and the "measuring of the body of God" set forth with so much laborious alphabetic arithmetic in Merkabah mysticism, surely anticipated and intended to represent these sweeping immaterial formulae that mediate between us and the absolutes of matter and energy. I continued to Esther, "And he had the nerve, this science type I was telling you about in the library, to more or less ask me to get him a grant so he can prove God's existence on the computer."

"Why are you so dead against it? You believe in God, or at least you used to."

Sensing her mood, I wasn't sure Richie should hear what would be coming out of her mouth; but we were all in the kitchen, where she, above all, had the right to be. Partake of her food, partake of her mood. "I'm sure I still do," I stiffly said. "But not because a computer tells me to. It trivializes the whole idea."

"Maybe this boy thinks God is more than just an idea."

"You sound remarkably like him."

"How tall was he?"

A curious question, but I answered. "Six feet, at least. Too tall."

"You gonna get him the grant?" Little Esther was being slangy, drawling and jauntily lighting a cigarette from the orange-hot coil of a burner on the electric stove. She lowered her face to within an inch of a ghastly maiming: a stumble, a mere nudge, and she would be forever branded.

"I do wish you'd stop your smoking," I told her.

"Who's it hurting?"

"You, dear."

"Everybody in the house, Mom," Richie pointed out. "They were saying at school how people who live with smokers have lungs almost as bad as smokers themselves." On "Gilligan's Island" a small man with a yelping voice was wearing a sarong and trying to avoid a heavyset blond man who, clad in a splashy-patterned bathing suit, was bombarding him with water balloons from a helicopter.

"I can't possibly get him a grant," I said. "That's not my department at all."

"He sounds like a rather touching young man," Esther told me, on no evidence.

Richie interrupted again. "Mom, what's twenty-seven to the base six? Dad won't tell me."

"Forty-three," she said. "Obviously. Six goes into twenty-seven four times with three left over for the units column. Read your book, Richie, for Heaven's sake. I'm sure it's all in there, that's why they give you the book in the first place."

I was nettled, sensing that she was siding with this unknown youth only in order to annoy me. I debated the wisdom of pouring myself a pre-dinner bourbon. Esther had poured another slug of red wine from the green Gallo jug, and just the way her hair had loosened up, its wings coming untucked, proclaimed her readiness for a fight. Were I to get drunk, it would help me in the fight but incapacitate me for the reading I had hoped to do tonight—the book, for instance, on Athanasius and the Cappadocian Fathers had been written by a former student, who was looking to me anxiously for a blessing and a bit of a boost up the Jacob's ladder of academic preferment. I compromised on the drink, denying myself the bourbon but pouring some of the Gallo into a glass of my own. It tasted thick, fusty. I prefer white. I really prefer champagne. "Since when," I asked my wife amicably, "have you become such a theologian?"

"I'm not," she said. "You know what I think. I don't think anything; I mean, I don't think *it's* anything. I think it's nonsense. But I'm amused to see you so vigorously defending your own style of nonsense against somebody else's style. All these emperors without clothes, you all have your turfs to defend. This boy comes in and offers to prove God's existence and you curl that upper lip of yours and

45

lower those eyebrows and obviously wish him dead, gone, out of the church. To you he's a heretic."

"I would not so dignify him," I said, all dignity. "He's very young, and I dare say a month from now he'll have another brainstorm. He's using God as a gimmick for a grant. This whole generation has grown up that thinks of nothing but grants. An academic welfare class." The wine was sour; it hadn't been just Esther's breath. Of course, fermentation is a kind of rot, much as life, from the standpoint of energy, is a form of decay. There was, though, a beauty, a certain soap-bubble shimmer of benignity, in feeling the first sips mingle with my blood and speed up its motion through my veins while my gaze was fixed on Esther's pursed, aggrieved little lips, tensed to unleash the next argumentative utterance. She spoke of my upper lip but it was hers that was complex; across her mouth there passed that wistful cloud, that sad sweet blur, a scarcely perceptible "hurt" look, a hint of some sudden tender sad song about to form a round *O*. She used to blow me a certain amount; indeed, when we were new to each other and the passion of courtship was upon her, the female passion of beating out another woman and securing a protector, I could hardly keep her lips away from my fly. In cars, while I was driving: her fluffy head would bump the wheel and make steering tricky. In my church office, as I sat back in the fake-leather easy chair my counsellees usually occupied in their spiritual confusion: my eyeballs would roll upward in the manner of Saint Teresa (who used, incidentally, to yearn at communion for a bigger host—*más, más, Dios!*). In bed, when we were spent: Esther would rest her lovely little sugar sack of a skull on my belly and hold me softly in her mouth as if for safekeeping, and in my sleep I would harden again. Now it was a rare thing, and she never failed to let me feel her disgust. I could not in good faith blame her: our emotions change, and the chemistry of our impulses with them.

"Why don't you bring him around?" she asked, as if innocently, her eyes also, it occurred to me, like my recent visitor's, awash with window light, though their blue favored the green end of the spectrum and my young visitor's the gray. My own eyes, to complete the chart, are a somewhat melting chocolate, a dark wet bearish brown that makes me look, according to the susceptibilities of the witness, angry or about to cry. Esther sarcastically added, "I haven't been around a brainstorm for years."

Underneath our sour exchange, Richie vented his exasperation. "All this dumb book does," he said, "is talk about sets and keep showing these like puddles of x's that don't have anything to do with numbers!"

With a sudden graceful acquiescence Esther bent low, as minutes before she had bent her face to the hot stove coil, and read the textbook over his shoulder. "When we write twenty-seven," she told him, "it's a shorthand way of expressing two sets of ten plus seven ones. To do it into base six, you must ask yourself how many sixes go into twenty-seven. Think. Begins with F."

"Five?" the poor child said, his brain frazzled.

"Four." Her voice barely disguised her disgust. She pointed into his book with a disagreeable scrape of her fingernail. "Four times six is twenty-four. With three left over makes forty-three. See?"

See. "Gilligan's Island" had momentarily yielded to a commercial. For catfood. A handsome, caramel-colored cat, an actor-cat wearing a bow tie, was shown snubbing raw steak and fresh fish and then greedily burying its face up to its throat muff in a dish of gray-brown pellets. Pavarotti in the distance was reaching toward one of the higher shelves of canned emotion. The ceiling above our heads, in our old-fashioned, servant-oriented kitchen, showed cracks and a worrisome yellowness, as if pipes under the second floor were slowly leaking ectoplasm. Through our big kitchen "picture" window—an improvement inflicted in the Fifties—I could see across our yard and fence into the dining room of our neighbors, the Kriegmans. Myron teaches bacteriology at the medical school and Sue writes children's books, and their three teen-age daughters are lovely in triplicate. Their five heads were arrayed in the light of the Tiffany lamp over their dining table and I could even see Myron's mouth moving—his low-slung face, his thick hunched shoulders, the choppy gestures of the hand not holding the fork—and the haloed coiffures of his women rhythmically nodding as if in a subdued rapture of agreement and adoration. Myron and I often meet at parties; he is an avid small-talker, "up" on everything and bored by nothing, except possibly his own specialty. Though we have exchanged thousands of words and spent hours pressed together with watery whiskies in one hand and slippery hors d'oeuvres in the other, he has never told me anything about the one subject, bacteria, where he might be truly informative; nor has he ever elicited from me any information on Christian heresies.

In contrast with the sour, quarrelsome atmosphere and deteriorating ceiling of our own kitchen, how happy the Kriegmans appeared in their dining alcove, their multicolored lamp just barely illumining the shadowy walls, which they, like most academic families, have strewn with clumps of eclectic objects—African masks and drums, Carpathian shepherds' horns, Ethiopian crosses, Soviet balalaikas—displayed as evidence of foreign travel, like the mounted heads of kudus or leopards for another social class, in another time and empire. I envied the Kriegmans their visible bliss, their absolutely snug occupancy of their ecological niche, which came equipped with a tenant couple on the third floor, as a tax break and hedge against burglary, with a summer home on a suitably underdeveloped small Maine island, and with uproariously unsuitable suitors for the daughters—such wastrel, drop-out boy friends (some of whom became husbands) being, I suppose, at our level of conspicuous consumption what yachts and summer "cottages" were to Veblen's rich. Esther and I, with our second marriage and single child and my relatively shabby job in the backwater of the Divinity School, didn't fill our niche as snugly as the Kriegmans did theirs, and we didn't even, unfashionably, put ourselves to the trouble of creating a third-floor apartment, preferring to use these old servant rooms as a storage attic and as Esther's studio, when one of her ever less frequent painting fits was upon her. In our decade here she had done rather lurid, abstractified views of the rooftops from all of the third-floor windows, in all of the directions of the compass, and thus used up her world. Her painting style had become over the years increasingly violent—great gumboish sweeps of the brush and palette knife, with dribbles of turpentine and unlucky houseflies accepted into the texture. Sue Kriegman's children's books, oddly, portrayed families in disarray: sundered by divorce, beset by financial emergency, or comically swept up in a frenetic untidiness, of too many cats and furniture spilling its stuffing, quite unfamiliar to those of us who visited her impeccably kept home—one street over, though its windows looked into ours.

"So why don't you?" Esther was asking, still looking to release her tension, to cap the outrage of her boring day, with a fight. For the past few years, beginning as a volunteer and graduating to underpaid assistant, she has been working at a day-care center in another part of the city, four days a week; but this activity only seems to exacerbate her sense of useless vitality, of her life's being wasted.

"Why don't I what? I was spying on the Kriegmans, envying them their happiness."

"That's the way we look to them, too. Don't worry about it. All families look great through windows."

"Cora Kriegman's a slut," Richie volunteered.

"What's a slut?" I asked him.

"Come on, Dad. You know." He took refuge back in "Gilligan's Island," where some kind of reconciliation seemed to be in progress, a mass embracing beneath the stage-set palms. The Pacific sunshine, made of studio lights, cast no shadows.

"Have him to tea," Esther clarified, "with your niece."

"Why should I have this creepy computer whiz to my own blessed home? I'll cope with him in my office, along with the other dirty work."

"It doesn't seem to me you *did* cope, though. You're acting very annoyed and upset."

"I am not."

"His ideas sound more amusing than you seem willing to admit, for some reason."

"I resent your poking at me about him. I also resent the way *he* poked me about Verna. He seemed to think I should be doing more for her than I am."

"Maybe you should. Don't you think it's unnatural, here she's been over a year in town and you haven't once called her up?"

"Edna told me not to. Over the phone. She said the girl had disgraced herself and her family, including me. Includ-

ing you and Richie, for that matter. Including the Kriegmans and Mrs. Ellicott, you could almost say."

"Don't rave, Rog. You don't care what Edna told you.
You've never been crazy about Edna."

"I can't stand her, to be precise. She was messy and
shallow and bossy. And I'm sure her daughter would be the
same."

"What a mean spirit I'm married to," Esther said. Her
green, hyperthyroid eyes had been tipped into glassiness by
her last sip of wine. One whole side of her hairdo had
collapsed and was falling loopily to her shoulders. "What
a cold, play-it-safe bastard."

I told her quickly, as one cuts short a student who is
garrulously bluffing, "My dear, you've been looking ever
since I came home for an excuse to attack me and I don't
think you've quite found it yet. I am not my niece's keeper.
When on earth is dinner?"

Richie, indignant at our quarrel—children take our
friendly adult give-and-take all too seriously—punched off
the television and said upward, "Yeah, Mom. When's dinner? I'm *starv*ing."

Simultaneously, Pavarotti, in the far-off living room, had
exhausted his string of sob stories and automatically clicked
off.

For fourteen years we've had the same cheap white timer,
a wedding present given to us by an old lady in my former
parish who didn't seem to realize that I had disgraced myself into an outer darkness beyond all such homey things.
The device had a docile little long-nosed clockface you
twisted to the required minutes; when the minutes were up,
it gave out its flat, furious peal. Looking like one of Shakes-
peare's slim transvestites, a bosomless boy in an unravelling
gingery-red wig, Esther bowed toward the timer as toward

a fellow actor. Dramatically extending one hand, palm up, she announced to her audience of two, *"Voilà. Le* meat *loof."*

"O mia cara," I said, thinking, *Más, más.* I love meatloaf; it's easy to chew.

Her wrist, thrust from her loose sweater, looked thin as a dog's foreleg. The faintly desperate impudence of this her burlesque of the housewife's role triggered in me that old enchantment, that fourteen-year-old sense of the space in her vicinity being sacred, charged with electrons agitating to one's own. Cathexis is, as Freud repeatedly says (where?), never lost, just mislaid, like a one-armed doll lodged among worn, rolled-up carpets and empty picture frames in the attic.

iii

Then a few days later I found myself walking in the steps of Dale Kohler as I imagined them, the afternoon he left my office. The trees held a few leaves less but the weather was otherwise similar, in-and-out, the blue-bottomed clouds twisting and fragmenting as they sailed their sea of air, the American flags shining in the sunny intervals. My route passed fire stations, schools, and other buildings where the public services of the commonwealth and the nation were distributed. I had looked up Verna Ekelof in the phone book, and was somehow astonished to find her there, to see that a girl with so few resources and little reason to be in our city had been allowed to procure a telephone.

Our city, it should be explained, is two cities, or more— an urban mass or congeries divided by the river whose dirty waters disembogue into the harbor that gave the colonial settlement its *raison d'être*. From the time when villages clustered here and there in the land, which the Indians had already partially cleared, there grew up municipalities each with its own city hall and power-jealous boards of administrators; but automobiles and their highways in this century have welded the whole area into one. We skim past boundary signs too quickly to read them. Bridges, some of painted steel, some of arched stone, connect the river's two sides. Lifted up suddenly out of a subway tunnel on one of the bridges—an old bridge, say, of sandstone hacked into big rough blocks and set there as if by a race of Titans, with buttresses and quaint conical towers and floriate lamp standards—the metropolitan transit passengers wince at the splendor of the sudden view, of the hotels and emporia of glass and anodized metal which glitter at the city's commercial center, of the roseate and powder-blue skyscrapers of the financial district that hovers above the brick silhouette of the old residential neighborhoods built on rubble-filled marsh a century ago, of the recently condominiumized warehouses and deserted churches, of the ribbon of Olmstead park along the riverbank and the bandshell and planetarium and the rented sailboats tilting on the river's sparkling plane, all these man-created wonders thrown into brilliant visibility by the impassive slant of our local star, the sun.

The university is situated on the duller, shabbier side of the river. Having walked a few blocks from the Divinity School, through the shady enclave of tall turn-of-the-century houses each of which, including mine, has doubled in value several times in the last decade, I came to the avenue called Sumner Boulevard in honor of that fanatic Yankee abolitionist now best remembered for having been beaten on his bald head by an equally self-righteous, if oppositely persuaded, Congressman; this unlovely broad way marks the end of university precincts. A big young man in a dirty loden coat, with a wide head of uncut curly sawdust-colored hair and a Mormon-style beard that left the area around his mouth clean of whiskers, stood stock still, as if signalling a boundary; he could have been an aging divinity student, or a TV repairman waiting for his partner to park the van or a madman about to strangle me in order to silence the voices in his head. Just the way this ambiguous stout fellow stood, unbudging in the center of the sidewalk, introduced a touch of menace to the neighborhood.

Sumner Boulevard stretched straight a mile, heading diagonally toward the river. A supermarket had boarded up the lower portions of its plate-glass windows, making it harder to break them. A drugstore advertised itself with a dead neon sign. Vinyl siding replaced honest clapboard; the houses took on that teetering three-decker look. Malvin Lane's lush back-yard beeches and oaks gave way to tougher city trees, scabby-barked sycamores and primeval ginkgos spaced as evenly along the sidewalk as telephone poles; instead of plump plastic pillows of raked leaves nicely set out by the picket fences for the trash collector, here dog-torn bags of garbage and stacks of flattened cartons were heaped up along the curb. There were no more Volvos and Hondas, just Chevies and Plymouths and Mercurys, rusted and nicked, Detroit's old big boats being kept afloat by the poor. Trans Am. Gran Turino. Sunoco. Amoco. Colonial Cleansers. Boulevard Bottle. Professional Podiatry. A triangular intersection was marked with the Italian name of a soldier killed in Vietnam. Imitation stone, oddly painterly in its mixture of artificial tints, wrapped around the little windows of a corner grocery store. On the asphalt of a gasoline station a puddle of an astonishingly pure green color meant that here a car had been bled of antifreeze; but I sensed that to Dale such utter viridity would have been a marvel, a signifier of another sort, a sign from above. To a believer of his elemental sort glory would have been in the air: the very width of this crass commercial avenue, and some lots where buildings had been torn down, flooded the eyes with light. Above the many intervening flat roofs and weathered chimney pots, against the backdrop of tormented clouds, the silver and emerald hems stitched at the tops of skyscrapers gleamed, marking the city's steely heart across the river.

A plumbing-supply store, advertising not Kohler but Crane fixtures, held in its dusty window a tree of toilet seats, padded or plain, white or pastel, and the lowest of them showing a pattern of nude Japanese women, drawn, disappointingly, without pubic hair or nipples. As the avenue gradually slanted downward toward the river, its tone worsened, its liveliness increased. Kung-Fu. Locks: Master Protection. Santo Cristo Center. Todo Para Casa. The Irish and Italians in this section had been supplanted by Portuguese and Hispanics, who now were yielding to Vietnamese, who were taking over the little food marts and had opened up several restaurants offering their spicy, insinuating cuisine. The Vietnamese women were no bigger than children, and the men had unlikable squarish heads on slender necks, and snaky wisps of mustache growing out above the corners of their mouths, and black hair of a dullness not quite Chinese or Japanese or Indian. We had dabbled overseas and in extracting ourselves had pulled up these immigrants like paint on a stirring stick. There was something about them distasteful and erotic, these remnants of an old adventure, yet something grand also in the global mixingness, the living anthropology of so many tints of skin jostling here, on this tough thoroughfare, the world's people partaking of and amplifying the energy of our American shopfronts and tenements, our cinder yards and body shops. Here came a couple, unmarried no doubt but indubitably matched: a tall pale black man and a Latino girl friend almost his coffee color, exactly his height, both of them in tight long-legged jeans and short black leather jackets, both with hair teased into tall oiled crests and wearing tiny earrings, kicking along in stride, one, two, arms locked, a stirring sight. Election Day was at hand and red-white-and-blue stickers were everywhere, on mailboxes and car bumpers and the plywood sheets closing off abandoned doorways and shattered windows. An old lady was trundling along a supermarket cart loaded with what seemed to be her possessions, including an ivory plastic radio; with her pink face and blue crocheted cap and raw white sneakers, she seemed a huge baby, toddling along. I was taking this walk in the steps of another and I felt his spirit invading mine, that greedy blind bliss of youth, when the world appears to be arranged by our impulses and full of convenient omens, of encouraging signs. A gaunt drunk in a Russian-style cap with fur earflaps muttered resentfully as I went by, at the alien innocence in my face and the blunt joy younger than my years.

The blocks here were broken into narrow old-fashioned shops. A flower shop, a beauty parlor, a laundromat, and a store proclaiming BAIT & TACKLE, the window full of lures and hooks that could not be cast into water for many miles around. In wobbly red letters a haberdasher was GOING OUT OF BUSINESS. A small dress shop on the corner advertised *Halloween Costumes for Playful Adults:* the faces of animals—pigs, a tusked boar, a snarling wolf—lay amid lingerie and lace underwear like slabs of meat on chips of shining ice. LARGE EGGS—*49¢ a Dozen! With Any $10 Purchase 1 Doz Per Customer.* The poverty all about me was being appealed to with the warning that dozens and dozens of eggs could not be appropriated by this come-on scheme. M E G A B U C K S *You Could Be Our Next Millionaire!* And yet those that did win, I had noticed, in their newspaper interviews seemed bewildered by the sudden burden of money, and some hesitated for days before claiming the loot, which would dwarf and mock the lives they had led hitherto.

The shops ceased and there was a blank in the boulevard while railroad tracks crossed it, the disused speckled tracks of some spur line that vanished into a region of large blank-sided buildings, a gypsum-colored pocket of hard industry not yet transformed into artists' lofts or high-tech labs. The newer university science buildings lay beyond this industrial tract. The university and its money permeate the city; the city's buildings and quadrangles are embedded in tracts of university-owned tenements, and there is even, many miles away, a hilltop preserve, bequeathed in the previous century, where forestry students in hard hats and leather leggings study and chop and thoughtfully chew twigs to earn their degrees.

I was seeing with Dale's still-religious eyes. Across the tracks, I saw on the renewed sidewalk a dog turd of extraordinary blackness, a coiled turd black as tar. A certain breed, or an unusual meal? Or an unvarnished wonder, an auspice, like the intensely green puddle? And then I passed a tombstone store, a glass-fronted office beside a gravel lot crowded with carved and polished marble. A rose-colored headstone held, in a niche between bas-relief pillars, an open book of just six words chiselled into its two pages:

MY PRAY
JESUS FOR
MERCY US

There was a typographic elegance to it, for the lefthand words got longer and the ones on the right dwindled. Dale Kohler, having left my office, would certainly have paused and mused here, grappling in his mind to make the connection between the frozen plea cut mechanically into this metamorphic stone and the cosmic furnace of the Big Bang amid whose grotesque and towering statistics irrefutable proof of divine supervision was locked. The spontaneous irregularities of the mottled texture of the marble were not unlike those minute but indispensable departures from homogeneity within the primeval cosmos, when all matter now installed between here and the farthermost quasars was squeezed smaller than a basketball and so hot the quarks themselves were still unglued, and monopoles were more than hypothetical and matter and antimatter engaged from nanosecond to nanosecond in a fury of mutual annihilation that by some mysterious slim margin of preponderance left matter enough to form our attenuated old universe.

The irrepressible combinations of the real! A very tall, willowy young black, with a shaved head and upon its baldness a many-colored skullcap, was carrying balanced across this spectacular head like a fantastic turban one of those padded semi-chairs, having a back and arms but no legs, with which people prop themselves up in bed; the thing was bright peach in color and wrapped in a transparent plastic that crackled as we passed, while crossing in opposite directions the sunken, tarred-over railroad tracks. Was this exotic black man, demographic studies to the contrary, a compulsive nighttime reader? Or was he dutifully taking this prop to an aged grandmother or great-uncle? The black family, though statistically in shambles, still has its sinews of connection; facts in summary never quite match facts in the concrete; every new generation gives America a chance to renew its promises. These hopeful, patriotic thoughts entered my mind straight from Dale's naïve soul.

A brick fire station, built at an angle to the street, bore high on its side a painted mural of George Washington receiving, without visible pleasure, what seemed to be an extension of credit from a delegation of similarly knickered and deadpan establishment men. Next to the station stood a huge old civic building, built in two-tone brownstone on the model of a Venetian palazzo; its deep Byzantine entrances were plastered with election posters, its soft steps had been worn into troughs by the feet of a century of petitioners. In the vicinity of these public buildings the street underwent a tiny surge of gentrification: a row of three-deckers painted in bohemian colors such as lavender and lemon housed a boutique, a health-food store, and, most venturesomely, a shop called ADULT PASTRIES, which advertised in the window *Erotic Cakes and Droll Candies.* What shapes this drollery might take I felt Dale's mind but lightly play with. The shape and mucilaginous infolded structure of our wrinkly human genitals did not, evidently, amid many phenomena that did, strike him as an argument for God's existence. I pictured his waxy face, breaking out in a masturbator's pimples. I felt superior to him, being sexually healthy ever since Esther took over from ungainly, barren Lillian. My second wife when unmarried had been a flexible marvel in bed, her underparts in the sunlight of our illicit afternoons fed to my eyes like tidbits of rosy marzipan.

After its jocular grab at prosperity, Sumner Boulevard

slumped downhill and its pedestrians took on a refugee desperation of appearance. On one curb paused an addled man so fat he looked like clothes hung out to air, swollen on the line by wind. In passing close to him I saw the skin of his enormous and preoccupied face to be afflicted with some foul eczema, layered like peeling wallpaper. On this same corner a building, its lower floor reshingled in stylishly irregular shades, had survived a fire in its top floors, which had left charred window frames empty of sashes; but the bar downstairs continued open, and sounds from within —the synthetic concussions of a video game, a muted, mixed-sex laughter—indicated a thriving business, well before the Happy Hour though it was. The view down the thoroughfare now included steel girders blotchily painted in anti-rust orange: a lead-in ramp to one of the bridges that cross the river, in whose polluted eddies, I now had reason to suspect, fish awaited local fishermen.

Prospect Street. Named for a view long since eclipsed. Here I turned, for Verna's telephone-book address was on this prospectless street, a few blocks farther along. Some of the houses still had pretensions to being homes, with mowed little front lawns and painted religious statuary (the Virgin's robe skyey blue, the Baby's face clayey beige) and flower beds still bright with the round hot button-heads of red and yellow mums. Most of the houses had given up pretensions: the yards were weedy to the height of a man's knees, and bottles and cans had been tossed into them as if into a repository. The façades were unpainted even where curtains or a tended flower box at an upstairs window indicated habitation. The owners had slipped away, whether through misfortune or an accountant's unscrupulous calculations, leaving the buildings on their own, like mumbling mental patients turned out on the street. Some had progressed deeper into dilapidation, and were plainly abandoned and no doubt trashed within, their doors and windows plywooded over though there must be back doors and basement windows whereby drug addicts and the homeless could force access. Even the trees here, weed ailanthus between the houses and a few spindly locusts staked along the curb, looked frightened, their lower branches broken and their bark aimlessly slashed.

I walked along, and in five minutes came to the project where Verna lived. I had driven past here perhaps a dozen times in the ten years we have lived in this city. Four blocks of run-down working-class neighborhood had been demolished in the JFK era to make a yellow-brick Camelot of low-cost housing. The architectural rigor of the interlocked complexes—U-shapes set back to back, each U enclosing a parking lot or a playground for the young or a small green space with benches for the elderly—had remained, but the sanitary vision of the planners had in many details surrendered to human erosion. Rude paths had been worn in shortcuts across sweeps of grass; hedges had been battered and benches hacked; some basketball stanchions had been bent to the ground as if by malicious giants. One received an impression of overpopulation, of random human energy too fierce to contain in any structure. Slowly the playgrounds, originally equipped with relatively fragile seesaws and roundabouts, had evolved into wastelands of the indestructible, their chief features now old rubber truck tires and concrete drain pipes assembled into a semblance of jungle gyms. A glittering sleet of broken glass fringed the asphalt curbs, the cement foundations. SE PROHIBE ESTACIONAR. Another sign warned that *Owners of* ABANDONED OR UN-REGISTERED AUTOMOBILES *Will Be Prosecuted.* No one seemed to be about, at this hour of mid-afternoon. As if under an enchantment I passed unobserved into the entry-way whose number, 606, corresponded to Verna's address in the telephone book. Inside the building, locks had been smashed or disassembled and replaced by padlocked chains threaded through the holes. The stairwells ascended through a complex cave odor of urine and damp cement and rubber-based paint, paint repeatedly applied and repeatedly defaced. TEX GIVES BEST HEAD, one fresh spray-can motto ran, signed with flourishes, MARJORIE. On the next landing, the same spray can, in an identical style of script, boasted MARJORIE SUCKS, signed TEX, with an elaborate X that somehow bespoke the signer's brave hopes for his future.

I had seen the name Ekelof pencilled on slot 311 inside the door down below, beside the tarnished mailboxes. On the third floor I walked down a long corridor. It was bare, though holes and irregularities in the walls remembered where things—decorations, amenities—had once been fastened to it. First I went the wrong way; the numbers mounted in even increments. I reversed myself and came to a door where the numbers 311 existed as faint ghosts, pierced by old nail-holes, in the celery-green paint. My hand was lifted to knock when on the other side of the door a small child babbled, babbled on the gleeful moist verge of language. My hand froze, then descended, not too solidly. Also from within I could hear music, a piping, brassy female singer. She sang rapidly, indignantly. I knocked again.

Something scraped, there was a slap, the babbling stopped, and I could feel eyes looking at me through the tiny peephole. It had been a number of years since I had seen little Verna. "Who is it?" Her voice was croaky and tense and faintly honking, as if a metal tube were involved in its production.

I cleared my own throat and announced, "Roger Lambert. Your uncle."

The door's smooth painted surface had a look of holding much evidence, were homicide detectives to come and dust it for fingerprints. Verna opened the door, and the draft of warm air this released carried a scent with it, a musty odor as of peanuts or stale spice, a sullen, familiar, Midwestern smell. I was stunned. This was my sister, Edna, when we were both young.

But no, Verna was an inch or so shorter than Edna, and had a coarse shapeless nose inherited from her blond fool of a father. Edna's had been rather fine, with sculpted nostril-wings that flared when she was being provocative and that sunburned all summer long. I sensed in Verna a dangerous edge that in my half-sister had been sheathed by middle-class caution. Edna had talked a tough and naughty game but ended by obeying the rules. This girl had been pushed beyond the rules. Her eyes looked lashless and had a curious slant. She stared at me for a long glazed second, and then quite disarmingly smiled. Her smile was childish, showing many small round teeth and bringing up a dimple in one pale cheek. "Hi, Nunc," she said, very slowly, as if my long-awaited arrival were obscurely delicious.

Verna's face was too wide, her skin too sallow, her light brown eyes too slanted, and the skin surrounding them too puffy-looking for her to be a beauty; but she had something, something that was trapped and spoiling here. She had curly, stringy hair, chestnut color with locks of induced platinum, and was wearing only a terrycloth bathrobe. The skin of her throat and upper chest looked pink and damp. "I should have called," I said, in recognition of the obvious fact that she had been taking a bath. "But this was rather on an impulse," I lied. "I found myself walking this way."

"Sure," she said. "Come in. Don't mind the mess."

The room was pathetically furnished, with a hideous purple shag carpet that must have come with the place, but it did have a view toward the center of the city: in order of recession, an opposite corner of the project, some asbestos-shingled three-deckers with many television aerials, a billboard advertising suntan lotion, a dome of the university's riverside campus, the summit of a skyscraper with its glassed-in observation deck and rotating skyview restaurant, and the day's hurrying clouds, their leaden centers and luminous unravelling edges. Beneath this view, on a plastic milk crate, a television set performed silently, the distressed actors of a daytime soap opera reduced to mime. Elsewhere, a few mismatched chairs stood around a card table: here someone, to judge from the many colors of stain on its cardboardy dark surface, painted.

"I was in the tub having a toke," the girl was saying in her small, rather endearingly reedy voice, "and I thought you were probably somebody else." This to explain the immodesty of her robe, which came only to the center of her thighs. Her legs, from which any summer tan had faded, seemed shapelier than I remembered Edna's as being, with smaller, pinker feet and tighter ankles. "Shut up, Poops," she said indolently to her little girl, who was pointing at me and crowing an almost-word that was "Baa" or "Daa." The child was topless, dressed in paper diapers. The apartment felt overheated, the radiators sizzling with steam. Perhaps the gentle stench of wasting food came from the room behind a drab maroon curtain hung with big plastic rings from a mock-gold bar. I was fastidiously conscious of my gray suede gloves, my Harris-tweed coat with leather-patched elbows, my gray cashmere muffler.

"As I say," I said, and had to clear my throat again,

"somewhat on an impulse, I thought I'd drop by and rather belatedly, I confess, see how my little niece is doing."

Music, turned up loud, came from the other room: *"She bop—he bop—a—we bop."*

"Cyndi Lauper," I said.

This impressed her. "How'djou know?"

"My son. He's twelve, and just plugging into pop culture. I would think, at your age, Verna, you'd be *un*plugging."

She saw me looking around the dismal room and made an affecting little shapeless gesture, her small pink hands lifting out as if to smooth, like a sheet on a bed, her environment. "Maybe so. If I didn't have Bozo here, I could get out and maybe get a job or an education or something. As it is, here is where I do my non-thing, except when we get our snowsuits on and go out and trade food stamps for all this carcinogenic garbage and stuff."

Like the young generally now, she had a vocabulary that already incorporates and neutralizes all possible discipline. When Esther found a copy of *Club,* borrowed from a classmate at Pilgrim, under Richie's bed, he told her disarmingly, "Mom, it's just a *phase.*"

"Da. Da-da." The tiny girl was plump, and a pretty color even paler than mocha or milky coffee, a honey tint. Her face was destined to be the site of a delicate war between Negroid and Caucasian features; at the moment, one was most struck by the great inky eyes, not brown as one might expect but a deep navy blue—fathomless life, pure globules of a dark distillate. Their shine showed she had been crying not long ago. Tear-trails darkened the skin of her cheeks.

"What is the baby's name? I should know but can't remember."

"Paula. My crummy dad's name is Paul and when the old fart kicked me out I called the baby after him to serve him

right." Her cold-blooded father, I remembered, would hold
forth at length, once he had gone from being an engineer
to an executive, about his efforts to streamline and de-
obsoletize the plant's operations; but it never occurred to
him, as an efficiency move, to resign his job and return his
bloated salary to the dying steel industry's coffers.

"I can't believe," I said, "he kicked you out quite as
brutally as it would seem." I said this, of course, merely to
hear his brutality confirmed.

Verna said, "Oh, he lets Mom sneak a check to me now
and then, but he's not kidding about never seeing me and
Poopsie as long as we both shalt live. My worker thinks his
trouble besides the racism they all have out there is his
religion. You know when I was little he had this cancer
scare with his prostate or one of those things men have and
got involved with this sect that advertises on the radio and
television and the funny thing was it *worked*, I mean, the
cancer went away. It really was a miracle I guess you'd have
to admit. So, boy, he's *really* rigid about what's good and
bad as he and the people who run this sect see it; they all
had false teeth was the funny thing I noticed. And the men
had these humongous big belt buckles. We even had to say
little graces over cookies and milk at home, it turned me off
the whole Jesus thing growing up and I could see it was
doing the same to Mom but she couldn't say anything. She's
really a coward, did you know that?" Verna tipped her head
back and looked at me as if I'd be especially interested. "It's
sad, since the way she comes on is as if she has a lot of
spunk. Anyway, maybe I shouldn't blame his religion since
you're kind of in the religion business yourself."

"Another end of it," I said, removing one glove. "Not
distribution. You might call it quality control. You said
your worker?"

"My social worker. She's big and black and *very* smart and stuffy. You'd like her. She thinks I'm artistic and should be going to the Museum School at the university. You could sit down if you wanted."

"*I bop—you bop—a—they bop!*"

"So money isn't what you think you need so much as education. I might be of some help with that."

"Yeah, my poor buddy Dale told me what a big non-help you were with this grant he wanted to help him find God on the computer. You sent him back down to the front office where they gave him these bullshit forms to fill out. I don't know much, Nunc, but this last year and a half I've gotten to fill out a lot of forms and I kid you not, those were bullshit forms. I told him to throw them out the window but I doubt if he did, he's such a wimpy nerd, poor guy. He means well, though. He wants to save us all from worrying about when we're dead. It's what happens when I'm alive that worries me."

I pulled off the other glove, finger by finger. In my field of vision beyond the stitched glove tips lay her blurred white legs. Someone, perhaps that social worker, had encouraged her to talk about herself. The new, garrulous poor. "We left it, I thought," I told her, "that I was not unenthusiastic, but the young man had to begin the process by proceeding through channels. I have no power over disbursements at the Divinity School, I'm just an employee, like your father at the steel plant," I added, trusting that a reference to her father would annoy her.

"Da? Eeya Da?" little Paula was asking, her sweet rounded arm, with its accessory crease between wrist and elbow, extended in pointing at me. Verna grabbed this small plump arm furiously; she lifted the child off the floor and shook her back and forth as if mixing chemicals in a container.

"I told you you shut up you little fucker!" she shouted down into the tiny crumpling face. "That's not Da!" And she let go of the infant's arm with a push that dumped Paula down on her diapered bottom, hard. The breath knocked out of her, she struggled for air with which to cry, her bare chest with its tiny nipples sucking in and out like a beached fish's gills.

In bending over to this maternal exertion, Verna had loosened her bathrobe and an entire breast had swung suddenly, luminously free. Without hurry she tucked it back behind a lapel and tightened her bathrobe belt. "She gets on my nerves," she explained. "My nerves aren't my best thing these days. My worker says one-and-a-half is hard, when they turn two you can talk to them and it's delightful. I loved it, in the hospital, when they showed her to me all wet and like lavender in color, I had no idea what color she was going to be, but it's been kind of downhill ever since. I mean, they're always *there*, right next to you. Kids."

"Be bop—be bop—a lu—she bop" issued jubilantly from the other room. The bed and the bathroom were behind this curtain, I had deduced; Verna had been lying in the tub doping herself while this juvenile music blasted into her soggy consciousness. I was groping my way into her reality and was ready to sit down; the best chair available seemed to be a porch chair of a type fashionable a decade ago, a straw basket on thin black metal pipe legs.

"Isn't that awesome?" Verna asked me, her strangely slanted, almost lashless eyes half closing in musical appreciation. "Lemme turn the tape, the next band's kind of soppy, even if it *is* number one on the stupid charts."

Now Paula had found her lungs and began to bawl. Taking a plunge, I placed my gloves on a rickety drop-leaf end table that may have cost all of ten dollars at the Salvation Army and sat down in the straw basket chair and reached and took the screaming infant into my lap. She was heavier than I had expected, more saturated, and furthermore made resistance, writhing in my arms and stretching her hands, their creased wrists and fat tapered backwards-bending fingers, toward her mother. She twisted, she squawked; I had the impulse to shake punitively this little tawny container of mixed bloods. Instead I jogged her up and down on my knees, saying, "There, there, Paula." I remembered a routine that used to distract Richie when he was an infant. "This is the way the ladies ride," I said. "Pace. Pace. Pace."

Verna brought her cassette player, a big dove-gray Hitachi with non-detachable speakers, out of the bathroom, set it on the end table on top of my gloves, punched the eject button, and reversed the tape.

"This is the way the gentlemen ride," I said in my deepest pedagogic voice. "Trot. Trot. Trot." The trick with an audience of students is to get a certain menace established in your tone at the outset. "And *this*," I urged into the tiny ear, compact and intricate and very flat to her skull, "is the way the *faaar*mers ride." Babies' skins run a fine little fever, so inviting I kissed her ear. Its complex softness shocked me.

"Here we go," Verna announced and, jiggling in her towellike robe, lightly swung in place to the calypsoish rhythm of "Girls Just Want to Have Fun."

Seeing this sign of benign life in her mother, the baby strained in my arms, her body still hiccupping sobs.

"Gallop, gallop, gallop," I hastily finished up.

The singer's voice was young, prematurely hardened, and lifted into some realm exhilaratingly above emotion. "*But girls they want to have fun, oh girls just want to have—*" The voice was cut off by electronic warbling, the inhuman proficient happiness of a synthesizer, like rapidly popping bubbles.

Verna accepted Paula into her arms and the two of them comically, softly bounced to the music. Verna's left cheek wore its dimple. The child's upturned eyes brimmed with dark blueness.

Sitting there, witnessing, I had a sensation of being Dale Kohler, earnest and awkward and himself needy, on one of his charitable visits. This moment of glee, of apparent rapport between mother and daughter, did a flipflop within me; I felt desolate. My gaze flickered away into depressed contemplation of the walls, which Verna had tried to animate with cheap Impressionist prints and awkward untutored watercolors of her own, of fruity still lifes assembled on the table at my elbow and of the view through the window, with its many bits of building crowned by the distant towers; their glitter now leaned toward the golden end of the spectrum, in the sun that lowered earlier every day. Daylight saving time would soon be withdrawn from our national firmament. The television set had left off its torpid daily drama, and was silently engaged in the greater animation, the more violent flickering of a commercial. For Preparation H: brow-wrinkling grimaces of anal discomfort, followed by bright-faced dramatization of soothing relief, proclaimed to an actor-druggist.

What was this desolation in Dale's heart, I thought, but the longing for God—that longing which is, when all is said and done, our only evidence of His existence?

"*I want to be the one to walk in the sun,*" Verna sang along with the music, while the half-black baby gleefully gurgled in her arms.

Why do we feel such loss, but that there was Something to lose?

The song ended, having at last exhausted its chorus; Verna sat Paula down on the purple shag carpet and asked me, "How about something, Nunc? A cup of tea? A glass of milk? I had a little bring-your-own party the other night and they might have left a little whisky."

"Nothing, thanks. I must get back to my own home, we're going out tonight to be, as they say, entertained. Tell me, though, Verna: how much do you see of this Dale?" I wanted to know if they slept together. In the movements of her dance, as electric and stylized and untouchable as the television commercial, the white inner side of one thigh had kept flashing out from the different-textured whiteness of her nubbly robe.

"Oh, enough," she said. "He comes around to see if I haven't shot myself or murdered the baby or anything. He asks me to pray with him."

I chuckled in surprise. "He does?" Preparation J, for the soothing relief of an afterlife.

She went on the defensive for him; her pouty smear of a mouth went smaller and her little round chin adorably stiffened, as Edna's would when, in our childhoods, I would try to control her thinking. "Whatever turns you on, Nunc," she said. "It's cheaper than smack. Dale's a sweet guy."

"He told me he met you at a church meeting."

"Oh yeah, one of these Isn't-This-Dreadful things. That's not really his bag, though. Dale thinks things are going to turn out gloriously, on Judgment Day if not before."

"How seriously does he take all this?"

"Oh, plenty. He doesn't talk that much to me about the numbers part of it, or what he does over at the Cube, just shows up once or twice a week to see how I'm doing, and sits there like you were doing playing with Poopsie."

"Do you—would you call it a serious relationship?"

"You mean, do we fuck? That's for you to ask and me to know, Nunc. No, actually, I could probably be talked into it, anything to kill the time, but I don't turn him on, funnily enough. He's like my worker, he sees me as a case. I guess the whole fucking world sees me as a case."

We do resent being typed. I have sometimes thought that the secret of Christianity's rampage through the Empire in those first centuries was Roman weariness with being typed: soldier, slave, senator, *scortum*. There is more to being a person than serving a function. But what is it? I asked. "What can we do to get you a high-school diploma and a job?"

"See—now you sound like Dale. I'm always having to tell him, Don't push me. I can't stand being pushed, it really bugs me. Mom and Dad, they were always pushing. Pushing and pushing. For what? So I'd be one more little married dolly in double-strand pearls wiggling my ass at cocktail parties over in Shaker Heights."

"We don't want that, necessarily. But, Verna—"

"I don't like the way you say 'Verna.' You're not my boss. You're not my mom and dad either."

She had a low boiling point. It was exciting, like an overpowered car that can kill you or shake itself to death. "True," I had to admit.

Her strange pale-lashed slanted eyes narrowed. "Has my mom been in touch with you?"

I inadvertently laughed, out of pity for her exaggerated notion of her mother's caring. For all this toughness, she was such a child she thought her mother was like God in the sky, always tenderly watching.

"No," I told her truthfully, and had to suppress my laugh reflex, since she so obviously would believe I was lying, and anticipating her belief made my reply ring like a lie in my own ears. I studied my thumbnail; I had cut too deeply with the curved face of the clippers, creating a notch where threads tended to catch. There was a virtually microscopic wiggle of thread caught there now. I tried to free it.

"I know all about you and her," the girl was going on, in the dead determined tone of the trapped. She had read my thoughts; she sensed that I had caught her out in naïveté.

"Oh?" The tiny thread in the notch seemed to be purple, though my coat and scarf were gray.

"She used to tell me a lot, some nights in the kitchen, waiting for Daddy to come home. She and you used to have some hot times, Nunc."

"We did?" I remembered nothing of the sort and wondered who was fantasizing, Edna or Verna.

"So don't come around here with your big-deal professor act, I don't want it. I don't need it."

"You need to get out," I mildly told her. My years of parish counselling were coming back to me; I was not afraid of this child, however much she blustered. You need to say little, just appear to listen, and the whole spool of grief will unreel in front of you. The whole twirled prayer wheel of standard human lamentation: Nature's purpose for us is not our purpose for ourselves.

"Yeah, how?"

"How do other single mothers do it?"

"They have friends."

"You must *make* friends."

"Yeah sure, *you* try it. This project is half old dagos and half black dudes you say 'Hi' to in the hall they think you want to get screwed. These guys, they can smell when you've been nicked, even without seeing Paula. Then they want to put you out on the street; their idea of a great success in life is pimping for a string of white girls. It really is." Her slant eyes went watery. "My parents were right, I guess; I've backed myself into this horrible corner. I'm lonely, I'm lonely all the time, you can't just talk to anybody like a man can, it gets to be a negotiation. And last night 'Dynasty' was on so I don't even have that to look forward to for a week." She tried through the tears to laugh at herself, her grief, her life already wasted.

"You shouldn't take it out on Paula," I told her.

Her mood turned angry; her emotions lay next to one another in a kind of watery film shimmering with nervous current. "So that's who this mercy call is all about. Little honey chile. Save your charity, Nunc, she can take care of herself. All the little bitch does all day is bug me. I sit out there in the playground for hours while she eats broken glass. But it never kills her, all that happens is her shit sparkles." She laughed again, at her own joke. I let myself smile. She wiped her stubby, shiny nose. Without that nose, and if she had lost ten pounds, she might have been pretty. "On top of everything else, I'm getting a fucking cold. You wonder why everybody doesn't commit suicide sometimes."

"One does wonder that," I said, and sighed, and stood. I had become oblivious to the smells of the place, the vague mushed-peanut odor, the ammonia from the child's saturated diapers. The room's ambience enclosed me as loosely and lightly as Verna's terrycloth robe enclosed her body. I was becoming too comfortable here. "Would a little loan help?" I asked.

Her tears, her words had become all one snuffle. "No,"

I heard her say, and then she shook her head to negate the word, and sobbed "Yes." She felt obliged to explain, "Dumb AFDC hardly covers the rent, and the WIC is just food vouchers. I could use cash to buy a decent chair or something for when people come to visit. I mean, this stuff is junk."

I took two twenties from my wallet, and considered inflation, and pulled out another, and gave her the three bills. I could walk by the bank on the way home and replenish my cash at the automatic teller, the little computer whose screen always politely says THANK YOU and PLEASE WAIT WHILE YOUR TRANSACTION IS BEING PROCESSED. When she held out her hand, its smallish plump palm was creased with lines lavender in color, like the newborn infant she had described.

Our transaction cooled us both off. Tucking the money into the pocket of her robe as she simultaneously removed a handkerchief, Verna sniffled one last time, wiped her coarse nose, and looked at me dry-eyed, with the defiant calm of a criminal. A wonderful moral plasticity seemed displayed before me, to go with her pliant pale flesh. "So now what?" she asked.

"I'll look into equivalency tests and night courses," I said.

"Yeah," she said, "just like you looked into getting Dale his grant."

I ignored this; it was time to reassert some dignity. "And I'd like to have you to my house to meet Esther and our son, Richie. Perhaps Thanksgiving would be a good time."

"Thanksgiving, Jeez-o, thanks," she said, mocking.

"Or, if you prefer, Verna, we could do nothing. I came here to investigate your attitude and now consider it investigated."

She hung her head. I could look down past her loose lapel at nearly the full curve of her young breast, its silken weight and faint blue veins. She was shorter than I, as was Esther. "Thanksgiving would be nice," she said humbly.

As we parted, I made an effort to see her not as a child but as a young woman, sturdy and to an extent competent, a biological success at least, and her life no more alarming than most of our animal lives as a hypothetical Mind might see them from above, their appetitive traffic apparently undirected but rarely producing a crash. "You were nice to come, Nunc," she added, offering her plump dimpled cheek for a kiss.

As I bestowed it (her skin had a startlingly fine texture, like flour when you dip your hand into it) I saw that little Paula had fallen silent on the floor because of an intense plucking interest in something discovered between the nubs of shag rug. Her lips were covered with fine purple threads. She looked up at me and droolingly smiled. I bent to caress her head and was startled and a touch repelled by her scalp's warmth.

Yet the secluded squalor of this unnumbered apartment pulled at me as I left. Its musty aroma searched out some deep Cleveland memory, perhaps the basement where my grandmother had laid up canned peaches on dusty shelves and where she did the week's washing with a hand-turned wringer, amid an eye-stinging smell of lye. Verna's place had for me what some theologians call inwardness. My own house, on its "nice" street with its equally pricey neighbors, felt sometimes as if the life Esther and Richie and I lived behind its large windows were altogether for display.

Outside the much-thumbed blank green door, I paused long enough to hear Verna shriek at her daughter, "Will you *stop* eating those fucking fuzz balls!" Then came the sound of a slap, and of whimpers breathlessly mounting into unstanchable wounded cries.

Hot times. I could not imagine what Edna had related; my only recollections of ever touching my half-sister were of wrestling in anger, over some toy or injustice. I vocally detested her and often protested to my mother my having to share a few weeks of summer with her. I called her, it came to me, Pieface; my mother enjoyed the malice of it, and the nickname was apt, as it would be for Edna's daughter. Broad, flat faces, a touch doughy. As she and I grew older, our physical tussles ceased, as best as I could remember; and if my pubescent thoughts had sometimes turned to her, a thin partition away on those hot "corn-growing" nights in Chagrin Falls, thoughts are not deeds, not on this mortal plane. How odd of Edna to say that, or of Verna to say she did.

Two limber black youths were mounting the steel stairs three at a time, in utterly silent bounds. They rose toward me at great speed, in their worn stovepipe jeans, their shiny basketball jackets and huge silent jogging shoes, and passed on either side of me like headlights that turn out to be motorcycles. My heart skipped and I nodded tersely, a second too late. In my tweed jacket and boyish gray haircut, I was the suspicious character here.

Along Prospect Street, the shadows of the half-abandoned houses extended from curb to curb, although in the sky overhead racing white clouds and negative patches of stark blue still spoke of bright day. At the rear of a vacant lot stood a marvel I had not noticed when walking this way thirty minutes ago: a shapely tall ginkgo tree, each of its shuddering fan-shaped leaves turned, with a uniformity unlike the ragged turning of the less primordial deciduous trees, a plangent yellow monotone. The tree seemed a towering outcry there in this derelict block, in a passing slash of sun. Along with a flicker of idle knowledge concerning the ginkgo—it had existed before the dinosaurs; in ancient China it had been grown around temples as a sacred tree; like the human species, it was dioecious, that is, divided into male and female; the female seed pods stink—came this stranger, certain knowledge that Dale, after his visit to Verna after seeing me a week ago, had also noticed this particular tree, and been struck by it, as by the green puddle, the black turd. His religious reaction passed into me. Peace descended, that wordless gratification which seems to partake of the fundamental cosmic condition. I even stopped, on the pavement of this unsavory neighborhood, to ponder more deeply that tall ginkgo with its gonglike golden color; there are so few things which, contemplated, do not like flimsy trapdoors open under the weight of our attention into the bottomless pit below.

II

i

The next time Dale came to see me in my office, sidling in with that embarrassed effrontery of his, his red knuckles and his acne the only imperfections in his generally waxen pallor, I felt fonder of him. Verna's assurance that he was not her lover had something to do with my kindly disposition: these young people come at you with their drawn sword of youth and it turns out to be a rubber prop, a nerf sword. They are no better at extracting happiness from their animal health than we were. He was still wearing his navy-blue watch cap but, as the weather got colder, no longer a camouflage jacket—instead, a denim jacket with a sheep-skin lining, its yellow-white tufts making a scruffy halo around its edges. A cowboy look, though he lacked the Marlboro.

"I filled out my forms and turned them in and thought you might like to have a Xerox."

"I would." My eye dropped past his statistics to his description of his project. *To demonstrate from existing physical and biological data, through the use of models and manipulations on the electronic digital computer, the exis-*

*tence of God, i.e., of a purposive and determining intelligence
behind all phenomena.* "Biological?" I merely asked.

Dale slumped into the chair of many woods facing my
desk and told me, "I've been looking a little into evolution
and Darwinism and all that; I hadn't much thought about
any of it since high school. You know, they show you these
charts with the blue-green algae on the bottom and primates
branching off from the tree shrew and you assume it's just
as much fact as the map of the Mississippi. But in fact they
don't know anything, or hardly anything. It's dogma. They
just draw these lines between fossils that have nothing to do
with one another and call it evolution. There are hardly any
links. There isn't any gradualism, and Darwin's whole idea
of how change comes about was of course by gradual increments, each tiny advantage consolidated by natural selec-
tion."

"Dogma," I said, shifting in my own chair uncomforta-
bly. The Admissions Committee, which once had but to sift
lightly through ministerial candidates from the genteel,
mainly Unitarian families of New England, now must yield
to the applications of untamed creationists from Nebraska
and Tennessee; an unattractive lot they tend to be, with a
curious physical propensity for wall eyes and jug ears and,
among the females, enormous breasts, which they carry
through our halls like a penitential burden slung about their
necks, suggesting those unfortunates in Dante's fourth circle "rolling dead weights with full chest pushing square"
(*"voltando pesi per forza di poppa"* [Canto VII, line 27] as
translated by Laurence Binyon).

"Yeah," Dale said. "Right at the beginning, all this easy
talk about a 'primordial soup,' where you have flashes of
lightning brewing up amino acids and then proteins and
finally a self-replicating string of DNA inside some kind of

bubble that was the first cell, or creature—it sounds great but just doesn't work, it's on a par with flies and spiders being spontaneously generated out of dung or haystacks or whatever it was the people in the Middle Ages thought happened. For one thing, the theory is based on the primitive Earth's atmosphere being a reducing one, that is, based on nitrogen and hydrogen and short of free oxygen. But if you look at the earliest rocks, they're full of rust, so there *was* oxygen. Also, the amount of information you need to make even the simplest viruslike piece of life is so great that the odds of its being assembled by chance are off the map. One biologist puts them at ten to the three hundred and oneth; another guy assumed there were ten to the twentieth planets in the universe capable of supporting life and he still came up with odds of ten to the four hundred fifteenth to one against its arising anyplace but here. Wickramasinghe, who I mentioned the last time, says the odds are ten to the forty thousandth, which is pages and pages of zeros; but that's just rubbing it in."

"We don't want to do that," I said, shifting my position again; he was the pea and I was the princess. I told him, "You keep citing these long odds to me as if the atoms and molecules had to fall into these combinations by purely mathematical chance; but suppose at this microscopic level there is some principle of cohesion or organization, comparable, say, to the instinct of self-preservation at the level of the individual organism, or gravity at the cosmic level, that would tend to encourage assembly and complexity. Then these long odds would go way down, without any supernatural intervention."

"That's not bad, sir, for a non-scientist; but your asking for another molecular law is asking for a bigger deal than you probably know. Also, there're all *kinds* of additional problems the 'primordial-soup' boys just plain ignore. The energy problem, for example: for that first little microscopic Adam to survive he'd need some energy system to keep him going, and right there you're in a whole other engineering realm. Enzymes, is another. You can't make proteins without DNA, but you can't make DNA without enzymes, and enzymes are proteins. How do you do it? They've been mixing up these electrified soups in the laboratory since 1954, and they haven't come up with anything like life yet. Why not? If they can't do it with all their controls, how come blind Nature did?"

"Nature," I pointed out, "had aeons of time, and oceans of material."

"That's what I used to think, too," the young man said, with that irritating, confiding aplomb of his. "But if you look at the figures, it doesn't check out. We have the purposive intelligence we say Nature doesn't, and if it was do-able on our terms we should have done it by now. What happens is pathetic, a mess of unrelated polymers. Soup produces soup. Garbage in, garbage out, as we say in the computer business. Out in California, they're trying to get nucleotides to self-assemble, and O.K., they do, but so slowly it just goes to show: one unit is added every quarter of an hour, as against a fraction of a second in nature."

"Well, but even that's indicative, isn't it, that we're dealing with a natural and not a supernatural process?" I studied my thumbnail. I had filed away the annoying small notch I had noticed before and now this nail was minutely, almost microscopically shorter than the other, with not quite enough white edge, as though I were a bit of a nail-biter. Verna's nails had been childishly short, I seemed to recall; whereas Esther's were too long. Fingernails: they tell time. In less than an hour I would be tackling my heresy seminar, the first of two full sessions spent on the Pelagians. Again and again (I would mischievously begin, to warm up the class) one is compelled to notice how much pleasanter, more reasonable and agreeable, the heretics in hindsight appear than those enforcers who opposed them on behalf of what became Roman Catholic orthodoxy. Who wouldn't prefer, for example, plump Pelagius (a "corpulent dog," fumed Jerome, "weighed down with Scottish porridge") and his amiable emissary Celestius and his silver-tongued apologist Julian, with their harmless hope that Man could do *some* good, could do *some*thing on his own to activate redeeming grace—who wouldn't prefer such humanists to irascible Jerome and to romantic Augustine, with his hysterical insistence on the evil of concupiscence (his own at last sated) and the damnability of freshly born babies? Once a Manichee, always a Manichee, Julian had shrewdly pointed out, apropos of our Algerian friend the bishop of Hippo.

The boy was refuting me while my absent mind rehearsed my lecture. "You sound just like the hard-core neo-Darwinists," Dale said. "They talk grandly about trends, and tendencies, and the inevitable imperfections of the fossil records. Imperfections! There's almost nothing there, just sheets of creatures that appear and disappear. The so-called gaps aren't gaps, they're humongous huge holes."

Where had I heard that word before, recently?

"Where are the pre-Cambrian fossils?" Dale asked. "Suddenly, multi-celled animals are everywhere, and seven phyla exist, and about five hundred species—arthropods, brachiopods, sponges, worms. Almost everything, in fact, except what you'd expect—protozoans. How did cells learn to congregate? For that matter, how did the prokaryotic cell, which is what the blue-green algae were, develop into our own eukaryotic cell, which has not only a nucleus but mitochondria, the nucleolus, the Golgi apparatus, and stuff they haven't even figured out what it does yet. The two kinds of cell are as different as a cottage and a cathedral—what happened?"

"Well," I told Dale, "something did, and I'm not sure I can myself see the hand of God in it. All this arguing backwards you do, from present conditions, saying they're so highly improbable—how much further does it get us than the cave man, who didn't understand why the moon changed shape in the sky every month and so made up various stories about what tricks and antics the gods were up to up there? You seem to think that God obligingly is going to rush into any vacuum, any gap of knowledge. The modern scientist doesn't claim to know everything, he just claims to know more than his predecessors did, and that naturalist explanations seem to work. You can't have all the benefit of modern science and keep the cave man's cosmology, too. You're tying God to human ignorance; in my opinion, Mr. Kohler, He's been tied to that too long."

I had made him sit up, his pale-blue eyes open wide. "Is that what I'm doing?" he asked. "Tying God to ignorance?"

I spread my hand with its still-imperfect thumbnail flat on my desk. "It is. I say, Free Him!" So Dale too had hit home; he had aroused passion in me. I cared about this. Free Him, even though He die.

Dale settled back, a smug or uncertain small smile on his lips, the fleece lining his jacket flaring behind his neck. "All *I* think I'm doing, Professor Lambert, is this: modern man has been persuaded he's surrounded by an airtight atheist explanation of natural reality. What I'm saying is, Hey, wait a minute, there's more going on here than they're letting you know. These astronomers, these biologists are staring something in the face they're not letting you in on, because they don't want to believe it themselves. But there it is. You can take or leave it, because that's the freedom God gave us, but intellectually don't be intimidated. Intellectually you don't owe the Devil a thing."

"Oh. You see the Devil at work."

"I do. Everywhere. All the time."

"And who is he, do you think?"

"The Devil is doubt. He's what makes us reject the gifts God gives us, he makes us spurn the life we've been given. Did you know, suicide is the second cause of death among teen-agers, second only to automobile accidents, which are often a kind of suicide also?"

"Funny," I said. "I would have said, looking at recent history and, for that matter, at some of our present-day ayatollahs and Führers, the opposite. The Devil is the absence of doubt. He's what pushes people into suicide bombing, into setting up extermination camps. Doubt may give your dinner a funny taste, but it's faith that goes out and kills."

"Look, sir. We're getting pretty far afield here, and I know you have those heretics to teach about in a minute. My point about evolution isn't that we don't know everything, but that the more we know the more like miracles things seem. People always cite the human eye, as impossibly complex. But take even the trilobite eye, right there at the beginning of the fossil record. It was made up of hundreds of columns, called ommatidia, with, some Swedish scientist discovered just in 1973, precisely aligned crystals of calcite and a wavy lower half of chitin all set up in exact accordance with laws of refraction that weren't known until the seventeenth century. Mind-blowing, huh?"

He looked toward me for contradiction, and I mildly

said, "That doesn't mean the trilobites understood the laws of refraction. It just means that some trilobites saw a bit better than others and that those tended to survive and pass on their genes." But my tone was non-combative; I had decided to let him argue himself into exhaustion. There is a name for this survival tactic: predator satiation. I lit up my pipe, sucking, the held match flaring, each gasping intake audible, as if a small death were in progress.

"Everywhere you look in evolution," Dale argued, "there is this problem of *coördinated* mutations that would have *had* to have taken place; it's the coördination puts the odds way off the board. In *our* eye, the retina, the iris diaphragm, the muscles, the rods and cones, the vitreous humor, the tear ducts, even the eyelids: it's fantastic to believe it came about by accident, by a set of random errors piled one on top of the other. For example, to make the lens, skin somehow got inside the meningeal coats of the brain. How could that have happened halfway? In all these things, there are these halfway stages where the adaptation wouldn't work at all and would be a pure handicap. You have these impossibility points where the graph of change as you'd have to plot it just won't go around the corner. From the standpoint of evolution, the mammalian ear is even more incredible than the eye. Bones that were rigid jawbones in the reptile migrated and became the malleus and the incus, the little hammer and anvil way inside. When the jawbones were becoming the middle ear, what were these intermediate creatures chewing on? Or the whale's tail: it moves up and down, whereas every land animal's tail moves from side to side. This is a bigger difference than it sounds; the pelvis has to get smaller, otherwise it would be fractured by an up-and-down movement. But if you imagine this process on the way to the whale, there would come a point when the pelvis would be too small to support the hind legs and still too big to permit the tail musculature! Or take even the archaeopteryx, which evolutionists are so proud of. They may not be able to show you anything between the gastropods and the chordates, or the fish and the amphibians, or amphibians and frogs, but, boy, they can sure show you how reptiles turned into birds. There are only a couple problems. One, true birds existed at the same time as the archaeopteryx, and, two, it couldn't fly. It had feathers and wings but also a sternum too weak and shallow to anchor the muscles you need for flight! At best it could have flapped up to a low branch."

"Like a modern-day chicken," I said. "Do you find chickens impossible also? And haven't I read somewhere that aerodynamic engineers have definitely proved that the bumblebee is incapable of flight?" Seeing the boy about to jump back in, I cleared my throat raspingly, inadvertently swallowing some smoke. It was time I asserted myself: to be lectured before a lecture is tedium upon travail. "The impossibility of the actual," I informed him, "is not an entirely original proof of God's existence. The Christians of the second century, when challenged to produce their supernatural credentials, tended to fall back on two arguments. *Not*, interestingly, Christ's miracles and Resurrection as sworn to by the Apostles, but, one, the fulfillments by Jesus of Old Testament prophecies, and, two, the very existence of the Church around them. How, they would ask, could a small band of uneducated Syrian fishermen in an obscure corner of the Empire have started up a faith that within a century had spread from India to Mauretania, from the Caspian to the barbarous tribes of Britain? Clearly, God's hand was at work. The Church, then, its rapid spread, was its own best evidence for the truth of what it proclaimed. Also, this line of argument goes, if Christ had been a fraud or a madman and the Resurrection had been a fiction, why would the Apostles have risked their lives in spreading the Good News? Here, too, you might say we have an 'impossibility point' you can't get around, in the evolution from an obscure Jewish heresy and tiny criminal skirmish into Constantine's imperial religion. I don't find the argument flimsy; but I do believe that there are plausible ways to get around it, given a certain historical *feel* for the first century. We don't have to postulate intentional fraud on the part of the Apostles, or the Gospel writers; first-century people just didn't have the same sense of factuality that we do, or of writing either. Writing was sympathetic magic, we should remember: writing something down was to an extent making it so, it was a creative rather than mimetic act, and all the outright falsifications we find in the non-canonical documents contemporaneous with the Gospels—and the entire fabulous birth tale in Luke, for that matter, or the Logos–John the Baptist bit in John—were simply, for the perpetrators, a way of dressing truth, of presenting the truth in the robes and ornaments *it should have.* So, given the general level of credulity, the existence of numerous parallel religious movements like Gnosticism, the Essenes, and Mithraism, not to mention later historical parallels like that grotesque Jewish episode of Sabbatai Zebi in the seventeenth century, where not even the supposed Messiah's apostasy to Islam disillusioned all believers, or, in Islam, the way the Mahdi's or the Aga Khan's turning into obese sybarites failed to affect their alleged divinity— given all this, we can begin to feel how it *did* happen, how the myth of the Resurrection, in particular, took hold. Not that in this age of UFO stories peddled weekly to supermarket checkout lines we need any special lessons in human credulity."

"Oh come *on,*" my young visitor exclaimed, his voice pitched as if he were squalling with a roommate. "The Apostles were beaten. On the run. Their leader was dead. Something changed all that. You think it was pure illusion?"

" 'Whether in the body, I cannot tell; or whether out of the body, I cannot tell,' Paul wrote; his epistles are the oldest texts in the New Testament, the closest to this particular 'impossibility point.' "

"He also wrote," my callow young opponent countered, " 'If Christ be not raised, your faith is vain.' Paul was very unambiguous about it, talking about Christ being seen of the Cephas, then of the twelve, then of the five hundred brethren some of whom are fallen asleep, and after that, of James and then all the Apostles, and last of all to Paul himself, as to one born out of due time."

"And then a little farther on he said—rather sadly, I have always thought—that if we have hope of Christ only in this life, we are of all men most miserable. But let's not quote the Bible at each other; there's much too much of that around here, and in my limited experience it proves only that the Bible was a very badly edited anthology."

"Sir, you started it."

"In self-defense. I was trying to make the point that, when we don't know and can never know the exact ins and outs of an event or process, a certain *feel* is all we have to go on as to what is plausible. When I look at the *National Enquirer,* with its accounts of these very circumstantial little green men coming out of UFOs or its latest absolute proof that Elvis lives, I get a vague *feel* for what might have happened early in the first century. When I look at the cases of fossils over in the university zoology museum and at the living animals and birds and insects and worms and germs all around and inside us, evolution to me, despite its gaps and puzzles, *feels* like a reasonable explanation of the tangled state of affairs." My pipe had gone out. I sucked on sparkless emptiness.

"But that's so *slop*py," the boy burst forth. "You're thinking in impressions, without looking at the mechanism. To say that 'Elvis lives' proves 'Jesus lives' is hokum ignores the fact that one is a parody of the other and everybody knows it, even the Elvis worshippers. To say that evolution *more or less* fits the bill ignores the fact that trained biologists are disturbed by all that it doesn't explain. There was a man called Goldschmidt, a geneticist. You ever heard of him?"

I shook my head. "The only Goldschmidt I know was the editor of a Danish magazine that attacked Kierkegaard."

"My guy," Dale told me, "fled Hitler's Germany and wound up at Berkeley. The more he looked at fruit-fly mutations, the more it seemed to him they didn't account for anything; you never got a new species or a really significant change. Point mutations—that is, single changes in the long strings of genetic code—don't add up. They happen, and are swallowed by the next generation, and a species remains a species. Goldschmidt published a book in 1940 in which he listed seventeen features of the animal world and challenged anybody to explain how they evolved on a step-by-step basis of small mutations. Hair. Feathers. Teeth. Eyes. Blood circulation. Baleen. Poison fangs in snakes. Segmentation in arthropods. Mollusk shells. Interior skeletons. Hemoglobin. And so on, into some I didn't understand. Well, who's come forward since 1940 to explain them? Nobody. Nobody can. Even something you think you can picture, like the giraffe's long neck, is much more complicated, more coördinated, than you think." Dale seemed happiest with this example. His hands slid up and down the imaginary neck, quickly cupping and uncupping to explain matters of hydraulic pressure. "To pump blood eight feet up to the head the giraffe has to have such high blood pressure that when he bends down to take a drink he would black out, except there's a special pressure-reducing mechanism, a network of veins, called the *rete mirabile.* Also, the blood in his legs would be forced out through the capillaries, so the spaces between the veins are filled with another liquid, also under pressure, and therefore his skin is terrifically strong and, what's the word, imperme-able. In whales—think of whales, Professor Lambert. They appear out of virtually nowhere in paleontology, and in less than five million years have produced eyes that correct for vision underwater, and the tail we talked about, and blubber instead of sweat glands to regulate temperature, and even a complicated mechanism to enable the babies to suckle underwater without drowning. And then you take the os-trich. The ostrich has these calluses—"

"Mr. Kohler, I don't doubt," I interrupted, "that you could sit there and regale me with the wonders of nature for many hours. The wonders of nature are of course an ancient argument for God's existence, as you can read in the Book of Job."

"But it's not *just* that they're *won*derful, it's *how*—"

"Exactly what God asked Job. How? I don't know, and Job didn't, and you don't, nor evidently did Mr. Gold-schmidt, but there is surely more at stake in theology than this, this mechanical-statistical approach of yours. If God is so ingenious and purposive, what about deformity and disease? What about the carnage that rules this kingdom of life at every level? Why does life *feel,* to us as we experience it, so desperately urgent and so utterly pointless at the same time? There is a whole realm of subjective existential questions you are ignoring. Men disbelieved in God long before Copernicus, long before thunder or the phases of the moon were scientifically understood. They disbelieved for the same reasons men disbelieve now: the world around them feels uncaring and cruel. There is no sense of a Person behind the—behind this wilderness of ingenuity you say natural phenomena present. When people cry out in pain, the heavens are silent. The heavens were silent when the Jews were gassed, they're silent now above the starving in Africa. These wretched Ethiopians are Coptic Christians, are you aware of that? They said the other night on television that the only noise you hear in the camps of the starving is that of hymns being sung, to the sound of drums and cymbals. People don't turn to God because He's likely or unlikely; they turn out of their extremest need, against all reason."

"*All* reason?" Dale looked at me with an unpleasant light in those pale eyes, an optical glow many of our students bring to us: the missionary light, the will to convert, to turn the water into wine, wine to blood, bread to flesh—to convert opposition to allegiance, to flatten all that is non-ego into mirror-smooth pure ego. This perennial presumption of students wearies and disgusts me, year after year. "You really have a stake in this, don't you?" Dale said. "You're not just neutral, you're of the other party."

"The Devil's party, you mean? Not at all. I have my own style of faith, which I don't propose to discuss with you or anybody else who comes wandering in here looking like a cowboy. But my faith, poor thing or no, leads me to react with horror to your attempt, your *crass* attempt I almost said, to reduce God to the status of one more fact, to deduce Him! I am absolutely convinced that my God, that anybody's real God, will *not* be deduced, will *not* be made subject to statistics and bits of old bone and glimmers of light in some telescope!"

I do not like myself when I become engaged. Passion of an argumentative sort makes me feel sticky and hot, caught in a web of exaggeration and untruth. We owe the precision of things, at least, a courtesy of silence, of silent measurement. I wished I could relight my pipe, but there really was no time for the ceremony. My hands, I noticed, were pathetically trembling. I clasped them together and rested them on the desk. In the pulpit in the old days they would tremble like this, when I fingered the lectern Bible for the page holding the day's text. Damnably thin, those big Bible pages.

Somehow this odd young missionary had gotten the better of me. I could tell from just the calm, cool way he stared, above his lopsided smile and flecked long jaw, and made no hurry to reply. He had got me to make a profession of faith, and I hated him for this. "Your God sounds like a nice safe unfindable God," he mildly observed.

"How's Verna?" I asked him, gathering up my notes. *Pelagius not a strict Pelagian. Offended by Augustine's tendencies toward antinomianism, Manichaean pessimism. Sin passed down from Adam as part of reproductive process? Corruption distinguishable from helplessness, in P. view.*

The boy, seeing my retreat from the debate, slouched back cockily into his university chair, and even slung one leg over a cherrywood arm. "Yeah. She said you came by last week." The look he gave me, from someone less highminded, might have been called sly.

"I wanted to see her setup," I confessed. "Not so bad as I'd thought."

"As long as she stays right in her apartment, it's not so bad. She goes outside, she gets hassled."

"By—?"

"By the brothers. A white girl that age with a black child has laid herself wide open."

"Do you think she should move?"

"She can't afford to." Was his curt answer a challenge, for me to give her enough money to move? He perhaps knew that I had given her sixty dollars already. How much, I wondered, was my pious young visitor part of a team, himself and Verna, bent on bilking me? This Eighties generation is capable of all sorts of self-righteous criminality along with their deficit-sponsored otherworldliness. Buddha says *Non-attachment,* Jesus says *Do unto others,* and the goods of others start getting detached. Well, who can blame them? Television goads them into begging for junk from the moment they open their eyes. The educational system keeps them as dependent as babies into their fourth decades. It's a throwaway world, all service industries and bubble wrap. The genius of Calvinism had been to make property an outward sign and a sacred symbol; in my old-fashioned way I was trying to gauge the extent of this young man's proprietorial claims upon Verna. I coveted his access to that messy overheated apartment with its captive girl all rosy from her bath. I had not quite believed her assurances that their relationship was sexless. Again old-fashionedly, I could not imagine two young people of the opposite sex locked in the same room and not copulating, or at least laying hands on each other's sensitive places.

I contemplated my visitor as he sat there athwart the shaft of light pouring in the neo-Gothic window at my back, and tried to sort out my feelings toward him. They consisted of:

(a) physical repugnance, at his waxiness, and the unreachable luminescence in his eyes, steady as a pale-blue pilot light burning in his skull;

(b) loathing of his theories, which couldn't have anything much to them, though some would need an expert to refute;

(c) envy of his faith and foolish hope that he could grab the hoary problem of belief by a whole new tail;

(d) a certain attraction, reciprocating what seemed to be his sticky adherence to me, since this second visit to my office served no clear purpose;

(e) a grateful inkling that he was injecting a new element into my life, my stale and studious arrangements;

(f) an odd and sinister empathy: he kept inviting my mind out of its tracks to follow him on his own paths through the city. He had mentioned, for instance, that he worked weekends in a lumberyard, and I had merely to think of this fact and the holy smell of fresh-cut spruce was in my nostrils, and the rough-smooth weight of newly planed and end-stained two-by-fours was thrusting against my palms, with a palpable threat of splinters.

I smiled and asked him, "Am I my half-sister's daughter's keeper? How much should I attempt to intervene?"

He surprised me by saying emphatically, "Not much. At least at first. This is her life, she's cooked it up, you have to let people have the dignity of their choices. The important thing, I would think, is for her to get out a little, and get some education."

"I agree," I said, pleased that our minds, on less than cosmic matters, could run along the same lines.

"Verna comes on very rejecting when you first put anything to her," he said, "but then the next time you visit her she's shifted around a hundred eighty degrees."

We were making of her, I noticed, a distant object of reverence, of wary speculation. This nineteen-year-old truant from Cleveland, with not a thing in her head but what pop music put there. I took a plunge. "One avuncular gesture I thought of making," I said, "was to have my wife invite her to have Thanksgiving with us and our son. We'd be happy to have you, too, if you have no other commitments." I rather assumed he did: a communal dinner, perhaps, at long tables in a big church basement, with a babbling, colorful host of do-gooding born-agains and demented street people.

His uncanny eyes widened. "That would be real nice," he said. "I was going to just eat in a cafeteria, they put on these turkey specials that are really pretty good, and I like the no-fuss atmosphere. Frankly, sir, holidays tend to freak me out. But that would be terrific, to meet your missus and your boy." Away from the urgencies of scientific explanation, his speech lapsed into a Midwestern folksiness.

And he was certainly less organized-religion-oriented than I thought proper for one of his fervor. Thanksgiving in a cafeteria? Christmas in a brothel? Of course, the Church has always been recharged unorthodoxly. Augustine was a pagan, then a Manichee. Tertullian was a lawyer. Pelagius himself had no ecclesiastical status, and may have first come to Rome as a law student. If the salt lose its savor, wherewith indeed? Jesus Himself, John the Baptist: raggedy outsiders. Insiders tend to be villains. Like me, I would smilingly tell my incredulous, admiring students.

ii

Dale Kohler's distaste for holidays formed yet another secret bond between us; in my childhood, bumpy monoxious
car rides out into the rural Ohio flatness, along what was
too aptly named Kinsman Pike, were my prime association
with American Christendom's tribal feasts. My deserted,
husbandless, pitiable mother and I would visit her "people," the men horse-faced and leathery and placidly sexless
but the women wide sloping mounds of fat trembling on the
edge, it seemed to me, of indecency, with their self-con-
scious shrieks of laughter, their hands at each shriek darting
to cover their mouths, their little teeth decayed and
crooked, and the steaming food they were copiously setting
on the table a malodorous *double-entendre,* something that
excited them, served up in an atmosphere heavy with barn-
yard innuendo as well as lugubrious piety.

In my great-aunt Wilma's house a praying Jesus, its colors sick and slippery, hung in the kitchen, against deeply
yellowed wallpaper, behind the black stovepipe too hot to
touch, and in the parlor the only book, with a little knobby
table all to itself, was the family Bible; its spine had ridges
as of cartilage beneath its terrible hide, creased like the skin
of a slaughtered animal, with that same soft stink of the
tannery, and a faded lavender bookmark, like a wide, forked
tongue, protruded from its gold-edged pages. There was a
smell of coal oil and, tracked in on the men's shoes, a musty
scent of mash, of livestock feed. These country outings
depressed me for days on either side, in anticipation and in
memory; and during the actual event my depression was
such that I seemed to sink beneath the table, so that my

visual memories focus on the embroidered tablecloth fringe and the knees and fat ankles and creased shoes hidden and shuffling in the strange dim cave beyond. When very young, I may actually have crawled in there, among the shoes and knees.

On the Fourth of July, the dismal holiday tableau was repeated, in a temperature ninety degrees higher, and sometimes outdoors, on rough tables set up beneath the backyard tulip poplars, pyramids of corn-on-the-cob shining with butter and platters of pork chops arriving charred from the grill amid cries such as might have greeted a Turkish belly dancer or the crucified Messiah.

The opaque, shy, menacing silence of the farm animals they tended had rubbed off on my country cousins, and like these beasts they tended to bump against things, as a way of perception. Dressed in sun-faded cotton, they bumped against me, and I feebly fought back, or hid, or else on rare occasions was lulled into a desultory game of quoits or a futile visit to some watercress-choked rivulet with a pole and hook and pinkish earthworms, to whose torments, impaled, my bumpkin playmates were placidly blind. The fish never bit. The afternoon, as the grown-ups grew more and more hilarious beneath the tulip poplars, never ended, but tailed into the blanched summer evening and at last the darkness of the Pike, my fragile, wounded mother at our old Buick's wheel, complaining of a headache and night blindness.

Edna was never along on these excursions, being safe with my disgraced father and wicked stepmother in suburban Chagrin Falls, where her tennis and golf lessons would be in full swing at "the club": here, in a palatial spread of mock-Tudor buildings and fenced-in courts at the end of a long curving driveway, there was a swimming pool where crew-cut boys executed splashy cannonballs in tribute to Edna's budding figure, and where she and her guests, of whom I was for my month of exile one, miraculously obtained endless Cokes and hot dogs from a poolside commissary simply by reciting a number, our father's chit code. Little as I liked Edna, who as pubescence took hold had added girlish vanity and a bubbly snobbism to her faults, these country relatives made me think fondly of her. The humid oppression of blood, of ancestry, of tedious tradition and the mummified past, that rural past when the stupid, sluggish, malingering earth spirits needed periodic human cavorting to remind them to switch on the next season— this was what holidays meant to me.

With a second wife, as my father had discovered before me, one's social obligations lighten. Esther and I at first, in the flush of my liberation from all the conformities expected of ministers, ignored Thanksgiving entirely, and even did without a Christmas tree, acknowledging our Saviour's (according only to Matthew) star-crossed birth with a pale supper of sole and champagne the night before, and a cursory exchange of presents at breakfast. My first wife, Lillian, herself a minister's daughter, had been a great proponent of the groaning board, of the rising at dawn to stuff the stuffed turkey into the grim oven, and of chaotically extended hospitality. These social ordeals soothed and flattered that within her which was mortally insulted by her biological inability—a ghostly cross we had carried in common until my sperm, produced by masturbation behind a swaying curtain into the clammy plastic substitute for a vagina the hospital had provided (it had also provided copies of *Penthouse* to stimulate the feat, and several tattered Bee-Line paperbacks: I read on and on, even into limpness, in a minor classic called *Hot Pants Schoolmarm*), was microscopically exonerated. Wandering students, bereft parishioners, distant cousins—we entertained them all, in a suffocating charade of fecundity. The Thanksgiving turkey, the Christmas goose, the Easter leg of lamb, the Labor Day rump roast—carving was giving me tennis elbow. Poor tall docile barren Lillian. Only briefly heartbroken by my defection, she took a secretarial degree after our divorce and disappeared into a corporation headquarters above White Plains, one of those with artificial lakes and abstract aluminum fountains and terraced parking lots; and then she married, most startlingly, money, a corpulent man with a half-ton of children by previous couplings. He adoringly takes her to Florida for four months of the year, like a New-World Persephone.

As Richie matured to the point of comparing notes with his peers, Esther and I have had to reconstitute some holiday observances. The house, in fact, with its baronial panelling and tile-faced fireplaces and high-ceilinged rooms, cries out for parties. When we do give one, usually in late May to celebrate the end of school, it seems, to my possibly too-delicate sense of it, underattended; I cannot escape my suspicion that the Kriegmans in their way and the Ellicotts in theirs are more adequate to this neighborhood than we, Esther and I, whose instincts tend toward a bohemian austerity—the book-choked foyer, the attic smelling of oil paints. Having scandalized a parish fourteen years ago, we still are, perhaps, shy. But for today I had laid and lit a fire in the living room, and its crackling dance ignited red echoes at the prismatic corners of our glass table and in the curved panes of our big bow window. Though it was cold outside, with a film of snow on the dead lawn and brick walk, the house smelled warmly of wood burning and food cooking, and Richie had been lured away from the parades and football games on television by the mystery of our guests.

They came separately, which weakened their liaison in my mind and pleased me. First, Dale appeared at the door, incongruous in a gray suit and button-down shirt; only his necktie, purple violently interrupted by green, struck the gauche note we expect from scientists. He carried a small paper cone of zinnias, the sort of bouquet young drug addicts sell now from traffic islands, and presented it to Esther, who had hurried down the hall in her apron. "How nice!" she exclaimed.

"You're nice to have me, Mrs. Lambert," he said. There was a smoothness to this boy I kept forgetting. Also, his easy tallness, which in the slant chapel light of my office he quickly folded into the university chair opposite my desk, here in my front hall loomed, all suited and combed, as a costume of grace, a form of potency. He was hatless. Because his curly, thinning brown hair had been combed back dark with water, his forehead was exposed and looked strikingly white, of the same unnatural candor as his eyes.

"Oh no," Esther said, slightly flustered, as women holding flowers do seem, "it's fun for us; Rog has talked about you quite a lot, you've made a big impression on him." She was wearing a frilly apron over a tight-necked dress of green velvet.

"Big, but mostly negative, I think," he said, giving her a smile I had never seen in my office, where his mouth was nervous and, in its eagerness to convert me, predatory, saliva sometimes bubbling in the corners. His smile at Esther didn't stretch his lips, but lightly shaped and parted them, as if in poised wait for her next move. I saw her through his eyes, my little wife, her tense and tidy figure foreshortened even more from his angle than from mine.

Her gingery red hair and its prim do had been loosened and fluffed by the work and heat of cooking; her bulging eyes were very green in the light from the front door. Esther had put on a glint, an alertness, an older woman's assured and ironic potential playfulness.

"Not at all," I intervened. "In fact, I was talking to Closson just the other day about your grant, and he thought it might bring in some amusing publicity, if it were known the school was underwriting computer theology."

Dale looked uncomfortable. "I don't see as how publicity would really help."

"Rog is saying," Esther told him, "that the school thinks it might help *them*. I'll go put your lovely flowers in water." She hurried off, clicking; her hips tugged the iridescent velvet of her green Thanksgiving dress rapidly this way and that, light scribbling zigzags on the folds.

I joked to Dale, anent publicity, " 'Preach the gospel to every creature.' "

" 'When thou prayest,' " he quoted back at me, " 'enter into thy closet.' "

He wore no topcoat, so there was none for me to take. I led him into the living room. "Hi," Richie said, guiltily rising up from beside the fire; he had plugged in the little Sony and had been watching tiny red men struggle against others in blue.

"Hi there. Happy Thanksgiving. Who's ahead, the Pats or Dallas?"

"The Pats stink."

"Not always. Eason's had some great days this season."

Again, I was surprised by the young man's savoir-faire, his quickness to make human connections, and I felt an unaccountable pang of jealousy: as if I wanted him, after our wordy wrestles on the floor of Creation, to be mine alone. He was promiscuous, in his untroubled conviction of his own righteousness, and this was another reason he should be destroyed. I offered to get him a drink, pointing out that I was having a glass of white wine. "Or a Bloody Mary? Some bourbon or Scotch?" He refused, instantly, softly, as one who habitually refuses, and asked me if I had any cranberry juice. I said I would see, and indeed there was, surprisingly, a half-bottle of this dreary liquid in the refrigerator. Cranberry juice depresses me, reminding me of bogs, of health food, of children with stained upper lips, and of old ladies gathering in dusty parlors to pool the titillations of their dwindling days. It looks dyed. When I returned with a glass of it, Dale and Richie were deep in conversation at the glass coffee table. Pencil and paper had been located, and Dale was saying, "A computer doesn't figure the way we do. Show me how you do a square root. Take the square root of, oh, say, fifty-two."

While the child was bending into the problem and slowly writing, Dale looked up at me and said, "This is a lovely home you have."

"You were impressed by the Divinity School, too, as I recall."

"Maybe I'm easily impressed."

"You seem to find me," I clarified for him, "always in posh surroundings."

"I'm sure you've earned them," he told me without smiling, and spoke to the boy seated beside him, on the red silk settee that was not quite close enough to the glass table for comfortable computation. "Hasn't he, Richie? Your father? Worked hard."

"All he ever does is read books nobody else ever does."

I was trying to recall all of the quotation Dale had thrown at me. It occurs in the passage in Matthew about hypocrites praying aloud. *Enter into thy closet, and when thou hast shut thy door, pray to thy Father which is in secret.* Thy Father, which is in secret, blessed be Thy name.

"How's the square root of fifty-two coming?" Dale asked Richie. I wondered how he had struck upon my age, for his number.

"I hate doing square roots. I get seven point two and then something little."

"Let's say seven point two one. O.K. Here's how a computer would do it. It makes a guess, then plugs that guess into a formula that's been programmed in, and gets a new number that then it plugs into the same formula, and keeps running it over and over until it gets the answer to within however many decimal places have been specified ahead of time. Here's the formula."

He wrote something on the piece of paper I did not bother to look at; I was glancing out the bow window to see if our other guest was arriving. Esther had talked to Verna on the phone and reported that the girl sounded bewildered and sullen and hadn't been sure she could get a babysitter on Thanksgiving. But she'd call if she couldn't, and she hadn't.

"Let capital N be the number, fifty-two in this case, you want to find the square root of, and y subscript one, y subscript two, three, four, et cetera, be the successive approximations of its root. Now you can see here that at any stage y is not going to equal N divided by y except in one case. What is that?"

My poor child thought; I could feel his brain's soft wheels turn, and turn, and not catch on anything. "I don't know," he confessed at last.

"Obviously," Dale said, "if y has become the true root. Otherwise, there's a difference, a discrepancy, between y

and N divided by y. But if you take the average of the two numbers—by that I mean if you add them and divide by two—you'll be a little closer to the answer, won't you? You *have* to be. Can you see that?"

"Y-yes. I guess I can." Light dawned, or pretended to. "I can!" the boy exclaimed, enthusiasm or its pretense causing his voice touchingly to crack. At times he reminded me of my mother, Alma, who often seemed to my childish sense of it to be trying to catch up, to recover the drift of a world that had moved and was still moving too fast for her.

"Great," Dale said. "So we call that new y 'y subscript two,' and substitute it for the old y in the formula, and keep going until we start getting the same answer—like I say, to a certain number of places. Then that's the answer, and the computer flashes it on the screen, in lots less than a second. But it's had to do dozens and dozens of little tiny operations, all in binary numbers. You know about binary numbers, don't you?"

"Kind of."

"What are they teaching you at school, Richie? Where do you go to school?"

"Pilgrim Day" was the embarrassed answer.

"Very posh," I announced from above them. "Very conservative. I think they still use Roman numerals." The view from the bay window, whose window seat Esther had long ago padded with cushions covered in a fabric whose Chinese panorama the sun had now faded to the dimmest of pagoda roofs and identically benign white faces, contained my brick walk, the shaggy back of our hedge, some supermarket sale fliers frozen into the snow-dusted lawn, a brown Milky Way wrapper, a curbside honey locust, and, across the street, the shuttered house of a former professor of Aramaic's corpulent and paranoid widow, but still no little

Verna trudging along; her stubborn plump face would be muffled against the cold, and her lashless eyes watery, red-rimmed slits.

"To finish up on this, Richie. You got the answer seven point two one. Let's be real crazy and substitute ten as our guess for the square root into our formula, even though you can see at a glance the answer's going to be seven and a little something, because why—?"

"Because," Richie said, after a pause. I was sweating for him now, my child on the spot. Ever so tentatively he offered, "Because the square root of forty-nine is seven?"

"Riiiight." Dale as big brother, as cozy "Y" counsellor, had the authentic blanketing concern, that made my skin crawl. "So if you put ten in, the new *y* equals one-half of ten plus—what's fifty-two divided by ten, come on, it's easy."

"Five point two?"

"Exaaactly." Coaxing, coaxing. The teacher's whoredom, teasing up the mental erection. "So that's one-half of fifteen point two or seven point six, see, already we're drawing closer to the correct answer, which we know to be—?"

"I forget."

"How could you forget? You just figured it out the hard way."

"Seven point two?"

"Absolutely. O.K. So the next time around, the new *y* is going to equal seven point six plus fifty-two divided by seven point six, which is going to give us, oh, six point eight, let's say, so that the sum divided by two is going to give us —what?"

"Uh . . . seven point two?"

"Which is—?" He couldn't wait for the boy to fill in the

gap. "—the answer, within one decimal place! Isn't that beautiful?"

My buffaloed boy nodded politely.

Esther came into the room, closer to naked without her apron on. A green-clad green-eyed lady elf. The elf of the house. The furniture, even the wainscoting, gathered about her in salute: the Queen Mab of Malvin Lane.

Dale hurried to his conclusion. "It's not *exactly* the answer yet, there is no abso*lute*ly exact answer unless N is a square, but when the difference between two successive answers for y is less than the decimal we've programmed in—point oh oh oh oh oh five if we want to be accurate within five places—the loop is broken and the computer goes on to whatever it's programmed to do next. A process that repeats like this is called an iterative algorithm, or a *loop*. You see, Richie, what our minds grasp by intuition and a kind of instinctive averaging out, the computer has to work through painstakingly with these loops. It doesn't mind all the little steps because electricity travels so fast and they've gotten the distances in the circuitry down to almost nothing now. A computer is much quicker than we are but it has no common sense, it's had no ex*peri*ence. With these loops the tricky thing is to make them converge toward the true answer; otherwise they can *di*verge, or, as we say, blow up, and get totally unreal." Dale looked up at Esther. "Bright boy," he said.

"Not in math, I fear. He takes after his father in that."

Dale looked at me, for the first time in our antagonistic relationship, with something like frank distaste. "Weren't you O.K. in math when you had it at school?"

"No. Not O.K. My psyche rebelled. Mathematics"—I was sounding, I realized, rather foolishly grand about it—

"depresses me." I needed more wine, and envied Esther her full glass.

"Oh it shouldn't be depressing," the young man said earnestly. "It's never threatening, the way some knowledge is. Geology, say. It's"—his big loose fingers made little circles in the air, describing unthreatening motion, a rapid kinetic music—"it's *clean*," he concluded, leaving suspended between us, above the glass table, between the crackling fire and the bookcase on which Esther had set in a slender crackled toast-colored vase his gift of zinnias, the implied mass of all that is unclean, that is dirty and sluggish and drags us down.

She, tilting a freshly lit, crimson-filtered cigarette with what I sensed to be an unusual jauntiness, bragged of herself, "I was good at math. My father told me he couldn't imagine anything more useless for a woman to be. But I loved it, as I remember. The way if you do what the book tells you the things all fit."

Dale gave her his freshened attention. "Or don't quite fit. There's a branch now of math, between math and physics, really, that you can only do on computer; they set up these cellular automata, little colored tiles each representing a number, with a certain small set of rules about what color combinations in the surrounding tiles produce what color of each new tile, and it's amazing, however simple the rules look, how these astounding complex patterns develop. Some end very abruptly, out of their internal logic, and some give signs of going on forever, without ever repeating themselves. My own feeling is with this sort of mathematical behavior you're coming very close to the texture of Creation, you could say; the visual analogies with DNA jump right out at you, and there're a lot of physical events, not just biological but things like fluid turbulence, that are what we call computationally irreducible—that is, they can only be described step by step. Now, on a computer you can imitate this, if you find the right algorithms. That's what they're beginning to use computers for, this study of chaos, or complexity. The implications are enormous: if the physical universe can be modelled by a computational system, and its laws regarded as algorithms, then on a sufficiently powerful machine, with enough memory, you could model reality itself, and then interrogate it!"

He was talking in a void. Only I knew what he was after. I told him, "If it's a faithful model, it'll plead the Fifth Amendment, just like the real thing."

"But Richie *loves* history, don't you, dear?" Esther asked the child in that slightly loud voice whereby we appear to talk to one person while really talking to another. "As long as it doesn't go back further than the age of Buddy Holly."

This seemed to me unnecessary teasing; what was she saying but, subliminally to Dale, *See what I'm stuck with here? A pair of dummies.*

It is not easy for me to know or picture Esther's attitude toward other males. At first, of course, in recoil at having taken me away from the ministry and my wife and our groaning boards and never-to-be-born children, she clenched shut upon *us,* Esther and Roger, and for four or five years was all ardor bred of shame, and loyalty bred of guilt. Then Richie began to go to nursery school, and my re-education secured my position at the Divinity School, and our private life, the hard-won and once-illicit intimacy in which we were like two gladiators whose heated grappling fascinates an entire arena, slowly, imperceptibly, became an enactment, a transportation hither and yon of lifesize representations of ourselves, while our real selves shrank to the size of dwarf puppeteers, unseen manipulators who when alone with each other at the end of the show had no voices left. I was old enough to accept our dwindling sex life as part of a general dying, a biological pullback; but Esther? Her nerviness and boredom seemed more intense at some times of the month than at others. This appeared to be one of the times; her movements of hand and mouth had an electric swiftness, and her hair pushed out from her head with unusual and unruly "body"; one felt she would be shocking to the touch, like a gleaming kitchen appliance that harbors a short circuit. Her hair was so vivacious she undid a clip and, holding its prongs between her teeth, regathered, coiled, and tucked tighter a piece at the back of her skull.

"The guy who I really like from that primitive era is Fats Domino," Dale said, after a pause, his eyes sliding toward my wife. It was as if he were speaking a foreign language by phrase book and were not a hundred percent certain that his output was also his listeners' input. I was beginning to get a headache. Holidays do that to me. A full glass of white wine had appeared in my hand, with no memory of how I had obtained it.

"Yeah, you see him on old film clips," dear Richie gamely, lamely responded. Except when rooted in front of his television set he seems generally at sea. "Along with Little Richard and Diana Ross before she was Diana Ross."

The doorbell rang—our vile doorbell, strangled in layers of rust and scrawking as if to set galloping all the families of rats domiciled in the lath and plaster behind our panelled walls.

"That must be your darling niece," Esther told me. "She took her own sweet time."

"I called her up," Dale volunteered, "to come over with

me, but she wouldn't answer her phone. She didn't answer it last night either."

They both sounded aggrieved. They were both good at math. They were welcome to each other. I marched to the door. The house is such that there is no quick way to the front door from the living room; you must pass under the archway, with its elaborate spindlework header, and then down the length of the hall. At the hall's far end, a door closes off the foyer; through its one big dirty pane, and then through the narrow leaded strip of glass beside the front door, I glimpsed Verna peeking dubiously in, her sallow broad face with its slant eyes. She looked cold, and scared. As I pulled open the various doors to admit her, the wood, dried by the reviving furnace and the arid air of late fall, crackled and popped alarmingly. Alarming not just Verna: she was carrying Paula, bundled up, and with a wool hood askew on her face so only one soft brown cheek and tearful dark-blue eye showed.

"Sorry, Nunc," Verna said in her reedy little voice. "I've had a fuck of a time. First the babysitter crumped out. Then the brother of the girl the babysitter said I might try came down to the apartment and tried to hassle me, so I had to throw a screaming fit to get rid of him. Then Poops here made a mess in her pants and had to have a bunch of cookies to keep still enough to let me dress her. So then I had to clean her face off of all these Oreo crumbs. Then the bus didn't come along the boulevard. And didn't come. And I began to cry, so these old bums and bag ladies waiting for the bus with me began to cluck and joggle the kid so much back and forth between them I got scared they'd kidnap her or something crazy. They're all crazy, you know, these people that sleep in doorways under cardboard and everything. I don't know where they were all going on a holiday, I guess to a handout somewheres. Then when the bus did come finally I got off a stop late and wound up in front of some chemical-research place that's being built onto and where nobody knew anything, just these nerds inside when I knocked. Oh boy. I feel I been hiking for hours. Just at the end of this street I was so tired I put Paula down on the sidewalk to walk a little, she can walk perfectly well when it's a question of getting into one of my drawers at the apartment and messing everything up, and the crummy little bitch just sat down on the cold bricks and wouldn't budge and screamed back at me until this old lady weirdo with a tiny white dog with hair hiding its face and its feet too came along and went right up sniffing her and gave her a scare so she decided I was the lesser of available evils. Now that I've picked her up again I think her snowsuit smells of dog pee. Every time I go outdoors something like this happens, I should give up trying. Sorry if I've made everything late. It's a real fuck-up."

This was all said, with accompanying sounds of avuncular sympathy from me, as she divested herself and Paula of their outer clothes. Esther had come out into the hall and heard the end of the recital and gave her in greeting a slim hand. Esther has intimidatingly slender hands, freckled on the backs and the fingernails grown so long lately I fear being inadvertently slashed when she rolls over in bed. "You poor dear. It sounds like a nightmare."

"It's more or less the way my life is," Verna told her, sighing and suddenly remembering: "Then on the bus some old sleezeball with this great mixture of rotgut-whisky and rotten-teeth smell coming out of his mouth tried to put a move on me, cuddling up to my friend here. She was giving him her cute smile. She's a real little hooker, aren't you,

Poops?" She shook the child a little harder than she needed to to cinch the joke.

Paula's great brimming navy-blue eyes had fastened on me, and her honey-colored plump hand, with its curling small conical fingers, reached toward me in recognition. Her father's blood was visible in the hard hall light: a flare to her little nostrils, and a gleam to the fine black wires of her still-wispy hair. Her hair had been pulled back into two pigtails, as if her mother had chosen to state, *This is my pickaninny.*

"Rog should have offered to pick you up in the car," Esther said, though she had never suggested it.

I defended myself: "I thought somehow Dale . . ." The fact of the matter was that the neighborhood has resident parking for cars with stickers; but many strange cars— Divinity School students, and an overflow of shoppers from Sumner Boulevard—crowd our area, and if you find a space in front of your own house you are loathe to unpark and give it up. I changed the subject, turning to Verna. "I'm surprised there was anybody at the Chem Annex on Thanksgiving."

"Oh, there were guys there, but I don't know what they were sniffing. They'd never heard of Malvin Lane, I can tell you that. And here I finally found it right around the corner."

"The two cultures," I lamented, insincerely.

"*Do* come in and meet our son," Esther said, leading us partway down the hall but then heading back into the kitchen, from which the aroma of our meal emanated like the stupefying incense that in pre-Christian times accompanied prophecy.

I led Verna in.

"Hiya, Bozo," she said lazily to Dale as he stood, or,

rather, froze in a crouch. They did not touch. Once more I tried to decide whether or not they had slept together, and decided not, yet failed to be satisfied with the conclusion.

She did reach out and touch Richie, shaking the hand he extended with that exasperating limpness of adolescents. "So you're the guy knows all about Cyndi Lauper," she said.

"Isn't she great?" he responded, startled, pleased. He needs friends. Esther and I must seem to him impossibly old and remote. The Kriegman girls and he used to play together, but Cora, the one nearest him in age, at fifteen has joined the other two in womanhood—become a slut, as Richie put it.

"She's O.K.," Verna told him, assuming the thoughtful tone of an adult. "Like all those rock types, it's not them actually so much, it's what you put into them."

She was charming, I saw; she had carried Edna's oozy old carelessness into an era where it could be a style instead of an undercurrent. She wore a brick-red wool dress with a wide scalloped neckline; for a nineteen-year-old, she carried her bosom low, and was equally heavy and down-slipping in the hips. Yet a coltish springiness and unpredictability hung implicit in her body. Her complexion was sallow and her bleach-streaked twisty hair fell in damp-looking careless coils to her shoulders, so there was something Pre-Raphaelite, tubercular and ethereal, about the glow she gave off. She carried her small head forward on a substantial neck, wide and flat at the nape. Her ears had been pierced several times and held two pairs of gold rings. She wore some rings on her fingers but unexpectedly so: a wide copper band on one index finger, a chunk of turquoise on a pinkie. Her fingernails were cut short, like a child's, and this did stir me. Her caresses would not scratch.

"Da?" Paula was saying. Her grimy snowsuit had been removed in the hall; the toddler's little bare feet gripped the nap of our Bokhara as if fearful of falling through. It was not clear whom she had addressed, me or Richie or Dale: a real little hooker, Verna had said. Elbows daintily, apprehensively uplifted and pointed outward, the child tottered on those precarious, narrow, uncallused feet to the glass table, whose surface she smearily slapped, upon arrival, in triumph. "Da!"

Dale, seated again, reached out and took her onto his knees.

Verna's head slowly rotated on its strong neck and she said, "Great place, Nunc. You professors do all right for yourselves."

"It's all a question of seniority," I explained. Actually, Esther's father had been generous.

The fire crackled, and abruptly tumbled upon itself in a spurt of sparks. Richie got up and rearranged the logs with the tongs. Paula leaned forward from Dale's lap toward a silver cigarette case that Esther's father, whose name is Arnold Prince, had given us on our fifth anniversary. He, an Albany widower, had "done well," as they say, and after five years of docile marriage we had earned this sign of blessing; also from then on he, in princely fashion, had begun to release to Esther fractions of her inheritance, giving her a certain nimbus of independence and added value. We had married at a civil affair in Troy, New York, the city nearest the town that had housed our scandal. What a decided pleasure, really, it had been, affronting public opinion: as sweet as returning soldiers sometimes admit the act of killing to be, as sweet as we know the discomfort and failure of others to taste. Yet fourteen years later I had slipped into conformity of a slightly reshuffled sort, my father-in-law's blessing, as represented by his polished gift, clutched in the slippery grip of my mulatto grand-niece.

I asked Verna, "Could I get you anything to drink?"

She said, "Oh, Lordy, yes, Uncle Roger. I thought you'd never ask. I'd love a Black Russian."

"Uh—what goes into it? Vodka and—"

"Kahlúa."

"As I feared. We don't have any Kahlúa."

"How about a Grasshopper, then?"

"And *its* ingredients are—?"

"Oh, come on. Guess." Was she playing with me?

"Crème de menthe?"

"To be sure; but then I don't know what-all they put in on top of it. Real cream, I know, and some other crème de something. Then they shake it all up with cracked ice and pour it into a cocktail glass and put it on the bar. It's delicious, Nunc; haven't you ever had one?"

"When do you go to all these fancy bars?" Dale asked her, from the settee. His big hands were cupped to keep the cigarette case from being dropped on the glass table. Paula was sucking one silver corner of the lid, which she had pried open. A wad of tinted, dried-up English Ovals had fallen out; they had been in there since our faculty party last May.

Verna smirked and preened at him, for having asked, and glanced sideways at me, sensing that I was interested. "They don't have to be all that fancy; the one down at the end of Prospect, with the burnt-out upstairs, makes a great Grasshopper."

"Who takes you there?" Dale asked, which is what I had wanted to ask.

"Oh . . . guys. What's it to you? A girl's gotta have *some* fun, you know."

"Like the song says," Richie said, amused at himself for

thinking of it, and cocky from handling the fire competently.

"Right," Verna said, to Dale. "Like the man says, like the song says."

There was in her manner something of learned vulgarity, imitated, I supposed, from punk girl singers, and from Cher and Bette Midler—from a certain vein of American brass going back at least to the Andrews Sisters.

"I could make you a Bloody Mary," I suggested.

"That'd be great," she drawled to me, as if to a bartender she was flirting with, to annoy the guy who had brought her.

A great concussion filled the room—possessed it, from Bokhara rug up to dentil ceiling molding. Paula had dropped the cigarette case upon the glass table. Dale and Richie looked startled and guilty; Verna, who had been lighting a cigarette, sighed so the match went out, and then struck another. "See, Nunc?" she said. "She's a bitch."

I went over and said, "No harm done," though my keen eyes detected an insect-shaped scratch on the glass, and a bent corner of fine sterling. I polished the case as best I could on my tweed coat sleeve, and dumped back in the tinted cigarettes, so desiccated that several of them broke in my fingers.

In the kitchen, Esther was wrestling with the food; her hair was flying apart, shedding its pins. She grimaced at me like Medusa and said, "Never again!" She says that every year, at Thanksgiving.

When I came back with Verna's drink and another glass of wine for myself, the young people had gone into a huddle by the table, and were muttering in a language I didn't know. Youth: the mountain range that isolates it in a valley far from our own grows steeper, I think, as capitalism ever more ferociously exploits it as a separate market, beaming at it whole new worlds of potential expenditure—home video games and rear-entry ski boots and a million bits of quasi-musical whining cut by laser into compact discs. Ever more informational technique, ever more inane information. I saw that they were huddled because Dale was sketching on the back of an envelope little boxes connected by lines. The envelope, I noted in my sociological mood, was the telephone company's: our nation's trust-busting guardians broke up AT&T, with the result that our bills have become as bulky as love letters, and the line crackles like Rice Krispies when we pick up the receiver. I saw that the boxes had words in them: OR, AND, NOT. The rudiments of the new Gospel. "And you see," Dale was saying, primarily to Richie, but Verna and even Paula appeared to be also listening as his pencil point raced along the lines, "a current and no current, a one and a zero in terms of the binary code, will give a hot output from the OR and not from the AND, but if the AND output then goes into a NOT, it comes out—"

"Hot," Verna said, since my dear Richie was silent, baffled. Young male heads, seen from above, so oval and shaggy and blind, invite in their helplessness a ruffling. The boy looked up at my fatherly touch with a scowl of annoyance. He was with older youth now and wanted to succeed, to blend in. I gave Verna her Bloody Mary.

"Right," Dale said. "And if instead of a single bit we put four together, in a half-byte, so it looks like this"—he scribbled some zeros and ones; his handwriting was messy and displeasing, as that of scientists for some reason tends to be, as if precision of thought precludes that of presentation, and *vice versa,* clergymen, especially Episcopalians, invariably sporting fine italic hands—"and then another, which looks like this, what is going to come out of the OR circuit?"

After a pause during which Richie was given a chance to answer, Verna offered in her scratchy voice, "Oh one one one."

"Hey, you got it!" Dale exclaimed. "And out of an AND circuit, the same input?"

"Simple," she said. "Oh oh oh one."

"O.K.! And, Richie, if the OR circuit was then linked up to a NOT?"

"One oh oh oh," I pronounced from above, after the silence had become painful.

"Obviously," Dale said, still sketching. "And you can all see how with just these three simple switches, or gates, you can set up any complexity of ins and outs to analyze your input. For example, you can run these same two four-bit numbers into AND gates along with their own inverses, produced in these NOTs here, and then take those two outputs through an OR; what the output tells you, oh one one oh, is where the original inputs agreed: it's cold where they did and hot where they didn't."

"Neat," Verna said. Half her Bloody Mary was already drunk. She was now smoking one of the English Ovals, a mauve-tinted one.

"You should be going to school," I told her.

"That's what I keep telling her," Dale said.

"Tell it to Poopsie here," she said.

"Eedy-da," Paula uttered, clutching at Dale's paper with saliva-slippery fingers and rumpling it.

He retrieved the paper, smoothed it, and prepared with his pencil point to attack our ignorance still again. "Not to overdo," he said, "but this gets us right into Boolean algebra, and it's so beautiful you've got to get at least an inkling.

Boole was some guy in the middle of the nineteenth century who developed an algebra for dealing with logical concepts, true-false statements basically, but it turns out to be just the math you need for the circuitry inside computers. An OR gate, for example, really adds, in the terms of Boolean algebra, where one plus one isn't two or zero, as you might think from the binary base, but one; I mean, positive plus positive is still positive. And an AND gate multiplies, really, when you think that anything times zero has to be zero, and so it takes two positives to produce a positive. What the NOT gate does is invert, really, so you write that with a hat like this over the number: the inverse of zero equals one, and vice versa. And that's basically all Boolean algebra does; but there're a lot of theorems that follow from these basics, and it's amazing what you can do. It tends to look confusing, but it's simple at heart."

"In a pig's eye it is," Verna said, a little blearily now. Richie had already eased away and was back to poking the fire: carbohydrates sinking back into the carbon atoms compounded in the heart of a star millions and millions of years ago. I thought of Dale's pencil point. Had the universe really been once that small? "Don't poke it too much," I warned my son. "You'll make it go out."

"We're about to eat anyway," Esther said, from the archway. She came closer in her zigzagging green velvet and said to Dale, "I was listening, a little bit, to your lesson. It sounded fascinating. I was wondering, would you ever like to come, say once a week, and tutor Richie? He's having a terrible time with bases."

"Mom, I'm *not,"* the boy protested. "Nobody in class is getting it, the teacher is lousy."

"The teacher is black," Esther told Dale.

"That shouldn't make any difference," Verna said quickly.

"I know," Esther sighed. "One of these young black women with some third-rate education that these expensive liberal schools feel they have to hire. I'm all for it in principle, but not when it's making the children stupid."

"Richie's not stupid," Dale said, entering the silence Esther had stunned into being with her illiberal declaration. "I'd be happy to tutor him, if we can find a time. My hours are kind of funny, with the time-sharing and all. For my graphics I have to split a VAX 8600 with a girl doing pattern recognitions."

"I'm sure," Esther stated airily, "we can find an hour to suit our mutual conveniences. Richie, come help me lift the turkey out." Peremptory, unrepentant, full of electricity, she turned her back on all of us.

"Nunc?" A small reedy voice poked softly at my side. "D'you think we could sneak another Bloody Mary in before all that food descends?"

Throughout the meal, the endless oppressive Thanksgiving feast that squeezes breath from the chest and all space of maneuver from the mind, I was conscious not only of Verna, whose sallow flesh with such confident indolence pressed against the bulging wool of her red dress, and whose flitting gestures and casual declarations seemed to my wine-tinted awareness infinitely if vaguely promising, but of Esther as seen through the eyes of Dale Kohler: an older woman, petite and wearily wise, yet with a maternal depth of tolerance and nurture beneath her crisp, taut-pulled manner.

"Does anybody want to say grace?" she had asked, the meal arrayed.

She knew it pained me to, though I could manage. The old words would roll, once my rusty mouth flopped open. I had actually composed the opening phrase and bowed my head when Dale's eager voice broke in: "I'd be happy to, if nobody else wants to."

Who could object? We were his helpless victims, cannibals to his missionary. He made us all hold hands. His evangelism had been learned in a folksy, nasal school. My ears shut as his words droned upward, in that voice we hear all the time over at the Divinity School, the singsong voice of homegrown Christian piety: believing souls are trucked in like muddy, fragrant cabbages from the rural hinterland and in three years of fine distinctions and exegetical quibbling we have chopped them into cole slaw salable at any suburban supermarket. We take in saints and send out ministers, workers in the vineyard of inevitable anxiety and discontent. The death of Christianity has been long foreseen but there will always be churches to serve as storehouses for the perennial harvest of human unhappiness.

A few of Dale's words bored into my brain, some kind of remembrance, before we stuffed our faces, of all the starving and homeless in the world, particularly East Africa and Central America, and my mind skidded off into wondering whether the UNICEF God Who would respectfully receive such prayers were not a frightful anticlimax to those immense proofs via megastar and mammoth tusk, and skidded further into thinking of meals and betrayals—the salt spilled by Judas, the chronic diet of Cronus, dinners whipped up by Clytemnestra and Lady Macbeth, the circle of betrayal established wherever more than two or three gather or a family sits down as one. Verna's hand was in my right hand and she had a rapid pulse; Richie's was in my left and there was heat here, too, the Oedipal animus, and on my side paternal coolness, the tigerish tendency to view the cub, once born, as a competitor as pleasant to extinguish as any other. A competitor born, furthermore, into the heart of one's own turf, which he fills with his electronic static and smelly socks and ravenous ill-educated appetite for what our cretinous popular culture assures him are the world's good things. Emerson was right, we all have cold hearts. And my frosty mind, as Dale's voice breathily aspired toward its final curlicue of blessing upon this food about to be so guiltily digested, skidded out of our house entirely, into the Kriegmans', whom I imagined, as Jews and atheists, to be taking the day more lightly, without any of the spiritual cholesterol implicit in our Puritan forefathers' self-congratulation, and to be having more fun. Jews are probably right: one Testament is enough. There were, in fact, quite a lot of Jewish converts to Christianity initially, but when the Messiah failed to reappear, as firmly promised to the first generation, and as an additional disappointment the Temple was destroyed in the year 70, they quite sensibly lost heart and let the Greeks take control of the expanding operation.

Dale's benediction at last launched and growing ever smaller in the stratosphere, we unlinked our sweaty hands, and there settled ineluctably into the center of my vision the turkey to be carved. Oh, those diabolically elusive, bloody, and tenacious second joints! And the golden-glazed skin that proves tougher than strapping tape! Esther, compared with Lillian, does a dry turkey, and you can slice the breast only so thin before crumbs and shredding compromise the slice. We were, at table, clockwise, Verna, I, Richie, Dale, Esther, and Paula, in Richie's dusty old high chair, which Esther had recovered from the third floor and in which the little girl, abruptly exhausted by her bus ride, long walk, and bite of silver cigarette case, kept slumping asleep. I, too, while I did not slump, lost consciousness for intervals: at least, there are great glutinous holes in my recollection of our conversation.

Esther, between doling out orange gobs of squash and white gobs of mashed potatoes, earnestly asked Dale what exactly his research in computer graphics involved. He said, "It's kind of hard to explain. A lot of it is looking for programming shortcuts that could bring raster-display dynamics closer to vector display in terms of image refresh time and memory cost. A vector display, you see, specifies to the screen two points and then draws a line between them, and even though there are a lot of lines and some of the instructions take a lot of crunching, it's as fast as the eye can take in, by and large: I mean, you see motion happening. With raster, it's like a newspaper photograph: you have a grid of dots, called pixels, maybe five hundred twelve by five hundred twelve, that's some two hundred sixty-two thousand separate pieces of output, and so each frame takes minutes to generate instead of microseconds, which is what you'd need for convincing animation. Thirty scans a second is what you see on television; you can get some sense of the refresh that's going on by wiggling your fingers in front of a live screen. Also, there's not just dimension and perspective, there's color and light, and light bouncing in certain patterns off of different textures—all that has to be programmed in. You look at this table now in front of you, there's a tremendous amount of visual information, I mean, a *ter*rifying amount, if you take into account, say, the sheen on that turkey skin, and the way it's folded, and the way the water in the glass refracts that bowl, and the way the onions are a different kind of shiny from the bowl, and then there's a little smoke, and look at that sliver of red in the stem of the wineglass from the cranberry sauce a foot away. The Japanese do an amazing job with that sort of thing—glass balls floating around in front of checkerboards and translucent cylinders and so forth. It means you have to calculate through the pixel, as if each one is a tiny window in the viewing plane, exactly how the beam of light you're shooting through that little aperture would go, and if it strikes something transparent, where it would go then; maybe it will even divide." His two lengthy forefingers went separate ways in illustration. His purple-and-green necktie began to look psychedelic, in the tawny low November filtered through our bare birches and our windows with their ornamental leaded lights of stained glass, a lurid gold and livid blue and the same poisonous red as Dale's cranberry juice. "Some pixels," he went on, "there's maybe five or six separate inputs to be averaged out. I mean, it's awesome, once you get into duplicating even a highly controlled set of objects, how it all blows up with complexity. It begins to scare you, in a way."

"In what way?" Esther asked, having eaten the morsels she allowed herself and now exhaling cigarette smoke, a billowing twin plume from her nostrils and lips, blue in the wan sunlight, a ball of smoke as big as her head.

"Well, I mean, just in trying to duplicate Creation on this one simple plane of visual information. You see, it's not quite like a photographer sitting down in front of a scene, or even a painter doing what's in front of him dab after dab. In computer graphics, you store the mathematical representation of the object, and then you can call up the image of it from every perspective, in wire-frame diagram or with the hidden lines removed, or in cross-section, say with a mechanical part you want to analyze. And it does it, generally —we're talking vector now—instantly, as far as our eye can tell, though even here with some of the crunching you can feel the computer begin to labor, and the delay can get up to a second, which feels like an eternity if you're used to working with computers."

An eternity. In a grain of sand. My eyes itched. Clouds of food particles. Receptors high in the nostrils can detect one particle in a million. Freud claims our sense of smell was freighted with poignant meanings when we walked on all fours, our noses closer to the dung-laden ground. We are base. A broad neck on a woman seems to invite a man to pounce, then lie there luxuriating like a fucked-out lion. Copulation from the rear nature's standard way; how did we ever get turned around? Frontal nudity, rated X. *In Adam's fall / We sinned all.* Verna was eating steadily, in silence. Could it be she was hungry? In this day and age can anyone not an African still be simply hungry?

"I like the way," Richie contributed, "they turn things over and over like in TV station identifications or in *Superman I,* where the three bad guys are condemned to space."

"Yeah," Dale said, "tumbling. That's fairly trivial to achieve, that sort of deformation and exaggerated perspective and so on, once you have the information; then it's just a matter of shifting and stretching coördinates under some pretty straightforward transformations. Simple trigonometry."

"Trig, ugh," the boy said.

"Come on, Richie. Trig is beautiful, wait till you get to it."

Wait till you get to sex, I hallucinated that he was saying. The odd thing, Richie, is, that's it. It's a grand surprise nature has cooked up for us, love with its accelerated pulse rate and its drastic overestimation of the love object, its rhythmic build-up and discharge; but then that's it, there isn't another such treat life can offer, unless you count contract bridge and death.

"The theory of it, I mean," Dale was saying. "And now with computers you don't have to do all that looking up in tables and long multiplication we used to do, the computers do it all for us. Just the little hand-calculators that cost ten ninety-five; in 1950 it would have taken a big refrigerated room to hold all those circuits you can put in your vest pocket now, if you wear a vest. But, hey, how come I'm doing all the talking? Professor, tell us about heresy or something."

"Yes, you should eat before it all gets cold," Esther solicitously told Dale.

"Nobody ever wants to hear about my poor heretics," I informed the table. "Tertullian, for example, whom I've been dipping into, to refresh my Latin. What a writer—crazy for language, when he takes off it's like Shaw, he'll say any mad thing to keep the ball rolling. Or like Kierkegaard, when he got the wind up. But Tertullian had a sweet, humanist side, too. He claimed, for instance, that the soul is naturally Christian: *anima naturaliter christiana.* And—you mathematicians—he did some of the basic Christian calculations. He invented the Trinity; at least he used the word *trinitas* for the first time in ecclesiastical Latin. And he put forward the formulation *una substantia, tres personae* for God, and for Christ the notion of a double essence, *duplex status,* rather nicely, *non confusus sed conjunctus in una persona—deus* et *homo.* An AND gate, I guess that would be, Dale?"

"Actually," the young man said, smiling and swallowing, "I think that's an OR. It's harder to get through an AND than an OR."

"Let the boy eat," Esther said. "That's very interesting,

dear. You notice, Verna, that nobody asked us about *our* specialties?"

The child, bless her, ignored my wicked wife and turned to me. "What made him a heretic, Nunc? He sounds pretty straight-arrow."

"Before I answer that very intelligent question, who would like some more of this bird, this homely half-hacked Paraclete of ours?"

Richie held his plate toward me. "Just white slices," he said. "Thinner than you cut them before."

"God damn it, you can't cut them any thinner with this dull knife; they fall apart!" My profanity startled even me: I traced it back to the third glass of white wine and the fact that Richie wears braces on his teeth, to which orange and white bits of food were clinging, a repulsiveness all the worse for his being unaware of it.

Little pigtailed Paula, having slumped to sleep in her high chair, half woke, and began, not to cry, but to make that mechanical noise of childish discontent, of air jouncing up and down the trachea, which is even more irritating.

Esther said, "Poor thing, falling to sleep in that awkward position, I bet she has a cramp."

"Do you, Poops? Or just think it's time to give Mom a hard time?" Verna pushed her face within an inch of her child's, merrily, mockingly, displaying to my angle of vision the delicious dimple in her round cheek, deepening.

Startled, challenged, Paula stared, hiccupped, and began in earnest to cry.

"In brief, Verna," I answered in an overriding voice, "he was a heretic because he was a Puritan, a purist, called a Montanist in those days; after doing battle against paganism, Marcionism, Gnosticism, and Judaism, he found the

Church itself impossibly worldly and corrupt. He was too good for this world."

"Just like you, dear," Esther said, and urged Verna, "Give her to me."

"There you go, Poops," Verna said, in the strength of her youth hoisting the child, tantrum and all, through the air on extended bare arms, into Esther's lap with an impact that visibly jarred my small-boned wife.

"You'll be interested, Esther," I called to her, "to know that one of Tertullian's works, *Ad uxorem,* is addressed to his wife and tells her that after his death she must remain a widow. Then he thought about it and wrote another tract saying that if she *must* remarry, it should be to a Christian. Then he thought still some more and in *De exhortatione castitatis* exhorted her to remain chaste, *not* to remarry, *even* to a Christian. Also, he thought that women, whether married or unmarried, should remain veiled."

"Don't you just hate men?" Esther asked Verna.

"I'll swap you Little Miss Nasty for a ciggyboo," Verna was saying to her.

"Also, he thought Christians should fast more and never serve in the Roman army. See, Dale, nobody's listening. My heretics lay an egg every time."

"I'd love one too," Esther responded. "But I don't have my pack with me, it must be in the kitchen."

"I know where there're some."

"Not with me," Dale said to me, adding to Esther, "I love these boiled baby onions. My mother used to make them, mixed with sugar peas."

"Oh those old things, they're so dry, they've been there forever," Esther called, seeing Verna leave the table and go into the living room, through the archway with its spindlework header, toward the glass table and the silver cigarette case that Esther's father had given us nine years ago.

"What's the *mat*ter with you?" I asked Richie, exasperated by his sulk. "Eat those thin slices you're so fussy about."

"You didn't have to swear," he said, near tears, his face bowed to his plate. That touching shaggy top of a young male's head again. A beast without eyes, butting through life.

"Our specialty," Esther rather operatically called over little Paula's wispy, frizzy head, as Verna returned with a handful of tinted cigarettes, "is cleaning up the messes men make. First they make a mess *in* us, then they make one *around* us." The wine was getting to her, too. When a middle-aged woman becomes overanimated, her throat turns stringy, a harp she herself plays. Esther's stringiness would lessen if she'd let up on that compulsive diet. It's as if she's denying me more than an ounce of woman over the marital quota.

"Maybe they can't help it," Verna said, slinging back into her chair with a soft and graphically unprogrammable multiple shift of volumes that, so vividly conveying the fluid heft of her body, made the inside of my mouth go dry. She lit a mint-green oval with a candle from the table.

"Christ, don't sulk," I muttered sideways to Richie.

"Leave the boy alone," Esther called, again in a clarion tone, as if the toddler's body in her lap formed a shield behind which she could launch spears at me. The tint of the cigarette pinched between her fingers was a high-toned pearl gray. "You've hurt his feelings."

"It's not me who's hurt his feelings, it's Thanksgiving depresses him; it depresses everybody."

"And don't tell us any more about that dreadful old bigot of yours; now he really *is* depressing. It's sheer perversity drove you, Roger, to specialize in those awful people, these antique fanatics not even skin and bones now, just dust, if that." She added in a tone slightly more conciliatory, "If nobody wants any more, you could clear, dear." She was pinned down by Paula, whose tint was milky brown.

"I'll help," Verna said, rising into her own smoke, so it swirled down her scalloped neckline into her bosom.

In the kitchen, we managed to bump bottoms, without acknowledgment, but twice.

"Scrape into the little middle sink, it has the Disposall," I told her, as if muttering a dirty secret. Reaching past her to get the dessert plates where Esther had stacked them, I brushed with my tweed sleeve the warm bareness of her forearm, that had lifted her child with Amazonian ease. Only my half-sister's daughter, I calculated: our shared blood had been divided and subdivided.

"I'll take the dishes in; if you could bring one of the pies warming in the oven . . ."

"Ooh," she exclaimed, "pumpkin! I love pumpkin, Nunc. Ever since I was a baby, I guess because it was so mushy. I've always had this terrible weakness for things you don't have to chew, like custard and tapioca."

"That's why I like meatloaf," I said. Setting the glass plates before Esther to serve on, I told her, "And then in *De monogamia* he concluded that marrying a second time was as bad as adultery."

Ignoring me, she was saying to Dale, "Just the little I overheard made it clearer to me than anything I've read or seen on television. You'd make a *won*derful teacher."

"Well, actually, I did teach a section of introductory calc two terms ago, but for some reason the university . . ."

I went back to the kitchen and took the apple pie from the oven: apple, the favorite treat of my somber boyhood, soaked with cinnamon and the crust marked by "bird's feet." Yet I was served it, as I remembered, very rarely, though there were orchards all around us in Ohio. My mother was always withholding things, not because they couldn't have been provided but in illustration of some life principle that she had painfully learned and was selflessly imparting. Since I had been weighing her belly down when my father decamped, I felt partially to blame for her life of "doing without," and accepted without protest my share of privation.

In the kitchen, Verna, before bringing the pumpkin, was pouring a neat shot of vodka into her empty Bloody Mary glass. The dregs tinted it pink. "You don't have to chew that either, do you?" I said.

She tittered and tossed it down. Her face was rosy, her slant eyes bright. "G'*wan,*" she said, in a Cyndi Lauperish voice, and this time did deliberately swing her ample wool-clad rump into mine.

"Let's not drop anything," I warned.

Esther, with Paula still on her lap, was explaining to Dale, "And then in the summer we *do* try to get away for a few weeks, but the idea of owning a whole *oth*er set of knives and forks, and *two* toasters, and double sets of bed linen, and kitchen chairs, and worrying about whichever house you're not in being broken into just strikes me as a *night*mare, I don't know how everybody we know does it. Dale dear: would you like pumpkin or apple or both?"

"A little bit of both, please."

"A *little* bit. Not enough to make a byte?"

He smiled; these flashes of suavity annoyed me almost more than anything about him. "No, that wouldn't leave any for anybody else. A byte is usually eight bits."

"One of each." She handed him his plate. "Does that make an OR, or an AND?"

That pleasant smile again, deeper on one side than the other. "If one of them wasn't there, and that made the one next to it disappear, that would be an AND."

"I see. Richie dear? You look so vexed with all of us. Forgive me, Verna, I'll get to you when it's ladies' turn. Let's serve the mighty gentlemen first."

Seeing before her eyes the knife and pie server flashing in Esther's narrow deft hands, the little honey-colored girl began to laugh. She reached for her own share. Her fingers sank deep into the point of a triangle of pumpkin. "I'll take that one," Verna said quickly, and rose to lift the child from the hostess's lap. "Damn you, Poops! You're a greedy bitch," she said.

Roughly restored by her mother to the high chair, Paula began to make again that dreadful grinding noise, of inner slippage; Verna ingeniously suppressed it by seizing the child's pumpkin-smeared hand and pushing it into her aggrieved, down-curling mouth. Grudgingly, then happily, Paula sucked.

"I said I'd look into high-school equivalency tests," I reminded Verna quietly, when Paula's fuss seemed subsided.

"Roger darling," Esther called. "We've forgotten you. Just apple?"

"Let me try a little pumpkin, too."

"Oh. I thought you hated pumpkin."

"I forget if I do, it's been so long since I had any. Please."

"Well. Aren't we being adventurous in our old age?" Her green eyes narrowed and shuttled, deducing some relation between the girl beside me and pumpkin pie. It was not my wife's methodical nature to let things pass, to let them lie undeveloped; otherwise, she might have slept with me on a few guilt-enhanced occasions and called it quits, and Lillian and I would still be entertaining the orphans of the parish at a long and childless table. Dear Lillian: I could not believe anybody could be happy so many months in Florida. Whenever I tried to picture her, she seemed an overexposed photograph.

"And apparently," I continued to Verna, under the clatter of dessert forks, "there's something called a GED, a General Educational Development Test, that's given once a month in any sizable city, and if you pass it they give you the high-school equivalency certificate. It's in five parts—English grammar, English literature, social studies, science, and mathematics—and each test is up to two hours long."

Esther was explaining to Dale in a carrying voice, "Of course, if you have *any*thing of a garden, you really can't leave for more than a few days at a time at any time up until August; it's silly, I know, to be an absolute *slave* to these flowers, but I honestly believe, and I know you'll think me absurd, that plants have to be talked to. They have to be loved." With the hand not holding the dessert fork, she kept tucking back pieces of stray hair. As she did this her slender hand visibly trembled. I was seeing her, while not forgetting Verna at my side, through Dale's eyes: the effect was of sudden living color, of a tuning adjustment on the UHF channel. She was dazzling and fetching, her green velvet shimmering in the dying holiday window-light, her gingery hair glistening in a multitude of bright points, her intelligent rounded forehead glowing, her prominent eyes processing irony and flirtation with electronic rapidity, and her wry lips lipsticked today a millimeter beyond their edges, to lend her puckish, almost miniature face a suggestion of the smeary, of the amusingly mussed. The aura of boredom had been tuned out.

Verna pensively ate, scarcely chewing. "Sounds kind of rinky-dink," she said. "Maybe it's not worth it."

"It *is* worth it," I insisted. "It gets secondary school out of the way and then you can start thinking about college. Or secretarial school. Or modelling school, or whatever you want to do. You're only nineteen, you have a *world* of possibilities." The old counsellor in me, revived, was breathing hard.

"I don't know shit about social studies," she said.

"You know about the checks and balances and the constitution and what you read in the newspapers."

"No I don't. And I don't read the newspapers."

"You listen to the radio. There's news on the radio."

"Not the stations I listen to," she said. "They're all music."

". . . they're such a *com*fort to me," Esther said at the other end of the table, "flowers," and turned her head, and I saw her close up, through Dale's eyes, the smeared edge of lipstick and the translucent filaments of whisker on her upper lip, this pensive upper lip's little reposeful ins and outs of muscle, and I felt a sexual stir in my lap, a blip of stiffening there, with his instinctive recognition, religious and information-saturated as he was, that this woman, in bed, once she had decided to be there, would do anything. The lightness of her, the provocative flexible smallness of Esther's frame, and the hungry green of her eyes with their gentle hyperthyroid bulge, all told him that. Anything.

"I don't know beans, Nunc," Verna whined.

"You know more than you think you do," I said, impatiently. I felt I had become an unwelcome voice on an all-music station.

Esther called down, "What's he trying to do to you, Verna? What's this test you're talking about?"

"I don't want to talk about it," the younger woman said miserably. "It's too embarrassing."

"The high-school equivalency test," Dale said. "I've been bugging her about it for a year. That's great you're going to do it."

"I'm *not*. We were just talking about it."

"It'll be easy," Richie said, coming out of his sulk. "It'll be a lot easier than going to Pilgrim Day every day."

"Professor Lambert can help you with the literature and grammar," Dale said, "and I can refresh you on the math and science."

"Oh no," Esther said to him. She laid her long narrow hand on his big knobby and red-knuckled one. "You've been signed up to tutor Richie."

Richie cried, straining for the right tone, "Go for it, Verna!"

"Everybody fuck off," Verna begged. "Why are you all on my case?"

There was a pause, during which Paula burped and tried to suck her other hand, which had no mushed pumpkin on it. Esther at last announced, "Why, my dear, because we're all *fond* of you."

In the kitchen, as we together cleared the plates and prepared the coffee to have by the fire (which had, thanks to Richie's ministrations, gone out), my wife said to me dryly, "We both seem to be getting into the education business."

"I'm always in it," I said, displeased that she appeared to be pushing (like those togaed old men, garrulous dust, who were my bread and butter) to have things better left ambiguous rigorously spelled out.

"I guess we all are," Esther conceded, with a sigh, lifting a distracted hand to her loosening hair and a wistful cloud passing over her puffy lips in a way that made her look rather mad and quite enchanting.

iii

All that December the weather held warm, as if the skies were bestowing their benediction upon our national choice, our re-election. God shone through the President, it seemed to many, and to the rest he was a force of nature it was idle to resist. Many who voted for his opponent were secretly pleased that he won; he asked so little, and promised so much. No, that is not quite true, for the promises, when examined, were ever sparser and vaguer: he was relieving the electorate of even the burden of expectation, and in this was perfecting his imitation of that Heavenly Presider whose inactivity has held our loyalty for two millennia (and indeed, if, *contra* Marcion, we consider the Jewish God and the Christian God to be one, for twice again as many millennia as that (assuming that Archbishop Ussher's date for Creation, 4004 B.C., also dates the commencement of active, sub-angelic worship and praise (though there is a sense, of course, in which even vacant space praises Him; and a holy fool like Dale might argue that the immutable and eternal laws of mathematics are precisely the form of this highly hypothetical praise))). Follow, you who can.

Esther had some years ago acquired a small, scarcely paying part-time job in a day-care center twenty blocks from our home, from seven-thirty to two-thirty four days a week. To save parking difficulties and the possibility, real enough, of vandalization of our invitingly marless new Audi, which had been described in the brochure as gray but had proved upon delivery to be a subtle swarthy Germanic color for which no word exists in English, she had lately taken to the bus and left the car available at the front curb or, less usually, in our small garage, which was crowded with gardening equipment and trash barrels and an obsolete swing set; and so I, on a non-seminar day, had no trouble walking back from my morning lecture and (after a glass of milk and a piece of last Sunday's quiche consumed standing in the chilly emptiness of the kitchen, as I spied on Sue Kriegman typing with fretful face in her upstairs study and ineffectually deliberated turning up the thermostat from Esther's stingy setting) getting into the car and heading for my niece's project. I had warned her by phone that I was coming, and had armed myself with a slippery big blue anthology of American literature that, in the befuddling stacked muchness of our university bookstore, had seemed possibly secondary-school level.

Driving along Sumner Boulevard, where I had walked a month before, I was struck by the loss of majesty. The sky no longer hovered tumultuous with wind-tormented clouds; instead, a fuzzy yellowish half-rainy wool merged with the blur of the now leafless trees and swallowed the tops of the skyscrapers at the distant center of the city. The stores that at a walker's pace had levelled a certain gritty merchandising spell appeared in the longer, swifter perspective from an auto to be hopeless makeshift tenants of tin-and-tar-garnished boxes scarcely more enduring than the cityscapes I would once fashion, on rainy Saturday afternoons in South Euclid, out of cereal boxes and egg cartons, Scotch tape and crayons. The people on the street, caught between the darkening time of year and the unseasonably tepid weather, appeared bewildered about how to dress, and showed every-thing from parkas to jogging shorts. Two young black women in long Medusa braids and Day-Glo miniskirts flitted along like negatived Alices who had passed through a besmirched looking-glass, their jaunty and girlish inno-cence a sign, somehow, of its very opposite. Poverty and flash jostled along the avenue, and I was tempted to sing, heading out of my accustomed neighborhood into one where possibilities were in squalor reborn. Indifferent Christmas tinsel spiralled up lamp standards and the win-dows of even the lock shops and the fishing-tackle store held the compulsory flecks of cotton snow and red cardboard.

I put on my blinker to turn left on Prospect and discov-ered, what I had not noticed on foot, that the street was one-way. I had to pass a block beyond, downhill, toward the end of the bridge that crossed the river; here, beneath its half-painted iron girders, there was a tangle of traffic is-lands, and in trying to turn left I found myself headed away from the city on a numbered state highway, and in turning off this rattling, shuddering route I found myself between brick factory walls, their tall windows mute with plywood or else erratically shattered, random panes replaced by rusted tin. It took me what seemed many impatience-stretched minutes to work my way back to Prospect, through rows of narrow houses whose porches were six steps up from the pavement and whose front windows and doors bore pathetic coarse touches of seasonal decoration. At the project, a cursory wreath with plastic ribbon hung on the scarred metal portal of each entryway. I parked, with a crunching of already pulverized glass, beneath the sign that in two languages warned off unauthorized vehicles. While I was locking the doors a small black boy, surely not yet ten years old, came up to me and asked, "You there mister: watch you car?"

The child was wearing a dirty rugby shirt—broad green and yellow stripes, and a white collar. It was warm for December, but not that warm. "Does it need watching?"

He blinked, unaccustomed to irony. Then he said earnestly, "You ain't suppose to park round here but if I watch it it'll be O.K."

"You must know the mayor."

He blinked again, beginning to worry, but not ceasing to stare up at me. "I don't know him any but I know guys that know him, that's for sure."

"In that case, here's a hard-earned dollar," I said, figuring that with just his bare hands and a sharp rock the child could do a thousand dollars' worth of damage to the Audi's perfect off-gray skin. I held the bill on high, out of his reach; I was getting into the swing of this encounter and warming up for the next. "How come," I asked him, "you're not in school?"

He still couldn't figure how seriously to take me. But I still had the dollar, so he answered: "They don't teach you none of the shit you need to know."

This seemed so acute and sad an analysis I lost heart for the game and gave him his protection money. "You're going to catch cold, you should wear a sweater," I told him for a final lesson, but here I went too far. The child stared me down in solemn, dumbfounded silence and, bested, I headed with my heavy schoolbook up to Verna's apartment. In the stairwell, the slogans involving Tex and Marjorie had been painted over, with a pinkish latex applied by roller.

I knocked on Verna's blank door.

"Nunc?" Her voice seemed to quaver, so that I imagined her terrified or, for some reason, in tears.

"Yes."

But when, with a rattling of the safety-lock chain, she opened to me, she was dry-eyed and, like the black girls glimpsed on the avenue, jaunty. Warned of my coming, she wore not that seductive short bathrobe but a denim skirt and a snug white long-sleeved jersey and—an odd, comic, debonair touch—a silk paisley kerchief tied around her neck. Its effect was not to diminish but to sharpen my awareness of the naked skin above the rather low neckline of the jersey, a bareness now sandwiched between strips of cloth like that bare pale belly which women's underwear, in the old days when panties and bras were substantial garments, used to frame so invitingly. There was an apache flavor to this neckcloth, a rakish vulnerability. A bow or knot carries with it the idea of being unknotted. The bumps of her nipples were conspicuous, but she might be, instead of braless, merely wearing a very elastic bra. Instead of being, as on my previous visit, barefoot, Verna had comp-leted her costume with little oval ballet slippers, too fragile for wearing outdoors in winter but in here announcing that she was primly dressed for study, and ready for avuncular instruction.

"Did you get the application forms? I'd like to see them," I said, removing the sheepskin car coat I had put on over my tweed jacket. It was boiling hot in the project. I took off my jacket as well.

"Well I went over there, and they wanted to see a birth certificate. You see, if I'm less than eighteen, they don't want me graduating ahead of what would have been my high-school class."

"Couldn't you show them your driver's license?"

"Yeah, I did; but since it's an out-of-state they can't accept it. The lady was terribly nice and all, but she said they just aren't allowed to, they don't know how other states verify or something, so she really needs a birth certificate. As if everybody has theirs just lying around. Mine's back there in my mom's safe-deposit box, if she hasn't lost it from the last time she took it out. I thought everything was on these computers down in Washington now; they just punched your Social Security number in and out came your fingerprints and blood type and who all you've slept with and everything."

"We haven't quite come to that yet. It's still only 1984. Have you called or written Edna yet?" Saying Edna's name, framing it in my mouth, was for me a kind of exposed skin, a distinct small dangerous pleasure.

"Not yet, Nunc," Verna said. This teasing and not quite friendly nickname was perhaps her way of registering an intuition that her mother's name excited me. "I found dealing with the bureaucracy just too depressing. I came home and took a bath and I must admit kind of forgot about it until you called this morning." She saw the disappointment on my face and explained in mitigation, "I had thought the place where you went would be just down the street, in those creepy old brick civic buildings across from the Domino—you know, the bar that had the fire—but it turns out I had to hike, pushing Poopsie here all the way in this clunky stroller with a bent wheel somebody on the floor below sold me for fifteen dollars, I should have paid five, up to some city high school I never knew existed, a humongous big thing with pillars, you wouldn't believe it, way up past ball fields and funeral parlors and adult bookshops for the pimple-faced kids, I guess, and junky used-car lots; it looks just like some incredibly hideous and pretentious jail, except it's up on a hill and doesn't have barbed wire on top of the fences. At least none that I could see. The lady in the office, actually, like I said, was nice enough; she said really anybody who could read could probably pass, but she advised not to take all the tests on the same day."

"Well, shall we see if you *can* read? I brought this anthology of American lit."

"For me? Nunc, you're too sweet. What's up with you anyway?"

Her apartment was tidier than when I had been here before. The apples and bananas in the salad bowl on her card table looked fresh, sharp-edged, as if waiting to be painted as a still life. Her television set was off, and the cassette player too. In the silence one could hear conversations, or televised conversations, from other apartments in the project. I asked, "Where's Paula?"

"Shh. Don't say her name so loud. The little fucker flopped off into a nap finally. She woke me up at five-thirty this morning, I could have killed her. Nunc, this book weighs an absolute ton!"

"You don't have to read it all. As I remember high school, American literature consists of 'Thanatopsis,' by William Cullen Bryant, 'The Cask of Amontillado,' by Edgar Allan Poe, and 'The Luck of Roaring Camp,' by Bret Harte. Let's begin with 'Thanatopsis.' It's the shortest."

Verna sat herself in the rickety bamboo basket chair, and something in the summery noises of its creaking beneath her weight, or in the shadows that clung at this dwindling hour of the gray day to the walls of her corner apartment and that crept down into the front of her jersey, which my gaze explored as I stood behind her, evoked confused echoes of a day or days with Edna in Ohio, summer days, when I was spending my obligatory month with my father, and we children sought shelter from the sun and insects and boredom in attic games. There were a number of us, not just

Edna and myself, but others from the neighborhood, thirteen- and fourteen-year-olds, and we had dared one another to play strip poker, there under the slanted roof, among cobwebbed trunks and cardboard boxes, on a rag rug we had unrolled to put over the dusty bare boards, and Edna's luck ran poorly, and she shed one by one her shoes and socks, and argued that barrettes could be counted and added two of those to her pile. Then, with a solemn look, her long curly hair having fallen loose, she reached into the neck of her summer-weight sweater to undo her dickey, a strange starchy butterfly pulled into the dim and secretive attic light. Dust in swirling formations moved through the thick shafts of sun from the little windows. Edna was down to her indispensable clothes, and began to argue and, it seemed to me from something choked in her voice, to cry, and we had a vote, whether to continue with the game or not, and since there were three boys and two girls the vote should have gone to continue, but I voted no, with the girls, and Edna gave me a little impulsive kiss of gratitude. But was it gratitude, I wondered all the rest of that summer, or somehow surprise and even pity? I had voted with the girls.

And of another summer, or was it the same?—we seem in my memory to be the same size, though I of course was a year older, but slow to grow, and never tall—I was tussling with her in a field, the two of us smelling of sweat in a sea of the lazy scratchy scent of grass drying out and going to seed, and as if pronounced the stronger by an invisible referee she stood up lording it over me and I was too lazy or breathless to stand, and looked up her legs as now I looked down the front of Verna's low bodice, and saw into Edna's shorts up to her underpants, which had been tugged in our struggles slightly askew, to one side, revealing dark hair, what seemed a lot of it. I had begun to have pubic hair also but I was older, she was hairier than I, she was right to lord it over me, this mysterious sweat-smelling powerful playmate and enemy who lived with my father while I didn't. While I couldn't.

Over Verna's shoulder I read silently,

> To him who in the love of Nature holds
> Communion with her visible forms, she speaks
> A various language; for his gayer hours
> She has a voice of gladness, and a smile
> And eloquence of beauty, and she glides
> Into his darker musings, with a mild
> And healing sympathy, that steals away
> Their sharpness, ere he is aware.

I could feel her eyes and mind moving along the same smooth, faintly resonant passageways of language. "He wrote this," I told her, "when he was younger than you."

"Yeah, Nunc—I read the little note at the beginning, too."

I was offended: I had not read the note and had been drawing upon my general erudition. "What do you make of the opening lines?"

"They seem flaky. 'Gayer hours.' "

"The word has changed meaning these last years. Just tell me in your own words what Bryant is saying here."

"When you're down, Nature seems down; when you're up, up."

"Good enough." My quickened sense of Verna's intelligence affected my skin; sexiness is a nervous condition, like hives, to which the intelligent are most susceptible. "Look," I directed, "at the ends of the second set of three lines. What can you notice about them?"

"They almost rhyme," she said.

"Do you know what that's called?"

"Almost rhyming?"

"Assonance. Assonance. If it's something like 'Peter Piper picked a peck of pickled peppers,' it's called consonance; the consonants do it. In assonance, the vowels."

"You think I'll have to know junk like that for the equivalency test?"

"It never hurts to know something," I said, struck as I said it by how untrue it was. "Read me these lines, from here on." I pointed, and the book in her lap yielded to my forefinger's pressure, and then bounced back. The skin of her chest as it sloped down and away from my eyes whitened in the shadows.

" 'Yet a few days,' " she read, " 'and thee The all-beholding sun shall see no more In all his course; nor yet in the cold ground, Where thy pale form was laid, with many tears, Nor in the embrace of ocean shall exist Thy image. Earth, that nourished thee, shall claim Thy growth, to be resolv'd to earth again; And, lost each human trace, surrend'ring up Thine individual being, shalt thou go To mix forever with the elements, To be a brother to th' insensible rock And to the sluggish clod, which the rude swain Turns with his share, and treads upon.' " Her voice, rather croaky in normal conversation, rose to a certain treble thrillingness under the stress of the lines, with me her only audience.

"Any words there give you trouble?" I asked. " 'Insensible'?"

"Out of it."

"Good. 'Share'?"

She guessed, "Plowshare."

"Terrific. And how do you feel about it, what you just read?"

"Not bad. Kind of bored. How do you feel, Nunc?"

"Horrible. I don't *want* to be 'brother to the insensible rock.' I don't *want* to surrender up my 'individual being.' The trouble with the poem is that its language lets you slide away from its very subject: death, *thanatos.* The title is Greek, 'view of death.' "

"Yeah, that's what it says in the little note."

"It's all too cool. The boy-poet sees the problem, but he doesn't feel it. The terror, the really quite radically insupportable terror. A few lines above, there"—the open book bounced again, in her cushiony lap, as I pointed to the place—" 'the stern agony, and shroud, and pall, And breathless darkness, and the narrow house': that really says it. 'Breathless darkness, and the narrow house.' Bryant was so young, you see, he could say it; an older poet's hand would have frozen with terror trying to write those lines. But then what does the kid do? He talks about these ancient kings and hoary seers who have already died and will keep us company, and tells us that 'All that breathe will share thy destiny' as if that's some kind of consolation, and without any benefit of religious avowal leaps to the conclusion that dying will be like lying down 'to pleasant dreams.' What evidence does he give that it will be like pleasant dreams? None," I told Verna. "The pattern here is the absolute pattern of every high-school valedictory address: big questions melting into fatuous, wishful answers."

The girl was studying. Her head, seen from above, was a depth of partly brown, partly blond curls, circle upon perfect circle like what cyclotrons reveal of matter's deep collisions. An aroma of shampoo arose from these deeps, and a faint tang more purely animal, the powdery warmth of her scalp. "He doesn't exactly say, Nunc, it will *be* like pleasant dreams; he says we should die as if it *would* be; we should go to our graves not 'like the quarry-slave' 'scourged to his dungeon' but 'sustain'd and sooth'd by an unfaltering trust.' "

"Unfaltering trust in *what?*" I asked. "In the utterly unconsoling fact that the 'matron, and maid, And the sweet babe, and the gray-headed man' shall all die also?" I stabbed at the place on the page I was quoting from, but this time she was holding the book firm, and it did not bounce. "Speaking of 'gay,' " I went on, trying to soften my approach, "isn't that rather terrific, just above: 'The gay will laugh When thou art gone, the solemn brood of care Plod on, and each one as before will chase His favourite phantom'?"

"Yeah, I guess it's all rather terrific," she said, letting the book relax in her lap so its speckled pages reflected the light and became twin blank sheets. "You shouldn't take it so hard, Nunc. We all gotta die, like Bryan, whatever his name is, Bryant says. If you don't want to die, you should talk to Dale. He says nobody does, it just seems that way. Anyways I thought this faith stuff was your business."

"Maybe it shouldn't be a business," I said, and the thought was enough of a Damascene revelation that I slightly swooned, lowering my face so that its skin and my pursed lips tingled with immersion in the clean explosive circles of Verna's hair.

She jumped like a cat at the touch, perching far forward on the bamboo chair and twisting to face me with amber eyes more widely spaced than, it seemed, a moment before. "So what's next?" she asked. " 'The Luck of Roaring Camp,' or are we going to fuck?"

"Fuck?" The word seemed an open portal, a superb sudden alteration in my house of narrow possibilities, of breathless darkness.

Her voice in the constriction of anger and fear had become reedier, more childishly lacking in timbre, than ever. "I know you have the hots for me," she said, "but is it the hots for me really or for my mom? I know about you and her. You wanted to screw her and never brought it off, though a lot of other guys did."

I took a breath and said reasonably, "I'm not sure she was exactly screwable then. It was a different world, Verna. Pre-Pill, pre-everything. We were children, and didn't much like each other."

In the years after our attic poker game, Edna had become more closed, ever less accessible to me in the coils of her own life, as we both matured in our different sections of greater Cleveland. From the age of fifteen on, she had boy friends, and sometimes, yes, I now remembered, she would tell me about them, would suddenly fling her secrets out at me, in those increasingly stilted, shorter and shorter stretches of summer when I would go stay with my father and Veronica, my corpulent and sugary-sweet stepmother—she, the trim vamp who had stolen him while I was asleep in my mother's womb, had been quite swallowed now by a middle-aged simpleton big into church work and canasta. As if our blood tie had neutered me, had indeed put me into the skirt and sweater and bobby socks of another teen-aged girl, Edna would on whim share her love life aloud, while we drove back sweaty from a tennis game at the club or sat with a pitcher of lemonade and a pack of furtive Camels on the long side porch in Chagrin Falls: she would tell me how far she let each boy friend go, what items of clothing the various ones were entitled to remove, where they could caress and for how long, all as if the male sex were one big many-armed and -fingered machine for the administration of an elaborate massage, a kind of carwash from which her

American body was to emerge a woman's, with polished bumpers and cavernous trunk, a virgin vehicle fit for marriage and the legal propagation of the race. Edna was certainly a virgin when she married, as was I.

I could not quite make out whether Verna were offering herself unconditionally, or only if I disavowed any affection for Edna. She said sullenly, like a child in the wrong, "I don't think you much like anybody, Uncle Roger."

We were back on ground where I felt secure: argument and counter-argument. "Tell me whom *you* like, Verna. Tell me about these mysterious men who hassle you, who take you to the Domino."

"They're O.K. All they see when they look at me is a white ass, but that's O.K. They respect me, for having an ass. You know: it's something of value."

"An asset, you might even say."

"Ha ha." Her voice croaked, and I recalled my impression, outside the door, that she had been crying.

"You have a mind, too, you know."

"Big deal. Next thing you'll tell me I have a soul. That's Dale's line. Everybody has a line. Oh, you really stupid intellectual men. Lemme start with these." She reached down and removed her ballet slippers, one and then the other, much like her mother in that far-off game of strip poker. My face felt windburned, as if I were clinging to a rocky height. Her feet were small, shapelier than Edna's, and pink along the sides, with rough golden heels.

"Tell me about Dale." My voice was shrinking, had lost all connection with my diaphragm.

"He's O.K., for a nerd." She stood up, her feet wide apart, like a judo fighter's, on the purple shag rug. "Come on, Nunc. Let's tangle. I feel horny."

I pretended I wasn't hearing her. "Do you know where this lumberyard is where he works?"

"Sure. Back up the boulevard two blocks, then three blocks to the left, along the tracks. Come on, let's just have a taste, you don't have to ring my gong. Little Shitface is going to wake up any second anyways."

I wondered if her language was designed to make her seem repulsive; for it was having that effect.

Her eyes were intense and stony and did not give me any relief, by moving from my own. "You got me all stirred up the first time you came in here, all those fuzzy shades of gray. You seemed so gray and broody, so *evil*. Why'djou think I flashed that tit?"

"You knew you were doing that?"

"C'mon, Nunc. You know about girls. Girls know everything. At least in that line they do." The dimple in her left cheek had returned, and I thought gratefully that this might all be a form of mischief. But then Verna crossed her plump hands at her waist and, smoothly, bowing forward as if in abrupt obeisance, pulled her white jersey over her head, with a lovely tumble of hair. She straightened up, pushing hair back from her face. She was wearing a bra, but a very little one; it seemed a dirty overburdened sling, and in her eyes was a watery something like pleading. "Don'tcha wanta play with my boobs?" she asked, so slangy and slurred I wondered if before I had come she had taken a drug which was just now coming to bloom in her veins. "Lick 'em, suck 'em?" Her hands lifted them, one under each.

I stood my distance from her, thinking how powerful the sexual impulse is, ever to leap the huge gap between the sexes. "Yes," I admitted.

"Wouldn't you like to fuck the bejesus out of me?"

The phrase seemed odd, forced. I felt what women must often feel: the irritating constraint of being inside someone else's sexual fantasy. "Do you have to keep calling it 'fuck'?"

The bra was beige and her shoulders had a ghost of tan and with the amber eyes and chestnut hair partly peroxided Verna seemed a portrait in sepia, in a deliberately limited palette, posed with a piece of the city off to her right like a poster. Her arms had gone limp at her sides in an awkward, defenseless manner. Her eyes went from watery to dreamy; her voice was a thin, croaky thread. "You're a funny guy, Nunc. Don't want to fuck, don't want to die. What do you want to do?"

"I want to end this tutorial session."

"But Nunc, what about us?" And she took a step forward and touched my arm, just below the shoulder, and I felt the question was sincere, girlish; she expected me to have an avuncular answer.

"You're my niece," I told her.

"But that just makes it friendlier. All that taboo stuff was just to avoid making pinheaded babies; but nobody makes babies any more." She was reverting a bit to her wised-up persona, the fun girl.

"You did," I pointed out.

"That was crazy. God, what a mistake." I was powerfully aware, now that her breasts had slipped from her own mind, of their glowing amplitude in the little elastic bra, the weighty breadth of them, and the depth of the sallow hollow between, inviting a finger, a tongue, even a phallus with its ache.

"But a mistake you must live with, Verna."

"Like you live with Esther."

"You think she's a mistake?"

"My mother thought so. She said it got you kicked out of the ministry. Getting laid by Esther."

"Small loss on either side. Me and the ministry."

"My mother didn't think so. She thought you really had it, you know, the bug. Even as a little kid, you were terribly *good*. Your mother was real neurotic and selfish and you just put up with it. Also, she liked whatsername, the first—"

"Lillian." Again, I had that sensation within my mind of skin, of some part of my soul that rarely saw the sun being stripped into view. "I'm sorry you don't like Esther," I said. "She liked you."

"In a pig's fart she did. She knew why I was there at Thanksgiving."

"Why was that?"

"For, you know. Balance. You know fucking well why."

In the other room, Paula cried. In the window, the short winter day was lowering; the heavenly wool, its promise of rain still undischarged, was turning black in foreshadow of night. Verna ignored the child's yammer, that protest children make when awaking, wet and hungry and exiled from their dreams, into the raw world; instead she stayed standing at my side, her hand frozen on the tweed of my sleeve, her head of hair a luxuriant tangy mass I again wished to immerse my face in. I had, after all, for all my quick retreat from her perhaps mocking response, made the first move, the "pass." Now we stood like a couple listening together, almost calm, waiting for punishing utterance, like that first couple our parents, welded together by guilt in the shadows of their leafy den. "That kid is out to get me," Verna confided to my lapel. "I brought her black into Whitey's world and I'm the only one around to blame."

"Where is her father?"

"Who knows? He split. It's not like it sounds; we agreed it would be best, I'd do better on my own, among whites."

"And yet here you are, in a project half black."

She flipped her head cockily. "Well, Nunc, it must be I like the jive. They dig me. Sorry you don't."

"Did I say that?"

"You sure did. You should have seen your face when I flashed both tits."

The child was becoming unignorable; her yammering had become a yell. Verna slashed back the maroon curtain and fetched Paula from the other room. The child's hair stood out from her sleep-creased cranky face in damp wisps. Verna—making some ironical point, squeezing down on her anger—held her tight against her, as if to make them one creature, pressing their faces side by side. I was struck by how nearly the same size their heads were, for all the disparity in height and weight and tint. Paula's eyes, puffy from sleep, also looked lashless and slanted. "See, Nunc? Mother and child."

"Lovely," I said.

The child reached out her hand with its pale-tipped fingers, but, instead of asking, "Da?," had the word for me today: "Man." Pronouncing it made her voice comically deep.

"White man," her mother amplified. "White man go bye-bye."

"I must," I said, and my desire to flee stumbled in reflex upon an aspect of the last time's parting. "How's your money holding out?" I asked Verna.

"But we didn't fuck, Nunc. No charge. No fuckee, no tickee."

I became confused, somehow startled that she would talk this way with the child in her arms. Her chest-slope of skin, above the skimpy bra, seemed to blaze with light. Of course, to her daughter this skin would not seem threatening: mother skin. "You're making a false connection," I said, as if to a student, even while fishing in my wallet for another loan.

"I know my assets," she said, echoing me as witty students will. "This must be advance payment. Girls like us don't usually get advance payment." She took the three twenties. The amount seemed stingy this time—we seemed to be progressing—so I added a fourth bill. Banks now automatically pay out cash in twenties; tens are going the way of the farthing.

"Man bye-bye," Paula recited, solemn animal wisdom brimming in her dark blue eyes.

"Read around in that anthology," I instructed, putting myself back into my two coats. "Try to find some stuff you like. I was just kidding about 'Luck of Roaring Camp.' Look at the Hemingway or some James Baldwin. Maybe I should bring a grammar handbook next time. Do you know what a predicate is? A participial phrase?"

Verna joggled the girl on her hip and in sympathy her breasts bounced. "Fuck next time, Nunc. There isn't going to be a next time. I don't know exactly what your creepy game is, but I don't want to get involved. Don't bother to come around here ever again, we won't let you in. Right, Poopsie?" She jiggled the child and made a cross-eyed face an inch from her face, so that Paula laughed, her spitty little baby-laugh from deep inside.

I suspected that this comedic turning to the child was a cover-up for her careless use of "we." *We won't let you in.* No doubt, there were shadows behind Verna, a population of shadows. "Don't be silly," I said. "Use me. You want a high-school degree and a better life. I'll help you make a start. You want to live in a project on welfare the rest of your life?"

Her face had gone stiff, in the manner of a child, for whom fury and panic are one emotion. "I don't see what good passing some dumb non-test would do me and if I did I could pass it myself. If you come back here any more I'll call up my mom and she'll have the police after you."

I had to smile at that. All this indignation and rejection of hers was a dance, the dance of the trapped. Was it Ortega y Gasset who said that once a man has gained a woman's attention, anything he does, anything at all, to keep her attention furthers his cause? It seemed to me I had made good headway today. After closing the door, I hesitated long enough to hear Verna say to little Paula, in a level voice, "You stink, you know that? You really do."

My chief concern, as I went down the familiar, echoing metal stairs, was how to pry Verna loose from this infant, so I could have the uninhibited use of her body in that deliciously shabby and warm apartment, in the room behind the maroon curtain, which I had never seen but could imagine: a secondhand crib, a mattress or futon on the floor for the mother, a cheap pine dresser enamelled some hideous girlish color like lilac or salmon, and the sadness of the scuffed walls relieved by rock posters and a few of Verna's mediocre, painstaking watercolor studies of the corners of her cage.

As I stepped into the misty chill December dusk, the answer came to me: Esther's day-care center. It existed to generate just such freedoms.

My Audi sat at the curb unharmed, though its little self-appointed guardian was nowhere to be seen. Several black women, wearing the grape-colored quilted long coats that have become a universal winter uniform in the city, sat

on benches while their toddlers utilized the minimal amuse-
ments of the shatterproof playground, its cement pipes and
rubber tires. It was not yet quite the time I usually returned
from the Divinity School (if Esther asked why I had taken
the car, I would say I had come back to the house for a bite
of lunch, her delicious quiche, and to pick up a book I
needed, on the Cappadocian Fathers, for a tutorial conference, and then had driven back to save a minute, and also
because I had left my sheepskin coat in my office and discovered the air to be turning colder); so I thought of detour-
ing past Dale's lumberyard, in order to satisfy my morbid
curiosity and to help erase the pulsing mental afterimage of
Verna pulling her stretchy white jersey upward and off in
an explosion of glossy shoulder skin and heedless, stringy,
semi-bleached, shampoo-scented curls.

Prospect was one-way the right way now. I drove down
it, past the semi-abandoned houses and the towering
ginkgo, which had lost all its leaves. Back up the boulevard
two blocks, she had said, and then to the left, at the railroad
tracks. And there *was* a street here, devoid of houses, that
led into an industrial limbo, surviving perhaps from an era
when this section lay on the edge of the city, a nest of mills
later engulfed and isolated, a wilderness of rusting sheds
and cinder-block warehouses, of factories whose painted
names had left ghosts of letters on the brick, in the ornate
style of the last century—vast shelters long since fallen
away from their original purpose of manufacture, rented
and resold and reused in fractions of floor space, and dropping ever lower on the rotting rungs of capitalism. An old
coalyard lingered in here, its tilted bins glistening with
lumps of graded size, and a sand-and-gravel company that
had created its own miniature gray mountains, had moved
mountains not through faith but with a rickety tall tramway

of triangular buckets on wheels. The asphalt beneath the Audi crumbled away, and the road became a chain of puddles and hard-packed spots in an earth saturated with oil and cinders and gypsum, with flattened containers and towering dry tufts of God's toughest, wiriest weeds. Yet this road—scarcely a road, a black path—kept going, and from the rear approached fenced acres of a lumberyard that fronted on a less informal street, with streetlights and gas stations though no visible pedestrians. GROVE, a modest orange sign proclaimed, scarcely legibly, for the day was turning to evening. Already electric lights burned in the sales office and in the tall sheds, roofed in corrugated iron, that housed the racks of lumber.

I turned into an opening in the woven-wire fence and parked well away from the bright office and crept out into the dusk, which was indeed turning cold enough to make me grateful for my sheepskin coat. Smells of pine, fir, spruce —resiny fresh corpses from the north, stacked in their horizontal phalanxes of two-by-fours, four-by-fours, four-by-sixes, some knottier than others, as with books and lives, but almost none without knots, without those dark resinous oblongs that, no matter how we shellac and paint and overpaint, weep through. I detected a faint holy whiff of cedar, of shingles and clapboards bundled with steel ribbons, and heard a distant stir of men banging wood and talking to one another within echoing spaces, toward the end of a weary day. I feared that Dale might be on duty. Above Grove's sheds and the shabby neighborhood, some of the university's science buildings, including that newish monstrosity, that nine-storied concrete bunker called the Cube, loomed surprisingly near—tall Argus-eyed beasts which by some twist of the city's geography had been allowed to creep close, and might pounce.

A bare bulb burned thinly in a far small stall. A circular saw blade gleamed beneath an apparatus of giant leather straps, the glint of its teeth regular as ticks of an atomic clock. Sawdust, its virginal aroma, permeated the crystallizing black air, and a multitude of straight shadows hurled transversely from within the open framework of the lumber racks suggested a silent diagonal toppling of trees. *Fear not.* I felt surrounded by a blessing, by a fragrant benignity, and yet with criminal haste hurried back into my car when a shadow of a man approached and asked if he could help me.

III

i

Quem *enim naturae usum, quem mundi fructum, quem elementorum saporem non per carnem anima depascitur?* For what use of Nature, what enjoyment of the world, what taste of the elements is not consumed by the soul *per carnem* —by the agency of the flesh? Tertullian wrote these words in *De resurrectione carnis* around 208, well after he had fallen away from orthodoxy into Montanism. Still, I could sniff out nothing unorthodox in his ardent exposition; on the contrary, the resurrection of the flesh is the most emphatic and intrinsic of orthodox doctrines, though in our present twilight of faith the most difficult to believe. Yet how incontrovertibly and with what excited eloquence does Tertullian build up his argument that the flesh cannot be dispensed with by the soul! *Quidni?* he asks—how not, how could it be otherwise? *Per quam omni instrumento sensuum fulciatur, visu, auditu, gustu, odoratu, contactu?* By its means all the apparatus of sense is supported—sight, hearing, taste, smell, touch. Then a rather delicate, Saussurian argument, linking the power of effectuation, glorified as a *divina potestas,* to the faculty of speech, in turn dependent upon a physical organ: *Per quam divina potestate respersa est, nihil non sermone perficiens, vel tacite praemisso? Et sermo enim de organo carnis est.* The *vel tacite praemisso* (literally, "even if only advanced in silence," i.e., tacitly indicated by the existence of speech, of words) seemed an especially scrupulous touch, and it occurred to me that *perficiens* above might be read as conceptualization, so that the Heavenly mystery of the Logos was made to descend, by means of a Platonic scaffolding of degrees of ideality, down into reality via ultimate dependence upon that repulsive muscle housed among our salivating mouth membranes and rotting teeth—the eyeless, granular, tireless tongue. *De organo carnis* indeed. The arts, too, rest on this slippery foundation: *Artes per carnem, studia, ingenia* (confirming my thesis above) *per carnem, opera, negotia, officia* (we must take a body to the office, every day) *per carnem, atque adeo totum vivere animae carnis est, ut non vivere animae nil aliud sit quam a carne divertere.* Did he mean to go quite so far, to assert that so totally is the soul's life derived from the flesh that for it to be separated is none other than death? To deny us, that is, O furious Tertullian, even the wispiest hope of a harp-strumming ghost in our machine, of an ethereal escape clause in this terrible binding contract with eyeballs, nostril hairs, ear bones, and edible gray brain cells, a contract that after all we never signed, which our ubiquitous agent Dan N. (for Nobodaddy) Amino initialled for us, without consultation? We want to break the contract, help! But our Carthaginian lawyer in his mad faith careers on, ever more zealously committing himself and us to an impossible miracle: *Porro si universa per carnem subiacent animae, carni quoque subiacent.* Further, if all things are subject to the soul *per carnem,* through the flesh, then they are also subject to the flesh. He knits us, soul and flesh, ever tighter, toward some smiling courtroom reversal. But the suspense is keen. *Per quod utaris, cum eo utaris necesse est.* That compression of old Latin: links of pounded iron; to paraphrase is to weaken the chain. What you use, with that you must use: *utor* here must have, like *fruor* above, the sense of "enjoy"—our poor body, used for our (the soul's, his implication is: we are, notice, *anima* and not *caro* after all) enjoyment, necessarily partakes of that enjoyment. Dear Flesh: Do come to the party. Signed, your pal, the Soul. *Ita caro, dum ministra et famula animae deputatur, consors et cohaeres invenitur.* So the flesh, up to now deputed the soul's minister and servant, is found to be its consort and co-heir. *Si temporalium, cur non et aeternorum?* If temporarily, why not eternally? Why not indeed? The thought of all our pale and rancid bodies jostling perpetually in some eternal locker room of a Heaven sickened me. And yet beyond the depressing mechanics of it, the general dim idea of our eternal survival, much as we are, athlete's feet and all, does lift up the heart. The old fanatic's logic and fervor and right grasp of our situation cannot be denied. Always, remember, he had Marcion on his mind— Marcion, who believed that Christ had been a phantom, a kind of holograph, on Earth and that no God worth worshipping could have dirtied His hands in the creation of this vile swamp of excrement and semen.

By finding ridiculous and sickening Tertullian's blessing of everlastingness upon our poor shuffling flesh, I was one with the heretics and heathens *(ethnici)* whose plausible objections he had outlined a few books earlier: *An aliud prius vel magis audias tam ab haeretico quam ab ethnico? et non protinus et non ubique convicium carnis, in originem, in materiam, in casum, in omnem exitum eius, immundae a primordio ex faecibus terrae, immundioris deinceps ex se-*

ROGER'S VERSION

minis sui limo, frivolae, infirmae, criminosae, onerosae, molestae, et post totum ignobilitatis elogium caducae in originem terram et cadaveris nomen, et de isto quoque nomine periturae in nullum inde iam nomen, in omnis iam vocabuli mortem? It is, that is, the heathens and not (as preening hedonists and mockers from Nero on would have it) the Christians who make an outcry against the flesh— its origin, its substance, its causality, its end—who accuse it of being unclean from its first formation out of Earth's feces and then uncleaner still from the slime of its semen, of being paltry (frivolous in its root sense of "weightless"), infirm, guilty (not so much criminal as covered with accusation, with slander), burdensome, troublesome. And then (according to the *ethnici*), after all this litany of ignobility, falling into its original earth and the name of a cadaver, and from this name certain to dwindle into no name, into the death of all designation. How terrible and true. Tertullian, like Barth, took his stand on the only ground where he could: the flesh is man. "All of him is flesh and by nature ought to perish," Barth roundly wrote, in his pleasant *Die christliche Lehre nach dem Heidelberger Katechismus.*

Weary of translating, I closed my eyes. I pictured a white shaft: tense, pure, with dim blue broad veins and darker thinner purple ones and a pink-mauve head like the head of a mushroom set by the Creator upon a swollen stem nearly as thick as itself, just the merest little lip or rounded eaves, *the corona glandis,* overhanging the bluish stretched semi-epiderm where pagan foreskin once was, and a drop of transparent nectar in the little wide-awake slit of an eye at its velvety suffused tip. Esther's studious rapt face descends, huge as in a motion picture, to drink the bitter nectar and then to slide her lips as far down the shaft as they will go, again and again, down past the *corpus spongiosum*

163

to the magnificent twin *corpora cavernosa* in their sheath of fibrous tissue and silk-smooth membrane, their areolar spaces flooded and stuffed stiff by lust; her expert action shows a calculated tenderness, guarding against her teeth grazing, care on one side and trust on another emerging *per carnem,* her avid cool saliva making Dale's prick shine in the attic light. For of course they have gone to her third-floor room, her seldom-used studio, the safest, most distant place, in case our awful clattering bell breaks into their rapture, and a place removed, too, from our second-floor bedrooms, which are haunted by the ghosts of her husband, his clothes, his shoes, his shaving lotion, his pipey smell, his bedside paperback *Kirchliche Dogmatik III,* and of their son, flesh of their flesh, his bedroom an innocent adolescent chaos of old homework papers and model spaceships and dropped underwear and rumpled *Playboy*s and *Club*s. Esther's paintings—big, slashing, angular, gobby, a far cry in education and sophistication from Verna's timid, pencilly, petal-by-petal watercolors—surround the lovers like a dappled forest, like patches of camouflage hiding them from the eye of Heaven, though from the third-floor windows they themselves can see ample of the world: the neighborhood rooftops and exiguous back yards and in this leafless season the twinkling distant heart of the city, and beyond the majestic skyscrapers the airplanes slanting downward toward the airport reclaimed from tidal marsh. January this year has been monotonously cold, so cold the inaugural parade was cancelled in Washington. Esther has an electric heater up here, and an old stained mattress dragged from a dusty storage space at the back, beyond her easels and canvases and some broken floor lamps and a faded velvet easy chair not worth re-covering. This junk has been transformed into the furniture of a room cozier than any below.

The heater's bright orange bar with its parabolic reflective shield casts a sharp arid heat onto their bare skins; their reflected pale bodies swim in the polished metal along with the glowing coil. The circumambient attic chill is no match for the coursing of their aroused blood; like their danger, their sin, it invigorates. She and Dale have already fucked once this afternoon on the filthy mattress. They sit upon it facing each other, legs crossed in yoga fashion, drinking white wine from squeezable plastic glasses. Then the willing wench, as porn novels say, takes note of his revived erection and puts aside her wine to bend her lips to its inviting hard-softness, its tacit standing homage to her. Esther loves being sluttish with this boy; he is so purely grateful and astounded and would never think to use it against her, to turn a gift into a demand and then a grievance in the manner of her gloomy, scowling husband. Also, she is thirty-eight and her womanhood won't be there forever to use. *Per quod utaris, cum eo utaris necesse est.* Her necessary time has come. This tall bony youth of shining skin and thrilling phallus has been somehow delivered to her. She gorges herself on his flesh until her jaws ache. In the respite, gasping and wiping her lips, she croons, "So big. Too big for my mouth."

"Not really, evidently," says Dale languorously, in a voice also made husky by concupiscence. His satisfied, relaxed voice implies that all this adoration is owed him. He has put his wineglass aside and leaned back onto his straightened arms, the better to be blown. His blue eyes are dazed like a summer sky. A smell comes off his prick that has low tide in it, all mixed with her eager spit. She wants to cocksuck a bit more. She bends down into it, tucking back her straying hair, its mussed strands of gingery red. Dale grunts and says, "You better not do that."

"Why not?" Esther's eyes look very green as she lifts her head to ask this. Her lipstickless mouth looks bruised. One long-nailed hand supports her weight on the mattress; the other hovers near her hair, to keep tucking it back as it strays. Her little breasts hang conical and white, but for the bumpy muddy-colored tips.

"I might come."

"Well . . . do." Taking thought, she smiles; her prominent upper lip looks swollen. "Do come."

"In your sweet mouth?"

"Would that amuse you?" The thought that it might amuses her.

"All over your pretty face?" He can hardly get the words out, the thought so excites him—the image, the words. *Et sermo enim de organo carnis est.*

Her own voice, usually so definite and shapely, sounds as if her throat is swollen shut. "I'd adore it, Dale. I adore your prick. I adore you."

His words like butterflies stagger from his lips. "Have you ever been so happy," he asks her, "your head hurts?"

Esther laughs whisperingly and flicks his one-eyed staring glans with her tongue. "Is that how you are?"

"It's just *pound*ing. As if my blood is too much for my veins."

"What got you so turned on?" Her words come out playfully, among darting ticks of her tongue, yet with that throatiness, that motherly husky woman-of-substance note that she knows is one of her holds over him, one of the charms that let her do anything she wants with him, that let her mold him like white clay. His pubic hair, when her nose pushes into it, smells of cedar.

"You ask?" he asks weakly, his voice like that of a child being squeezed in wrestling and asking for mercy. He is close to coming. That kick at the root of his prick, the *crura,* is developing, that push from the prostate that in older men makes the hard-working old anus hurt after intercourse.

"I mean before," she says, up through the cloud of her hair. "When we were just sitting there talking and drinking wine."

"You," Dale gets out. "The way, the way you were sitting there, in the lotus position, with your legs spread so casual, and your pretty fur," he gasps, "just so *there,* all wet and sweet and mussed, your little pink cunt peeping through." These words do it. The kick is taking over, from underneath. "Oh," he says, "oh," wanting to name her, to give her a name. "Esther" feels like another tongue's property and "Mrs. Lambert" too formal; for him she has no name, is simply that Other that faces us, that elastic wall that takes our punches, yin to our yang, pit to our pendulum, woman to our man.

He is coming. She stares at the little dark eye, the *meatus urinarius,* and with stern helpfulness gives a downward tug at the base of his engorged phallus with her encircling hand —how small and fragile and even shrivelled, she thinks, her hand with its long nails looks around the root of that helpless alabaster shaft—and when the first gob comes, as if in slow motion on a pornographic film, she has to have it herself, inside herself, all that startling pure whiteness; ravenously nimble, she straightens up on her knees and wades to him so she seems to his blurred *sensus* a bobbling warm giantess and, holding him firm with that hand at his kicking root, centers her cunt above his prick quickly and impales herself, settling her split self to its limit, so she feels shot through with light from underneath, up to beneath her heart, my faithless Esther's heart. Catching his climax as it prolongedly subsides, with that desperate pumping energy of youth, she wraps her arms about his head and grinds the crest of her *os pubis* against his and catches up while Dale's own heart is still beating as if to burst his veins and has her own climax, possesses it, wraps it around with her *anima,* moaning and then crying out in that faintly theatrical and yet well-intentioned way of hers so that, if anyone were even in the basement of the house, say a dope-crazed Haitian burglar from some other part of the city, he would hear her. Even Sue Kriegman, pecking away at her next children's book (tentative title: *Scott and Jenny Run Away to Wyoming*) next door, would hear Esther's proud and operatic cry of joy but for the double-glazed caulked storm windows that Myron has prudently had installed on all sides, to stand guard against this January's monotonous cold.

Then our house slowly feeds its silence up to the lovers: the muffled knocking of the steam in the radiators, Esther's great-grandfather's eight-day Waterbury clock tolling the quarter-hour with its high-pitched chime, a creak of wood settling, an almost inaudible concussion that sounds like a footstep. Like the sea returning from a long suck and ebb, guilt floods the silence; the empty house fills with the ghostly stirring of guilt. *Frivolae, infirmae, criminosae, onerosae, molestae . . .*

Esther feels it and makes a wry impatient mouth, as if brushing a buzzing fly aside. She disengages herself; milky strands of semen link their underparts, their interfaced *pudenda* (the plural of *pudendum,* "that of which one ought to be ashamed," a grammatically neutral form whose onus has been patriarchally shifted onto the female genitals alone), like tenuous umbilical cords. *Immundioris deinceps ex seminis sui limo.* Elsewhere in that same chapter, Tertullian has his scoffing heretic or heathen very sensibly ask, of our bodies in the afterlife, *Rursusne omnia necessaria illi, et* *inprimis pabula atque potacula, et pulmonibus natandum, et intestinis aestuandum, et pudendis non pudendum, et omnibus membris laborandum?* Pudendis non pudendum*—the style at its most savage, and least translatable.

She feels the guilt in the air, in the ghostly disturbances of the great house that stretches beneath their semen-stained mattress, as a manifestation of me; her long-accumulating anger with me, her boredom, leads her to brush the sensation aside and to rejoice, more deliberately now, in the well-knit pale body of her awkward young lover. She kisses him on the lips (wetwarm, pushsoft) and then gazes into his eyes, making him return the gaze, knowing her eyes have been flushed a richer, kinder green by her orgasm. "I wish I did have a pretty face," she says, reminding him of his remark in passion. "I did once but it's got all dry and bitter, with tiny little wrinkles."

"I don't see them."

"And what if you did?"

"I'd love you anyway."

"That's the answer. What else can you say?" she asks, a bit dryly. "And I'm sorry I didn't let you come in my mouth. I just had to have you"—the manner of a faculty wife, courteous and superior, is slipping back upon her as her blood cools; she lowers her lids—"down *there*. Next time, I promise."

Though this is a delicious promise, sworn with the strength and generosity of a woman's giving heart, her mention of the "next time" reminds them of the time (did the Waterbury clock strike four-fifteen or four-forty-five? Richie returns a little after five, to be tutored in the tortuous

---

"Will it have all its needs there again, especially food and drink, and the floating of the lungs, and the surging of the bowels, and the not being ashamed of the shameful organs, and the laboring with all the limbs?"

bases) and reminds him of his running commitment, somehow evolved in these weeks since Christmas, to make love
to her, to betray me in my own house with my lawful wife's
body, not impulsively in an ungainsayable burst of mutual
longing but mechanically, by schedule, from three o'clock
on, Tuesdays and Thursdays, on and on into a future whose
only horizon is their unthinkable, unbearable parting.

"Maybe we should meet out of this house," he says.

Esther's eyes widen. "Why? It's perfectly safe. Rog never
leaves his precious office before five-thirty, and even if he
did you could just stay up here until he was out of the house
again. I'd get him out."

"But it feels, I don't know, *wrong,*" Dale ventures. "Like
trespassing. All your nice things, room after room. I feel
him watching us, somehow."

To him, yes, our things would seem nice, luxurious, even
—our few stately antiques from Esther's mother's Connecticut ancestors, the rugs and red settee and glass table, the
mahogany dining table and chairs in the Danish-modern
style still fashionable when we were newly wed, Richie's
room with its wealth of rapidly defunct electronic games
and gadgets. As he mounts the stairs behind Esther's tight
ass he must feel that he is boring upward through a wad of
money. In truth, our house, compared with that of the
Kriegmans or the Ellicotts, is shabby and underfurnished.

"I have a room," he tells her. "I mean, my roommate's
hardly ever there. He studies over at the tech library and
has a job evenings parking cars at a movie-theatre lot."

"But, darling—what's the building like?"

"Oh you know," he says, as if she has been there other
than in his masturbatory fantasies, or as if all faculty wives
know how perpetual students must live. "In one of these old
three-deckers all broken up into studio apartments."

"Full of messy kids," she says, wishing for a cigarette but knowing that if she goes downstairs to her bedroom to get one it will signal the breakup of the day's tryst, it will begin the dressing and the tidying up and the putting on of suitably joyless faces to greet Richie when he returns from school, and wanting instead to linger in this easy nudity, to keep gazing at the image of herself cast back by the mirror of this young man's flesh, and tasting the briny taste of herself he puts in her mouth. "I can imagine it. You all hear each other's rock music through the walls and have to thread your way through a crowd of beat-up bicycles in the downstairs hall."

He nods, on his side also thinking sadly that they are winding down, when what he'd like to do, after another glass of wine, is go at her another way, burying his face between her legs where she's wet and at the other end of their conjunction making her make good on her kind offer, even though the poor cunt wriggle and gag like a hooked fish. *Inprimis pabula atque potacula.* This older woman is for him a sensual field in which his incarnation has room at last to run and roam to the limit. She even holds out, in her fantastic willingness (engendered of the desperation dutiful years work upon a woman), the possibility of his being cruel; this possibility is in his hands like pulling, burning reins when they are making love; when the love is over, the possibility has flown.

"I'll feel ridiculous," she says, in that superior drawling voice she uses socially, sitting there casually cross-legged leaking his jism onto the blue-striped mattress ticking, "going into a building like that. What could I be doing there, in my little wool suit and Gucci shoes, but coming to be fucked? When a woman gets the first gray hair, Dale dear, there are suddenly certain places where she simply doesn't go. To be a woman is to be very unfree."

"I just thought," he says, embarrassed by his refused offer, "the day-care center where you work isn't so far from my neighborhood."

"The days I don't take a bus, I park on one certain street, always in front of the same house if I can, and walk up the sidewalk looking neither to the right nor the left. This much, I'm permitted. If I were to park in the next block up, I'd be in trouble." She stands, and in standing rises above him in her flesh so that Dale recalls how when she had waded to him on her knees she appeared in that moment of predation a giantess, her small breasts huge and her compact hips enormous and split by desire like worlds dividing.

"It's great, by the way, your taking Paula off of Verna's hands some of the time."

"She's a sweet little girl. I can see why there's tension between her and her mother."

"Verna's not sweet?"

"Oh God, *au contraire.* Hard. Selfish." In contrast, the implication is, to her own soft, extravagantly giving, quite vulnerably naked self.

"She's already passed the English grammar and literature parts of her equivalency tests, and now I'm helping her with the math."

"Does it occur to you, my darling, that Verna uses people?"

He considers this a second, enjoying the friendly sight of Esther wiping herself between the legs with Kleenex and then stepping into her lacy bikini underpants. Not two hours before, having rushed home from the day-care center, she had put these on with him in mind, after taking a quick shower, and powdering her crotch. She had thought of putting in the diaphragm but in her haste and at her age had decided not to bother, to gamble. *Immundioris deinceps ex seminis sui limo.* Dale glances around the attic floor for his own discarded underpants, boyish Jockeys, while asking her, "Isn't that what we're here for? To use each other? Isn't that what you and I have been doing?"

Esther is slightly shocked, as I have on other occasions been, by this unexpected coolness of his, a poise that seems to arise somewhere beyond his earthly manifestation as a penniless misfit, a perpetual graduate student.

He hears the rebuke in her silence and goes on apologetically, "That's what makes me feel guilty toward your husband. I'm using him, he's helping me get my grant, and yet here I am, with—" His gesture floats past her nearly naked body to include the entire attic, subsuming the entire house, in the fact of his entrée into lives where he does not belong.

"Fuckable old me," Esther finishes for him. "Maybe *he's* using *you.*"

"How? How could he be?"

"I don't know. Rog is strange. He never should have left the ministry, though at the time I thought I was rescuing him. He needs to manipulate people, and when he had a church that's what the people asked for. Anyway, Dale dear: don't you feel guilty toward him. That's my territory, and I don't."

"Why not?"

She picks up another lace-trimmed snippet of underwear from the floor and shrugs. "He's a tyrant. Husbands tend to be. It drives their wives into a constant war of liberation." Sensing his desire for her reawakening at the sight of her in her scant underpants, even seeing physical evidence of it as his long pale young body lies languid on their shabby mattress, she pushes her lips forward and says, "I want you to feel guilty only toward *me*."

Dale is entranced by her fragile-seeming awkwardness, her pointed elbows, her facially expressed determination to find the right snaps as she puts herself back into her bra. She tucks in a sliver of tit pinched below by the elastic and straightens up, looking about her as if for a fight. He asks, "Why?"

Esther mock-pouts. "Because you haven't told me I'm a great lay."

Rursus, Tertullian goes heartbreakingly on, *ulcera et vulnera et febris et podagra et mors reoptanda?* In our bodily afterlife, are we to know again ulcers and wounds and fever and gout and the wish for death—the renewed wish for death, to give the *re-* its curious, heartbreaking force. And yet, my goodness, pile on the cavils as you will, old hypothetical heretic or pagan, we *do* want to live forever, much as we are, perhaps with some of the plumbing removed, but not even that would be strictly necessary, if the alternative is being nothing, being nonexistent specks of yearning in the bottomless belly of *nihil*.

"Oh, but you are, you are a great lay, my God," Dale says, led into blasphemy.

When he came into my office, he seemed uneasy, uneasy in a way new since the time he kept looking over my head out of the window and at my walls of books with their many Japanese prayers of bookmark. Instead of the denim jacket he had put on, in deference to the monotonous cold, a mustard-colored parka that had greasy stains as if used to wipe a griddle. He took off his knit wool cap. He had had a haircut, so his ears stuck out. "How's it going?" he asked, with an affected jauntiness that ill became him.

"I was going to ask you the same thing."

"I mean about the grant. Have you heard anything?"

I imagined that he seated himself in the chair of many woods rather tenderly, as if his bones ached. His waxy face had added to the pink scrapes of acne along his jawline bruiselike patches below his eyes, the kind of shadows that, we boys used to kid one another in high school, indicated too much masturbation. "As I said," I said, "Closson is not uninterested; the unusualness of the proposal amuses him, much as it does me. But, in view of this same unusualness, he wants to meet with the full Grants Committee and would like you to appear before them to make an oral presentation and submit to a few questions."

A weary "Oh Jesus" escaped him.

I smiled at this sign of deterioration. "It would be a relatively painless little trial," I said. "Let me describe Closson. He's a man of about sixty, rather stout, with a curious square head, almost like a box of bone, with this thinning hair combed all the way across from just above his ear"— I was quite vain of my own fluffy gray mop, with no sympathy for the touching stratagems of the bald—"and an absolutely unquenchable—what can we call it?—*twinkle*. He was born a Quaker in Indiana, and studied in Germany just after the war. Heidegger's his baby. He believes nothing you could put into writing, but there's still that inner light, that Quakerness, which makes him rather holy. He looks at someone like me as a sort of paleontologist, and the period of the Church Fathers as absolute darkness, a battle of dinosaurs. Closson was curious, specifically, as to what *of your own* you were going to bring to these scientific points you allude to, and that I described to him as best I could. How does the computer, he asked me, come into it?"

"As the means," Dale said, "to pull it all together, to make the universal model that we can, I don't know, sift.

Also, it throws some new light on old questions, like the body-mind problem."

"Ah," I said, "the body-mind."

His hands began to trace circuits and connections in the air, and our shared awareness of his being saturated in intimacy with Esther—shining with it as a fish fresh-pulled from the ocean shines with saltwater and its own slime— shuttled to the backs of our minds, much as the herpes virus hides at the base of the spine. "There's a general impression," he said, "that it's all settled, what with psycho-pharmacology, increasingly sophisticated brain anatomization, the chemical understanding of synapses, all this trendy fiddling with the cerebral hemispheres and the *corpus callosum* and so on, and above all with the rise in the last twenty years of computers, that we know just what mind is: it isn't an immaterial substance; it's a function, like a haircut is a function of hair."

"I see that you got one," I said. I had also noticed that Esther lately had trimmed her dangerously long nails.

"It gets to feeling scratchy after a while," he explained. "People make this analogy with software/hardware: the brain is the hardware, and mind, so-called, is the software. But if you take that analogy seriously, you get right back into dualism, because software can exist without hardware. Or, rather, it can function with a variety of hardwares. If a computer running a program is destroyed, you wouldn't have to reconstruct the computer to get the program running again; you could put it into a new computer, or even work out the same logical relationships with pencil on paper."

"A paper afterlife. 'A paper moon,' " I quoted, smiling, " 'floating over a cardboard sea.' "

He was too young to know the song. He went on, "All

this talk about computers that think is to anybody on the inside a terrific non-issue. You can link up all the computers from here to Palo Alto and you still won't get self-consciousness out of those billions and billions of bits, out of all that stored memory and algorithms: you're just as likely to get it out of the telephone company's wires and switchboards. You won't get sensation, you won't get emotion, you won't get will, you won't get self-reference. Hofstadter can talk all he wants about Strange Loops, but until he builds one that can make a computer reprogram itself or get so bored inside its box it commits suicide, it's in the same category as life assembling itself in the primordial soup. The category, I mean, of fantasy, of faith. Materialism is a faith just like theism: only it asks a lot more in the way of miracles. Instead of asking we believe in God it asks we don't believe in ourselves; it asks we don't believe in our own awareness, our own emotions and moral sensations."

I winced at the width and violence of some of his gestures; I wondered what moral sensations he felt, fucking my little Esther. "Tell me, though," I said. "How do you feel about a dog's circuitry? Is there self-consciousness there? Anybody who's ever owned a dog would assure you there's emotion. Certainly there's memory, and isn't what we call self mostly memory? There's even free will; you can *see* dogs trying to come to a decision, waffling and wavering, and then feeling guilty about it. Imagine," I said, "a hierarchy of organisms up from the amoeba—which *does* respond to certain stimuli, like heat and light, so there's *some* degree of apprehension there—up through the spider and the lizard, and the mouse and the squirrel, to the dog and the dolphin and the elephant and the chimpanzee: surely by the end term of this sequence you're getting into brainpower not qualitatively different from ours, and personality, and emotion, and sensation, and those other good things you say a computer could never have. Where do they come in, at what point in the complication of the neuron structure? What will prevent that same point from being reached as computers become ever more complex?"

Dale leaned his unhealthy pale face toward me. The haircut had subtly distorted its proportions, so that some moral imbalance or inner torque seemed expressed. Zeal to speak pushed little bubbles into the corners of his mouth. "Because I *know*," he said, "what's inside a computer; it's just little switches, tiny little switches that move current around in certain patterns so that calculations result, all in terms of zeros or ones—off or on, high or low, hot or cold, full or empty, whatever. The speed is fantastic but the basic event is totally simple, and no matter how many billions of connections you kludge together there is basically nothing there, spiritually speaking. How could there be?"

I could see I had led him onto ground where he felt shaky. I lit my pipe. The smoke of the first puffs built up like sculptures of bluish stone in the shaft of sun; though the month's cold had been relentless, the sun was strengthening every day—at our backs, as it were. "But mightn't our own brains look exactly the same way, to an electrical engineer?"

"In theory, Professor Lambert, but only in theory. In practice, there is something there nobody wants to talk about: you. When you hear a noise—those bulldozers over there, for instance—vibrations compress the air and move through the glass and stone and touch the little bones in your ear, they communicate the disturbance to the eardrum, which passes it on to the fluid of the inner ear, and that moves some filaments that generate electrical impulses that travel along the auditory nerves to the brain. But *who* is hearing the noise? Not the brain by itself; it's just a mass of electrochemical jelly. It doesn't hear anything, any more than a radio hears music it plays. Who, furthermore, decides to get up and go to the window and see what's making the noise? Something makes those neurons fire that move the muscles that move your body. That something is non-physical: a thought, a desire. People are willing to admit that the brain affects the mind—creates the mind, you could say—but, illogically, don't accept the other side of the equation, that mental events create brain events. Yet it happens all the time. The world we live in, the subjective world, is a world of mental events, some of which set up electrical signals that move our bodies. This is the most obvious fact of our existence and yet materialism asks us to ignore it."

The eddies his breath set in motion were destroying the smoke sculptures I was erecting. The pipestem was warm on my lower lip and I thought of lip cancer. I often think about how I will die, what disease or surgical procedure will have me in its tarantula grip, what indifferent hospital wall and weary night nurse will witness my last breath, my last second, the impossibly fine point to which my life will have been sharpened. I picked up the pencil stamped PILGRIM DAY and studied its point; I sighed and said to Dale, "That mind-electricity jump is a hard one to picture."

He said quickly, "But electricity-mind doesn't give you any trouble."

I answered slowly. "It seems to me we *do* have to watch out for semantic confusion. Not everything we can put a word to is a thing in the same way. Like haircut and hair. When a materialist says 'mind' he just means to speak of a way the brain operates, as one says 'seeing' or 'sight' of the eye. This reification of abstractions and processes is what Ryle, among others, tried to clear up; ever since Plato, we've been stuck with it, and Christianity seized upon the confusion wherever it suited it. In the beginning was the Word. In the beginning, that is to say, of our wishful thinking."

"On the other hand," my young opponent said, shifting his weight so actively that the university chair protested with a cracking noise (the boy was still less enfeebled by adulterous guilt than I would have liked him) "materialists ever since Democritus have had to explain away consciousness as an epiphenomenon, as an illusion. Yet it's all we have—"

"Which doesn't mean we'll have it forever."

"—and now quantum physics tells us it's intrinsic to matter: a particle doesn't become actual until it's observed. Until the observation is made, it's a ghost. According to Heisenberg's uncertainty principle—"

My blood was up, too; in my haste to interrupt I swallowed some smoke and fought a cough. I told Dale, "If there's one thing that makes me intellectually indignant around here it's the constant harping of calf-eyed students on quantum mechanics and the Heisenberg principle as proof of that hoary old philosophical monstrosity Idealism."

Dale leaned back and smiled. "Blame the physicists themselves. They keep coming up with it. Einstein hated the quantum theory. He said it was 'spooky.' On several occasions he tried to refute it; but experiments proved him wrong, most recently the Paris experiments of 1982, with oblique polarizers. But Young's old two-hole experiment from, gee, way back in 1800 demonstrates the basic oddity: a succession of single photons will create wave interference patterns as if each particle is passing through both holes at once!"

"*Certum est,*" I murmured, "*quia impossibile est.*"

"What's that?" the young man asked. He did not know Latin. But, then, he might say, those who know Latin do not know the language of computers. We all know, relatively, less and less, in this world where there is too much to be known, and too little hope of its adding up to anything.

" 'It is certain,' " I translated, " 'because it is impossible.' " Tertullian. His most famous sentence, in fact—usually misquoted as *Credo quia absurdum est:* 'I believe because it is absurd.' He never said that. What he was talking about, in the relevant section of *De carne Christi,* is shame, embarrassment. Intellectual embarrassment. Marcion, the fastidious heretic, was evidently embarrassed by God's supposed incarnation in Christ. But what is more unworthy of God, Tertullian asks, more likely to raise a blush—being born or dying? What is in worse taste, being circumcised or crucified? Being laid in a manger or in a tomb? It's all something to be ashamed of. But, 'Whoever is ashamed of Me,' God says, 'of him will I be ashamed.' 'I am safe,' Tertullian says, 'if I am not ashamed of my Lord'—not embarrassed, that is to say, by the incarnation and all the awkwardness that goes with it. The son of God died, Tertullian says: it is absolutely to be believed, because it is out of place, in poor taste—*ineptum,* the Latin adjective is. And was buried, and rose again; it is certain, because it is impossible.' "*

"Yeah, well," Dale offered. "What particle physics has to

Quid enim indignius deo, quid magis erubescendum, nasci an mori? carnem gestare an crucem? circumcidi an suffigi? educare an sepeliri? in praesepe deponi an in monimento recondi? . . . Quodcunque deo indignum est, mihi expedit. Salvus sum, si non confundar de domino meo. Qui mei, inquit, confusus fuerit, confundar et ego eius. Alias non invenio materias confusionis quae me per contemptum ruboris probent bene impudentem et feliciter stultum. Crucifixus est dei filius; non pudet, quia pudendum est. Et mortuus est dei filius; prorsus credibile est, quia ineptum est. Et sepultus resurrexit; certum est, quia impossibile est.

add to that is that reality is intrinsically uncertain and in a very real way dependent upon observation. There's this physicist named Wheeler down in Texas who says the entire universe had to wait for a conscious observer before it could be real. Not just subjective-real, but real in a very real way. The two-hole experiment, Wheeler points out, can be rigged to be retroactive—that is, the observation that ties down the particle can occur after the hybrid behavior. By hybrid I mean both states of, say, a particle position exist until measurement. Until you look into the box, that is, Schrödinger's cat is both alive and dead. Mind really does affect matter in this sense. There's another physicist called Wigner—"

"Please," I interrupted. "This is very charming, but isn't it, honestly, rather stretching it? The reason people don't make too much of their minds is that they see how totally at the mercy of the material world the mind is—a brick drops on your head, your mind is extinguished no matter how indeterminate are the motions of the individual atoms composing the clay in the brick. Life, thought—these are no match for the planets, the tides, the physical laws. Every minute of every day, all the prayers and ardent wishing in the world can't budge a little blob of cancer, or the AIDS virus, or the bars of a prison, or the latch of a refrigerator a child accidentally locked himself into. Without some huge effort of swallowing shame such as Tertullian outlines, there is no way around matter. It's implacable. It doesn't give a damn about us one way or another. It doesn't even know we're here. And everything we do, from looking both ways when we cross the street to designing airplanes with huge safety factors, acknowledges this, this heartless indifference in things, no matter what crazy creeds we profess."

The expression on Dale's face told me I had become impassioned, and he counted this, in the insufferable way of evangelists, as some kind of triumph. "So that's how you see it," he said.

"Well, it's a way of seeing it," I said, embarrassed. "In relation to you I have to be a Devil's advocate."

" 'Crazy creeds,' " he repeated, his blue eyes bisected by the light from the tall Gothic window at my back. "You're really a very angry man."

"That's what Esther sometimes says. I don't see it that way; to me, I'm as calm and good-natured as the human situation warrants—a little more so, even."

Color, I imagined, had crept into Dale's waxen cheeks at my mention of Esther. He tried to stay with our theological tussle. "You know," he told me patiently, "when Christ said faith could move mountains, He didn't say it would instantly move them, or open up refrigerator doors; your way of thinking is miracles or nothing. But surely you can see that mind, our desires and hopes, do change, can change, the material world. I mean, what we're all coming to from about twenty different directions is a holistic—"

"Next to the indeterminacy principle," I told him, "I have learned in recent years to loathe most the word 'holistic,' a meaningless signifier empowering the muddle of all the useful distinctions human thought has labored at for two thousand years." I added, "Richie's math—how is that coming?"

Blood, that warm traitor, visibly surged beneath his skin; it was his turn to be *pudibundus,* to shoulder the shame of being. By evoking Richie, fruit of her womb, I had evoked Esther. "Good. He's a sweet boy, really; so willing. But I'm never sure how much he gets; one week we have it all together and the next session he seems to have forgotten everything. I tried to work around his mental block on bases by bringing in computers, to make it more concrete, the way they're not only binary in principle but employ, a lot of them, hexadecimal numbers for printout, sixteen being, of course, four four-bit binaries and simplicity itself to convert. But, I don't know, I guess he takes after his father. With that natural sweetness of his, he'd make a great minister."

I didn't want to hear this. I didn't want to hear most of what Dale told me: he had a knack, like the dental hygienist with her fine-edged scraper, for the soft and tender spots of my enamel. I wanted to keep him close to the carnal, to images recalling him to his sin. "But his mother is so number-minded," I said. "Do you want to know something interesting about Esther? It's rather intimate."

"Sure," he had to, hesitantly, say.

"She gets on the bathroom scales naked, and whenever she sees she weighs over a hundred pounds, she eats nothing but celery and carrots until she's back to exactly one oh oh."

"That's pretty compulsive," Dale admitted, in a voice that sounded reedy, like Verna's. I knew the reference to our shared bathroom would wound him; our casual, sanctioned nudity, our damp towels and washcloths promiscuously interchanged, our mingled medications and dental floss and mouthwashes and red discarded Band-Aid threads would torment him with the realization that there were many rooms below the attic where he and she enacted their charade of hopeless love—rooms of reality, of shared possessions and wedded tasks, of memories with worn corners and chipped paint, of shelter I could give her and he could not. Well, when you venture into adultery you must expect to trip over the husband's dental floss.

"I always find it exciting, somehow," I confessed to him, "to think of her as being exactly one hundred pounds of flesh, of meat. Tertullian calls it *caro, carnis,* which seems a more satisfying word. An argument for the mind-body split you didn't mention is the estrangement we all feel from our bodies, the disgust we have to fight in dealing with them. Feeding them, wiping them, watching them get wrinkled. Imagine how much worse for a woman—the unwanted body hair, the bleeding, the secretions staining the underpants, all those little malfunctions that result from God's having packed too many functions into those little round bellies of theirs. . . ."

"Sir, I don't want to make you late for your seminar," Dale interrupted.

"You won't, there isn't one. It's exam period. Next term, we do the post-Nicene heretics—mobs of the poor buggers. The Cathari, the Waldenses, the Apostolici, and then on into the Lollards, the Hussites, the Beghards and Beguines, not to mention you and me."

"You and me?"

"Protestants. We did away with the middleman. Faith alone. Phooey to works. Phooey to the Pope and his indulgences. It all gets very political and economic and rather dreary—the Templars, for example, weren't heretics at all, just victims of the greed of the King of France and Pope Clement the Fifth. A lot of it had to do with the rise of cities. City religion spells relief from the city, and as such tends to be mystical. Anti-organizational. The Church couldn't have that. Everybody, from Saint Francis to Joan of Arc, wanted their own direct pipeline, and the Church couldn't stand that either. I much prefer the ante-Nicene part of the course, before the bishop of Rome became quite such a brute. In those first centuries there was something intellectually creative going on; they were trying to work

out what had happened—what was the exact nature of
Christ. What is it, do you think?"

"What's what?"

"The nature of Christ. You're a Christian, yes? You keep
wanting to prove the existence of God via natural theology;
where does Jesus figure in your diagrams?"

"Why"—his embarrassment had shifted ground but kept
its color—"wherever the Creed says He figures, as God
made Man, come down to redeem our sins—"

"Oh, please. We don't need to have our sins redeemed,
do we? What sins? A little greed, a little concupiscence?
You call those sins, compared with an earthquake, compared with a tidal wave, a plague? Compared with Hitler?"

"Hitler—" he began to argue, hitting on my weak link.

"And don't talk to me about *the* Creed: *which* Creed?
The Athanasian has a totally different emphasis from the
Nicene. The Apostles' is a cover-up, a company hand-out.
How do you see the two natures of the God-Man combin-
ing? Like the Arians and Adoptionists, with the God part
tuned way down, or like the Monophysites and Apollinari-
anists, with the Man part just a phantom, a pretense? Or
like the Nestorians, with the two parts so independent poor
Jesus couldn't have known Who or what or where He was?
How do you feel about His sex life? Any? Some? None? He
had a way with the ladies, you must admit, sweet-talking
those sisters of Lazarus or just sitting around in the house
of Simon the Leper getting expensive oil poured into His
hair, and telling everybody not to throw the first stone.
Think of being Jesus Christ at age fifteen, back home in
Nazareth after Your impish behavior in the Temple has
been forgotten and everybody thinks You're going to be just
another carpenter, just like Your dad. Do You masturbate?
Do You go out behind the stack of wood scraps with the

little Canaanite girl next door? Do You have wet dreams that not even old Yahweh at His most forbidding could hold against a boy? Don't be embarrassed. This is the kind of thing the ante-Nicenes thought about day and night, this was their bread and butter, and now it's become my bread and butter. When Esther gets up over a hundred pounds, it's this bread and butter she's had too much of. She's ravenous, have you ever noticed? The woman loves to eat."

His blanched irises shuttled with fright at my manicky mood. "You talk about me and blasphemy," he weakly accused.

"Yes," I said simply. "All this Heaven-storming you want to do. If God wanted His tracks discovered, wouldn't He have made them plainer? Why tuck them into odd bits of astronomy and nuclear physics? Why be so *coy,* if You're the Deity? Tell me: are you ever afraid of looking too deep and having your eyes torn out?"

Dale blinked and said simply in turn, "Yes."

The defenseless answer touched me. I felt myself abruptly, vomitously brimming with that detestable stuff ἀγάπη.

He confided to me, "Ever since I began to go into this seriously, my prayers at night—they feel unheard. I've broken some connection. There's an anger."

"Of course there is," I said, spreading my hands on my gray, stained desk blotter and noticing that once again I had cut the one thumbnail too short, with a notch in it. It must be my way of holding the clippers. "You're trying to make God stand at the end of some human path," I told Dale. "You're building a Tower of Babel."

"And in my personal life," he huskily, tearily began to confess, seeing that he had awakened the old minister in me. But I didn't want to hear about Esther, however he disguised her. If he were allowed to confess and weep, the wound would start to drain and stop festering. I held up my hand. "Ah well, *that*," I said. "We all have something. In these circumstances down here everybody has to be a bit kinky. Don't be afraid of the Earth. The flesh. You know what Tertullian said? He said, 'There's nothing to blush for in Nature; Nature should be revered.' *Natura veneranda est, non erubescenda.* He goes on in rather interesting detail, about men and women. He says when they come together the soul and the flesh discharge a duty together; the soul supplies the desire and the flesh the gratification. That the man's semen derives its fluidity from the body and its warmth from the soul. He calls it, in fact, a drip of the soul. Rather charmingly, saying that he must risk offending modesty in his desire to speak the truth," I said to Dale, leaning forward as if to activate in the space behind his eyes the licentious images that he and Esther had stored there, "Tertullian says that when a man comes he feels his soul has flown, he feels faintness and his sight goes dim. He goes on to point out that Adam was made from clay and breath, and that clay is naturally moist, and so is the semen that springs from it.* Nothing to be ashamed of, in short. *Non erubescenda.*"

"It's funny," Dale confessed. "But at night I sometimes

In hoc itaque sollemni sexuum officio quod marem ac feminam miscet, in concubito dico communi, scimus et animam et carnem simul fungi, animam concupiscentia, carnem opera, animam instinctu, carnem actu. Unico igitur impetu utriusque toto homine concusso despumatur semen totius hominis, habens ex corporali substantia humorem, ex animali calorem. Et si frigidum nomen est anima Graecorum, quare corpus exempta ea friget? Denique, ut adhuc verecundia magis pericliter quam probatione, in illo ipso voluptatis ultimae aestu, quo genitale virus expellitur, nonne aliquid de anima quoque sentimus exire? atque adeo marcescimus et devigescimus cum lucis detrimento? Hoc erit semen animale protinus ex animae destillatione, sicut et virus illud corporale semen ex carnis defaecatione. Fidelissima primordii exempla. De limo caro in Adam. Quid aliud limus quam liquor opimus? inde erit genitale virus.

—De Anima, XXVII

want to talk to you. I think of arguments. You disturb me, I guess. You tell me not to be afraid of the Earth. I could say the same to you. You're always bringing up earthquakes, the horrible hugeness and heartlessness of it all, war, disease. . . ."

"Yes." I urged him on; I wanted to hear his solution.

He was still blushing, rubescent; his eyes slid away when I sought them. "That sort of thing can be said, of course, and maybe *should* be said; I mean, it's God speaking within us, this indignation. This rebellion. It's what makes atheists so religious, in a way, so self-righteous and proselytizing. But"—he forced himself to look at me, my many shades of gray—"what I framed one night to say to you is this: you should realize that our loyalty to God will not go away, because it is basically loyalty to ourselves, if you can follow that."

"I can," I said, "and it sounds dangerously close to humanism to me. There has to be an *Other*. As you know. And once you get the Other, He turns out to be a monster, full of terrible heat and cold and breeding maggots out of the dung and so forth. Anyway, you were good to say it. I know it's hard to express these things we store up. You were good to want to comfort me."

We were both, indeed, in a crisis state of discomfort; our eyes, our souls, were sliding back and forth like ghostly eels. The cold blank sky of this January cast a stony light into the cathedral space of this office. My feet felt cold on the floor; I felt in my bones the weight of all the books lining my walls. My pipe had died. "How's Verna?" I asked, for something to say, as relief from God and these terrible, perilous attempts to pin Him down, to caress the divine substance.

"I don't know," Dale told me. "Something's eating her.

She was all up for a while, really exhilarated, it was great to see it, about getting the diploma, and getting going in the world, but something's pulled her back down. Have you been over there since Christmas?"

"My last visit didn't feel like a success," I said, though this hadn't been quite my feeling at the time. In truth I had been afraid to pursue my advantage, for fear I had imagined it. "We tried to read 'Thanatopsis' together."

"She passed the English part of her exam."

"Yes, I know."

"You do? How? She just told me herself over the phone the other day."

"Esther told me." Esther again. Verna had told Dale, Dale Esther, Esther me.

He didn't flinch. "You ought to go make a visit, honest. Verna respects you."

I had to smile. I remembered her angry face, her exposed breasts. "That's not the conclusion I've drawn."

"You're her only relative in the area."

"It may be she came to our fair city to get away from her relatives."

Dale now seemed much as when I had first met him— the shy yet cocksure do-gooder, the Jesus freak in jeans and camouflage jacket; for the moment he had forgotten (how could he!) that he was in love with my wife, her hundred-pound sack of membrane and guts. Poor Esther had flown from his mind as he worried about hapless Verna. "You wouldn't be checking on just her, Professor Lambert, you'd be checking on Paula. She's the one I worry about, really."

"Why?"

He paused. "Verna does get pretty frantic."

"But the child is going to the day-care center five mornings a week. Free." Esther had seen to the financial arrangements.

"That doesn't help the afternoons and nights, somehow. I don't know. It's like if you take the pressure off a little bit, it's worse when it comes back. I mean, she realizes now what she's been missing. I really wish you'd at least give her a call; I just don't have the energy to focus on her any more."

"Where is your energy going instead?" I mischievously asked. His skin seemed slightly to cloud, and the knit of his long face, its cartilage and cheek fat and underlying bone, to loosen, creating bluish pockets such as a baby's flesh has. Our exchange of $\dot{\alpha}\gamma\dot{\alpha}\pi\eta$ notwithstanding, I did intend to crush him, and this determination felt delicious and solid and gristly, like an especially circumstantial paragraph in Tertullian.

"My project, I guess. I keep groping around in my mind for the way to frame it, to model reality on the computer, and really it's too vast. Just to store the data of how a city block, say, looks, let alone the atomic and chemical structures underneath, would take more megabytes of storage than I think exist between here and Berkeley, even if you posit an omniscient and lightning-fast programmer who had the time to feed it all in. Just the commercial project I'm working on—the problem is to bounce a ball, with the lettering and logo of a certain kind of pet-food can mapped onto it, across a little pebbly patch of landscape that's already been generated, piece by piece. Sounds simple, but every time the ball bounces you have to show it slightly flattening, otherwise it looks like a glass ball and like it should shatter, and then in mid-air the elasticity makes the shape rebound, so what you have is not a circle but some linked spline curves, not exactly symmetrical, because the ball flattens on one side—all this can be calculated, of course, even in three dimensions, but when you get the functions piggybacking and the mapping going on on these constantly distorting surfaces thirty times a second, not to mention the highlighting and reflection and texture diffusion and all that, well, the crunching, the number crunching, becomes significant. If the system you're time-sharing is loaded you can sit there for minutes waiting for the processor to grind it out. And this bouncing ball is a relatively trivial animation problem. Cartoon figures made up of cylinders and truncated cones and bicubic surface patches are more complex by another order of magnitude or two. But really, with graphics and robotics both, it's the elasticity of organic substances that puts the mathematics of it out of sight."

I had understood little of what he had said. It depressed me to try. I nodded, saying, "It's appalling to think about."

"Well, the machine does most of the thinking for you," Dale reassured me, "the gritty stuff." His hands had begun to dart and slide in mid-air, as he empathized his way into the computer, into the problem. "I've been thinking, for the proposal, that trying to model the world from the outside bit by bit is ridiculous; that what I have to imitate is not Creation but the Creator—that is, if I set up a system of, whatever, not molecules and neutrinos and galaxies and microbes, but just a few thousand color blocks, say, and program absolute randomness into the proliferation of one set and tilt another a bit toward teleology by injecting some cellular-automata rules, maybe a planning and reasoning subsystem of some kind, I don't know, just something mathematically to represent an element of intention, of divine purpose more or less, and then crank up this planner and crank it up again to see if some parallels emerge with the observed world, that is, if the absolutely random set resembles reality less than the teleologically tilted set, we might have a bit of a package to present to your Grants Committee. When did you say they want to meet with me?"

"Soon after spring term resumes. Early February, I would think."

He stared over my head, into space. "Oh boy. That's almost immediately. It's all still so vague in my mind, it's like this beckoning cloud. I'm not sure I'm the one should be attempting this; I feel too stupid sometimes."

"Well," I told him briskly, "perhaps stupidity is one of the qualifications. It has been for a number of noble enterprises." I heard in my voice a valedictory note, and Dale heard it too, and stood and departed. The angles of his neck and shoulders signalled discouragement; I pictured him making his way down the long second-floor hall with its chocolate-brown linoleum and closed classroom doors, the limestone staircase, its broad oak railing, its slit-windowed landing like a little side chapel, and then the first-floor hall, past the bulletin board with its overlaid announcements of banjo-accompanied Eucharists in downtown ghetto churches, of moonlit rap sessions concerning "The Development of a Jewish Feminist Spirituality" and "Liberation Theology at Work in North America's Third World," or of an address by a visiting M.D. on the sticky matter of "Intimacy and Trust in the Era of AIDS."

I felt lightly covered in slime after our spiritual grapple, our "reaching out." I hated to have my most intimate views, my hot Barthian nugget insulated within layers of worldly cynicism and situation ethics, dragged toward the light by this boy's earnest agony, his obstinate refusal to let me go until I blessed him. I kept my distance from my students and resented this interloper from another department, from another side of the university altogether, tracking his big hush-puppy footprints where so many others had never trod. For many, even square-built Corliss Henderson with her dogged melancholy butchifying of the saints, would have liked to know me better, to "get in touch with" impeccably gray-swaddled Professor Roger Lambert, who had made his deal with the universe and was damned if he was going to welsh on it.

ii

Tentatively I knocked on the blank green door; I had never been here in this kind of daylight before. The morning sun stood at the end of the stripped, scarred hall, and there was a chaste silence to the project—children off at school, adults off at work or still in bed with their sins. Verna opened the door in a prim charcoal skirt and lilac-colored cable-knit sweater. Of course: she had been up and out, walking little Paula to the day-care center on this crisp morning in Epiphany. She had opened the door quickly, as if expecting someone else. When she saw me instead, her wide sallow face— her pieface—underwent a transformation that erased its dimple, and she pulled me into her apartment and collapsed in my arms. Through my several coats I felt the smearing pressure of her breasts, the heat and pulse captured in her young-woman's fragile cage of ribs. She was sobbing, her breath and tears hot on the side of my neck. "Oh Nunc," she was gasping, in her reedy immature voice. "I wondered where you'd got to."

"I've been in town," I said, stunned. "You could have telephoned if you wanted to see us. Me." My pronouns reflected, first, a pretense that it was Esther and I together, as surrogate mother and father, whom she might have needed, and then a reflection that she and Esther must see each other at the day-care center and a glad acceptance that it was I myself alone the child wanted to turn to.

She seemed loath to let go. For the first time in fourteen years I knew what it was like to embrace a female who weighed more than a hundred pounds. But my grip was light, confused, apparently avuncular. "Oh Christ," the girl bawled and sniffled. "It's been horrible."

"What's been?"

"*Ev*erything."

"I hear you've passed part of your tests," I said. "And don't you like having Paula off your hands every morning?" We had disentangled, though a kind of heat shadow of her body lingered on the front of mine, mussing my shirt, my trousers.

Her sniffling became a snort. "Poopsie," she said scornfully. "She's the least of it." Verna looked at me with her amber eyes. They had the lashless squinting shape of a disgruntled cat's. She was putting a bold face on the words to come. "I'm making another, Nunc."

"Another . . . baby?"

Verna nodded. Her stringy bleached curls bobbed deeper over her low forehead. Her voice came out squeezed as if by apology. "I don't know what there is about me; it's as if these guys just have to wink."

"Guys?"

"Well, come on, Nunc." Brightly, as if quoting from *Cosmopolitan* or some breezy advice column: "Today's young woman plays the field."

The repeated "Nunc" felt like a jeering; but she *had* been relieved and grateful to see me at her door.

"Didn't Dale tell you?" she surprisingly asked.

"Not exactly. He thought I should check on you, though."

"So that's why you're here. Thanks."

"So what are you going to do?" I asked.

She shrugged, and the abstracted way she glanced around the apartment suggested she had put the problem, along with her outburst and embrace, behind her. The radio was on in the other room; the music was repeatedly interrupted by a rapid joking voice, a female voice that proceeded in insolent fits and starts. "Hey there, all right now," the voice said, as if disoriented. "Station W-I-L-D!" The television set was off, and sat dully on its milk crate. The room looked more like a student's room. A little white-painted bookcase had appeared; its contents consisted of some fashion magazines and the slippery-blue anthology I had brought her. And there was a new chair, a vivid overstuffed armchair that reminded me of something, I didn't know what.

My question, somewhat like the theological questions with which Dale and I irritated the space between us, had been a voicing of what should be left unsaid: Verna kept forgetting that actions have consequences. Her unstable face threatened to dissolve again into panic, as when she had greeted me. "I don't *know.* I don't want to do *any* thing."

I decided to become directive. "You can't just *have* it," I told her. "That would put you deeper behind the eight ball."

It came to me what her new chair reminded me of: that peach-colored corduroy bed rest I had seen the willowy young black carrying on his head the time I had walked to this place, down Sumner Boulevard, before Election Day. Not that the colors or shapes were exactly the same, but they shared an aura, of doomed hopefulness. I touched the chair's tangerine corduroy. "I see you've spent the money I gave you."

"That's my uncle's chair," she said, imitating a little girl. "For him to sit in when he comes to visit. If he ever does." I sat in it. Its cushions had the stiff resistance of new air-foam. "How many periods have you missed?" I asked.

"I think two," she said sullenly.

I realized I had compromised my dignity by sitting down. My face was at the level of Verna's hips. My nerves still glowed with the sensation of holding her: her body, the weight, denseness, and responsibility of it. There is an odd erotic illumination that comes over us when for a moment we see women as simply the females of our animal species, another set of forked creatures condemned to a daily round of ingestion and defecation, of sleep and exertion. We are in this together. *In carnem.* "You *think*," I said sternly. "Can't you count?"

"The third would be about now" was her grudging re-sponse. Her hips in their charcoal skirt swayed; she was idly beginning to flirt.

"Well then," I told her. "No problem. Have the abortion. You're lucky to live in a time when you can have one for the asking. When I was your age you had to creep and crawl and beg to have it done. It was illegal, and dangerous, and women died of it. And now these idiots want to bring the dark ages back."

"Did you ever have to creep and crawl, Nunc?"

"No. My first wife," I said, reluctantly, "couldn't have children. It was the tragedy of her life."

"If she had been able, would you have made her risk her life and kill the fetus?"

"We were married, Verna. There is no comparison between our situation and yours."

"You know, Nunc, I agree with those idiots. The fetus is alive. It shouldn't be killed."

"Don't be grotesque. The fetus, as you call it, at this point is about as big as a peanut, as a minnow. If you've ever eaten sardines you should be willing to have this abortion."

"Don't *you* be grotesque. It's inside me, not you. I can *feel* it wanting to live. There's a movie they show, of how they crush the baby's head."

"Stop thinking baby. Think Verna. What do you want with another little tarbaby when the one you already have drives you crazy and is dragging your life down?"

There is a point in an argument, however heated, when the center slides away from the topic being ostensibly discussed, and the participants' actual interest has slid to the heat itself, the back-and-forth of passion being generated. Verna's flirtatiousness had increased; it clung to her hips like a sarong. Her voice had lowered, gone sultry. "Who says the baby's a tarbaby?"

I was still shrill. "Whatever the color: that baby can be as white as snow and there's no room for it in this world. Why let it in just to torture it?" I wished I had brought my pipe.

"You wanna know something, Nunc? I love having babies. Feeling it grow, and then that incredible thing of being split and there suddenly being two of you."

I rested my forehead on my fingertips and thought no answer at all would be most impressive.

She sashayed closer to the chair. "You want to know something else?"

"I'm not sure." My throat was drying.

"My mother wanted to have me aborted, but my daddy,

'cause he was pretty religious even before his cancer scare, wouldn't let her. That's why I can't get too mad at him for being such a prick about Poopsie and all. Without him I wouldn't be here. I'd be nowhere, Nunc."

Someone knocked on the door. The acoustics of her underfurnished room were such that the knock seemed enormous, and as hard as a gun held against our heads. Yet the knock actually had been gentle, insinuating.

"Verna?" The voice was a mellow baritone, with a sediment of gravel. "Verna you there honey?"

She and I had frozen, me in the chair and she standing, her thighs a few inches from its square padded arm. I was looking up at her and she down at me, her chin creased into chins; she smiled a sly motherly, dimple-making smile, to seal our conspiracy of silence.

The man at the door knocked again, more sharply, and then could be heard to shuffle his feet and softly whistle through his teeth to dramatize his patience. "Verna, you playing possum?"

Verna's smile and her maternal gaze down at me did not alter; but her chubby short-nailed hands at the sides of her gray skirt bunched and lifted the cloth, lifted it, rustling so faintly only my ear could hear it, higher, up above her thighs. She was wearing no underpants. My mouth went utterly dry, as if raked by the dentist's saliva vacuum.

"O.K. you Verna," the voice said, to itself, and the back of its knuckles tapped an absent-minded little rhythm on the door. Her thighs were sallow shining curved columns; her pubic bush was broad, like her face, and darker than the hair of her head, and even curlier, so that arcs of reflected light glinted in it and random congruences of the circlets made little round windows through to the skin. The man at the door heaved a stagy sigh, and, though his footsteps were stealthy, by the vibration of the walls we knew he was going away. She lowered her skirt and backed off, still smiling but her eyes solemn and hostile.

"What was that for?" I whispered.

"Oh," she said in her normal, reedy voice. "Just something to do while we were killing the time. I thought it might interest you. You don't have to whisper. He must have heard us talking and just did that to bug me."

"Who was he?"

"A friend, I guess you'd have to say."

"Is he the father?"

"I doubt it, actually."

"Could Dale be the father?"

"Would that make it better? Could I keep it then?"

"I wouldn't think so. But if he were, then you and he could decide together."

"No way, Nunc. Like I told you in the first place, he and I don't fuck. He's not like you. He doesn't think I'm nifty."

"I do think you're nifty, yes." What she had displayed to me remained in my mind as a distinct creature, a sea urchin on the white ocean floor. When she lifted her skirt an aroma had wafted out, cousin to that musky crushed-peanut-shell scent from my deepest childhood, but with an origin beyond even that, back to the birth of life. Moisture was slowly returning to my oral cavity.

She moved about switchily, pleased with herself. "If I do get an abortion, Nunc, it's not exactly free."

"I thought they were, at a clinic. Isn't the whole idea of a clinic to save teen-aged girls like you the embarrassment of telling your parents?"

"Yeah, but they like to charge something now, it's part of Reaganomics. Anyway maybe I don't want to go to a clinic and stagger out an hour later. Maybe I'm terrified of operations and ought to go to a regular hospital. Also if I go through with it don't you think I should get something for mental suffering?"

I sensibly asked, "Why should I bribe you to do something for your own good?"

"Because you want to fuck me. You want to lick my cunt."

"Verna. Your language."

She grinned girlishly. "It's great, isn't it? Mom could never have got herself to talk like that."

I asked, to test the depth of her corruption, or to discover the price of a fetus, "How would three hundred suit you?"

Her lips came forward as if her tongue were fiddling with something caught between her teeth; a Fifties mannerism that made her look remarkably like her mother. After considering thus, she said, "I have to think about it. I'm not just kidding, Nunc, I feel it's a sin to do it."

"We all feel it's a sin. But the world is mired in sin. In this mire we try to determine the lesser of available evils. We try to choose, and take the consequences. That's what being a grown-up is."

"Come on—you believe even little babies are bad?"

"Augustine did. John Calvin did. All the best Christian thinkers did. You have to; otherwise the world isn't truly fallen, and there's no need for Redemption, there's no Christian story. Anyway, Verna, it's your life, as you said. Your sweet body."

The project was quiet around us, as if only we existed. Snow on the windowsill blew upward, sparkling. Though not much snow had fallen, January had been so cold that what had fallen remained, had failed to melt away, squeaking and shifting underfoot and blowing back and forth in a thousand little glittering pseudo-storms.

Verna seemed restless, captive. But where did she have to go, on this bright morning, without a car, without a job? "My sweet body, huh?" she said.

"Should we be doing anything," I carefully asked, my throat gone parched again, "about my finding you so nifty?"

She didn't at first know what I meant; her eyes widened, then narrowed. "Oh, I don't *know*," she said at last. "You feel funny about fucking when you're in a family way, like eating on a full stomach or something." Her refusal, like most tentative positions, was lavishly overdetermined. "Anyways, I was going to do a watercolor. Dale said he wanted one to show somebody, and also he gave me this book to brush up on math with, for the equivalency tests. Also I promised my worker I'd swing by and get some AFDC forms, they keep changing the rules. You know," she told me, her eyes widening again, "I could make an extra seventy-four dollars a month from AFDC, having another baby."

"Verna," I scolded. "What a way to make money. Making babies."

"No worse than making it by having abortions."

"I wouldn't be paying you, I'd be compensating you."

"That's a pretty cute distinction." She looked down at me again, in that way that creased her chin. "About you and me. Wouldn't it feel funny, you being my nice uncle and all?" She touched the top of my head, that thick silvery hair of which I am vain. "You could kiss me, though. That would be friendly."

I moved to push up out of her new armchair but she moved closer and said, "Don't get up. Here," and lifted her skirt again. Some boyfriend must have once told her she had a beautiful pussy. There was a tender pale valley, with the faintest blue buried veins, where her abdomen met each thigh, and I chose the one on the right; a few pubic hairs stood like sentinels on the edge of the woolly homeland, at the side of the mons Veneris. Far above me Verna giggled. "That's a tickly place."

I kissed with more pressure, to reduce the tickliness. As I thought of moving my lips leftward she backed herself away and flipped down her charcoal skirt. I was pleased to notice below my own waist the beginning of an erection. Not every female can reach into your reptile brain; it's a matter of pheromones, an obscure fit of neural notches. Nor does this reach have any relation to the lady's societally admirable qualities; if anything, these dull the interlock. We mate not to please ourselves but the great genetic pool lapping all around us.

Verna was back in her girls-wanna-have-fun mood: "It'd be fun maybe at least to take off our clothes," she said. "If you don't reject me again."

"I never reject you, do I?"

"All the time, Nunc. It's devastating. You tease me."

"Odd. I could have sworn you were teasing me."

"I bet you wonder why I don't have any underpants on."

"I made my speculations, yes."

"I like the feeling. When I walk out in the air it's like I have this secret."

"Among your many others."

Her slant eyes narrowed and took up the challenge. "Not as many as you think. You think I'm really a slutty person."

As she spoke and stared, a wall of glass materialized between us; the little links forged when my face nestled beside her belly were all broken, and I saw this common-minded delinquent girl as meaning less to me than a department-store mannequin. The sensation was a relief; as soon as her invitation to be naked together was delivered, I had been besieged by darting thoughts of AIDS, of herpes, of the man at the door returning with a strengthened fist, of the mountain of performance I should have to climb, of my rickety and undependable fifty-three-year-old* flesh, of the mockery I would risk from this unstable teen-ager, of drunken and hilarious descriptions to dark strangers down at the Domino. "I think," I solemnly corrected her, "you're a person not doing the most she can with her life."

"Well, fuck you, Nunc, that's the last sniff of my pussy you'll ever have. And I don't need your money either. Like we were saying I have an asset."

"Christ, don't start doing that, you'll really hit the skids. How are you and dope, anyway?"

"I never have a joint until after five o'clock. I only snort coke when somebody else has paid for it. It depends on the date I'm with."

"Dear me, what a bad girl."

"I'm a *good* girl, Nunc."

We were drifting into patter. I was already looking into my wallet and planning the stop at the automatic teller on the way back to the Divinity School: THANK YOU FOR USING OUR SERVICES AND HAVE A NICE DAY. "Here's eighty-five, it's all the cash I have. Just as a little cushion for right now. *Do* go to the clinic, Verna. I'll go with you if you insist. Would it help you to talk it over with Esther?"

"*E*sther?"

"She's another woman."

---

*Since the outset of this account I have suffered, in the margins, a birthday. I was born on one of the shortest days of the year, and my mother with her narrow pelvis writhed from dark to dark. Fifty-three! How old had Tertullian been when he composed his carnal paragraphs? At a certain age and beyond, the best sex is head sex—sex kept safe in the head.

"That snippy little snob, she doesn't give me shit when I see her over at day-care."

"She probably thinks you don't want to talk to her. She's shy, with most people."

"Boy then I guess I know the wrong people."

"What does that mean?"

"That's for you to ask and me to know, Nunc."

I did not dare ask if Dale had been talking. I wanted thoroughly to be away from this musty-stinking, dead-end project apartment and back at the Divinity School, amid the limestone, the ancient and rarely troubled books (the other day I opened up a squat two-volume edition of Tertullian, published by the Jesuits of Paris in 1675; the pages in over three centuries had never been cut): amid the majestic patience of the place.

Yet, so volatile and nonsensical was my relationship with my niece, we had an affectionate kiss, full on her warm unpainted lips, at the door, and no sooner did the door close than the image of her naked, treasure I had spurned, overwhelmed me like a giant wave one has misjudged, body-surfing.

I was going to do a watercolor. Dale said he wanted one to show somebody. Esther looks and says, "Touching. Under all that brass, this little pot of violets. Such pale little violets."

"Maybe she doesn't have the right paint to make them purple," says Dale loyally.

Both are naked. White, white their bodies, no fat on either, suspended like elongating globules in a tall beaker of the gray shadows and grime of our wintry city. She has agreed to come, in the cause of love, to his dingy student apartment near the university's scientific buildings, those domed and antennaed structures supported by mysterious vast financial infusions from the Pentagon and the corporate giants. He lives in a block of three-deckers owned by the university but not yet consigned to development—a parking lot or new academic facility. She has walked up the unpainted porch steps careful not to catch the pointy heels of her red leather boots in a rotten board. With beating heart she has picked her way through the crowd of rusty bicycles in the foyer and, above a bank of battered mailboxes with doubled and tripled name cards, rung KOHLER/ KIM.

Who is Kim? One of those hardworking young Orientals who, by the twenty-first century, will have a grip upon all the levers of the world. Dale has briefly described him to her, his flat colorless face and straight black hair, his unexpected barks of humor. His first name, or his last, it is not quite clear, is Tong-myong. Dale has promised that jolly, brilliant Mr. Kim will not be here—he will be attending his hydrogeology seminar and then parking cars at the movie theatre—between two-thirty, when her stint at the day-care center ends, and the time two hours later when she must return to Malvin Lane to greet Richie and then Roger, home from their respective schools.

With gloveclad finger, Esther, my Esther—I can feel her heart beating! I can feel the watery sensation in her underpants—punches this button and waits with her hand on the brass door handle for his releasing buzz to sound. The extensive wear on the thumb latch, those thousands of thumbs, first working-class Irish thumbs and now student thumbs of all global races and God only knows what procession of weary aching thumbs between, reminds her of something: what? She remembers: those foot stands the old-fashioned shoeshine chairs used to have, oddly graceful, baroque curves lifting up this narrow metal mirror-image of a shoe sole and heel, the heel lower than the sole. Her father as he climbed in the business world had been a great man for shoeshines, and as a little girl she had more than once been made to wait beside one of those multiple thrones, once so common in the hotels and depots of Albany and Troy, with their smell of polish and cigar butts and their waxy rags and brushes and their old black men chuckling and bobbing their heads as they snapped the rag; waiting at her father's ever-shinier feet, little Esther was aware of rough men's eyes on her and of her father's voice more growly and dragged-out than when he talked at home and of how dirty the shoeshine man's dark hands would be on her dress if they decided amid the growling and chuckling to touch her. The shoeshine man's head wobbled as he applied the last vigorous swipes; his palms and the under-side of his fingers were the color of pink silver polish such as Mama used with the maid once a month. On those strangely graceful foot stands, as on this thumb latch, the brass had been worn down to its golden core: atom by atom the world wears out.

Esther is wearing suede gloves and a fawn cloth coat and looks every inch, with her fur hat and furrowed brow and oxblood boots, a faculty wife—saucy and mousy, dashing and prim, a well-dressed woman on the edge of middle age. So what is she doing here? Perhaps she is a tenant's mother, or some kind of caseworker. The buzzer rasps, almost as ugly in its sound as our own front doorbell, and the door with a push and a click gives way, and she ascends the stairs carrying her proper, beating, timid heart like a baby smuggled beneath the thick lapels of her coat. At each landing, from behind closed doors, student sounds—typing, rock music, Bach fugues, loud voices tangling in male horseplay

—threaten her; as she ascends she is praying that, or should we say that her mind is looping again and again through her intense desire that, no door open and no coarse young person see her, confront her, catch her stealthily climbing toward her tryst.

Dale lives way up, on the fourth floor. Straining her neck, she sees his pale, beloved, guilt-strained face hanging over the landing railing above her like a kind of sickly sun. Her heartbeat strengthens; she is pulled up the stairs by a force stronger than the fear of social embarrassment. When she reaches his landing, with a young man's clumsy strength he pulls her into his gaudy room, which overloads her senses with its blatant posters and tattered disarray and the pungent scent it has of young males cohabiting in a small space. He locks the door, slips the tarnished chain lock across. She becomes his mistress, a hundred-pound packet of shameless, tender carnality. They strip, they fuck.

But first—wait, willing words!—they kiss: together they pry open above the thickness of Esther's chilled clothes a window of warm lips and saliva, a warmth that from this small puckered point of origin spreads throughout their bodies, beneath the clothes, and reasserts their acquaintance, the claim they have staked over each other's blood. She has never been to his room before and even while feeling his kiss expand within her tries to notice through fluttering eyelashes the Escher prints, the posters where the bodies of women and of automobiles flow one into the other, the custard-colored walls of gently buckling plaster, the single tall window with those tall old thin panes whose corners have cracked in a century of winds and been patched and repatched with Scotch tape that has sharply yellowed. A touch of Korea: a large black folding screen, decorated with busy bunched people in odd box hats and carrying all at the same slant complexly braced parasols, divides the room into the separate areas where the two young men sleep, exuding the odors of self-forgetfulness. The space left has been jammed with desks, hi-fi equipment, bookshelves concocted of cement blocks and pine planks from Grove Lumber, a few director's chairs with the hinges breaking and the canvas coming unstitched, and an incongruous collection of dolls, all furry, scaly, and metallic.

"Those are Kim's," Dale apologetically explains. "He collects space dolls." E.T. with his mournful potato of a head, R2-D2 the dome-headed robot and his silver butler of a sidekick, C3-PO, sagacious Yoda with his long green ears, those furry chattering Ewoks from the *Star Wars* sequel after that—Esther recognizes them thanks to her association with Richie, and the movies she used to take him to, when he was a few years younger and not embarrassed by being taken. Someone, jolly Mr. Kim presumably and not her serious Dale, has gone to the trouble of tricking out the bigger of these figures with freakish sunglasses and those visored hats that she associates with men on farms but which now come stamped with the logos of all the beers and are worn by people in the city, a kind of redneck chic. "Kim does all that," Dale confirms. "These Orientals, they're not exactly like us, it turns out. They love the grotesque. They love Godzilla."

On the wall, beneath a poster of Reagan with Bonzo, hangs a big computer printout that when Esther squints becomes a naked woman on her side, pubic triangle and heavy breasts and hanging hair all done in mathematical and alphabetical symbols of varying density. And beneath a shelf laden with big paperback computer texts, above the bed that must be Dale's, hangs a small black cross, four right angles. The room's one window looks not across the river toward the skyscrapers at the heart of the city but back beyond the domes toward the virtually suburban neighborhood where the humanities buildings, the Divinity School, and her own home are located. Esther can make out above the treetops the limestone university chapel spire that, when she was newly moved up here with Roger, she would use to find her way back to Malvin Lane from shopping expeditions.

"You think you can feel relaxed here?" Dale shyly asks. "Would you like a cup of tea?"

"I would," she says, briskly turning from the window, aware—as if in pivoting she has traversed a decade—of herself as a woman nearly forty, in the wrong part of the city, an adulteress in the long view from the chapel spire, a wicked woman who must look, by the merciless light admitted by the tall cracked window, her age—the skin beside her eyes etched and the backs of her hands freckled and so dry they are chalky. Coming straight from the school, she had no opportunity to prepare herself, to shower, freshen, apply a moisturizing lotion. "I had juice and a cookie at ten-thirty, and then a peanut-butter sandwich at noon." She tells him this as a wry joke on herself, this child's diet, but also as lovers tell everything about themselves, trusting the other to care.

"You may not want to, you know, make love here," Dale says, busying himself in the tiny kitchen, just an alcove where a double hotplate sits on top of a half-refrigerator. He sounds almost hopeful this will be so. She unbuttons her coat and drapes it over a frazzled director's chair, which nearly topples under the weight. She sets her fur hat—ruddy, like her hair, like her oxblood boots—on top of the coat, and then her wool scarf. A resentful wave of lust has risen within her at his remark. She watches his body make

angles in the little alcove as he reaches up for a box of
Pepperidge Farm cookies, down to the cabinet for the red
box of Lipton teabags, into the refrigerator for the milk
carton, and up again for the sugar bowl. He stoops over the
kettle of water on the hotplate, anxiously waiting for it to
boil. How touching men's backs are, that whole blind side
of them they can't defend. At the base of his long back
Dale's ass looks cute, a tightly stitched package in his worn
jeans, the tail of his plaid shirt half out. He wears a broad
cowpuncher's belt, she has noticed before, with a buckle
showing in bas-relief the head of a staring longhorned steer.
She sits on his bed to pull off her high-heeled boots. The
faces of the children she has been dealing with all day, the
multiracial waifs of working or lazing mothers, float in the
red behind her eyelids, and lift away with the boots. She
wonders what substance the little cross is. It doesn't seem
to have a grain, like wood, or any rims, as metal would. Can
it be plastic? She wants to touch it but he might see her and
think it presuming. Cupid and Psyche. She resolves, *Later,*
and goes to stand beside him and to wait with him for the
water to boil, knowing he will find her sudden drop in
height sexy, and the sight of her stockinged feet on his
uncarpeted tenement floor boards. She puts her hand on his
cute, defenseless ass.

Then her arm drifts around his waist, and her fingers
explore the little triangle of skin the torn shirt has bared
above his belt. He toys in response with the back of her
neck, his fingers sliding beneath the pinned wings of her
gingery hair to the softer finer looser wisps at her nape.
Away from her house and that attic crowded with her own
broad wild brushstrokes she has sacrificed authority; here
in this unaccustomed room the lovers are shy, as they might
be if suddenly thrust out into the world, a mismatched

couple absurd except to themselves. In a spasm of remorse and protectiveness Dale embraces her, and the molecular reactions of their chemistry take hold. The water boils, the kettle sings. They never bother to make the tea. *God,* she thinks, taking him into her flattened body; he was so suddenly aroused, she is slightly dry, and hurts at first, but then her smarting yields in the redness behind her closed eyelids to that swelling sense of completion, of being so filled that the fear of death itself is thrust beyond the rim, an eclipse of roundnesses, of holes and suns, which she does not recall Roger ever giving her, though he must have, for she had loved him enough to take him away from his wife, and attach her own life, which had already developed some fibers of independence, to his.

Dale is above her, sobbing. The smooth white curve of his bony back reveals to the fingertips of her left, caressing hand a few pimples, while her idle right reaches out and touches the cross. As she thought: not wood, not metal. Plastic. No little plastic man on it, however, no space doll about to mount His rocket. Just the empty launching pad, the slingshot. "That was amazing," Esther says. "You were so ready. Why are you crying?"

"Because it was. So fucking perfect. We shouldn't be doing this. The worst thing is, I don't mind that we shouldn't be, except it means we'll have to stop some day. Some day soon." He sniffs back his phlegm so hard the little bed heaves.

"Oh," Esther says idly, toying with the shaved back of his neck while her mind ascends, travelling out the window toward the spire, travelling upward with the ascended Jesus like a helium balloon she once accidentally released from her hand at a sleazy cotton-candy fair her father once took her to when she was perhaps eight. She had gotten sick on a mixture of candy apple and crab cake, and Mama had been furious with her father when they got home. Then after a while, years that seem now days, her mother had died, and Daddy and she could go where they pleased. "You could carry me off."

"I can't," Dale says, with a shudder of his chest that shows he has considered it. "I can't support you. I can't even support myself. I live on pizza and those little transparent packages you boil for twelve minutes. Kim jogs every morning but I don't go with him because I don't want to use up the calories. And what about Richie? What about Professor Lambert?"

"Oh, Professor Lambert. I think he'd manage."

"How could he, without you?"

"I'm not the same with him as I am with you," Esther says.

"He adores you. He must."

"He did, but that was a long time ago." She is beginning to find Dale's weight on her chest oppressive: it is nearly twice hers, even on his supposed poverty diet. His self-description of living on pizza has made him a bit repulsive. Tears look repulsive on his waxy face; they slide down toward his chin in little fat clouded balls. After all, she offered to be carried off, and he has declined. She made the definitive female gesture of total helplessness, and he has cast her back on her own resources. She says to him, "Such a sad little plain black cross." She lets him see her stroking it, with the fingers that minutes before had grasped his lovely alarmingly large warm ridged cock, steering it home. The ridges were as of gristle, suggesting to her touch the rippled ice on a river that freezes on a windy day. "What is it made of?"

"I don't know. It's not mine, it's Kim's. A lot of Koreans

are Christian, you know; look at Moon and the Moonies. Some kind of horn, I think. Could there be a kind of yak or arctic musk ox or something with smooth dark horns like that, that the Koreans might shoot?"

"Looks like plastic," Esther lazily insists.

"I just remembered. You were interested in Verna's watercolors and I got her to do me one. It's over there on the desk." He withdraws from her body and the bed. His slimy semi-erection swings loosely from side to side, like a snake looking for what has annoyed it.

While he is up, Esther calls, letting her thighs lie flopped open as he has left them, "Could you bring me a couple of Kleenex or a paper towel? I'm absolutely *swimming* in your sperm."

Touching. Under all that brass, this little pot of violets. Dale doesn't tell Verna that; he lies, "She really admired it, she thought you have a very delicate color-sense. She thinks you have talent, and she would know."

Verna is angry. She is angry at many things, but Dale is the person who has shown up, on this Groundhog Day, a sunless Saturday, following a day of freezing drizzle. Paula is sick, with a fever, so Verna can't go out. "I wouldn't have given it to you if I thought you were going to show it to that stuck-up cunt. When do you see her, anyways?"

"When I tutor Richie. Sometimes she gives me tea afterwards."

"Better watch it, big boy. These sex-starved snobby housewives, they'll take anybody for a stud."

"She's really nicer than you make out," Dale tells her, blushing.

"You know, Bozo," Verna tells him, staring hard at his

face as if having suddenly come to a decision. "You're kind of a non-person. You really drive me crazy."

He goes into his maddeningly patient, benign, slightly dazed mode. "It's not *me* driving you crazy," he says. "It's something in yourself, Verna."

"Spare me the sermon." She is wearing her bathrobe and there is a smell of hot water and bubble bath and of something acrid-sweet in the air. Her eyes look pink and poorly slept, and her face seems fatter, though this might be his being accustomed to Esther's lean, top-heavy face, with its clever, wry, wistful mouth.

"What do you think's the matter with Paula?"

"Who knows? The flu or something. They have a million germs over at the day-care center; I'm thinking of pulling her out."

"You shouldn't do that."

"Who says?" Verna's mouth gets an ajar, blankly stubborn look.

"You need the, the freedom. You need to develop your own potential. Are you doing anything about your remaining equivalency tests?"

"No. I don't do a fucking thing but smoke cheap dope and feel sorry for myself and listen to Paula say, 'Da? Da?' Actually, she talks better than that now. I dread if she gets a couple years older, the questions she's going to ask."

Dale asks, "Could I have a peek at her?"

"Help yourself." She lights a cigarette. Dale pushes through the maroon curtain that divides the two rooms. The little girl is asleep in her barred crib a few inches from where the Hitachi cassette player is blaring. "Aaaall through the night," sings a raucous female voice gone tender and croaky, "I'll be awake and I'll be with you." Paula seems darker, less the shade of Diana Ross and more now

215

that of Natalie Cole. Her breathing is snuffly and clogged, in the little flat-bridged nose with its whorled solemn nostrils. He touches her forehead. It is hot, velvety, furious as even the deadest things are furious with the motion of atoms.

Back in the other room, he asks Verna, "Are you giving her anything? Baby aspirin?"

"I broke a Tylenol in half but the little bitch wouldn't swallow it."

"If she doesn't get better in a day or two, you should take her to a doctor."

"You ever been to one of these clinics? You sit there two hours in the waiting room with these morons, inhaling every germ God ever invented. Then the doctor is some Iranian or something who can hardly speak English. Christ, you're stupid, Dale."

On the brick windowsills, the sparkling snow has at last melted, carried away by yesterday's cold rain. Some twigs of the battered gray trees still hold ghostly casings of ice. "What questions," Dale asks, "are you afraid she's going to ask?"

"Oh, like 'Why were you always screwing around, Mommy dear?' What do you care anyways? What do you care if I take those equivalency tests or not? What good would it do me? Are they going to get me out of this?" Her walls, her windows, her rug, her chairs. Her clothes, her skin. Her face, with its deceiving dimple and plump cheeks, undergoes a convulsion, submits to rage. She cries out, "Can't you see I'm miserable? Can't you see I have things to think about? Why do you keep coming around here with your goody-goody asshole smile? Why don't you do me a favor and let me the holy shit alone?"

"I love you."

"You *don't,* I *know* you don't, that's *such* a dumb thing to say!" Tears afflict her already reddened eyes. Their being there, for him to see, watery evidence, enrages her further. "You don't, and I don't want you to. I think you're a nerd, a simp. Go away. You're a worm in my head, Dale; you gotta stop bothering me. Can't you see I've been knocked up again? Oh, God, please go away."

She begins to hit him, so ineffectually at first, like a kitten's experimental batting, that he begins to laugh, lifting his forearms in defense; but then his laughing drives her to hit harder, harder, trying to erase his benign glassy smile, to wipe him away as her own face, its lashless amber eyes, seems wiped away by blind rage. She makes a small guttural noise, a kind of apology, with each attempted blow, a grunt such as the younger tennis players now attach to every serve. "*Bas*tard, *bas*tard, *bas*tard!" she utters; Dale backs out the door, still trying not to laugh, though she has begun to kick too, and this might do some damage. When the blank green door is shut in his face he hears thumps and shouts of protest from other residents of the project, who have had to overhear the brawl.

Knocked up again. Esther strokes the black cross made perhaps of Korean yak horn. "Tell me," she asks, with a just-fucked woman's presumption, "how much does this mean to you?"

He wonders whether she means the fucking, and is about to assure her how very much, when he sees with surprise where her fingers and eyes are resting. These same slim fingers have dropped the sopping Kleenexes to the floor.

"Quite much," he says, yet hesitantly. "I can't follow all the details of the doctrine the way your husband can. . . ."

"He thinks they're funny," she says. "With him all those men arguing and killing each other over these ridiculous distinctions are just a kind of cruel joke."

Dale is minded to argue, slightly, in my behalf—we men have our loyalties, through thick and thin, against these presumptuous, elastic others—but then senses the honest openness of Esther's question, and makes a lunge of sincerity. "Without it," he tells her, "I become too frightened. I become so frightened I can't act. I get terribly lethargic, as if I'm at the bottom of the sea. In Idaho that year, with these woods all around, to the horizon on all sides, and the little noises they would make—it just seemed all so hideously *God*less, if that makes any sense. I mean, I could *feel* the Devil. He was *out* there. . . ."

Her motherly and loving instincts are aroused, as he half expected; she hugs him again to her slenderness, her hundred pounds of womanly flesh and vein and bone. "You poor darling," she says.

He goes on into her ear, urging the moist words home, trying to explain. "Without it—faith, I mean—there's this big hole, and, what's strange, the hole is a certain shape, that it just exactly fills. That He just exactly fills."

It all seems so messy and sad and hopeless to her that she squeezes his curved, bony back, its cool skin constellated with patches of raised pimples. Why does it make her want to be fucked, this confession of terror and despair from this boy, with only the toy, the ramshackle antique rig, of Christianity distracting him and enabling him, along with the rest of us, to live from day to day, from sleep to sleep? "Are you always frightened?" she asks.

"Oh no," Dale says. "At times, much of the time in fact, walking down an ordinary street for instance, I feel exultant, with the sureness of it. Really. It's only at moments it feels fragile. And you have to have those moments of despair, the New Testament is full of them, not just Peter but Jesus Himself; they're part of it. They're what you earn it with. And you survive them. That's the proof, right there. You come out the other side. All you need, as it says, is as much as a mustard seed. Pray with me sometime, Esther. Not today. Not here, I know this place feels grubby to you. But sometime. That would be so nice. For me."

Under this barrage of his breath in her ear her soul is so strained by desire that she can scarcely call out, as if on the verge of fainting. "Is there anything I can do right now," she manages to ask, "to get you hard again?"

"I don't think," he answers in much the same strained voice, "you'll have to do much."

iii

The Grants Committee usually meets in the Roland L. Partch Memorial Room. Partch's father, grandfather, and great-grandfather had been Presbyterian ministers, and although Partch himself heeded instead the call to invest in inner-city real estate—he smelled gentrification coming before there was a word for it—pangs of benefaction overtook him in his middle age, as if in anticipation of his sadly early death, when the propane tank fuelling his outdoor grill exploded. His son, Andy Partch, was an apple-cheeked student here in my first years, and now, I believe, enjoys a pleasant parish in suburban Maryland, in the neo-Biblical town of Bethesda. The Partch Room had been formerly a part of Hooker Hall's storage basement; as our interview of Dale Kohler proceeded, the ground-level windows above our heads flickered like a set of television screens with the insigniaed running shoes and woolly ankles and torn pants cuffs of students passing on the cement walk outside, and the intermittent apparition of a flying saucer slanting across the white sky—an early-season Frisbee game being played on the campus and its late-winter mixture of matted brown grass, mud, and grime-speckled leftovers of snow.

I have described Jesse Closson. He is square-headed, ex-Quaker, ecumenically imperturbable. He is broader, in shoulders and wrists, than I may have conveyed, and unexpectedly rank, since he takes snuff, not up the nostrils but against the gum. When he turns his great boxy head toward you with a comradely brown-toothed smile, the spittoon stench is almost unbearable. But make no mistake: he knows his Husserl and Heidegger, his Schleiermacher and Harnack, his Troeltsch and Overbeck.

Rebecca Abrams, our female professor of Hebraic, Old Testament, and intertestamental studies, is thin, tall, curt and nimble in her motions, with long nostrils, glinting steel spectacles, mannish eyebrows, and black hair pulled back in a bun; yet her hair in its kinky energy sets a halo of frizz around the severe do, and her face has that Jewish way of abruptly hopping into a transcendent warmth and confident charm, like the gush of water when Moses smote the rock in Horeb. Jeremy Vanderluyten, the black on the Grants Committee, from the Faculty of Ethics and Moral Logistics, is a grave man the color of iron filings; he moves in his three-piece suits with a certain stiff heaviness, and his lower lids pinkly droop as if they, too, feel the weight of Christian praxis. And Ed Snea (two syllables, Sne-a), a specialist in Bultmannism and holocaustics, is a short, slight, fair nominal Presbyterian who has become, by one of those tricks of fashion that animate academic communities, the Marrying

Sam of Godless weddings; when the Czech-émigré astro-physicist's daughter marries a Japanese Buddhist graduate student in semantics, it is Ed who tailors the rite to their exact shade of polite disbelief, silently rolling his eyes upward when a single spoken word of Heavenly appeal would be too much. For those to whom even the vaguest mention of natural harmony or everlasting love would savor unduly of barbaric theism, Ed, with his touch of Southern accent and his suede-colored smudge of mustache, has a way of intoning empty phrases so that not a pinfeather of the agnostic couple's integrity is ruffled while the bride's staunchly Episcopalian step-grandmother (who doesn't hear too well anyway) leaves the service also placated. He has not gotten rich on this sideline, but he has partaken of much champagne and vanilla layer cake; indeed, Ed is so well known to the local caterers that he sometimes hitches a ride home in their van, and takes his neglected family a feast of leftover chicken livers wrapped in bacon and speared with tinted toothpicks.

Dale didn't look well for this interview; his waxy pallor had slid over into the sickly. He seemed to be sweating, and he had put on a checkered sports jacket over his lumberjack shirt, with discordant effect. He had confided to me beforehand that he had been up all night at the Cube, crunching out additional research.

I was allowed to be present at his interrogation because of my prior involvement, but was not supposed to speak. From where I sat, at the side, in one of those old-fashioned wooden classroom chairs whose left arm atrophied and whose right has enlarged like a lobster's fighting claw, the faces of the four committee members were seen in three-quarters profile, in shadow but for the tops of their heads, Closson's bald pate pathetically modified by raked stripes of uncut side-hair. Dale's checkered shoulders were turned somewhat away from me. When, in some agony of inquisition, he twisted, I could see in profile his speckled, laboring jaw and the many nervous blinks of his long eyelashes. Up above this tableau, indifferent feet constantly flickered past in mid-February's stark sunshine.

Dale described to the committee, as he had to me, the remarkable unlikelihood of the extremely delicate balance of fundamental forces evidently struck in the instant of the Big Bang, a balance of forces which alone could have produced a universe sustained and stable enough to evolve life and, in the case of our planet's leading primates, consciousness, abstract thinking, and morality.

The committee listened in shadowy silence, beneath the flickering bright feet. When Dale got a little lost in the relation of the strong force to deuterium production and thence to nuclear reaction, Jeremy Vanderluyten, out of conversational mercy, cleared his throat and with his elegant and grave elocution observed, "That's all of indubitable interest, Mr. Kohler, but—correct me if I'm wrong—these figures have been on the table quite a few years now. Cosmologies change, and I expect have changed not for the last time. What strikes *me,* if I may interject, is the manner in which our ethical and religious concerns persist no matter what the prevailing cosmology. Think of the eighteenth century and how convinced its scientists were that mechanistic materialism had all the answers. The universe was like a wound-up watch, they said, and Newtonian physics was deemed airtight. Yet what happened within the Judaeo-Christian faith? Pietism, and the Wesley revival, and the great missionary surge to every part of the globe. Look at the young people today, when the so-called death of God has been certified over and over: the most religious generation in a century, and all out of inner imperatives." The black man laid his hand across his rep necktie, and his iron face, deeply creased, seemed on the verge of smiling. "The stars alone won't do it; it's the stars *plus*. Plus ethics. Do you remember what Kant said?"

I could see Dale's poor unkempt head shake negatively. It was not a good haircut, seen from behind. Had Esther given it to him, in a Delilahlike spirit of erotic play? Verna?

"Der bestirnte Himmel über mir," Jeremy pronounced in ringing tones, *"und das moralische Gesetz in mir.* 'The starry heavens over me,' " he obligingly translated, holding up a lengthy forefinger, then tapping his necktie, " 'and the moral law within me.' The two things together, you see."

"I see, of course," poor Dale said, impatient in his fatigue, and out of his field. "It's just that people should *know,* you see, that the universe has these kinks, these telltale signs, so the moral impulse and our will to believe have a place to grab hold, if you follow me."

"We follow you, Mr. Kohler," Rebecca Abrams said tartly. "We're here to follow you. So where else are you leading?"

He outlined to them, with increasing agitation of his hands, the kinks in evolutionary theory, its unavoidable strangeness once you looked closely, from the impossibly long odds of the first self-replicating unit assembling itself in the so-called primordial soup on up to the absurd hypothetical leaps, utterly unattainable by any gradualist accumulation of accidental small mutations, of such actual wonders in the world as our eyeballs and the whale's tail. The giraffe's neck and the ostrich's calluses, as before in conversation with me, were cut short in explication.

Rebecca sighed impressively out of her stately nostrils. Her nose had no Semitic hook to it and in its straightness reached abnormally far from her face, giving her, when she removed her glasses, an extended, challenging look. "But, Dale," she said, putting him on a first-name basis and leaning toward him and then pulling back so rapidly that her nose left a white smear on the shadows, or so my retina reported, "do you really find creationist doctrine more comfortable? How do you picture *those* events? Do you really see God's hand coming down and fiddling with the clay and patting it smooth? As you know, 'Adam' does mean 'clay,' 'red earth.' I say creationist doctrine, but there isn't any, of course; they don't attempt to explain *any* detail of how matter took form, or why there are so many extinct species, or why it all took so much *time*. All they offer you is the first chapter of Genesis, verse twenty on. Even there, of course, it says God said, 'Let the waters swarm, let the earth bring forth,' et cetera: *'Vayyomer elohim tose ha'ares nefesh hayyah leminah,'* et cetera. Simple subjunctives. '*May* this and that happen,' in other words. As if He can hardly help it, really, is just giving permission, a kind of blessing. Otherwise"—she sniffed, again magnificently—"and if you take it all literally, you get into exceedingly grotesque positions, such as arguing the rocks aren't really that old, they all began in 4004 B.C., that they're not even as old as bristlecone pines where you can actually count the rings, some of my creationist students, oh, the poor dears"—she looked around at her fellow faculty members, who knew what she suffered—"you could actually feel sorry for them, if they weren't so exasperating." She challenged Dale: "Is this what you're offering us?"

I felt sorry for *him,* as I studied the spiky back of his ill-trimmed head. His hair stood up as if he had freshly pulled off his wool cap, releasing its load of static electricity. He said, "I'm all for science, ma'am"—he paused, doubting that the word was adequate for a lady professor, yet unable to think of anything better—"whatever it can show us; I *love* science, and never meant to get into any of"—his gesture was so vague as to seem despairing; it loosely included this room, the sky beyond the basement windows, the five of us—"this divinity business. I was taught I guess the Bible in Sunday school but I've never, frankly, paid a lot of close attention to it since. The God it shows us was what the technology, the social awareness of the times was up to but he looks pretty brutal now, all that sacrifice and smiting enemies and *I am What I am* and so forth. I don't want to knock it but no, I don't exactly picture a hand coming down into the clay, I don't know what I picture. I do know at times I feel *I'm* being touched inside and molded, that something is reaching down and touching *me*, but if you want to call that a subjective sensation or a hallucination or hysteria or whatever, I wouldn't argue; I think a lot of times the words we put on things just show our feelings rather than anything about the *thing*. I mean, some say 'vision' and others say 'hallucination' and these express opposed opinions about whether or not anything was *there*."

Closson said, perhaps feeling the boy was floundering and wanting to help him along, "And as Berkeley and Husserl and in his way Wittgenstein among others have indicated, the basic issue of whether *any*thing at all is there or not, and if so what its nature is, is by no means undebatable, it has to do quite a bit with how we define *there*. *Esse est percipi*," the old Quaker added in kindly manner, tilting back his big head so that his reptilian wrinkled eyelids leaped in the thick curved glass of his half-spectacles. His brown gums showed in a twitch of a smile.

"I'm not even saying exactly that," Dale said, twisting in

his chair, getting excited in spite of his fatigue, in spite of the terrible drag that Esther's love and lips, sucking, sucking, had placed upon his body and the movements of his mind. "I'd like to see religion get away from all this hiding inside the human, this sort of cowardly appeal to so-called subjective reality—to wishful thinking, in a way. What I'm trying to offer, since you ask me what I'm trying to offer, is what science is trying to tell us, objectively, in its numbers, since the scientists themselves don't want to, they want to stay out of it, they want to stay pure. There are these numerical coincidences," he explained, and he told the committee about ten to the fortieth power, how it recurs in widely varied contexts, from the number of charged particles in the observable universe to the ratio of electrical force to gravitational, not to mention the ratio between the age of the universe and the time it takes light to travel across a proton. He tried to explain the remarkable coincidence whereby the difference between the masses of the neutron and the proton almost equals the mass of the electron, and furthermore whereby this difference times the speed of light squared equals the temperature at which protons and neutrons cease transmuting into one another and the numbers of both in the universe are frozen. Equally marvellous, to him, was another equation, which showed how the temperature at which matter decoupled from radiation equalled that at which the energy density of photons equalled that of matter, mainly protons. Also, the element carbon, so crucial to the forms of life, is synthesized in stars through an extraordinary set of nuclear resonances that apparently just happen—

Ed Snea, whose ceremonies were all laudably brief, began to interrupt: "Mr. *Koh*-luh, I'm a-wonderin'—"

Jeremy Vanderluyten jumped in heavily. "As I said before, this all seems in the nature of rehash, of eclectic synthesis. Where is the original content that would warrant our financial encouragement and support?"

Dale pulled from the breast pocket of his unaccustomed tweed jacket a wad of computer paper, accordion-folded and with perforations on both sides. I could see from where I sat the paper covered with columns of numbers, masses of gray. "One of the reasons I'm so groggy," he explained to the panel, with such translucent, care-worn engagingness that Rebecca tilted her bright nose up and Jeremy cast his stern eyes down, "is I was up a lot of last night running some of the universal constants through some random transformations, trying to come up with something for you people."

"And what might that something be?" Closson asked, rolling his lower lip in a restive, snuff-craving way.

"Something unexpected," Dale said. "Something more than random."

His voice had strengthened. He tipped his chin up, facing these inquisitors. We like, it occurred to me, being challenged. That little adrenal rush washes away a lot of problematics and puts our life on the line, where it wants to be. Better see red than be dead. We like a fight because it shoves aside doubt.

Dale unfolded his grotesquely long printout, which tumbled between his knees, and said, "For instance, the speed of light times Newton's gravitational constant, both in SI units, of course, and one of them a huge number and the other very tiny, comes out almost exactly to the simple number two—one point nine nine nine five three two six." He looked up. None of the panel had blinked. "That's an incredible coincidence," he explained. "Another unexpected unitary result was that the Hubble constant—that is, the rate at which the galaxies are moving away from one another and the universe is expanding—divided by the charge on the proton, which of course is at the other end of the scale of cosmic constants, comes out to twelve and a half, with no remainder. I got to looking at that, last night about two o'clock, and after a while I noticed that all over the sheet there seemed to be these twenty-fours jumping out at me. Two, four; two, four. Planck time, for instance, divided by the radiation constant yields a figure near eight times ten again to the negative twenty-fourth, and the permittivity of free space, or electric constant, into the Bohr radius yields almost exactly six times ten to the negative twenty-fourth. On the positive side, the electromagnetic fine-structure constant times the Hubble radius—that is, the size of the universe as we now perceive it—gives us something quite close to ten to the twenty-fourth, and the strong-force constant times the charge on the proton produces exactly two point four times ten to the negative eighteenth, for another. I began to circle twenty-four wherever it appeared on the printout: here"—he held it up, his piece of striped and striped wallpaper, decorated with a number of scarlet circles—"you can see it's more than random."

"I'm not sure I *can* see that," Jesse Closson said, peering over his half-glasses. Dale held the paper higher and we could all see that his knobby big hands were jerking, shaking. He was holding the universe in those hands.

"Randomness or the lack of it is no kind of category—" Jeremy Vanderluyten began.

"Mah friend," Ed Snea pronounced, as if calling a jabbering lawn party to order, "what do these interrelations between these numbers *mean?* Aren't you adding apples and oranges, as they say, and then dividing by grapefruit?"

"These aren't just numbers, they are the basic physical

constants," Dale told him. "These are the terms of Creation."

"Oh I *like* that," Rebecca gushed. She was, I realized, Dale's first ally on the committee, and he realized it too.

He turned his head to face her, one on one. "These numbers," he said intently, with an almost paternal earnestness and yearning for understanding, as the feet flickered over her head, "are the words in which God has chosen to speak. He could have chosen a whole other set, ma'am, but He chose these. Maybe our measurements are still imperfect, maybe my transformations weren't the most intelligent. . . . I was getting so tired, and nervous because of this meeting today; there might be a differential equation that would yield something definitive, I just don't know. But there has to be something here, if anywhere. You don't like the way the speed of light times the gravitational constant comes out to two?"

"Oh, *I* like it," Rebecca repeated, with a different emphasis, "but—"

"This is kabbalism," Jeremy Vanderluyten rumbled. "Numbers can be made to say anything, you fiddle enough. Just to satisfy my curiosity: see if you have a six six six anywhere there."

Dale, his head moving in little quantum jumps, looked over his printout and announced, "Yes, sir, I certainly do. Not just three sixes but ten of them, right in a row. The Bohr radius divided by the Hubble radius."

"See," the black man said. "Now that's the number of the Beast, and supposed to mean the end of the world is at hand."

"Or that two is being divided by three," Closson said, a pepper of impatience creeping into his bland manner. "These calculations have for me, young man, a certain savor of desperation. As Heidegger might say, your *Verstehen* has been overtaken by your *Befindlichkeit*." The other committee members tittered.

Dale with dignity admitted, "I do feel desperate, sometimes. But then I think, Why should God make it easy for me, what He's denied to all of mankind up to now? There was a moment," he said, "last night. I was tired, and I guess exasperated if not desperate, and began to punch commands at random, and in the middle of the garbage I was getting on the screen there flashed suddenly this beautiful number: one point zero zero zero zero zero zero zero zero, I don't know how many zeros, maybe ten, and then a one. Now nowhere in nature is a calculation going to yield such an odd amount, one and one-ten-billionth or whatever it was. But the numbers being generated kept scrolling past, and when I tried to go back to it and take a printout, the computation was gone."

There was a silence. It occurred to me that not once had Dale glanced in my direction. He and Esther must have had an exceptionally hot time yesterday, in the attic. She had been languid and saucy when I returned at five-forty-five; she and Dale and Richie had been bent above the dining-room table like a sentimental Biblical mezzotint under the Tiffany lamp, their three heads forming a triangle, standing Esther's the apex. They had been working at hecadecimal numbers. "And two D?" Dale had asked. "What would that be, Richie?"

Silence had stretched, while in the kitchen the refrigerator consulted with itself about making more ice.

"Forty-five," Esther at last had drawled. "Obviously."

"Your mom's right," Dale had said, embarrassed for her. "See, Richie," he had explained, "the two on the left means two sixteens, so that's thirty-two, and the D represents—because, remember, we have to assign a letter to the two-digit numbers under sixteen—" He had waited a second, then himself supplied, "Thirteen. Thirty-two plus thirteen makes—?"

"Forty-five," the child had said in a weak, troubled voice.

"Exactly! See, you're getting it!"

"About time," Esther had said languidly, saucily. Her mouth, even under a fresh application of lipstick, had looked chafed, and her green eyes had glowed, I felt, with how far into nature she had tunnelled and rooted a few hours before. That night, last night, in our dark conjugal bed, out of concupiscent momentum she had fumblingly offered to apply some of her filthy tricks to me; I socked her naked shoulder with the heel of my hand and turned my back, protecting what they used to call roguishly, back in Ohio, the family jewels.

Ed was asking Dale, with delicate distaste, the crucial question. "Do you have any other thoughts as to how to use a computer in this search for"—he could not make his lips, beneath his minimal, as it were demythologized, mustache, pronounce the gawky old monosyllable—"the Absolute?"

"Or did this shoot your wad?" Closson crackled, too much a Quaker innocent to know, I think, how vulgar the phrase was.

Rebecca did know, and leaned forward to smooth things over, to mother the young man. "Dale, what did you visualize as the end-product of your researches? A technical paper, or something more inspirational?" She sat back and removed her steel-framed glasses from her long white nose, and this changed her aspect for us. She was a woman—Eve, *Hawwah*, "life." I felt within me Dale's heart yearn toward her, a spot of warmth within this chilly trial. She smiled and continued, "What I'm trying to ask is, How could we *use* your theories, to justify a grant?"

Jeremy, still irritated by the lack of respect paid *das moralische Gesetz,* asked, "What you trying to prove, shuffling these numbers around?"

"Sir, I'm trying to give God the opportunity to *speak,*" Dale said, rousing himself to forcefulness. He described to them, more fully than he ever had to me, his notion of making a model of reality along the principles of computer graphics. Shapes, he told the committee, can be subtracted one from another, once they are represented in machine memory as solid primitives, and cross-sections can be computed at any angle, and along any slice, once a few commands are given. In computerized industrial design, such as the making of a die or a mold, negative shapes have an importance equal to that of their positive counterparts; also (and here his expressive hands came into play, elaborately), solid shapes can be created by moving a planar figure along a specified path in space. By making such systems interact, and by injecting local rules for the evolution of these shapes, and by using more global planning algorithms, Dale felt he could simulate our actual world, not in its content so much as in its complexity, at a level that would yield graphical or algorithmic clues to an underlying design, assuming one exists. It was a little like, he said, the common process in computer graphics whereby first a "wire-frame" image of a solid object is generated by vector lines and then, with a simple formula operating on the z coördinate, the hidden edges are eliminated, the edges that in the "real" world—that is, the world we experience with our senses—would be hidden by the object's opacity; theologically speaking, we move through a world with its hidden edges removed, and Dale's attempt, with the committee's indispensable support, would be to restore those edges, removing the opacity and giving Creation back the primal transparency in which, since the Fall, only a few mystics and madmen and, perhaps, children have seen it. Or, if the committee would prefer an analogy from particle physics, his effort would be to subject the macrocosm, transposed into computer graphics, to a process like atom smashing.

Yet Dale's presentation was halting, and at points his voice dragged to a long pause; it was as if he had rehearsed this moment in his mind so often that when it finally came he had no energy to give it. He was at the end of his strength. He seemed resigned to rejection.

Smelling blood, Jeremy said, in his gravelly grieving dark voice, "Since Kant and Kierkegaard on up through William James and Heidegger, religion has planted itself within subjectivity. Subjectivity is religion's proper domain. We must not let ourselves be tempted out of that domain. You start poking around with this sort of pseudo-science, you'll be right back to magic and fundamentalism of the least defensible sort. Good-bye, moral imperatives; hello, voodoo."

Rebecca said, "But, Jere, aren't you really being a bit un-Biblical? The God of Abraham and Moses wasn't a subjective phenomenon only; the Israelites experienced Him with their total being, as history. They argued with Him, even wrestled with Him. They were *covenanted* by Him. You wouldn't want to be the one to say to God, You can't come into history, You can't come into the objective world!"

"Every day of the week," Closson said, clearing his throat with a nicotine-induced scrape, "prayers invite Him in; and the damnedest thing is, nobody knows, after all these years, if He's come in or not!"

"What *Ah* worry about," said the Reverend Ed Snea with

his ceremonious Southern twang, "is, supposing these computers in the kind of array that Mr. Kohler has described to us *do* acquire something like intelligence, doesn't that mean they will acquire a subjectivity also, and so even if one of them testifies that in the objective sense there is an Absolute, is that going to mean any more than the testimony of some Jesus Saves hillbilly from the backwoods of Tennessee?"

"Or than that of the Aztec maiden who believed enough in Huitzilopochtli to let the priests tear her heart from her living breast." Closson's reptilian eyes twinkled and his foul brown mouth creaked open in a little silent laugh. Religion, it came to me, had never ceased to amuse him.

"What *Ah'd* like to do," Ed said, "is give these computers enough rope to hang their selves. Computers in my book are just fancy filing cabinets."

"In *my* view it would be a sorry misappropriation," Jeremy said, "in this day and age when black and women's studies are starving for funds—"

Rebecca interrupted, "Some of the women I talk to are tired of being studied. Is being a woman *all* we do? Can't we say anything about ourselves except that the patriarchal society has forced deodorants on us? My sweet little militants, they look as if they've never washed their hair or cleaned their fingernails, as if it were *men* who invented bathing—" She knew she should stop but went on, with an irresistible swift smile, "I think it's *charm*ing that this young man wants to come over from the science end of the university and give us a helping hand."

Closson cleared his throat once more and turned his big overstuffed box of a head toward me. "Roger, do you have any insights or thoughts you'd like to share with us before we excuse Mr. Kohler?" One of his cover-over strands had come unstuck and waved out from the side of his head like an inquisitive antenna.

It shocked me, to be called out of my apartness, my existence as purely a shadow. "You know me, Jesse," I said, with a false jocosity that barked in my own ears. "A Barthian all the way. Barth, I fear, would have regarded Dale's project as the most futile and insolent sort of natural theology. I also agree with Jere: apologetics mustn't leave ground where it's somewhat safe for ground where religion has been made to look ridiculous time and time again. Like Rebecca, I don't think God should be reduced purely to human subjectivity; but His objectivity must be of a totally other sort than that of these physical equations. Even if this were not so, there are additional problems with provability. Wouldn't a God Who let Himself be proven—more exactly, a God Who can't *help* being proven—be too submissive, too passive and beholden to human ingenuity, a helpless and contingent God, in short? I also see a problem with His facticity, as it would be demonstrated to us. We all know, as teachers, what happens to facts: they get ignored, forgotten. Facts are *bor*ing. Facts are inert, impersonal. A God Who is a mere fact will just sit there on the table with all the other facts: we can take Him or leave Him. The way it is, we are always in motion *toward* the God Who flees, the *Deus absconditus;* He by His apparent absence is always with us. What is being proposed here for us to finance, I'm sorry, just strikes me as a kind of obscene cosmological prying that has little to do with religion as I understand it. As Barth himself says somewhere—I can't give you the exact reference offhand—'What manner of God is He Who has to be proved?' "

After this Judas kiss, Dale for the first time glanced my way. His acne, my visual impression was, was clearing up, thanks to Esther's ministrations. His blue eyes were dazed, clouded. He didn't understand the favor I had done him.

Jesse, of course, is an ecumenicist and a sentimental Tillichian, and Ed a professional Bultmannite, and Rebecca not insensitive to the streak of suppressed anti-Semitic feeling present in Barth's professed philo-Semiticism,* and Jeremy a social activist and an ethical logisticist; by bringing Barth, the scornful enemy of religious humanists and accommodators, the old foe of Tillich and Bultmann, so thumpingly into the discussion, I had swung the committee against me: that is, toward Dale.

Jesse hawed a bit and tried to sum up: "Well, yes, the Ground of All Being has to *be* in a somewhat superior sense, I suppose, He can't be just one more being. But that poses a whole slew of interesting questions, whether being, *esse, Sein,* is a simple either/or—a binary condition, in Mr. Kohler's language—or whether there are degrees, intensities. . . . This is *all* very interesting, actually: you've gotten us to think, young man, and that's not easy in academic circles. Heh. Heh-heh. You should be hearing from us within two weeks."

When, ten days later, I told Esther that Closson had let me know that the committee had voted to give Dale a provisional grant of twenty-five hundred dollars, renewable upon application next September subject to his submission by June first of a forty-page paper summarizing his concrete

---

*See—and then absolutely no more footnotes!—Barth's letter of September 5, 1967, to Dr. Friedrich-Wilhelm Marquardt: ". . . in personal encounters with living Jews (even Jewish Christians) I have always, so long as I can remember, had to suppress a totally irrational aversion, naturally suppressing it at once on the basis of all my presuppositions, and concealing it totally in my statements, yet still having to suppress and conceal it."

and original results, she said, "That's too bad. That's terrible, in fact."

"How so?"

"Now he'll feel he has to come up with something, and it's impossible, what he's trying to do."

"O ye of little faith."

"He's losing his faith. This will do it in entirely."

"How do you know he's losing his faith?" I asked.

She turned on her clacky heels and swished down the hall, giving me that back view from which even the smallest woman looks somehow grand, a piece of the Earth. She was wearing snug khaki slacks; she had been out in the garden, doing some fidgety winter pruning, wondering when the mulch should come off, finding the first snowdrops hanging their heads over in that sun-warmed corner of our fence toward the Ellicotts' tool shed. "Aren't we all?" she called back to me, before vanishing into the kitchen. I had never thought of Esther as having any faith; that had been part of her charm, the succulent freedom she had held out.

I had asked her to take Verna to the abortion clinic and she refused, saying that she was my niece and anyway Verna had conceived a dislike to her; she was quite rude coming into the day-care center. Where, incidentally, she brought Paula less and less faithfully, and when she did bring her the poor child was filthy. Things were deteriorating on *that* front, she said. As if there were any number of fronts, and she and I were campaign headquarters.

Over the telephone Verna had been quite clear that she didn't want to go alone. She said it was my idea anyway. I said I would take her, then. Better that than let her wriggle out. I was determined to see this through. On the appointed afternoon a babysitter from within the project crumped out at the last minute, typically. So little Paula had to come with us. It was a time of day, late afternoon, that until recently had been pitch-dark and that now surprised us with its light, the daylight lingering on the three-decker rows, the corner stores with their grated windows, the leafless sycamores and locusts, the bent and spray-painted No Parking signs. The light embarrassed me as I chauffered this nineteen-year-old woman and the one-and-a-half-year-old girl in my solid, unmarred, slightly racy Audi along these streets lined with the rusted bloat of Detroit, cars frozen here like wads of lava. I had no business here. But I did. I was killing an unborn child, to try to save a born one. Two born ones. The clinic was a low building of white brick, the building not exactly new and the brick only white enough to make the mortar look dark; it was a number of blocks beyond the project, deeper into that section of the city where I never used to go.

It embarrassed me, too, to go into the clinic office attached to this mulatto toddler and this slack-mouthed, sallow-faced, slightly overweight teen-ager. For this event Verna had contrived to put on her most thrift-shoppy outfit, a collage of wide pea-green wool skirt and canary-yellow turtleneck and orange leather vest under some kind of plaid serape; she looked like an ingénue bag lady. And her hair was done up in oily curls—that wet, snaky look, as if fresh from the shower, which you see more and more, even on the secretaries at the Divinity School.

The fluorescent lights inside the clinic, faintly buzzing and humming, made little headway against the sullen air. There were two desks in the anteroom, staffed by a nurse and a secretary. The nurse looked up and gave me a look that seemed accusatory. To fill out the forms, Verna had to pass Paula into my arms, and the child felt heavier than when I had last lifted her—not only the outdoor winter clothes but growth, new muscle demanding satisfaction from the world. How tiny she was, yet how fully alive, with personhood's full unitary value. She was getting leggy. Her face now wore a more complex, thoughtful expression. In my grasp she felt restless, her little muscles softly rolling, yet undecided as to whether or not to make a strenuous effort to break free. From inches away she looked me straight in the eyes, unsmiling, appraising. "Not faw down," she said, singsong. Her eyes, which had once looked navy-blue to me, had become brown, shades deeper than Verna's.

"Paula not fall," I agreed. "Man hold tight." I wondered what the little smell was, coming off of her as she warmed in my grasp; I remembered Esther's "filthy" but this was not excrement, it was a musty comfortable odor from deep in my life, savoring of the enchanted spaces behind bureaus or of closets whose shelves were lined with oilcloth. I remembered this child's grandmother in the slant-roofed attic that day, the dust motes, the sad gray-white of her dickey as Edna reached inside her sweater to undo it. I remembered the longing that our poor minds press against the bodies of others, like water against the bodies of swimmers.

"Nunc, mind if I put you down as next of kin?" Verna asked in her scratchy and conspicuous voice. Several faces turned toward me. There was a row of chairs to wait in, in this room with its flickering fluorescent ceiling, its Venetian blinds hiding the view of the street, its wall panels of institutional pastel. An odd thick interior silence diluted the swish of traffic outside; the plastic bucket chairs, in different primary colors as in an elementary school, were a third occupied, by young women, mostly black, and a few desultory escorts. One prospective mother chewed bubble gum, with virtuoso deadpan placing perfect pink spheres in front of her lips, repeatedly, expanding and popping and growing again. Another wore a Walkman and her eyes were shut upon the din filling her head. A black boy who looked little older than the child who had guarded my car was urgently murmuring into the ear of a girl and offering her drags of his cigarette. She had wet cheeks but was otherwise impassive, an African mask, her lips and jaw majestically protruding.

"But I'm not," I said, stepping closer and whispering.

"Bad man," Paula said close to my face, testing, flirting. Her rubbery wet fingers probed my mouth and tugged at my lower lip. Her tiny fingernails scratched.

"I don't want to put down Mom and Dad," Verna said, carelessly loud. "They say fuck me, I say fuck them."

Another bubble popped. A car with a broken muffler snarled tigerishly out on the street. The nurse, with a blue cardigan worn like a cape over her starchy white uniform, led Verna into another, brighter room. Paula and I could see her inside the ajar door sitting in a chair, having her blood pressure taken from a bare arm. A thermometer tilted upwards jauntily in Verna's mouth. The child became agitated, fearful that her mother was being hurt, and I carried her outside.

Outside on the sidewalk, night had come. From the distant heart of the city, where a dome of light stained the sky and the airplane-warning lights at the tops of the skyscrapers pulsed, there arose a muffled roaring, an oceanic sound as if the stalled surge of traffic had taken on an everlasting meaning. This neighborhood seemed almost suburban; a grocery store glowed on one corner, and faceless pedestrians moved back and forth across the street, snapping off words of greeting. Paula bucked in my arms; she was apprehensive, hungry, and increasingly heavy. She kept kicking me softly through my sheepskin coat and scratching curiously at my lower lip. Rather than venture back into that flickering waiting room, I took her into the shelter of the Audi, and on the car radio tried to find a song that would please her. I tried to find that song with all the bops in it, but in the jungle growth of new songs and new stars, Cyndi Lauper was nowhere to be found, from one end of the softly glowing dial to the other.

"Music," Paula observed.

"Wonderful stuff," I agreed.

"Awesome," she said, in her mother's exact tone, slightly trancelike.

"You could say that."

I ransacked the dial, trying to find music instead of the news or the talk shows that proliferated as the evening deepened. Half of the callers were drunk, and all were stirred into garrulousness by the miracle of their being on radio. I marvelled at the practiced rudeness with which the hosts shut them off. "O.K., Joe. We're all entitled to our opinion. . . . I'm sorry, Kathleen, you got to make more sense than that. . . . Take care, Dave, and thanks a ton for calling." Paula fell asleep; I moved her to the passenger seat and realized she had made my lap damp. I switched off the radio, its Tower of Babel.

A spiritual fatigue descended upon me, a recognition that my life from the age of fifty-three on was a matter of caretaking, of supervising my body like some feeble-minded invalid kept alive by tubes and injections in a greedy nursing home, and that indeed it always had been such, that the flares of ambition and desire that had lit my way when I was younger and had given my life the drama of fiction or of a symbol-laden dream had been chemical devices, illusions with which the flesh and its percolating brain had lured me along. There is, as the saints knew, a satisfaction in this fatigue, as if in sinking beneath despair and acedia we approach the abysmal condition that drove God in His vacuum so diffidently to say, *Let the waters swarm, let the earth bring forth.*

I pushed down on the door handle and listened to hear if the noise woke Paula. Her breathing snagged for a second, but then resumed its trustful oblivious rhythm, and I went back out into the air, the street. A gentle cold drizzle had materialized, darkening the asphalt, tingling at my face. We do love being touched from above—by rain, by snow. I thought of Esther moving about our kitchen, her motions slowed by wine and inner reflection, and of Richie mechanically putting food into his mouth while his eyes gorged on the shuddering little screen, and I was happy not to be there for once, to be out in the tingling air in this strange part of the city, as strange to me and as pregnant with the promise of the unknown as Tientsin or Ouagadougou. I wondered if I had left one of the Audi windows cracked to let in a little air, as you would for a dog, and went back and checked. Paula asleep looked not worth stealing, a bundle of rags. As seen by the sodium glow of the streetlight she had no more color to her face and her little limp limbs than a newspaper photograph.

The nurse was gone from her desk and the secretary said my niece would be a while yet; there was only one doctor on, so he was running late. Of the three young black women I had originally seen, only the African mask was left. Her escort was gone, and her tears had dried, and she was impassively regal, princess of a race that travels from cradle to grave at the expense of the state, like the aristocrats of old. I found myself wondering how many hours it had taken to do up her hair in so many fine braids, interbraided with colored beads and tiny ringlets of imitation gold.

When Verna did at last emerge from the unseen chambers of the clinic, ten minutes before eight o'clock, she, too, was impassive; she moved carefully, as if walking on feet she could not feel touching the floor. She was carrying into the milky, flickering light pieces of paper, both big—official forms—and little: prescriptions to be filled. Also a small parcel, something yielding wrapped in tissue paper. I offered her my arm, when her brief transactions with the secretary were over, but she ignored my helpfully bent elbow. Perhaps she didn't see it. Below her eyes there were delicate mauve cushions, as if her face had been inflated and was not quite collapsed back onto its bone. "What's in your little bundle?" I asked.

"Pads," she said. In a loud ironic voice she imitated an enthusiastic child: "They gave me the cutest little pink belt to wear, free!"

Outside, the rain had subsided to a mere mist, yet I still wanted to shelter her, to be a canopy as she walked to the car one floating step at a time. Like butterflies about a statue my concern fluttered uselessly about her stoic upright figure. I found her dignity alarming, asserted now against a personal history of indignity and clenched around a determination to be revenged. She stood at the passenger door while I gropingly, clumsily poked at the little curvate handle slot with the ragged key. While patiently waiting she looked in and saw Paula's tumbled body through the dark glass.

"Well Nunc," she said, in that deadened voice of hers which seemed exhaled through a tube too narrow, "one down, and one to go."

IV

i

Toward evening of this first Friday in April, Dale proceeds, with a cooling hot-pastrami sandwich in a grease-soaked paper bag, plus a small carton of high-fat milk and a pair of broken oatmeal cookies in a plastic envelope, to the building, erected in 1978, that houses the university's violently expanded facilities for computer research and development. A concrete cube with nine times nine windows on a side, it looms above the tattered and doomed rows of tenements that stand in this section of the city, real estate that is all owned by the university and awaiting its developmental fate. Mere daily life seems meagre in the shadow of this great housing, its many windows identically deep-set in sandy-gray sockets bevelled like the slits of a bulletproof bunker. The sky this evening is turquoise, and the smaller, more nervous clouds of spring have replaced winter's stolid mantle. Everything, suddenly, is tugging, from greening tree-tips to mud underfoot, to be something other than it is. Dale's stomach feels high in his body, its lining chafed from within by guilty apprehension. He has accepted money for his project; he has bitten off more than he can chew.

Though the normal world's working hours are over, and the great rose-marble foyer of the Cube is deserted but for one lackadaisical guard who checks Dale's laminated pass, on certain upper floors truly creative activity is just beginning, having yielded the daytime hours to more assuredly profitable projects than its own. Dale enters one of the powder-blue elevators. He punches the number 7.

The first floor of the Cube is given over to reception space, the offices of the public-relations staff, and a technical library of computer science and the great programming languages (LISP, FORTRAN, PL/1, Pascal, Algol with its ancestor Plankalkül and its descendant JOVIAL), plus a small and amusing museum displaying abaci, Inca quipus, a seventeenth-century slide rule, diagrams of Pascal's toothed and ratcheted calculation wheels and the stepped wheels of Leibniz, a wall-sized enlargement of some engineering specs for Charles Babbage's epochal Analytical Engine with its Jacquard cards and thousand wheels of digit storage, reproductions of selected pages of the Countess Lovelace's mathematical notebooks and also one of her actual embroidered linen handkerchiefs, samples of the Hollerith punched cards used in the U.S. census of 1890, significant pieces of the Automatic Sequence Controlled Calculator put into operation at Harvard in 1944, and a disassembled accumulator, consisting of ten ring counters comprising in turn ten vacuum tubes, from ENIAC, the first true electronic computer, designed in Philadelphia to calculate the trajectories of quaint, old-fashioned bombs and shells.

On the second and third floors the administrators of the Cube have their offices, and there are conference rooms and a small all-stainless-steel kitchen in which luncheons and heavy hors d'oeuvres can be concocted for significant visitors. For the benefit of the Cube's workers there are a gymnasium (with Nautilus equipment and a balcony running track), a meditation room (equipped only with mats and zafus), a three-bed infirmary, and storage space for bicycles and mopeds, which must be brought into the building lest they be stolen outside.

The button to the fourth floor, in most of the elevators, is taped over, and even in those elevators where the button is exposed it achieves no response unless a numbered code, changed every week, is punched into a small panel. The work done on the fourth floor is secret, and yet from this unmentionable work stem the funds upon which the entire Cube rests. The men who work on the fourth floor never acknowledge it but can be identified by their relatively formal attire—suits and neckties, whereas even the head of all research and development, a jubilant Italo-American named Benedetto Ferrari, goes about in a turtleneck or a silk shirt open at his throat to disclose a thick gold chain or some old love beads of no-longer-fragrant cedar. Once a brilliant mathematician, with his fine Italian flair for elegant shortcuts, Ferrari dazzles trustees and even charms, over the telephone, those weary men in Washington who like coal heavers of old must shovel out their daily quotas of the incessant national treasure.

The fifth floor is mostly devoted to Ferrari's pet project, the development of adaptive brainlike hardware silicon chips for artificial intelligence—though what benefit might be brought to mankind, already possessed of so many disastrous intelligences, by the mechanical fabrication of yet more is less clear than the immaculate, feral smile of approval and encouragement that the boss bestows on all sides when he visits his favorite department. His happiness, perhaps, is that of Pygmalion, of Dr. Frankenstein, of all who would usurp the divine prerogative of breathing life into clay.

The sixth floor holds the guts of the place—the massed ranks of CPUs—VAX 785s, Symbolics 3600 LISP machines, and the Cube's own design, the MU—churning and crunching through calculations twenty-four hours a day; thunderous fans keep them from overheating, and a floor of removable segments protects yet renders accessible the miles of gangliated cable connecting their billions of bytes with not only the floors of display-processing units above and below but also, through high-speed modems and satellites, with terminals as remotely, strategically placed as Palo Alto, Hawaii, West Berlin, and Israel. Dale, to cool his mind, sometimes likes to wander around in here on the shuddering floors, up and down the aisles of encased circuits and racked spools of magnetic tape, amid the gigantic hum of something like spiritual activity, yet an activity mixed with the homely leakiness and vibration of a ship's engine room, complete with the reassuring human curses of grimy-handed mechanical engineers wrestling with cables and hand-tightened connections.

The seventh and eighth floors hold the cubicles of the lesser minions of the Cube, and the ninth holds the air-conditioning equipment—the ninth-floor windows are dummies, installed to satisfy the architect's post-modern need for insincerity, for empty symmetry. Dale gets off at floor 7, which also holds the cafeteria, closed after five o'clock, and a hall of rather weary machines that at any Godforsaken hour will accept coins and supply coffee, tea, bouillon both chicken and beef, candy bars, potato chips, cans of soft drinks, and even triangulated, bubble-wrapped sandwiches, all by encoded number. Working soldiers in the computer revolution, these big scarred boxes operate at a

level of dogged, fumbling reliability interrupted by sudden
spurts of rebellious malfunction—the coffee that will not
stop pouring from its limp white nozzle, the bulb-lit red
legend claiming OUT OF STOCK even though the desired bag
of Fritos is in plain sight behind the plastic pane.

This seventh floor is also a realm of refuse, of paper cups
and discarded wrappers, of posters overlaid one upon another like raster-display windows that cannot, oddly, be
moved at the touch of a button but need fingernails to pry
loose the thumbtacks and pressure to push them back in.
There is, on the bulletin boards and the office doors of these
seventh-level computer wizards, an atavistic population of
comic-strip animals, of Snoopy the blobby white dog and
Garfield the chunky striped cat, of Booth's bull terriers and
Koren's gleeful shaggy anthropomorphs, as if a certain
emotional arrest has been the price of the precocious quickness of these young minds. Few of Dale's peers are at their
posts at this in-between hour; also, spring and its holiday
have called many of them home. Allston Valentine, an
Australian roboticist, can through two doorways be
glimpsed, as it were in clipped image, amid the rickety
wreckage of a disassembled many-elbowed arm, while its
leverage schematics patiently glow in vector sketch on the
display terminal. Isaac Spiegel, who has been struggling
since his junior year at MIT with the unreachably deep
structures of computerized translation, sits with a bronze
can of Michelob in a cubicle lined with dictionaries and
grammars and Chomskyite charts branched like impracti-
cal antlers. Language, that spills from every mouth as naturally as saliva, turns out to be even more resistant to analysis than enzymes. Spiegel is growing bald in the service of
his specialty; he looks hairy everywhere but wears on the
back of his head a bald spot the shape and size of a yar-

mulke. He is overweight; his stretched shirt shows pumpkin seeds of skin between each pair of buttons. He looks up at Dale suddenly in his doorway and says, "Don't scare me. You look like a ghost. Where've you been, Fuck-off?"

"Around," Dale says.

"Not like you used to be around. What's the distraction? Where's the old dedication? Frontiers of reality, and all that?" Dale's mouth gropes for the answer, and Ike supplies, "It's gotta be a cunt. Or an asshole; but I don't think you're into those."

In truth Dale's desire, with Esther's connivance, to possess her completely, her slender perishable body, has led them lately in their lovemaking to that smallest, tightest orifice as well. Dale remembers the grip of the cold greased sphincter and the sight of the nape of her dear neck tense at the other end of her spine and blushes and marvels at Spiegel, the fat man's nonchalant clairvoyance, his fearlessness in the face of nature, his *groundedness.* God's anointed. The blacks and the Jews are the magical people in America, and our blanched, gentile, protesting race the dead weight, the ancient chafe, the persisting saddle sore. "Something like that," he confesses.

"Come on in later, I have some jokes for you." Spiegel pivots in his swivel chair back to his overloaded desk, the unchartable morphemes swimming in their sea of human ambiguity, of multiple signification.

Dale goes to his own cubicle, which he shares with a blonde, poignantly breastless graduate student called Amy Eubank. Her project in computer graphics concerns a quantitative approach to pattern recognition, from bird and insect markings to the bizarre individuality of human beings, each one of which can be recognized by family and friends from distances at which all quantifiable markings and proportions should have quite broken down. We can spot an acquaintance from the back, swaddled in clothes, a block away. How? From Amy Dale has disturbingly learned that insects see farther into the ultraviolet end of the spectrum than we do and that flowers accordingly are marked with nectar guides that we cannot see, as are moth wings with courtship signals; an entire angelic conversation transpires invisibly all around us. This revelation disturbs him—irrationally, for of course there are languages Dale cannot speak, and it is a standard item of Christian faith that there are realms of knowledge beyond us, that God's ways are not ours. Dogs smell and hear worlds more; migrating birds somehow read the Earth's magnetic lines: yet the thought of flowers striped in patterns that only insects see insults him. The eye is the soul's window, and we atavistically trust its information to be complete. *Percipi est esse.*

Like Dale with his animation graphics, Amy needs to use the Venus, the VAX 8600, which costs four hundred thousand dollars; to have undivided access to the machine, he and she must schedule away from each other, in four-hour slots, so they rarely are in the cubicle together. This suits Dale well, since Amy's fragile femininity, though she is six inches taller than Esther, reminds him—especially around the wrists and in the sudden anxious way she tilts her head, as if listening to sounds he cannot hear—of his mistress and agitates him with both the resemblance and the possibility, suggested by this resemblance, of other women, women not ten years older than he and not awkwardly married to a professor of divinity. Even Amy, stripped of her blouse at one in the morning up here on the quiet seventh floor, might show something to suck, if not exactly Esther's surprisingly substantial, downward-conical breasts with their bumpy mud-colored nipples, the left one of which has around it a few unnecessary hairs. She likes, Esther, to thrust her breasts alternatingly into her young lover's mouth while her wet nether mouth stretches around his prick; with Esther it all becomes a matter of mouths, openings interlocking and contorted like the apertures and intersections of hyperspace, Veronese surfaces graphed in more colors than nature can normally hold and that not even insects could see. Dale feels at times, intertwined with her, caught up in an abnormal geometry, his body distended on a web of warping appetite. Were he to make love instead to Amy (her body shyly immobile under his, in the conventional missionary position), she could afterward calmly discuss with him such blameless technicalities as hidden line algorithms and buffer refresh times, cabinet versus cavalier projections and Hermite versus Bezier parametric cubic curve forms, instead of lying there smoking, as Esther does, with an exhausted wry air of foreseen tragedy and, beyond the tragedy, boredom, boredom of a privileged, professor's-wife sort. Amy would seem a kind of sister afterwards, lightly mussed and sweaty as if after jogging, and Dale would not have that disturbing sense of being—his bony young body, his obedient and astonished ardor—a luxury deliberately enjoyed on the edge of death, on the edge of a long sliding down into death.

The sky, he sees from his window, now is indigo. A single star shines in it as upon a jeweller's felt. Bevelled planes of the big sandy-gray pebbles of the Cube's texture frame the view. Down below, sections of other science buildings and of tenements owned by the university thrust up murky rectangles lightly loaded with perspective; there are gravel roofs and water tanks and ducts and sluggishly twirling fans. The lumberyard where he sometimes works is a black hole, but for weak night lights by the office and the saw shed. A notched gulf in the middle distance, a snippet of Sumner Boulevard, glows with the neon signs, like flowers in their tender beckoning, of a Chinese restaurant, a bowling alley, an adult cinema.

The pastrami in his sandwich is so tepid now, so nakedly greasy, that Dale has no appetite; instead he tears open the milk carton and dunks the oatmeal cookies. He punches his log-in name and password followed by a call to his program, **DEUS.** He taps the keys that conjure up the menu of transformations, each with its little symbol and viewport along the screen's left edge, each available to the bright triangular cursor controlled by the electro-optical mouse under his right hand. Another phrase on the keyboard causes to appear, with a quick yet not imperceptible electronic scrolling, a list of objects—**Tree, Armchair, Water Mite, Carbon Molecule**—that he or other students of computer graphics have modelled in wireframe, vector by vector, angle by angle; some are pure polygon meshes, constructed of points and straight lines, while in others curved 3-D surfaces are patched together with polynomial equations whose transformations in 2-D space involve calculations large relative even to the CPU's oceanic capacity. In every case a complete, mathematically specified representation, an application-dependent solid, is stored in an ideal space that physically exists only as a huge string of 0s and 1s, closed or open switches, full or empty electronic pockets, within the gigantic RAM to which Dale, threading his way through the requisite keyboard strokes and processor commands, gains access.

The world, in stylized and specimen form, exists at his fingertips. Awe, or fear, touches him as his hands hesitate. He has no precise intention, no program of manipulations to produce the end result spelled out in his program's Promethean title; he proceeds by faith, trusting his prayerful intuition to guide him ever deeper into this maze fabricated to duplicate, in its essentials, created (can it have been uncreated?) reality. He knows that the graphics procedures available to his program represent a paltry number of objects as against the objects that exist on Earth, let alone in the universe; but his hopeful sense of it is that the number of bits involved in his representations and his transformations of them already approaches a number so high that, though infinitely (of course) short of infinity, it nevertheless cannot be regarded as a special case. The odds approach the infinitesimal that a conclusion true of a sample set so large will be untrue of the grand set, the enclosing and all-inclusive and divinely appointed set.

To warm himself up, Dale sets his luminous, nervously responsive triangle-pointer at **Carbon Molecule** and, setting his view volume at $10.0 \times 10.0 \times 10.0$, rotates it parallel to the screen's y axis, through $x = 100$. He taps out:

```
(rotate
      (molecule      (protein 293))
      (angles
          (from      alpha)
          (to     delta)
          (steps     (*      0.001      (- delta alpha))))
      (shade     S3)
```

Slowly, recalculated every thirtieth of a second, the leggy luminous molecule twirls, spidering on the invisible filament of the y axis. Cruelly, Dale calls for perspective projection and moves the viewpoint closer in, so that the calculations, the rapidly and tabularly approximated cosines and sines, arrived at tortuously through loop after loop, begin to excel the image refresh time and to impart a jerky, perceptibly effortful motion to the altering vector lines: the spider's limbs are creaking, the atoms composing carbon, represented as vertices, space themselves across the docile gray screen widely as stars—stars, those scattered, raging proofs of cosmic madness, those sparks in the velvet void of the overarching brain!

Next, to work himself into the program and its blasphemous (I say) attempt, Dale calls up from Memory the model labelled **Tree**, generated fractally—that is, "grown" by certain implanted principles of random subdivision tuned as closely as possible to the principles of organic arboreal growth. With a few rudimentary adjustments of parameters, indeed, the branching pattern of the **Tree** can be made to resemble the upward reaching of an elm or a Lombardy poplar, the downward droop of a willow or a pin oak, or the stately sideways spread of a dogwood or a beech. A tree, like a craggy mountain or a Gothic cathedral, exhibits the quality of "scaling"—its parts tend to repeat in their various scales the same forms. By an ingenious algorithm that Dale himself supplied in a bygone, more tranquil epoch (before Lambert! before Esther!!) the trunk and lower branches proportionately thicken as the twigs, tracing the fine lines of their branching, multiply. This **Tree** once its growth has been terminated and its mathematical specifications have been stored, can be conjured up from any angle, in part or (with much detail lost in screen resolution) as a whole, and submitted to yet further lightning-swift ingenuities that the computer depths can trigger. Dale tilts the **Tree** perpendicular to the plane of the screen, along the z axis, and slices it in section with a plane, simply by setting the front and back clipping planes to the same depth. At $z = 300$, a roundish pool of dots appears—the topmost twigs in transverse section. Moving the setting of z higher, Dale moves down the **Tree** to where circles and ovals— thicker branches intersected at various angles—appear, and then to where the twigs—dots, black on gray, and segments of lines where these happen to lie exactly on the display plane—retreat to the edge of the screen, whose center now is occupied by blobs that enlarge and merge as forks are encountered and their copulating outline impassively relayed to the CRT. At last there is only the single, fractally irregularized trunk to be sliced across.

Dale on his plastic keyboard, its electrically supplied patter as delicate as the scrabble of rats, moves back into the viewing space, away from the plane of the screen, up again into the **Tree**, where dots and small ovals indicate the height to which small boys, if projected into the mathematical woods, might safely climb. Each element of the array has its equation, which the machine can be made to disgorge in hexadecimal form, and which the dot-matrix printer on the other side of the cubicle—where Amy Eubank sits when Dale is absent and where she leaves her lipstick-stained Styrofoam coffee cups like love letters in another system of notation—will obediently print, in what is called a "dump." Dale takes readings at $z = 24.0$, $z = 12.4$, $z = 3.0$, and $z = 1.1$, and the machine—another rat-noise, a terrible terrified high-pitched chattering—spews out, with a syncopated, somehow irritable bumping rhythm of rapid platen rotation, line after line of figures: these Dale scans for an abnormal, a supernatural pattern of recurrence. He especially checks the long accordion-folded sheets for 24 or any striking incidence of 2 or 4, which he has half decided are the sacred numbers in which God will speak to him— higher powers of the machine's brute 0 and 1, astraddle the traditional weary trinity, and one short of the ominous 5 we find grafted onto our hands and feet.

He encircles in red felt-tip 24s as they occur in the hundreds of polynomials and coördinates the computer has supplied. He cannot decide if the dancing activity of the red marks—the sense of a subliminal message activating mysterious connective currents—in the periphery of his vision flows from a trans-random statistical anomaly or from his own fatigue. He starts sweating, from the probable futility of it all. Since receiving his grant he has slept poorly. Some deep trespass yearns to reveal itself to him in the dark. In the affair with Esther, her demands have become more rapacious, and her manner, simultaneously, less courteous. A fretful, disappointed impatience has been extruded by her into the heated mix of their mutual passion, and several times he has registered this uncongenial element with impotence. Sexually, she seems bent on performing stunts, rolling up new records, and his body has protested its mechanical role as her partner in these feats. Its refusal has surprised him as well, for beneath his intellectual and spiritual aspirations Dale has since adolescence harbored a sly genital pride: he thinks his erect penis rather beautiful, its marble pallor and royal-blue veins and dusky-rose bulbous glans, and the way its tapering shape curves slightly backward as if to nestle that suffused, single-eyed head in his navel. He feels, erect, split into two creatures, of whom the much smaller has much the greater share of vitality, even of spirituality. Esther's power over him is nowhere felt more strongly than in her spontaneous and frequent discovery, within his witness, of a phallic beauty that up to now he has always admired alone, with a sense of shame, mostly by touch, beneath the covers, on the edge of dreaming. Esther has brought his furtive beauty boldly into the waking world and made him stand before the mirror of herself.

What is *she,* the question always arises in these hetero-sexual matters, getting out of it? She wants him, Dale's feeling is, to rescue her from the dour, tweedy villain who hangs like a dark cloud with his oppressive eyebrows and melting eyes over every luminous and acrobatic encounter, a sullen husbandly nimbo-cumulus that at any moment may release a chilling outpour. Though he deeply needs to rescue somebody from something—witness his extravagant plan to redeem mankind from the intellectual possibility that God is not there, or his feebler-minded dancing of attendance upon poor stoned Verna—Dale wonders, vis-à-vis Esther, if this particular package of redemption is not too cumbersome, with too many sharp corners, for him to handle. He cannot help observing that she, however dwindled her love for her cuckolded husband, is securely attached to the social role and domestic furniture that come with her wifery. She has tended to avoid Dale's own minimal, Kim-flavored apartment, with its faint underscents of jogging sneakers and soy sauce, after a few experiments there, and again insists on entertaining him in the upper reaches of her house on Malvin Lane, where the leafy signs and birdy sounds of early spring now infiltrate through the third-floor windows, left open a crack as if to simulate winter's invigorating drafts; at their lightstruck attic height the lovers, as they wade into each other with a hearty smack of secretions, are serenaded by the hesitant warble of lovely Miriam Kriegman, in bikini top, practicing her flute on our neighbors' sun deck. The prim neighborhood, its fences and greening yards, murmurs and coughs beneath them like an awed circus audience while they do their acrobatics. Dale has sensed, at times, that his mistress's passionate contortions have something in them of exhibitionistic defiance, of "showing" an invisible third party, of effecting a balance involving factors that preceded his arrival on her scene. He figures, in short, as part of an ongoing transaction. He resents this; but could pallid Amy Eubank (say) lift him so far up the spiralling interlaced tracks of sex, the dizzying double helix at the center of things carnal? Would her mouth and eyes be anything like as avid, her ass so paradoxically tight yet pliant and penetrable?

Since $z = 2.5$ constitutes a plane, then by setting z equal to the transformed coördinates of the model carbon molecule atoms Dale creates a series of more complex intersections, an array of traces on the gray screen that shifts as the angle of the **Tree** is shifted and the viewport and its scale are modified. He watches the screen intently, waiting for some pattern—a snowflake, a face—to emerge. The black dots dart and swarm from one edge of the screen to the other like midges above a summer pond, but Dale fails to see any message, any indicative configuration, in their staccato sway.

His idea (as I, on the other side of the sciences/humanities divide, intuit it) has the simplicity of desperation: given that the three-dimensional primitives accumulated in this computer memory sufficiently represent the array of created things, by crashing them together—using one set of phantom polyhedra to clip another with its defined edge-planes—he is giving God the opportunity to insert His version of the shape, the talisman, beneath all forms. Mathematically, since all these polyhedra and fractal patterns (as in the **Tree**) are stored as strings of binary numbers, a certain limit will be approached in the churning that constitutes, for God, an opportunity to declare Himself, even more clearly than He has declared Himself in the preposterous odds of Creation, the miraculous aptness of the physical constants, the impossibilities of evolution, and the consciousness that flits above the circuitry of our neurons. The Devil's advocate within Dale, the intellectual conscience, might argue that God's opportunity already lay, sufficiently abundant, in the colossal vocabulary of form and information that stretches from here to the quasars, and that even upon our cosmically negligible planet exists as a virtual infinity of declared, achieved entities. If God, that is, did not speak clearly in the rain and the grass, or through Behemoth and Leviathan, why would a computer's plenitude of logic gates give Him voice? Because, Dale might answer, on the computer screen numbers become points and vectors of light and are available to our apprehension with the purity of syllogisms. Vector lines are potentially the bright bones of what is, as Wittgenstein put it, the case. Really, Dale's reasoning boils down to no more or less than prayer, a way of making himself vulnerable to visions: Byzantine saints and Plains Indians sought the same end with sleeplessness, flagellation, and hooks beneath the skin. In his nocturnal project there is something of self-mortification, an ordeal in which the computer is made to share.

The display file library contains pre-generated images of airplanes and cubes, duodecahedra and starfish, three-dimensional letters used in animated television-station logos and even a small animatable man, with stovepipe legs and B-spline–form shoulders and a face composed of over a hundred tiny tinted planes and bicubic patches attached to difference equations whose variables can be manipulated to produce expressions of joy or anger, grief or concentration, and to shape the mouth, cheek muscles, and eyes in ways appropriate for pronouncing syllables of speech; the effect, when rounded by Giroud shading and illumined from a single point by the same algorithms that remove hidden surfaces, is eerily real, though the man moves relative to the way we do as mercury moves relative to water —in quicker jerks, and with a more pronounced tension when static. As midnight tiptoes past, Dale crashes these volumes together, calling up for display now the points and planes of intersection and now, subtracting volume from volume and sweeping the remainder in an arc along a cubic curve, producing marvellous moldings such as would decorate a mansion in Pandemonium or a picnic pergola on Mars's far side. Having switched into the double-buffered color raster now, he was calling upon the host computer— housed on the floor below, where a fan cooled its brow— to load the data bus with prodigious amounts of visual information, twenty-four bits per pixel, 1024 × 1024 pixels on the screen, each refreshed every thirtieth of a second. In crackling lurid color the strange forms rotate, rotate in silent spasms that hint of the storms of computation behind each hesitant visual tug. Discontented even with the stripy and dimension-aping marvels conjured up, Dale taps into the mechanism additional strictures and permutations. Commands in a rigid little language (**setq** . . . **defun** . . . **mapcar** . . . **eq** . . . **prog**) cause electricity docilely to run through the circuits, the flipflops, the adders and half-adders, the endless infallible transistor gates, each a mere twenty microns in dimension, less than the finest hair on Esther's breast.

The images on the slightly outcurved screen aggregate and extend; he rotates them, in obedience to a persistent panicky sensation that something lies behind the generated garish objects, some spider or coin hiding in the illusionistic space where even shadows and reflections can be conjured with the right commands. The computations cannot swing the altered viewpoint into place fast enough, and Dale seeks to trick his unseen opponent by calling for a tilted mirror to be placed behind the occulting images—a relatively simple procedure in computer graphics wherein, each pixel being considered as a tiny peephole, the line of sight passing through all non-occulted x and y values is specified **bounce** at a certain value of z (a sliding value, since the mirror is tilted). This **bounce** command, attached to a specific angle of "reflection" ($12°$ in this case), collects from the graphics memory store, pixel by pixel, the information defining the back surface of the occulting object, converted at the average rate of 160 nanoseconds per pixel. The back side looks much like the front; Dale still cannot find that lost gold coin, that spider spinning its web, that hostile secret the computer is harboring.

The merged images, as the heaped-on transformations dispassionately work upon them, look increasingly like skeins of glutinous polychrome yarn. They look organic, as if a certain process of magnification and refinement is bringing up into view a core fibrosity in things. There is, Dale supposes, on the analogy of the real world, a crystalline level beneath these fibers; but the powers of computer graphics, unlike those of the electron microscope, are not yet powerful enough to reach it. Dale reasons, however, that the computer world, being man-made, will hold its analogous deep structure at a coarser level than the world God has knitted out of quarks. He has devised a composer program that applies torque to his chaotic accumulations, squeezes them as a giant machine might press layers of shale for a drop, a glistening drop, of underlying principle. This drop will show itself, he believes, as an oil leak fans outward from a leaking engine, spreading its peacock sheen between the rusted and sodden accumulations of debris. This statistical iridescence is what he is looking for, an aligning like that of the rods within the ancient trilobite eye. From time to time he stops to take a readout of the equations being visually expressed or to make a hard-copy design on the laser printer. He has been running these experiments and accumulating this ingenious chaotic evidence for some weeks now, all through Lent. But tonight he feels a climax approaching, a crisis and an atonement, atonement in its root sense of *at one;* after some hours he feels his fingers on the keys tingling as if electricity were flowing into *him:* his nerves and the majestical electronic architecture of the CPU and its memory are kludged together.

At some point in the evening he must have eaten his unappetizing pastrami sandwich, for the crumpled and grease-spotted bag lies on the terminal table, next to the drained milk carton and gray control mouse. At some point he must have arisen and gone to the bathroom down the hall past the vending machines and on his way back spoken to Ike Spiegel, for he finds in his head dirty traces of his doing this, leftover punch lines of jokes. "Two: one to call the electrician and one to mix the martinis." *"Nu,* don't vorry, I *like* sitting here in the dark." "So boys will talk to them." Spiegel laughed. The hairy spaces of skin between his shirt buttons framed by double elliptic arcs jiggled. Even sitting down, Ike had a stand-up comedian's rapid mirthless patter. Take it or leave it, here comes another. The lead-up to the third punch line comes back to Dale. "Why do girls have vaginas?" Like a punched button, he laughed; but it seemed less a joke than a mere sad truth.

His fingers flicker with their rat-scrabble on the feather-light plastic keyboard, crashing together yet two more ag-glomerations of vertices and parametric cubic curves. Out of the instant ionic shuffle a face seems to stare, a mournful face. A ghost of a face, a matter of milliseconds. How little, after all, it takes to make a face. A few dots on a piece of white paper will cause an infant to smile and reach out in recognition. Amy Eubank's studies show that we can distinguish a friend from a stranger at seven hundred yards.

The face is gone. A screenful of gluey polychrome yarn has replaced the image that had seemed to stare out, its eyes deep sockets of undying, grieving life. Dale tries to think how to re-execute the computation—polygons clipped by polygons—but his mind is so blank that the first half of another of Spiegel's jokes comes into it: How many WASPs does it take to change a light bulb? He asks the machine for a dump, and across the cubicle the printer chews away with its frantic pointed teeth. In his agitation Dale lifts up from the sticky warm swivel chair and goes down the hall for a Diet Coke. The machine grinds loose the desired red-on-white cylinder from within its guts and after a second's tumble slaps it into the waiting trough. Then, as if taking thought, it with an offhand clatter spills back his two quarters and dime. Some wise guy has rigged it to refund. These clumsy machines are constantly being outsmarted by the smart alecks on the floor. And how many Jewish mothers? Maybe you had to be Jewish to understand that joke.

The face, he seems to remember, had long hair but no beard; the traditional iconography is evidently wrong. Men of the Middle East that you see on television giving interviews all seem to have three-day accumulations of bristle. How do they manage that, every day? Like putting the lawnmower on a higher setting.

The long cream-colored hall with its pinned-up Snoopys and baby pictures is silent. In Dale's skull echoes the sound, perhaps a half-hour old, of Spiegel packing up and leaving. The linguistic analyst stamped flat a beer can on the floor beside the trash receptacle and shouted good night. Dale has this entire brightly lit sector of the Cube's seventh floor to himself and, back in his cubicle, falls to his knees between the swivel chair and the display terminal. He prays for an illumination that will relieve him of this tension, this guilt, the tension and guilt of being a thinking animal. There is a swimming reddish void behind his eyelids; the void vaguely pulses and has some structure, a microscopic grain with a rapid downward movement, like rain on a sheet of glass. He leans his brow against the slightly outcurved screen; it is cooler than he, yet slightly warm. Radiation. Give himself cancer of the brain. He backs his head away and stiffly stands, resolving to keep at it for another hour or so. He feels on the edge of a breakthrough. Yet he postpones sitting at the terminal.

He goes to the window. The city as seen from the window is settling slowly, like the ashes of a still-glowing fire. In the post-midnight sky a wide-awake moon, five-eighths full, glides amid flakes of cirro-cumulus, a broadening scattering, a lake of luminous wavelets. Seven stories below, the little trapezoidal park, with its bronze statuette of Lady Lovelace, shows a softening of the trees, their twigs no longer, as in winter, merely linear, but now blurred, thickened by buds, tip droplets aching to unfold into leaves and get the photosynthetic cycle rolling again. Dale's eyes sting; his body, too long bent into the sedentary position, longs to stretch out, to lay its length on a bed, beside Esther, her green eyes thirsty for his slime, her slender questing trembling hands. They have had, like many of the classic lovers, no decent bed, ever—a dirty mattress in an attic, a narrow student's pallet beneath a plastic cross.

He returns to the terminal and tries again to find that trace, that divine hint. He takes the numerical printout of the crank-up that produced the ghost of the face and has the computer count the 2s and 4s for random recurrence; indeed, he does find a small statistical edge over the strict .200 that probability would indicate for two digits—.208673, the .0086+, even if consistently generated, not quite enough to base a theology on. More promising, however, is the deviation from the .01 that should represent the statistical incidence of the configuration 24 in integer pairs from 00 to 99. Instead of .0100, the computations showed an incidence of .013824, an almost inexplicable nearly four in one thousand more than chance alone would have generated, and it ends with a 24! The same statistical tests, run off on non-biological primitives—tables, chairs, airplane wings, polyhedra, Koch curves, old fractals used for texturing—yield frequencies within .001 of the predictable random norm, which indicates to Dale virtually beyond doubt that his statistical dusting of the biologically derived models had revealed, if not one of God's fingerprints, a whorl or two. There *is* something there.

But beyond all this numerical quibbling Dale still hopes —he is greedy, spiritually greedy; he is climbing his Tower of Babel—for a graphic confrontation, a face whose gaze could be frozen and printed. Refreshed by yet another Coke with its increments of caffeine and carbohydrate, he tries to retrace the steps that gave him his haunting glimpse; he tries to ascend, gate by gate, through the immense binary maze that the mere touch of a button can reshuffle and double. He alters angles, he zooms, he changes parameters. He loses track of time. The small morning hours are much like one another. Vague sounds from elsewhere in the building—elevator doors opening and closing, cables singing in the black shaft, surges of humming on the floor below— indicate the presence either of other night workers or else of automated workings, of timers and thermostats inflexibly sending their signals. It has grown colder, outside and within. The coldness that, beginning in his fingertips and on the backs of hands, has travelled up through his wrists and forearms toward the cage of his chest he takes for Heavenly inspiration; in the microscopic maze where a single fleck of fallen dust would block a passage like a boulder and the finest hair come crashing down like a cathedral beam, he is drawing closer to the dragon, to the fire-breathing secret. As a child he would feel thus timorous descending to the cellar, where his father, in that Akron house with thin walls, had set up the Christmas train, and whose obedient switchings and reversings proved to the boy a fascination and a mystery, as if a kind of corpse lay down here waiting to be activated, a spindly metal body with a narrow, heavy, alive head, the locomotive. The locomotive had a glowing single eye and, when touched to the tracks, its wheels would angrily spin. Working alone, conquering his awe and feeling of trespass, Dale became more adept at the mysteries of the Lionel than his father, and began to buy new equipment— more track, a more versatile transformer—out of his allowance. He was on his way.

Increasingly often he encounters on the screen the protest **Insufficient Free Memory** or **Are you sure?** Beneath his commands the levels of operational hierarchy, language overlying language down to the elemental binary vocabulary, slide one within another like crystal spheres as the screen supplies Dale's eyes with striped toroidal surfaces displaced in a jagged twinkling by others. He has loaded the simulator with a transformative function that subjects each successive crash to new parameters derived from the polynomials of the preceding phase: a kind of spiral that should tighten, he reasons, toward cosmic essence. Yet the displayed configurations do not simplify but, rather, fragment and complicate. They are blowing up.

The face again is what he hopes for, and yet dreads. Perhaps the coldness overwhelming his body is dread. Within these hollow small sliding hours his sensation enlarges that the presence cringing within the mazy electronic alleyways of the computer is inimical: It hates Dale's seeking It, and will extract vengeance if he finds It. Suppose, in seeking God along these pathways, he takes a wrong turn and encounters a false god, one of the myriads who have tormented men, Moloch or Mithra or Siva or Osiris or transformed Lucifer or that Huitzilopochtli who demands and eats the living heart? Nevertheless, our young man presses again the keys that spell **repeat,** and the striped colors and cells of the screen shudder like grease-marbled water into which a pebble has been dropped. The new display resembles the one before, save that its patches are finer in scale and have been subjected to a torque that has generated whirlpools, concentric intensification of color layers that appear to tunnel downward like the fingers of a rubber glove. With a slight squint and an adjustment (how? who is tapping that keyboard?) of the visual-interpretative cells within his brain, these same patterns appear to be cones rising toward him. In the crumpled strata between two of these cones, something anomalous seems embedded, in several colors. Dale zooms in, setting his viewpoint closer and enlarging the window. The anomaly, in shades of green intermixed with orange, appears to be illegibly foreshortened; he maps its image on a plane tilted first 85° on a vertical axis, and then a more cautious 72°, and thus arrives at an image he can read. It is a hand. A hand, patched of colors as if dabbled with glowing camouflage paint but its form emergent, even to palm creases: a hand relaxed on its back and its fingers curled together and not strictly distinguishable, but the knobbed form of the opposed thumb unmistakable. Its relaxation is curious. Is it relaxed because it has been slain, a hand nailed limp to the cross? Or is it more like the hand of the sleeping Samson, flung into the folds of Delilah's lap while the enfeebling shears are plied? Is its limpness that of Adam before he was touched with life, or a limpness of exhaustion, of final despairing surrender? Dale inspects the image and can see no dark trace in the palm of a spike or stigma. The phantom configuration's anatomy, fitted into the ambiguous three dimensions of the tortured, abstract pattern, appears complete to Dale; he believes that, with higher resolving power than the VAX 8600 can summon, knuckles and even fingernails and cuticles would emerge, just as the tendrilous graphics of a Mandelbrot set can be infinitely enhanced. Gazing at the hand transposes him to another plane and gives him peace: rapture passes through him as if its path had been cleared by the coldness he has been feeling for hours, his own selfish vitality ebbing from him as the night progressed. Frozen along his veins, scarcely daring breathe lest he jar loose a pivotal electron, he taps the commands to take a printout of the pattern. From the other side of the cubicle, near Amy Eubank's lipstick-stained Styrofoam cups, that inhuman shrill chatter of the dot-matrix printer is launched. Imagine being consumed alive by such avid, implacable teeth! Dale is feeding God, that tender shadow on the underside of our minds, to those teeth.

The printout is disappointing. It looks faded; the color ribbons need to be replaced. The hand hardly shows—a dim mottled ghost flat on the paper where the glowing points beamed onto the screen from within presented the eye with a living intensity. Still, he now has evidence, of a sort. His own hands, pale and with sparse tufts of hair between the knuckles, hesitate above the keys, to repeat the transformative function once more. The next change might wring the matter dry, presenting him with an entire body, or an empty tomb. He feels cold to the pit of his being; his stomach is possessed by an unstoppable shudder. The very hum of the computer feels to him like a cry for pity, a craven pleading silence as the electron gun races back and forth refreshing the static screen, scanning back and forth in alternating attraction to the two magnetic fields generated by the deflection yoke while the control electrode relentlessly, repetitively modifies the beam of electrons freed by heat from the barium and strontium oxides coating the cathode. All this is performed with a precision and rapidity that seem miraculous until one has been taught (as was Dale, years ago, at Case Western) that these sub-atomic particles behave in this invariant way, wave and particle both, because they can't help it, there is no other way. So a mechanism that would itself arouse worship in a New Guinean savage whose only glimpse of civilization is of the Godlike airplanes flying overhead is for Dale simply a means. He is like (as I picture him) a bat in this night, monstrously evolved so that webs enabling his soaring and flickering fluttering stretch between his hugely elongated fingers.

He types **repeat.** The screen ripples; seconds pass as the necessary crunching is performed. The stripes and concentric tunnels of the preceding display have been subdivided into geometric fish scales. The hand has been folded in, has vanished, unless its shape has been reduced and transformed into the single green scale at the lower right of the screen, in the position of an artist's signature. Elsewhere, orange-red dominates; the fish scales have a certain optical alignment that leads the eye in, while yet remaining surface, remaining excited points in a film of phosphors backed by a super-thin mirroring film of aluminum. The machine is still locking him out of its secrets. Greedily, impatiently, his fingertips ask the VAX 8600 to **repeat** its gigantic loop once more.

The screen goes a cool gray, saying in unanswerable black letters **Insufficient heap storage.**

Dale feels wasted. He pushes himself back from the terminal. The skin of his eyes, the interface where vision meets light, hurts. The coldness of the place and hour have gone right through to his bones. He limps stiffly to the window; the moon is gone. The shreds of cloud have come to form a continuous blanket whose pewter color takes a yellow tint from the unsleeping streetlights of the city. In all the rectangular silhouettes of university and city buildings only a few windows are lit—bright slots spelling, in binary code, a word here and there. But of course, actually, a row of dead windows, of empty slots, spells words just as well. Zero is information also.

ii

"Nunc? Is that you?"

It was night, nearly ten. I had settled in my study with some lightweight old Tillich—*The Socialist Decision*—while Esther was finishing up a bottle of sweet vermouth and a tape of *La Bohème* in the living room. The phone had rung.

"What's wrong, Verna?" Her voice sounded strange: hollow, charged.

"Oh God," she burst forth childishly, "everything!" Yet

it was not grievance or indignation that dominated her croaky voice, but fear. "Look"—she was tearily begging, sinking into her manipulating self—"could you possibly get your ass over here?"

A soft click told me that Esther had picked up the phone in the living room. To clue her in, I said to Verna, "You want me to come over there *now?*"

"Oh *please,* you *got* to." She spoke in little gasps, almost hiccups; fear had knocked the air out of her lungs. "It's not anything to do with me so much; it's Poopsie. It's Paula."

"What about her?" My own voice sounded strange.

"She can't walk; honest to God. Or else the little bitch won't. She isn't screaming any more but she doesn't want me to touch her."

That numbness that overtakes us with too much reality was slowing my mind, my tongue. "When did this start?"

"I don't know, maybe fifteen minutes ago, the worst part. The whole thing's been going on ever since supper. We've been having it out."

"Having it out?"

"You know, hashing it over. Girl to girl."

"With a one-year-old?"

"She's almost two now, wake up. Listen, don't give me a hard time. It wasn't my first idea to call you; I tried to call Dale but he doesn't answer his phone."

"You say she won't walk?" I repeated this not so much for Esther's benefit as to help the picture form in my mind.

"It's like"—the reedy voice hesitated, gasped, and then broke rapidly into the free air of confession, of pronouncing the terrible and thus dismissing it—"something's wrong with her inside. So she *can't* walk. I put her up on her legs a couple times and all she did was flop down and bawl at me."

A faint light dawned. "Have you been hitting her?"

A silence, then with a childish slide: "I gave her a little push. She was bugging me. It's the fault of that little dumb bookcase I bought when I was gonna be a hot-shit high-school grad; she sort of flew into it at kind of an angle and maybe caught one of the edges on her leg, I don't know, I wasn't paying exact attention." Another silence, then: "Are the police going to have to hassle me?"

I felt her mind working against some resistant stuff, some chemical that piled up in waves and then thinned enough for reality to frighten her before the waves piled up again. "Verna, hold on a second," I said. Carefully, so she wouldn't know I had left her, I rested the receiver on the arm of the chair, next to *The Socialist Decision* splayed face down with Tillich's handsome, uneasy face glowering from the back of the jacket, and raced stealthily out into the hall and into the living room. "What do you think?" I asked Esther in a whisper.

She put her hand over the receiver through which she had been listening; the gesture seemed slow and oddly graceful, like a diver's adjustment underwater. When she looked up at me, the whites of her eyes seemed enormous, and blood-shot. Her lips framed a tiny black *o,* as if she might whistle. "Go," she said softly, wide-eyed. "You must go."

To Verna in the middle of the night? But I had her blessing. In needless excuse I said, "Probably all much ado about nothing, but—"

Gracefully holding the smothered phone, Esther sat with an air, perhaps drunken, of great composure. She was wearing her fawn cashmere cardigan (bought on the same day, in Trimingham's, as my camel V-neck) over a yellow turtleneck, and she perched on the edge of the red silk settee with her bare knees pressed against the edge of the glass table. Through the glass I could see the white ribbon of pressure on her kneecaps, refracted. Her face looked glazed, perhaps from the heat of the dying fire, and I had an impression of her being less surprised by this development than I was. She had turned the volume of the cassette player down, but the little red light and the rotating hubs in the plastic windows told me the opera was still moving toward its climax. Poor Mimi. Poor Rudolfo.

I rushed back to the library phone to tell Verna I was coming. The receiver buzzed. She had hung up. In the hall I put on my plaid-lined Burberry, my gray wool scarf, my Irish bog hat. Though there had been a day or two of melting sunshine, April is still in our part of the world a cold, damp month.

Esther came to me in the hall. She seemed to be having trouble walking, though she wore no clacking heels; her feet were bare. For her gardening she wears rubber Wellingtons or else a tattered and muddy old pair of tennis sneakers, without socks. Her feet have broadened and grown homely in these fourteen years of marriage, but since they have acquired their warped nails and yellow calluses in my service, in the performance of tasks for our common household, there is for me a certain affecting beauty about them. Our bones spread, the knit of our flesh loosens, no matter how we diet. She was sweating, as if the affair with Dale, all those attic afternoons of shameless and vengeful adultery, her turning herself inside out like a porn queen, her wallowing in a young man's semen and innocent heat, had pickled her in something faintly acrid that now was being exuded from her pores. Like all sinners she was stewing in her own juice. She had brushed back her damp hair and her prominent curved brow shone. "How long are you going to be?" she asked. Could she have it in her tipsy heart to arrange a swift tryst, an electronically quick coupling with our computer whiz?

"I don't know what's going on," I said. "It could be a while, if the child needs medical attention."

"The child—?"

"Paula. Or Verna, for that matter. You go to bed. You were right about the girl; we should have left her alone."

"You were just trying to be a good brother to Edna," Esther said, I couldn't tell how ironically. My heart was beating so hard as to dull my senses. I yielded to a rare impulse and bent down and kissed her. Startled, she softened her mouth in response just as I was pulling away. How nice, nevertheless, it was and is, to bend down to a woman! With Lillian, my sensation, kissing, had been of ceremonially greeting another man, a fellow politician. Tillich was right: as creatures we are not only incorrigibly religious but incorrigibly social. As I left to rescue another woman, I felt lust for my wife, steeped though she was in another man's brine.

And she? The look on Esther's face reminded me of how, fourteen—fifteen, in fact, it was getting to be—years ago she used to look when, after a session of illicit lovemaking at her apartment, she would send me to back to confront Lillian and the turbulence and guilt of my breaking home. *If I never see you again,* her bulging green eyes seemed to say, as I shut the door in her face, *we've had this much.* She thought like an accountant.

The Audi was parked at the curb out front. I got in and drove it. Our city is divided into zones that, blurred during the day, at night take on a certain sharpness; the denizens of one zone do not pass unnoticed in another, even if it is only to stand a moment at the take-out counter of a Chinese restaurant. Subtle matters of dress, or make-up and voice and even of personal bearing, shout out in the city lights and betray a trespasser. So it was with a slight sense of danger, sustaining my heartbeat at its high muffled pace, that I drove down Malvin Lane out of our neighborhood of barny faculty homes and headed into the realm of three-decker rows, of shuttered shops and blue-lit self-serve gas stations, of little clusters of the young and the tough gathered with the nervous watchfulness of grazing animals on the pavement outside of bars, beneath neon names. These bars leaked music; I could hear it dimly through my rushing windows. The Audi's tires bounced on the rotted, potholed, overused asphalt of the Boulevard. At the edge of my headlights' travelling cones, elongated shapes flitted along or hung on the curb—spectral, faceless shapes, *od ombra od omo certo.* The top lights of the tall center city showed far to my right, beyond the river, lights red and white like the lights of the airplanes slantingly descending into the airport still farther beyond. What were the planes descending and ascending toward, for what purpose were these shadowy clusters gathered on this raw spring night? The same force, no doubt, that had propelled me out into this potholed city, fragrant through all its asphalt of fertile spring.

Having learned my lesson that Prospect Street was one-way, I turned a block before the burnt-out bar, up a similar, half-abandoned street, whose windows were either dark or dimly signalling with television's fluorescent flicker. Parking near the project was more difficult than in the day: the birds came home to roost. I circled the blocks and finally squeezed into a space illegally near a hydrant on Prospect, across from the gap that revealed the ginkgo tree, now coming again into bud. The struggling curbside saplings, spindly maples and taped-up locusts, were not yet leafed out. I locked the car and strode, not so swiftly as to appear to be running, beneath some smashed streetlamps toward the sulphurously illuminated project.

Though darkness had overtaken some of my winter-afternoon visits to Verna, I had never been here at night before. The black children who used the playground of truck tires and concrete pipes had been replaced by older youths who, chilly as it was, with the damp breath of the harbor in the air and a luminous mist thickening between the buildings, had congregated on the benches and the steps leading up to the iron doors of 606. The swift-moving white man in his fancy raincoat was so quickly upon them that they had time only to lean away from my footsteps as I scuffed briskly through a startled mass of denim, quilted dacron, and rounded hair glistening with drops of the night mist. There were girls—fat, with fat Afros and fat rubber-dark rounded arms and fat false pink pearls—among them, and this mitigated my sense of danger. Foolishly or not, we do associate females with safety, all history's murderous mothers, frenzied Bacchantes, and self-mutilated Amazons to the contrary. All it takes to kill, after all, is to perceive another as an enemy, whose destruction will do us good; and such perceptions are surely not exclusively male. Sadism, however, is—sadism as a philosophical protest. The capacity for indignation at the nature of things, this cankerworm that has helped inspire men to such prodigious feasts of torture, lies stillborn in the hearts of the daughters of agreeable Eve. Women rage in frustration and plot out of spite but do not, it seems, exult in demonstrating to the universe its scandalous toleration of pain.

These thoughts—or the sketchiest inner rerun of them, for I had been over this ground in my mind before and even in my classroom, as in my discontinued seminar in blasphemy (readings in Villon, Rabelais, Sade, Verlaine, Ba-

taille, and others [French not a requisite but desirable])—
carried me through the entryway and up the cement-and-
metal stairs. On the landings, the love-boasts of Tex and
Marjorie had been effaced by rollers of paint itself now
overlaid by some graffiti art so artful I could not read it; the
message or signature seemed dashingly scrawled in something like Thai or Japanese. I listened for footsteps rattling
in pursuit of my wallet and heard none. But as I attained
the third-floor landing, the origin and purpose of my mis-
sion overtook me, and dread rubbed the floor of my stomach, and that numbness of too much reality returned. Those
musty, doughy women of home: they had been too much for
me, I had successfully fled them, why was I courting this
disaster?

I walked down the bare hall to the door with 311 in
ghostly numbers. I rapped lightly, hoping no one would
answer. Verna, in her terrycloth bathrobe, her curly hair a
partially bleached mess, the chestnut roots grown out several inches, opened the door instantly, pulling it so eagerly
hard that she bumped herself, and the chain lock jangled.
Her sallow broad face looked puffy and had been stained
pink by the passage of tears. Mascara had run in dark lines
downward from the outer corners of her eyes; I thought of
a Japanese mask. To let me enter she stood aside with a
demure ceremonial stiffness that went incongruously with
her dishevelled appearance and the air of dislocation that
had invaded the room, of its all having been tipped and
hastily righted. Nothing, even the window, seemed to be
quite where I remembered it.

Yet out of her pitiable condition her first words were an
attack: "Jeez, Nunc. You took long enough."

"I had trouble parking," I said. "Where's the child?" My
voice surprised me with its deadly calm; long intimidated

by Verna, her luminous and boneless flesh, I had been given the upper hand.

She bowed her head and said dully, "In here."

I shoved through the maroon curtain ahead of her into the dismal small room that contained the child's cot and an unmade futon. A faint sweet smell, of female animals. The cassette player was sitting on the floor outside the door to the bathroom but was silent; into the silence dripped sounds from the other apartments—reggae, a toilet being flushed, a distant quarrel that might have been something on television. Paula lay in her cot, motionless, in a paper diaper whose white swarmed in the dark. Her liquid live eyes were awake and stared up at me. She had been attending to some inner issue and her eyes only slowly focused on my giant white face as it loomed above her. "Da *bad,*" she said solemnly, and then smiled. Her curly long upper lip, her two small spaced front teeth. There was a red welt below one eye.

"How did that—?"

"I hit her," Verna said at my side. I sensed her skin inches from mine, through our clothes. "All day, everything I told her to do, she did the opposite. When I said, Put your toys in the basket, she dumped those that were in out. After I put her shoes on to go outside, she took them off and threw them behind the bed. When I fed her supper, she let the food go in little repulsive dribbles down her face and laughed at me." Verna's list of accusations felt prepared, for some court where her guilt would be decided. "Then she wouldn't go to sleep, and wouldn't and wouldn't. . . ." Her reedy voice became croaky and broke.

Of Paula's little honey-colored limbs, her two arms were held limp at her sides on the bare mattress of the cot and one leg was bent like that of a comedian about to take a sideways sliding step.

"The little bitch," Verna went on, in this room whose walls were leaking small noises. There came a gush of unmistakably televised laughter, that canned product there is no mistaking for any real thing. "I had read her a story, a Little Golden Book about that gingerbread man, I used to hate it when Mom read it to me, about how little pieces of him keep getting eaten off, now they've cleaned it up so he just runs and that's boring too, anyways"—she sighed greatly, so I felt at her side her lung capacity, her Amazonian solidity and power—"I had put her down finally and thought she was asleep, and was taking this bath ever so quietly, and she was standing up in her crib and had thrown her cuddly bear and her Pilly and Blanky and everything out, Nunc—she'd even pulled up the rubber sheet, and that takes strength! So I tapped her," Verna confessed, "and then she set up such a howl and made me feel so fucking guilty I lifted her out and carried her into the other room and tried holding her till she calmed down, me still wet from the bath and without a stitch on."

Even in her misery she went out of her narrative's way to tease me with that.

"Why were you taking a bath?" I asked.

"Can't a person just take a bath because they feel like it?"

"They can," I said, "but I was wondering if you were planning to sneak out once Paula was asleep, which is why you were so impatient with her not falling asleep. You wanted her to fall asleep so you could go out. I suspect you do that quite a bit."

The child under our eyes was holding uncannily still, staring, like a person with a Walkman singing in her ears.

"I wasn't impatient, Nunc. You should have seen me,

I was fucking Mother of the Year. But she wouldn't shut up, she wouldn't settle down, and it was getting later and later—"

"You had a date," I told her.

"O.K., Smartass, I did. Big deal. What are you anyways, some kind of chastity belt or something?"

I sighed, weary, really, of this half-formed child, of the something half-formed and clumsy about all this abortive to-do we call life. "Why did you hang up?" I asked.

"When?"

"When you were talking to me. You called the house and I said wait a minute and when I came back you had hung up."

"I didn't like your going off to consult with that stuck-up wife you have and talking about my case. I knew what you were doing, you two."

I sighed again, and under my eyes Paula stirred. Her good leg moved. She was expecting me to do something to shut off her inner music. I ducked back through the curtain into the other room and Verna followed, squinting against the light. "So when did Paula become unable to walk?" I asked.

She straightened; her chest puffed out, in the loose neck of the terrycloth robe. "After I dumped her out of my lap and knocked her into the little bookcase I got when you and that dumb Dale were goosing me along to get a fucking worthless high-school certificate." She gestured at it; she had fastened on the bookcase as the problem, the culprit. "Here I was," she said, beginning to cry with self-pity, the tears flowing readily from their warmed-up ducts, "being so *good* and patient, I don't care what you say, and the little cunt, who'd been really *such* a cunt all day, squirms in my arms and reaches out and knocks my drink all over this watercolor I had nearly finished and had let sit on the table to dry!"

"I can't quite picture this," I said. "You were drinking?"

"Yeah and I finished up an old joint in the bathtub, maybe that's why I was so mellow at first, trying to be this picture-book mommy like you and all the other creeps want."

"I'm not sure that's what we all want. We want you to be your best self."

"Tell me about it."

"And then was that when she couldn't walk?"

Verna nodded, her tears as quickly dried as they had appeared. "She fell kind of funny, sort of wedged against it at an angle for a second, and then lay there yowling in this new kind of way, sort of startled and, you know, like she *real*ly meant it now. So I picked her up and held her and she didn't like that so I tried to put her back on her feet and she just kept going limp and falling back down on the floor, so I—"

"So you what, Verna?"

"Slugged her again. I had been *so* mellow, Nunc, so sweet and reasonable, all naked, holding her and sort of singing, you know; that's what the dinge do—you get all mellow and then they take advantage, they pop their pricks out or knock your drink over or something to let you know you're just dumb white dirt. I'd been working so hard on that watercolor, and getting really pleased, you know, and then her ruining it showed how pathetic and useless it all was, not just then but all along. And you want to know something else?" Her voice was growing smaller, into a whisper.

"What else?" My heart was racing as if I had just climbed the stairs, and I wondered if it had ever slowed, since the moment the phone had startled me in the midst of Tillich.

"It felt great. The best. Whacking her that last time, when she was down. This poor little colored girl, not even two years old, as hard as I could. Isn't that something?"

"That's something," I agreed, unable to decide whether her theatrically drugged-sounding voice was an ironical act, seeking a reaction from me, or the best she could do, locked as she was behind that flat amber gaze, which seemed focused on a point beyond my head, where the recent past was being rerun. I asked, "How did she get back into the crib?"

"I dumped her in."

"Did she cry out when you lifted her?"

"Like I say, she was yowling pretty much all the time. I was getting all this pounding on the ceiling, and shouts through the walls. One lady across the hall yelled she was calling the police. She always yells that. She's a wino."

"I mean, did Paula act as if something were ruptured, or sensitive?"

Her gaze altered and slowly alighted on me. "Oh my God. You think I really hurt her."

"Don't you?"

In the other room, Paula, hearing us talk, cried naggingly, halfheartedly, like the grinding of a non-starting engine that has drained its battery. We went in to her. I touched her, gently palpating. That miraculous silken texture of a young child's skin. My touch hypnotized her into silence until I came to her left leg. Her little scream was equally of pain and of protest, her inky round eyes indignant and astonished from deep within. These eyes no longer seemed at all blue. Her father's genes were also taking firm possession of the child's flared nostrils, her everted upper lip, her squarish ears so nicely close to the skull.

"A hairline fracture," I guessed. "Or maybe just a sprain. There's no visible dislocation."

"Oh my God," Verna moaned again.

I told her, "Better that than an internal injury. A ruptured spleen and she could be bleeding to death. But she isn't guarding her abdomen. We must get her to a hospital. Get me a blanket—two blankets, that one of hers on the floor and one of yours from your bed." My mind had that curious clarity that fatigue with its tunnel vision brings.

Verna moved away but it was not to follow my order; she went into the bathroom. I shouted after her, "And while you're in there, wash your face! You look like a circus clown!" I heard her retching, as I swaddled Paula myself. Women throw up so quietly, I have noticed: as if this function, too, is less unnatural to them. "Paula," I explained, "I know this hurts, but I'm being as gentle as I can. We're going to go ridey-ridey in the car-car." A phrase that came back to me from the days when Richie was small.

She stared up at me solemnly from within the blankets. "Go home," she said distinctly. It was a command.

"As soon as I can," I promised. I wondered now if I should have checked her diaper. It had not seemed wet on the outside, but then these new paper-and-plastic ones are deceiving.

Verna came back to us; her face was clean and less luminous, less white. "Yukky," she said. "But I think I got my head back on a little better. God, Nunc, I'm a mess. I should be put away."

"Get dressed," I told her. "And please check if Paula's diaper should be changed." I went into the other room and tidied up somewhat and gazed out at the city lights. Paula whimpered. Verna sang to her croakily: "Aaaall through the night . . ." They at last appeared, the child blanket-wrapped and wearing a Sherpa-style hat with earflaps, Verna in a gypsy blouse and wide plaid skirt and her serape. I thought the outfit a bit impudent for the occasion, but held my tongue.

The city has many hospitals, all of them expanding, commandeering block after block of their surrounding neighborhoods, as if the healing art has itself become a cancer. The hospital I know best (from an appendectomy of Richie's when he was nine, and a gynecological scare of Esther's that came to nothing) lies just across the river, a set of clinical skyscrapers among which the original granite temple of medicine with its copper-green dome is hidden like an Easter egg. The emergency entrance is reached by driving up a concrete ramp to a sweeping semicircular new annex named after a local hi-tech magnate's first wife, who died young.

Inside, all was brightness. While Paula, amazed into forgetfulness of her injury, sat wriggling against her cocoon of blankets in my lap, Verna dealt with the admissions desk. Her dealings with the welfare system had given her a certain bold sense of her rights. In the silence of the Audi, as we crossed the old ornate bridge, her tears of guilt and fear had begun to flow again, their trails down her cheeks glinting as the lamps in their floriate standards flashed by. These tears should have lubricated the admissions process; but the female bureaucrats on the dead man's shift at the hospital's portals saw grief and misfortune on a steady basis and were not moved by it. They had the almost-poor's prim contempt for the truly poor, for the indigent and useless. Early though the night was, the underclass had already dispatched some delegates to the hospital; the young derelict with his missing teeth and winter tan, the muttering bag lady with her bleeding forehead, the family of Haitians protectively bunched around some nocturnal wound—all these waited their turn in the merciless brightness. Only when I rose and plunked down my credit cards and established myself as Dutch uncle did the portals creak open and the wheels begin to turn; people in white uniforms appeared and lifted Paula's pain from our hands.

The child was taken out of our blankets, for a first step. But Paula shrieked "Banky!" when they removed her fuzzy infant blanket, with its blue-on-white teddy bears, and she was allowed to keep that one with her. She was laid on a rubber-wheeled gurney and trundled down corridors where interns examined her and X-rays were taken. Throughout these dazzling experiences she clung with her great dark eyes, so brimmingly alive, to her mother's face; Verna seemed the passive and helpless one of the two, dragged like a balloon after the child, trapped within this tiny child's field of need. Myself, I clung to the Sherpa hat and to the rejected blanket, whose rough folded mass weighed on my arm with a dreamlike adherence, a physical fragment of Verna's actual apartment, those sequestered and musty chambers I had so often visited in erotic fantasy.

The young intern who spoke to us was short and blond, with an unconvincing bandit mustache and aviator-style, pink-tinted eyeglasses. He had a way of speaking in three-quarters profile, as if half to himself. "Yes," he told us, somehow embarrassed. "A fracture. The kind we call a green-stick. That means the break didn't go clean through. No big deal setting it, but . . . could you tell me how it happened?"

Verna's pale slotlike mouth sagged open and the lower lids of her slanted eyes lifted in the effort of answering the question. I realized that she was too panicked to lie and stated, in my most professorial and incontestable voice, "The child fell. On the playground, off a swing."

He glanced at me, then at Verna. The tinted lenses placed a thin cloud, as of diluted blood, above his eyes. "And the bruise on her face, did that occur in the same fall?"

"Yeah," Verna answered weakly.

I said, "She let go the chains on the swing and fell forward."

The young man was the type who, though hesitant and shy and unable to look the world in the face, has a dogged stubbornness, a burrowing will. He said hesitantly, "The break isn't the type we usually associate with such a fall. You get arm breaks off a swing. And I didn't notice any grit in the facial contusion, it looks almost like—"

I interrupted: "We washed her face. Obviously. What is this interrogation, anyway? We've brought you an injured child and we were made to wait for half an hour at the front desk and now this. Is this a hospital or a court of law?"

"—almost looks like she was struck," the young man blinkingly continued. "And we noticed some incipient bruises in the posterior area. We're supposed to report cases that look like child abuse. You see some terrible things— cigarette burns, infants that have had their legs yanked apart and their pelvises snapped. . . . You wouldn't believe it unless you saw it." He was half talking to himself. His tone shifted: "Sir, were you present in the playground when Polly had her fall?"

"Paula," I said sharply, buying some nanoseconds with the correction but unable to come up with a plausible alternative to "No." I added, "She phoned me as soon as the accident took place."

"When was this?"

"I didn't look at the clock."

"Pretty late, to be out on a playground."

"That's none of your fucking business," Verna told him. "I keep her up late; that way she sleeps later in the morning." She was trying, I realized, to come to my rescue.

But I had tried to outclass him and he didn't want to let me off easily. "Funny," he said to me, as if Verna weren't there, "that she didn't bring the child directly to us. Or Saint Stan's, the hospital two blocks from where she lives, according to this form." A flimsy blue copy of her admissions particulars had followed us in here.

"She has no car. She's new to the area." One answer would have been enough, though both were true.

He turned to Verna, glancing at the form. "Mrs. Ekelof—" he began.

"Miss, thanks," she said. She was trying to outclass him, too. "I'll get married when I'm good and ready."

He looked at us both out of the corners of his tinted glasses and without another word walked out of the room, returning in a minute with an older man, a balding black man with a dancer's smart carriage and a severe expression upon his face, which was the color of a dark tobacco leaf. He had a stethoscope in the side pocket of his white jacket and was evidently the intern's superior. They conferred in murmurs at a little distance from us, and then the black man faced me to ask, "Sir, what is your relation to the young lady?"

"Uncle."

He smiled. "One of those. That's nice." He had a voice, lazy and tired but confident, that could have sung the blues to the accompaniment of a twelve-string guitar. "Sir, we appreciate your input, but since the mother was the only one present at the mishap, we'd very much like to hear her account."

"It's just like my uncle says," Verna said. "I always tell her to hang on tight but the—but she disobeyed. She's been big into disobedience lately; my worker says it's a phase she's getting into, the terrible twos."

"My associate and I were asking ourselves, Isn't the child a bit young to be on a playground swing?" As he softly, courteously spoke, the doctor's hands, slender with shapely pale nails, touched Paula's toes where they peeked out from under Blanky. Absent-mindedly he strummed them lightly.

His overworked, rubbed-looking eyes, with yellow, bloodshot whites, came to rest on Verna, and instinct told her that this was her chance to squeeze by. "Maybe so," she said, in that plaintive little-girl voice of hers, as if pushed through a tube. "I won't do it ever again. No more swings till she's big enough to hang on."

A certain sugar-daddy twinkle had lit up the doctor's creased features. "Promise?"

An electricity had been set up, and Verna, dishevelled and drained as she was, yearned forward into it, bending back her head so her throat made a white curve and her breasts lifted within the thin cotton of the gypsy blouse. She was near tears again. "I promise." She unexpectedly sobbed, one syllable.

"Because," the doctor went on, in a preacher's musical tone, "a little child like this is a precious gift placed into our hands, and we sure don't want any harm to come to her, now do we?"

Verna shook her head, once, twice, slowly.

"No matter how much stress and exasperation we feel, now do we?"

Verna repeated the motion as if hypnotized.

The young intern and I had watched this transaction with

fascination. Now the black doctor, breaking the spell, abruptly frowned and said, "Let's get this leg prepped."

A nurse appeared and gave Paula a sedative injection, even though the child, in sheer exhaustion, had amid the sound of our voices fallen asleep, green-stick fracture and all. Her little lulled body looked pathetically small on the gurney. The needle went in just below the edge of the paper diaper. She didn't wake. We were allowed to follow into a bright small room where she was transferred from the gurney to an operating table; while the older doctor watched, the intern laid strips of plaster-soaked gauze around the small brown leg, swallowing it in a whiteness that wounded our eyes, beneath the cruel blue lights. Her toes, a row of round digits, seemed a fragment left over from some visual collision or subtraction.

The cast when completed went from the middle of Paula's foot to the middle of her thigh. At some point in the process her eyes had come open again, in amazement. They scanned our faces and settled on the doctor's. He held out one tobacco-colored forefinger, and her little plump square hand seized it. He told her, "Honey, I bet you were a really good walker. I bet you really stepped out."

She smiled, in agreement or in simple pleasure at hearing him talk. The gap between her two round front teeth showed.

"You remember how to crawl?"

This struck her as so amusing her smile widened and she managed a laugh, a gurgle.

" 'Cause you're going to have to go back to crawling for a little while now."

The intern removed his surgeon's gloves of whitish transparent rubber, and Verna's stubby and grubby-nailed fingers fiddled with a corkscrew curl at her temple. The clock on the wall said eleven-forty-two. It was utterly round and black-and-white and its clean numbers were swept every minute by a long red second hand. Its institutional perfection reminded me of Esther, her exactly one hundred pounds. I should call her. But such a call would plug up this vivid little pocket of freedom I had won, here in the middle of the night, where muddle seemed about to break into a whole new meaning.

Verna's submissive daze was wearing off and in the role of mother she asked the doctor, "Are there any pills or medicine I should give her tonight?"

The answer came very soothingly, with a wry smile. "We'd like to keep little Paula with us overnight," he said. "With her mother's permission, of course."

Verna blinked, not yet scenting danger. "Why is that? Isn't she all fixed up?"

"Her leg you could say is fixed up, but there's some few more medical attentions she might need. We would like to keep her under observation. I think she'll have a good rest here, won't you, honey?" His tone of voice as he shifted from Verna to Paula didn't much change.

"You mean you think there still might be some internal injuries or something? But I'm sure she doesn't have any of those. We're all sure, aren't we?" She looked from the doctor to the intern to the nurse—the nurse, I noticed for the first time, was an uncommonly tall gray-haired woman, as tall as Lillian, with that same tense, too-good, sterile air. Verna saw that she was trapped. "You're not going to call DSS!" she blurted out.

I had to step in. I told the doctor, "I'm a professor of divinity at the university, and I'll personally vouch for this little girl's safety."

The doctor wearily smiled and said, "I don't doubt you

will, Professor, but there wasn't much vouching going on a few hours ago." He added, more pleasantly, "We just want to hold onto her until we can check out a few things."

"Don't you dare call fucking dumb DSS!" Verna said. "They don't know *any*thing, they're a bunch of non-persons freeloading on the taxpayers, they couldn't get a real job if they tried!"

I said, "If the mother wants the patient released—"

"Then I think," the doctor said, "we better get a policeman and a Department of Social Services representative over here for our own protection. In our judgment this injury may not have been inflicted as described."

"It *was!*" Verna protested. "It was a total accident. I gave her a little tap and she threw herself against this idiotic bookcase they made me buy. It was her own stupid fault, practically."

She had forgotten about our playground swing.

Now she remembered, and furiously pushed on. "You twerps can't keep her here without my say-so. I know my rights. I want my baby, and my baby wants me."

Edna, too, could do this pose, I remembered: the lady affronted, the *grande* suburban *dame,* the Chagrin Falls matron indignant over her servant problems. Edna had imitated it from her mother after Veronica, having stolen my father with Heaven knows what sluttish stunts, had put on weight and become involved in church and garden-club circles. In Edna's eyes her mother had been to this manner born; but now the pose, passed down to yet another generation, had become quite bedraggled and hollow.

"Da bad?" an inquisitive voice said from the operating table. Little Paula was looking up at her mother. Her dark irises were dyed blue in the hospital light, her pupils no bigger in diameter than pencil leads. Her mouth was curling downward; she was beginning to whimper in fright. I held out a forefinger and she softly, stickily grabbed hold. My fingernail, I noticed, looked dirty, and a touch lopsided.

"Let's let her stay, Verna," I said. "She'll be in good hands here."

"Only if they promise not to call DSS. I have enough trouble with those creeps." Perhaps "creeps" was meant to soften the earlier "twerps."

No one spoke.

I sighed and offered, "I'm sure they'll only do what's best for Paula."

"I'm not signing anything," Verna said.

The doctor spoke, weary of being seductive. "You don't have to, young lady. You just come to the front desk around nine-thirty tomorrow morning and if everything has checked out the little girl is welcome to go home with her mommy."

Verna thought. "Actually," she said, "I have an art class and there's some things with the teacher I should get straightened out. Suppose I came by around noon?"

"That would be most gracious," he said, without smiling. "I of course will be off duty at that hour, but the E.R. chief will be informed as to the case. The cast should be checked in two weeks and can come off in three or at the most four. Our bones heal fast at that age." Our bones if not our souls, he seemed to be implying. To me he said, "A pleasure to meet you, Professor. I'm a great admirer of those that make it possible for the rest of us to keep the faith. My daddy was a preacher."

"I'm not surprised," I said.

The nurse and the intern had transferred Paula back to the gurney. Verna went over to it, to kiss her good night. As she bent her wide pale face down to the child's smaller, darker one, her heavy bosom swayed in the low-cut cotton blouse. She adjusted Blanky under Paula's chin, and bent low again to kiss lightly the toes that stuck out of the cast. From my angle, she was flashing both tits. I wondered if she knew it. "These nice people are going to put you to bed, Poopsie. Mommy will come for you in the morning. You be good."

The child's sharp little chin crinkled and she began to cry, with a panicked fury. The hospital staff crowded about the noise like a set of smothering white pillows. I pulled Verna from the room, and as I steered her back through the rooms and curving corridors to the entrance she too was crying. Her chin crinkled just as Paula's had.

In the Audi, as we glided through the streets, her crying continued, now loudly, now inaudibly. Her words came out with difficulty. "When I bent over her, Nunc . . . I could feel all that hard plaster—in my stomach, like some kind of rock. You could see in her eyes she didn't know what the fuck was up."

"Well, few of us do, exactly."

"They're going to take her from me, aren't they? That smooth old dude is going to call DSS even though he promised not to."

I told her, "I didn't hear him promise. What I heard was the silence of his not promising. As he explained, Verna, the hospital has to protect itself. Not just against being accused of breaking the law but of lawsuits." Neon and sodium flickered in the windshield; we went around a traffic circle and up a looping ramp and then were on the bridge, with its Art Nouveau lamps and blocky old sandstone towers.

"And then the assholes are going to hassle me," Verna was going on, "and ask me to crawl and eat fifty-seven varieties of shit, and if I don't they're going to . . . they're going to take away my baby!" This last phrase emerged with a shriek; she lifted the serape from underneath and pressed it against her eyes, her mouth, as if to stifle another outcry. More role-playing, I said to myself. And not especially well played. Westerners have lost whole octaves of passion. Third-world women can still make an inhuman piercing grieving noise right from the floor of the soul, as you can see and hear on television clips from Lebanon and Ethiopia.

Aloud I said, "I don't think so. They may ask some questions, but remember it's a hassle for them to take a child from its mother. What do they do with it then? The state isn't that anxious to become a massive orphanage. If you listen to what Reagan and the others are saying they're begging the family to resurrect itself, to take some of all this responsibility back out of their hands."

She was indulging her hysterical vision: "First you all make me kill that one baby and now you're going to take this one from me!"

It occurred to me that, like many visions, this was a wish fulfillment: she wanted little Paula to be taken from her.

I went on reasonably, "If you'd just stuck to our story—"

"It wasn't *our* story, it was *your* story. It was a *dumb* story."

"It was better than *no* story, and that's what *you* seemed to be coming up with, in your fabulous brilliance." Edna and I used to have quarrels that would go on and on, a whole stale hot Ohio afternoon, *you did, I didn't, I know you did, I know you know I didn't;* it was a kind of tussling, when we were too young and green to touch, and brother and sister besides.

Verna kept pressing the serape into her face, grinding its rough wool against her eyes. For the first time, by the light of loss, Paula seemed to have become real to her. "She was so . . . fucking brave, wasn't she, Nunc? She hardly cried, once she saw we were doing something about her, and had produced these other people."

"She was very impressive," I swiftly agreed. We were not many blocks from Prospect Street. We were traversing that gorge of gaudy light Dale had seen, earlier this April, from his window on the seventh floor. I wanted to dump Verna and get swiftly home. Esther would be up, smoking and drinking and her mind browsing back and forth between anger and worry. I knew her mind, I could feel it nibbling on the possibilities. Long after love goes, there is still habit. Esther was my habit.

"She's really so sweet," Verna was saying, struggling for breath. "*Wants* to be so sweet. We have a lot of fun, sometimes, listening to music. You can see the poor little thing . . . watching me, trying to figure out . . . how to be a human being. I'm the only one she's got. It's not just that . . . *I'm* so alone I mind, it's that *she's* . . . so alone."

I felt now that her sobs were being deliberately orchestrated and said irritably, "Don't exaggerate. Paula's no worse off than a lot of children in this city, and in many ways better."

Her sobs haughtily dried up. "You mean because she's connected, sort of, to swell people like you and that snooty wife of yours with your dumb kid. I'm sorry, I shouldn't say that, he seemed nice, actually, that Thanksgiving; he was giving it a try, being nice to the stranger and all. He knows you both think he's a dumbo, too." I was hurt by this; if true, it was a distasteful truth. But it couldn't be true. We loved Richie. Verna was burbling on, "But don't you see, that makes it worse, for her and for me; until you showed up in all your snappy coats and gloves and your funny hat and everything, it didn't occur to me there was something else, just my horrible parents I was so happy to get away from. God, I was happy. I used to wake up some days and start singing, me and my baby in those little rooms. The project isn't much, I know to you it looks horrible, but it was a life, if you didn't think there could be any other and if other people didn't keep coming and telling you how crummy it is."

I stopped the Audi right there, at the project, double-parking. It occurred to me that thus dropping her off at that hideous, childless apartment was somewhat heartless, even by my modest standards. "Or would you rather," I asked, "come home and spend the night with us? We have a spare room. There's a whole third floor. I know Esther will be still up."

I prayed the girl wouldn't accept; the sordidness of this evening was sinking in, and her noisy grief and confused self-defense reminded me of why I, too, had been glad to leave Cleveland: these heartland people have such an inex-haustible, tiresome gift for *self*—self-defense, -deception, -dramatization. Self-examination and moral acrobatics all day long; every bedroom, every breakfast nook an apologetical forum haunted by the hand-wringing ghosts of Biblical prototypes, hairy-nostrilled old Jews that would never be admitted to the country club but that enter into every event from mortgages to masturbation. Our Puritan heritage. How did those old Israelites get their hooks into us so deeply, sticking us with their frightful black Bible and its imprecations while their modern descendants treat the matter as a family joke, filling their own lives with violin music and clear-eyed, Godless science? *L'Chaim!* Compared with the Jews we Protestants do indeed dwell in the valley of death.

Verna's voice in the shadows of the Audi was so quiet I could hardly hear it above the muffled explosions of the idling engine. "No, I don't want to do that, Nunc. But couldn't you come up for a minute?"

Streetlight fell on the edge of her ragged cloud of hair, but her face was a featureless oval from which this husky small voice emerged as if from a gray hole. "Please. I can't stand to be alone with myself just yet. I feel lousy and scared. I know I've been a pretty crummy human being."

A musty warm attic smell had come into the car, from the heater. The clock on the dashboard said twelve-eighteen. *Pretty late, to be out on a playground.* The hospital visit had taken only two hours; it could just as well have taken three. The sly hand of Providence pulled a card from its sleeve: under the streetlight just ahead a car was pulling out, leaving a free space. I asked Verna, with an edge of scolding, "Why would my coming up make you feel less crummy?" I spoke as if to one more poor or failing student who has used up her hour yet still clings to the professor's presence in the vain hope that this proximity may magically achieve what in fact can only be done alone, in work and study.

Her voice had shifted; hysteria had evaporated and a soft deadness, a knowing calm, had drifted in. She had become the teacher. As if we had entered some scalded and parched terrain where only she knew how to live. "I think you want to come up," she said, almost singsong. "It might make you feel less crummy, too, and that might help me."

"Who says I feel crummy?"

"Everybody can see it. Look at your frowny face sometimes, Nunc. Those eyebrows. The way you look at your own hands all the time. Come on up." Her voice had gained authority. "Give something to somebody for a change."

Her voice and not my hands and feet seemed to glide the

automobile forward into the space of asphalt beneath the streetlight; the space was so long I did not even have to back in.

The project felt deserted; the human presence on Earth was reduced to vestiges: burning light bulbs, old graffiti, use-worn stair treads. In the apartment, Paula's strange absence greeted us; that the child was not there, asleep behind the maroon curtain, could be tasted in the air of the place, its familiar peanut-husk scent as still as pondwater where the silt has settled.

Ignoring me, her shoulders hunched in elderly, plodding fashion, Verna punched through the curtain and disappeared. I could hear her open faucets, close a door, sniff, cough, begin again—a suppressed and furtive noise, like that of her retching earlier—to cry. I stood in her living room looking toward the tall crystalline center of the city, marvelling at how many of the skyscraper windows were lit. The waste. I felt numb, my body swollen by blows it had forgotten receiving.

"Nunc?" her snuffly voice called. "Aren't you coming in?"

"I thought you might be coming out," I said, and carefully sidestepped through the curtain.

This room had only one window, over in the kitchen area, beyond the black edges of a cabinet and small fridge, and my eyes took some seconds to adjust and find her. She was on the floor, in her bed, her futon. All but her wide pale face was beneath the covers: a child waiting to be tucked in with a kiss and prayers. I had to squat to her; both my knees loudly cracked.

"Aren't you going to take off some clothes?"

"Oh, I don't think so, surely," I said. "I must be getting back almost immediately." As my pupils expanded, I could make out a shine on her face, more tears or the dampness of a washcloth. The musty smell was strongest here, and comforting. Perhaps it was something the futon was stuffed with.

"I wish you'd just stretch out and hold me a minute," she said.

"It would muss my shirt and trousers," I said. The words as I pronounced them had the firmness of a slightly doubtful fact in a lecture (*e.g.*, Pelagius was born in Scotland).

"That's why you should take them off."

What she said made sense. I obeyed, as far as my underclothes and socks, and lay down on top of the covers and put an arm around her blanketed, shapeless bulk. Like me, she felt swollen. Her breath, so close to my face, had the innocence of mint, a whiff of antiseptic mouthwash. I remembered hearing her spit catlike as in the other room I watched an airplane descend like a gently dislodged star. I could see the white of her eyes as she stared at the ceiling. After a minute of our lying still she asked, "How shitty a person do I seem to you?"

"Not at all," I lied. "Just a little, ah, in over your head. I think the way people were designed originally the tribe used to raise the children, once the young mother had them. There was an overall program and everybody shared it. Now there is no tribe. There is no overall program. It's hard."

"Yeah, but other people don't make a mess like I just did."

"Who's to say," I asked her, "what's a mess? When I left my first wife for Esther, it looked like a mess but it was really very clarifying. In God's eyes"—I corrected myself —"according to the Bible, what looks like a mess may be just right, really, and people that look very fine and smooth and shiny from the outside are really the lost ones." *A stool may be high enough and the longest ladder too short.*

"I like it," she said, "when you talk about God."

"I gave it up years ago."

"Because of Esther?"

"She was an effect, not a cause."

"You sound very natural when you talk about these crazy things."

"I was much admired, actually, in my pulpit days. Raise the doubts, then do the reassurances. People have no idea what they're hearing, they just want a certain kind of verbal music. The major, the minor, and back to the major, then Bless you and keep you, and out the door to the luncheon party."

She shut her eyes; her curved eye-whites were eclipsed. "Sounds nice."

I changed the subject. "I'm sorry you don't like Esther."

"No you're not" was the flat answer.

I changed it again. "It's getting cold out here in my underwear."

"You're cute, Nunc. Come under the covers."

"No, I think you've cock-teased enough now and I should be heading home."

"You think I cock-tease?" The idea seemed to awaken her, to sparkle on the surface of her numbness. "Maybe you pussy-tease. Take off those funny boxer things and fuck me."

"I'm scared," I said.

"What of, baby?"

"Of getting VD. There seem so many new kinds, since I was a boy."

"Boy, you just ain't kidding. Do you think AIDS is going to gobble us all up? I do."

"Well, if not it, something else."

"If that's really the hang-up, I could just blow you."

It had once enchanted me to discover, in my sneakered seminary days, when Latin and Greek were fresh springs in my desert of ignorance, that, far from its taboo meaning's being derived from any inexact and displeasing analogy with wind instruments, "blow" is etymologically kin to the Latin *flāre* and the Greek φαλλος. Verna's plump and naked arms had snaked out from beneath the covers and she was pulling at my maligned undershorts, trying in clumsy sorrowful fashion to undress me, while her uncovered breasts slewed about on her chest. At her attack, the delicious flutter of ambiguity beat its wings, necessarily two, through all my suddenly feminized being. Not either/or but both/and lies at the heart of the cosmos. "This isn't right," I ventured, limp in some parts, stiff in others.

"Nunc, it's no big deal," my childish seductress reassured me. "I mean for me; it is for you. You wanted to fuck my mom all those years. Fuck me instead. I'm a better piece of ass, honest."

"How do you know?"

"It goes with the times. Screwing has made real progress. Come on. Let me do something nice for somebody today; otherwise my self-image will be totally crappy."

"But," I said sharply, and her busy hands stopped tugging at my old body. "I'd like you to want it too."

Her face was again the featureless blur of luminous shadow it had been in the car. "Yeah, I do," she whispered. I wondered if I had wrung this from her oppressively but then, the universe being so patently imperfect on many other counts, overrode the scruple.

What followed is less distinct in my refractory mind than my flexible wife's many pictured infidelities with Dale. In the dark warmed space beneath the covers, the musty aroma of childhood poker beneath the attic eaves became abruptly powerful, resurging from the past; or was it in fact the futon's stuffing, or my fifty-three-year-old flesh in a sweat of deferred pleasure? Verna's nakedness was smooth and ample. There is lodged in my obstructed memory a sensation of billowing, of an elaborate fatty unscrolling, of something like a folded, watermarked letter fitting nicely into its creamy, lined, and well-licked envelope, though her cunt (if I may risk offending modesty in my desire to speak the truth) proved youthfully tight and resistantly dry, as if her compliance were absent-minded and her invitation had been somewhat formal. At the moment of entry I was reminded of the sensation of that plastic vagina into which, a lifetime ago, I had ejaculated (with a boost from *Hot Pants Schoolmarm*) so that my and Lillian's joint barrenness might be analyzed into its lonely components.

When I was spent and my niece released, we lay together on a hard floor of the spirit, partners in incest, adultery, and child abuse. We wanted to be rid of each other, to destroy the evidence, yet perversely clung, lovers, miles below the ceiling, our comfort being that we had no further to fall. Lying there with Verna, gazing upward, I saw how much majesty resides in our continuing to love and honor God even as He inflicts blows upon us—as much as resides in the silence He maintains so that we may enjoy and explore our human freedom. This was *my* proof of His existence, I saw —the distance to the impalpable ceiling, the immense distance measuring our abasement. So great a fall proves great heights. Sweet certainty invaded me. "Bless you" was all I could say.

"You're quite a horny old fart, it turns out," was her compliment in return.

"How's your self-image?"

"Better."

"Think you can sleep now?"

"Yeah," she said. "I'm beat."

As I struggled up from the floor and into my clothes, her infantile lassitude and passivity annoyed me. "Shouldn't you be doing something about not making yet another baby? Take a douche or put in some spermicide or something?"

"Relax, Nunc. I just had my period a couple days ago. Anyways I could always get another abortion now that you've showed me how."

I saw that she was teasing me with the possibility of her pregnancy and supposed that she had the right. I let myself out. The hall shocked me by being lit, as if its glaring vacuity, lined with shut doors, had been all this time eavesdropping.

Sex surprises us with how little time it actually takes. My Omega's hands were splayed at the apogee of the dial face: five of one. I danced, considerably lightened, down the vibrating project stairs and into the Audi, its tan paint sucked empty of color by the sulphurous streetlamp overhead. I got in and drove away. Sumner Boulevard at that hour, though not totally devoid of people—isolated hunters, poised in the doorways and spindly as Giacomettis— or of automobiles, had a rolling empty splendor and seemed wide as a noontide wheatfield. The stoplights had automatically shifted to the blink mode. A drunk hailed me as if I were a cab, and some Scarlatti, played with authentic period instruments, came on, daintily tintinnabulating, the university radio station. Music as I prefer it: on the verge of the inaudible. Go, Scarlatti, go! Keep telling it to those angels!

Any Wagner or Brahms, and reality might have crushed me.

The two phosphorescent hands of my Omega had merged —five after one—as I pattered up my porch steps to face Esther. She was still up, as I had foreseen; her face looked puffy, and her wondering green eyes hyperthyroid. Her unruly hair was strangely neat, as if let down and then repinned.

"I was getting terribly worried," she said, and I realized that though my presence gave her no pleasure my absence gave her pain. I recounted the evening accurately, allowing thirty-five undescribed minutes to be absorbed by the hospital's white spaces and tranced procedures.

"So poor little Paula is being held for her own protection against her own mother in the hospital."

"That's a way of putting it."

"But Verna, how did she take that? I would be devastated; any mother would be, good or bad."

"She cried," I agreed, cautiously, for the untold part of the evening loomed under me like a tiger trap covered with loose thatch. "But I think she expects to get the child in the morning and that things will go on as before. I'm not so sure they will."

Esther wasn't quite listening; she was looking at my face. "It happened, didn't it?"

"What? What happened?"

"Whatever it is has been building between you and Verna ever since you went calling on her the first time last autumn. That was quite uncharacteristic of you, Rog—playing the uncle. You hate those Cleveland people. You couldn't even stand it about Lillian that she reminded you of them. At least that's what you used to tell me."

As if her sensation of my lying now made me a liar then

and always. I counterattacked blindly. "It was that damn Dale Kohler," I said. "He came around with his lugubrious face and told me I should try to help her. That's the trouble with these holy rollers, always stirring things up."

"Don't change the subject, you're always doing that. We're not talking about Dale, we're talking about Verna. Did you just drop her off, at the project?"

"Actually," I said truthfully, trusting my face, that thin-skinned traitor, to back me up, "I suggested she might come back here and sleep somewhere. Maybe on the third floor."

Esther's eyes narrowed a bit, and her lips with them. "There's nothing on the third floor," she said. "Just those old paintings I never work on any more."

"You should paint again. You were really loosening up, I *liked* those big angry abstractions you were doing last summer. Verna's evidently taking art lessons now; she has one tomorrow, that was the reason she gave for not coming back here. So"—I sighed, genuinely exhausted—"I just dropped her off."

"You didn't tuck her in? You let her go into that dreadful place unescorted?"

"Baby"—where did I get the "baby"?—"she *lives* there, she's the big white queen. That project is to her as water to a fish, as the briar-patch is to Br'er Rabbit." Even I, I did not say, was feeling more at home there; like any ecological niche, it was more accommodating than one might at first think. Cocky, light in the balls, I pressed my luck: "As to the third floor, I seem to remember an old mattress up there. She wouldn't have minded that; she sleeps on what they call a futon. The kids now, they think it's more spiritual than a mattress."

Esther's eyes sparked, making unspeakable connections. She said, "I don't want that slutty girl in the house, I don't want Richie exposed to her any more than absolutely necessary." She angrily turned, giving me my favorite view, that iconic view of a woman from the rear.

I went into my study and rescued poor Tillich, another fool for love, from his undignified position face down on the armchair arm beneath my still-burning bridge lamp. Esther and I have different territories within the house, and our estrangement is such that she had left the library in its evident disarray untouched. Since it might be an aeon before I looked into this volume again, I glanced at the last pages, strident with concluding italics. *"The salvation of European society from a return to barbarism lies in the hands of socialism."* This had been written in 1933, when Hitler came to power and I had just learned to toddle. Like so much Tillich says, it seemed both true and false. Barbarism had come, and some of it had called itself socialism.

In bed, Esther's slender, scratchy hands sought me out, to inspect and test me; but though I felt such cheerful lust for her as not for years, I did not trust my elderly body and feigned a sleepiness that insensibly became true sleep, freighted with atrocious dreams of garbled, slashed, babyish bodies displayed on flat surfaces, under strong light.

V

i

In a stable society, traditions accumulate; it has become our custom, Esther's and mine, to give a large cocktail party in the second week of May, at the juncture where classes give way to the looser travail of final examinations. She insisted that Dale be invited; I did not ask that Verna also be included. She was not an academic—indeed, not even a high-school graduate, for all my guidance and advice—and would have felt ill-at-ease amid our brilliant company. Her comportment at Thanksgiving had not impressed me as discreet, and now we had an achieved small secret to protect.

Since our joint immersion in despair after depositing broken little Paula at the hospital, our communications had been perfunctory, restricted mostly to the enlarging shadow of the Department of Social Services over our tenuously connected lives. The department had been that next morning informed of the curious nature of Paula's green-stick fracture, and when the diligent art student did show up at the hospital—closer to two o'clock than at the promised noon—to retrieve her child, she found there her "worker," who had been described to me as big and black and very smart and stuffy and who was by no means amused at having missed her own lunch while Verna dawdled over hers. In her panic at seeing access to her daughter barred, Verna invoked my respectable name, for which I did not thank her. Messy depths had opened under me, where poverty and government merged. You sleep with somebody in a moment of truth and the obligations begin to pile up nightmarishly.

Esther, bless her, accompanied me to our conference in the big brick city building across from the adult-pastry shop, and it was she, unusually animated and authoritative, who proposed the acceptable compromise to the two executors of welfare present: Verna's plump but muscular worker, her gilt-and-ruby half-glasses attached to a velvet cord that drooped regally from either ear, and a fretful gaunt white man with skin as dingy as paper shuffled with carbon paper. A Form 51A had been filed by the hospital, he informed us, and it couldn't be filed away without notation of action.

Esther had worked for a lawyer and they, of course, like social workers and clergymen, dwell in that chiaroscuro where our incorrigible selves intertwine with society's fumbling discipline. The board that sat behind Verna's social worker, much as the Nicene Council sat behind the barefoot and bibulous village priest in *those* imperfect centuries, had recommended that Verna seek psychiatric counselling along with her parents. Esther pointed out that her parents were many states away and that the father, as a resolute Christian, had turned his back on his daughter.

I chuckled at that, but no one else even smiled; they saw no paradox. Nor did our Saviour: *He that loveth son or daughter more than me is not worthy of me.*

There also was the embarrassment, from the standpoint of social order, that (as Esther further pointed out) no one had admitted or could prove that Verna had injured her child. Paula herself, Exhibit A, sat there in her mother's lap, in a leg cast upon which Verna had painted in watercolor some realistic flowers and idealized hearts. Perhaps these hearts softened the social workers'; or perhaps it was Esther's firm-sounding offer that Verna would voluntarily seek counselling. And we, she and I, she unexpectedly volunteered, would promise to share the guardianship of Paula with her mother; the day-care center already had *de facto* custody of the child for much of most days, and we would be willing to take the child for as many nights as Verna felt she needed to recover her poise and take possession of her life. These last pretty phrases startled us all and gave a kind of glistening frame to what had seemed a rather shabby picture.

In the end, warily and wearily, Esther's assurances were accepted, with due notations clipped to form 51A, as the best deal the system could strike until Paula's next leg was broken and the state could move with due process to assume custody and place her in an official foster home. This threat was delivered by the male worker, whose smudged features were eerily mobile: his lower lip kept sliding into prominence with a kind of rubbery preening as he chewed his melancholy, chastening words.

I watched to see if Verna and Esther made eye contact at any point in these transactions. The chemistry between two women we have fucked fascinates us, perhaps, with the hope that a collusion will be struck to achieve our total, perpetual care. Though Esther in her animated gestures several times reached out to touch Verna as one would Exhibit B, I saw no actual contact occur; rather, Esther's long-nailed fingers froze an inch above the skin of Verna's forearm, whose fine hairs responsively rose up, bristling. The girl was holding Paula on her lap with the stunned obstinacy of one who resists having a tooth pulled even though it hurts. Her short-lashed, slightly slanted eyes pinkly filled with tears from time to time and then dried, emptying down her cheeks, at which she bumped ineffectually with the back of one hand. In her lap, Paula— lighter in tone than Verna's worker by three notches, yet with an identically shaped, bridgeless nose—prattled, cooed, solemnly stared in mimicry of our grown-up solemn stares, and gave friendly pats to the knee of her cast, where the stem of a rather skillfully rendered purple iris curved with the plaster. Verna's art lessons were paying off.

And so it was that some afternoons and evenings and nights Paula came to stay with us on Malvin Lane, while Verna exercised elsewhere her constitutional right to pursue happiness. My sexual jealousy roused itself only after midnight, in that casket of an hour, the clock's weest, wherein she and I, poppets ever smaller with the passage of time, had copulated. Esther, drugged by her dose of synthetic motherhood and noisily converted to mouth-breathing by this May's onslaught of pollen, snored steadily at my side. Even then, I remembered my niece's unscrolling, fatty, yet tightly valved white body with more dread than desire; two weeks had passed and I had night and morning checked myself by the bathroom glare for signs of any of those new state-of-the-art venereal diseases that have nipped the sexual revolution, so to speak, in its buds. No intimate pimple or furtive urinary burning had yet shown, but I did not feel safe, would never feel safe. I had been contaminated, if not by herpes or AIDS, by DSS; from my corbelled limestone academic precincts I had been dragged down into that sooty brick parish of common incurable muddle and woe from which I had escaped twice before, in leaving Cleveland, and in leaving the ministry. Now I had an illegitimate mulatto child under my roof, along with an adulterous wife and a son with learning disabilities. By what you use, you are used, *per carnem*. I have filed as mere psychological data the sublime buoyancy, the joy of release with which I had driven home from Verna that moonless misty night, through the wheatfield of waving skeletons while dead-as-dust Scarlatti jubilated on and on.

Indeed, it has occurred to me that in my sensation of peace *post coitum*, of sweet theistic certainty beneath the remote vague ceiling, of living *proof* at Verna's side, I was guilty of heresy, the heresy of which the Cathars and Fraticelli were long ago accused amid the thunders of anathema —that of committing deliberate abominations so as to widen and deepen the field in which God's forgiveness can magnificently play. *Más, más.* But *thou shall not tempt the Lord thy God.*

ii

To the party came Closson with his shrivelled little pretty wife, Prudence, her clear blue eyes as hard and intense as enamelled beads baked in her lifetime regimen of health foods, spring water, militant pacifism, and illusionless goodness, and the Vanderluytens, to give our gathering the factitious jolly racial mix of a Coca-Cola commercial on television, and Ed Snea, who was "working things out" these days with Mrs. Snea and brought in her stead a flaxenhaired, starry-eyed, and utterly hipless graduate student in problematics to whom his relationship had evidently ceased to be purely advisory. Rebecca Abrams brought a female lover, a rosy-cheeked square-built Englishwoman who knew all about Mochica and Nazca pottery shards, and Mrs. Ellicott a middle-aged son by one of her many fatal marriages, a tall bald person with a rapid eye-blink and a tic that caused his mouth, every minute or so, to shoot sideways toward one of his ears. Though quite nicely spoken, he had an odd, ineradicable air of not having dressed himself, of other hands having done up his buttons. Rebecca's escort, on the other hand, plainly put herself every day into the same impenetrable plaid suit, equally sound for a dig or a party, its wool so thick and tangled as to awaken envy in a tweedy type like me.

Some of my graduate students came, but no one could imagine my having an affair with Corliss Henderson; she instantly gravitated toward the bushy Englishwoman to quiz her on the issue of whether, in pre-Columbian cultures, pottery had been the product of (as patriarchal doctrine had it) male or (as she firmly believed) female hands. The Englishwoman, in her boxy skirt and mud-colored flat shoes, stated with loud relish that the Inca woman was a beast of burden, pure and simple. The wife of a tall economist famous for his readiness to appear on talk shows begged to differ, on the strength of last winter's trip to Machu Picchu. The husband of a Bolivian poetess *persona non grata* with the present regime had his own slant on that, the Latin-American feminist question. Has North America, for all its vaunted suffrages, ever had a figure like Eva Perón? Or Gabriela Mistral? And so it went. The party brimmed with guests to remain nameless in this narrative yet all with some claim, via beauty or brains or birth, to be considered exceptional, to be among what in an earlier New England would have been called the elect.

On all sides, while I greeted guests and ushered them, clucking absurdly and trying to remember for the sake of small talk the names of their children and pets, and Esther hustled on her clacking heels back and forth to the kitchen, where skulked the two pathologically shy Irish girls hired to pass the hors d'oeuvres, there arose a shrill unanimous deploring of the President's latest blunder, more than a blunder, the downright atrocity of his laying a wreath at some German cemetery. The party munched, munched, munched upon Reagan's absent body; each President in turn is offered up to the vigorous though untested conviction of the university personnel that they could run the country better than the elected authorities that do. And yet it seemed to me that we all existed inside Reagan's placid, uncluttered head as inside a giant bubble, and that the day might come when the bubble burst, and those of us who survived would look back upon this present America as a paradise.

I wanted Dale to meet the Kriegmans, and luckily they all arrived together—Dale looking, in his gray suit and violent necktie, pasty and gaunt, while the Kriegmans, all five of them, radiated health and heartiness. Myron and Sue always bring that extra touch to a party: forsythia and magnolia had given way in our adjacent back yards to dogwood and azalea, and the amusing Kriegmans had snipped their hot-pink azaleas *en fleur* and woven matching garlands for their heads. The three daughters had restricted themselves to single blossoms tucked into their semi-punk coiffures. These *jeunes filles* were nicely spaced at nineteen, seventeen, and fifteen years old, and their names—Florence, Miriam, and Cora—could be remembered by their happy consonance with Flopsy, Mopsy, and Cottontail. I introduced them all to Dale, and told the boy, "You must talk to Myron here about your theories. Unlike me, he's a real scientist and can give you some intelligent feedback."

"What theories?" Myron asked hungrily. His intellectual appetite is as keen as his thirst for good wines and good times; over the years his constant intake has shortened the distance between his head and chest so that his large, swarthy face seems rooted below his shoulders, his several chins engulfing the knot of his necktie. His three daughters, each a distinct shade of loveliness in stencilled pastel tank top and baggy painter pants, picked Dale over with their eyes and decided they'd better move deeper into the party. Indeed, he did look terrible, terrible from within: the inner worm was gnawing lustily.

"I'll be getting back to you, young fella," Myron promised him. "I can't absorb theories without a glass in my hand."

The Kriegmans moved down the hall into Esther's theatrical embrace and, although Dale's blue eyes (their cool serenity somewhat qualified since he and I first met) travelled over my shoulder to seize the sight of his mistress in the frilly costume of a wife, I held him a moment, as if solicitously, there beside the bench loaded with the wrack of theological books the tide of troubled faith deposits at my door.

"How's it going?" I asked him, in the urging, conspiratorial whisper we use with the sick.

"How do you mean?" His eyes dulled, and without turning my head I could see, as in a rearview mirror, Esther passing from his field of vision.

"The project," I urged.

"Oh, O.K. There's some interesting things turning up. I

still haven't got the methodology a hundred percent straightened away, but maybe in a week or two, when the pressure eases on the daytime stuff, the animation graphics."

"You're expected to come up with something substantive before June," I reminded him. "To get the grant renewed."

Dale removed his gaze from the distances where Esther might reappear and tried to focus on me, his friend and enemy. I felt him, with a soft snap of will, vow to be honest. "Maybe it shouldn't be renewed, Professor Lambert. Maybe the whole thing is too big for me."

"Nonsense," I told him. "You persuaded *me*, and I've been a hard-core fideist since the age of fifteen. How did you fancy those young Kriegman ladies, by the way? A little young—but my intuition about you is that you like 'em young." This was vulgar, but a party forces us to become many people, none of them entirely pleasant.

"I didn't notice them all that closely. They looked pretty typical," Dale said. Again, that soft snap, deciding to be frank with me: "I don't much want to discuss my theories with their father, for that matter. They feel a little strange to me right now, my theories." Astonishingly, in his unkempt and somewhat curly brown hair, allowed to fall over his forehead perhaps to hide the thinning at the temples, a few white hairs had appeared, all the more shocking for being, as yet, very few.

"Nonsense," I said again, playing the bluff professor-host, unafraid of repetition. "Kriegman has an open mind. You'll bowl him over."

Poor Dale. He feels sick. He sits down, on the red silk settee. The inner worm is gnawing high in his stomach, where the esophageal tube joins and ulcers begin. The sight of Esther, clacking and flurrying back and forth through the loud and gaudy garden of her party, stuns him with some wrong so deep at the base of things as never to be reconciled with his own inner *Gesetz*. For this occasion my wife is wearing not the suave and iridescent green velvet of Thanksgiving but a lighthearted frock of pollen yellow, trimmed with floppy frills at the sleeves and hem and striped black across the hips so that she seems a giant bumblebee. That this crisp, overanimated, quasi-official female presence could ever have lain naked on his narrow cot in the room smelling of sneakers and soy sauce, that those same hips bound in black stripes could have parted for him in the contortions of love to reveal the rose-brown dent of her anus, and that that prattling painted mouth could have stretched to engulf his inflamed and veiny manhood now seems a dream, a Boschian vision frozen on a cracked canvas, an old Hell priceless on its burglar-alarmed museum walls. He feels, my poor Dale, a futile raging possessiveness, a helpless desire to reclaim, to wrench Esther loose from the solid and lively social matrix in which I have embedded her, and to extend into a lifetime those few ecstatic hours she has wantonly granted him, for reasons of her own which, like all else in this sublunar world, are not immutable. In the two weeks since Paula has become a part-time tenant, the lovers' attic trysts have fallen off; they parted last time with no appointment for the next. An Estherless void confronts him, and now her glances convey only an irritation that he keeps gazing toward her so soulfully, where the flower of our local academia can observe and take note.

Richie senses another orphan and sits down beside him, here by the glass table. The fireplace ashes have been swept away with the winter and a big fluffy vase of peonies set in the black cavity. A few petals have fallen onto the hearth bricks and are turning brown at the edges.

Dale gamely asks, "How's it going, Rich? How're the bases coming?" Their tutorial sessions have not been resumed since the Easter vacation, another sign from his mistress's direction of diminished passion.

"I flunked the last two tests," the boy admits, already too inured to failure to sound an apologetic note. "I thought I had the theory of it down but I guess I didn't. You multiply something by something else but I didn't remember what, it all goes sort of inside out in my head. My mother thinks I'm dyslexic."

"Does she though?"

"Where's your girl friend?"

"Girl friend?"

"You know, Verna, who parks her baby with us now sometimes. I like her. She's funny."

"What does she do funny?"

"Teases Dad. A lot of the times you can see he doesn't know he's being teased."

"She was never my girl friend, just a friend. Maybe she wasn't invited because she teases your dad too much."

"No, it's because Mom doesn't like her."

"She doesn't?" The mere introduction of Esther into the conversation gives Dale's heart rise. Love tumescent in every cell fans through his skin, as when a punched-up spread sheet arrays itself on the screen, left to right, up to down. "Why not, do you suppose?"

"She thinks she's slutty. She doesn't want me to talk to her, but I do anyway, when she comes for Paula or drops her off. Once I showed her my *Club*s and she laughed. She said those girls weren't really horny, they were just pretending. It's all exploitation."

Dale wonders about pretending, women pretending. Had Esther been pretending? *Impossible,* he thinks. But the thought makes his body burn with shame beneath his clothes. He wants to ask this boy a thousand questions about his mother—how she looks in the morning, what she eats for breakfast—but decides this would be exploitative, and changes the subject. "How do you like having Paula around?"

"She's a pain," my son says, "but I guess she can't help it. She's this funny color, too, but I guess she can't help that either. I teach her stuff, like how to use the remote control on the VCR. She's smart, she can do it."

Dale wonders if Richie, who will never be a mathematician, might become a teacher or a clergyman instead. The boy has his defects but seems kind. There are people people and thing people, Dale thinks, and reflects of himself that he was a thing person, from that Lionel train set on. Personifying things is perhaps as big a mistake as reifying people. Some mistake has certainly been made.

Esther comes over to where the two of them are sharing the settee. Her stripes are sudden bright bars on Dale's eyes. He doesn't dare lift his eyes to her face, that aggressive cushion of an upper lip and her slender jaw with its middle-aged slack. Her voice descends, speaking motherly to Richie. "Darling, would you *please* like to go help the girls pass the hors d'oeuvres? All they want to do is hide in the kitchen and giggle, and if the chicken livers wrapped in bacon aren't served hot they become greasy and mealy."

These last remarks seem to be addressed to an adult, and Dale hopefully lifts his eyes. Her face, so far above him, gazing down, has a neutral, questioning look, as if he were a bit of tissue on a slide, whose pathology has not been quite determined. "You aren't having a very good time," she observes.

"No. I am. This is a great party. It's nice to see the house all full of people." Evoking the times they have had it to themselves, as Adam and Eve had the wilderness.

Her mouth compresses into a circle, a bumpy bud, of flesh. "I prefer it with more select company," she says, still conversationally but her voice so lowered that only he can hear.

She still loves him, wants him. His inner leap of renewed belief drives him to stand, but this is a mistake; his raw height alarms her, his bony unusable size, and makes them as a pair conspicuous. "Richie tells me he's flunking again," Dale says. "Maybe he could use a little tutoring. I sure could use . . . the money."

Esther looks distracted, checking on either side to see who is standing close. She is smoking a cigarette. "It's so near the end of school," she tells Dale, "I wonder if it's worth it. Roger and I really don't know what to do about Richie; maybe Pilgrim is just too academic for him. So many clever Jewish children, and now these appallingly motivated Orientals." She exhales irritably, stubs out the cigarette in our silver ashtray, distractedly looks into the silver case, finds it empty but for a few crumbs, and lets the lid slam shut.

Dale says, "You're the boss." His sense of incapability seems to him in the midst of my party a costume of degradation, a beggar's rags smeared with dung. If only they were naked! She couldn't fail to fall to worshipping his beautiful erect prick. He would tease her with it, torture her; when she opened herself on the stained attic mattress to be entered between her spread legs, instead he would kneel to her little face and rub it across her lips, have her kiss it balls to tip, her tense, distracted features subdued and grateful in the dreamlike loosening of concupiscence. "You have my number," he tells her. He receives a glimmer, through his mental picture of their love play, of the possibility that women are stirred to such feats of love by the sensation of their own power, by the joy of power, and that having proved their power lessens their interest; and, further, that enacting the role of hostess at a party like this, in such a substantial and correct house, proves power of another sort, and provides another agreeable sensation.

"I do," Esther curtly agrees, and in turning bumps into Myron Kriegman, who is bearing down, wineglass in hand, garland on head.

"Whoops. Sorry, Es."

"Myron, you all look divine."

"Sue's idea. I feel like a damn fool."

"I *must* check on the kitchen; ghastly things are happening."

"You go, sweetheart. O.K., young fella, hit me with those theories of yours."

To Dale at the moment these theories are as hatefully irrelevant and obscure as the exact words being exchanged in the cheerful cacophony of these many rooms of mine, where the word "Bitburg" keeps sounding like a bird chirp. Esther's closeness, and the ambiguity of their conversation, have tantalized him; his renewed glimpse and scent of the woman-lover, that radiant animal who waits crouching at the head of the stairs, at the end of all these crooked, noisy, obstructed social corridors, have left him dazed. His mind aches like an overexercised body. Yet he politely offers, as on the other side of the world priests peddle candles in the clamor of the weary holy places, the cosmic arguments: the hugely long odds against the Big Bang's having worked out so well, the horizon, smoothness, and flatness problems, the incredible necessary precision of the weak- and strong-force constants, not to mention that of the gravitational-coupling constant and the neutron mass, were any of which different by even a few ten-thousandths the universe would have been too explosive or diffuse, too short-lived or too utterly homogenous to contain galaxies, stars, planets, life, and Man.

Kriegman hears all this out with bursts of rapid nodding that bounce his chins on the knot of his necktie and wag the blossoms of the azalea garland he still wears. As if better to understand, he has put on large squarish horn-rims, trifocals; behind their lenses, between sips from his flexible plastic glass of white wine (Almaden Mountain Rhine, $8.87 per three-liter jug at Boulevard Bottle), his small eyes jump and change size as they jiggle among the three levels of focal length. "Well," he says at last, smiling like a man who even as he talks is listening to a background music with sentimental associations, "nobody denies the Big Bang has a few wrinkles we don't comprehend yet, we may never comprehend for that matter; for example, I was reading the other day that even the oldest star clusters show traces of the heavy elements, which is strange because there's no older generation of stars to have cooked them up and as you know the particle mechanics of the Big Bang could only have supplied helium and hydrogen, right?"

Dale wonders if he's supposed to say, "Right." He foresees that he will not have to say very much.

"Listen, there's always going to be wrinkles," Kriegman is telling him with a fatherly gruffness. "This primal fireball et cetera, and all this field theory in those first fractions of a second, we're talking about virtually incomprehensible events, ridiculously long ago. These astrophysicists are just whistling 'Dixie' three-quarters of the time."

"Right," Dale says. "That's what I say."

"Yeah, but no need to go all obscurantist either. Let me

give you a homework assignment. Want a homework assignment?"

Dale nods, feeling weak, with a child's grateful weakness when he is told he is sick and must be put to bed.

"Look up in *Sky and Telescope,* one of last summer's issues I think it was, a helluva funny piece in this connection they reprinted from some book in which a bunch of rotifers —you know what rotifers are, don't you?—microscopic aquatic doohickeys with an anterior retractile disc of cilia that makes them look like their heads are spinning—of course they aren't really, any more than owls can turn their heads clear around, it just gives that impression—*any*way, a bunch of these rotifers are imagined in learned conversation concerning why their puddle had to be exactly the way it was—temperature, alkalinity, mud at the bottom sheltering methane-producing bacteria, all the rest of it—it was clever as hell like I said—and from the fact that if any of these things were even a little bit different—if the heat necessary to vaporize water was any lower, for example, or the freezing temperature of water any higher—this Little Puddlian Philosophical Society, I think it was called, but you can check that when you look it up, deduced that the whole operation was providential and obviously the universe existed to produce their little puddle and *them!* That's more or less what you're trying to tell me, young fella, except you ain't no rotifer!"

Kriegman's constant benign smile widens into an audible chuckle. His lips are curious in being the exact same shade of swarthiness as his face, like muscles in a sepia anatomy print. As he raises his glass to these exemplary lips Dale intervenes with "I think, sir—"

"Fuck the 'sir' stuff. Name's Myron. Not Ron, mind you. *My*ron."

"I think it's a little more than that, what I'm trying to say; the puddle analogy is as if the anthropic principle were being argued from the Earth as opposed to the other planets, which of course we can now see, if we ever doubted it, aren't suitable for life. In that sense, yes, we're here because we're here. But in the case of the universe, where you have only one, why should, say, the observed recessional velocity so exactly equal the necessary escape velocity?"

"How do you know there's only one universe? There might be zillions. There's no logical reason to say the universe we can observe is the only one."

"I know there's no *log*ical reason—"

"Are we talking logic or not? Don't start getting all intuitive and subjective on me, my pal, because I'm pretty much a pragmatist myself on some scores. If it helps you through the night to believe the moon is green cheese—"

"I don't—"

"Don't believe it is? Good for you. I don't either. Those rocks they brought back didn't test out as green cheese. But my daughter Florence does; some zonked-out punk with purple hair tells her it is when she's as stoned as he is. She thinks she's a Tibetan Buddhist, except on weekends. Her sister Miriam talks about joining some Sufi commune over in New York State. I don't let it get to me, it's their lives. But you, if I size you up right, young fella, you're pulling my leg."

"I—"

"You really give a damn about cosmology, I'll tell you where the interesting work is being done right now: it's the explanation of how things popped up out of nothing. The picture's filling in from a number of directions, as clear as the hand in front of your face." He tipped his head back to see Dale better and his eyes seemed to multiply in the trifocals. "As you know," he said, "inside the Planck length and the Planck duration you have this space-time foam where the quantum fluctuations from matter to non-matter really have very little meaning, mathematically speaking. You have a Higgs field tunnelling in a quantum fluctuation through the energy barrier in a false-vacuum state, and you get this bubble of broken symmetry that by negative pressure expands exponentially, and in a couple of microseconds you can have something go from next to nothing to the size and mass of the observable present universe. How about a drink? You look pretty dry, standing there."

Kriegman takes another plastic glass of white wine from the tray one of the Irish girls is reluctantly passing, and Dale shakes his head, refusing. His stomach has been nervous all this spring. Pastrami and milk don't mix.

My dear friend and neighbor Myron Kriegman takes a lusty swallow, licks his smiling lips, and continues in his rapid rasping voice. "O.K.; still, you say, you have to begin with *some*thing before you have a Higgs field; how do you get to almost nothing from abso*lute*ly nothing? Well, the answer turns out to be good old simple geometry. You're a mathematician, you'll dig this. What do we know about the simplest structures yet, the quarks? We know—come on, fella, *think.*"

Dale gropes. The party noise has increased, a corner high in his stomach hurts, Esther is laughing on the other side of the living room, beneath the knob-and-spindle header of the archway, exhaling smoke in a plume, her little face tipped back jauntily. "They come in colors and flavors," he says, "and carry positive or negative charges in increments of a third—"

Kriegman pounces: "You've got it! They invariably occur

in threes, and cannot be pried apart. Now what does that suggest to you? Think. Three things, inseparable."

Father, Son, and Holy Ghost floats across Dale's field of inner vision but does not make it to his lips. Nor does Id, Ego, and Superego. Nor Kriegman's three daughters.

"The three dimensions of space!" Kriegman proclaims. "They can't be pried apart either. Now, let's ask ourselves, what's so hot about three dimensions? Why don't we live in two, or four, or twenty-four?"

Odd that the man would mention those almost-magic, almost-revelatory numbers that Dale used to circle painstakingly in red; he now sees them to have been illusions, ripples in nothingness such as Kriegman is rhapsodizing about.

"You're not thinking. Because," the answer gleefully runs, "you need no more or less than three dimensions to make a *knot,* a knot that tightens on itself and won't pull apart, and that's what the ultimate particles are—knots in space-time. You can't make a knot in two dimensions because there's no over or under, and—here's the fascinating thing, see if you can picture it—you can make a ravelling in four dimensions but it isn't a knot, it won't hold, it will just pull apart, it won't per*sist.* Hey, you're going to ask me —I can see it in your face—what's this concept, persistence? For persistence you need time, right? And that's the key right there: without time you don't have anything, and if time was two-dimensional instead of one-, you wouldn't have anything either, since you could turn around in it and there wouldn't be any causality. Without causality, there wouldn't be a universe, it would keep reversing itself. I know this stuff must be pretty elementary to you, I can see from the way you keep looking over my shoulder."

"No, I just—"

"If you've changed your mind about wanting a drink, it's not Esther's going to get it for you, you should ask one of the girls."

Dale blushes, and tries to focus on this tireless exposition, though he feels like a knot in four dimensions, unravelling. "I beg your pardon," he says, "how did you say we get from nothing to something?"

Kriegman lightly pats himself on the top of his head to make sure the garland is still in place. "O.K. Good question. I was just filling in the geometry so you can see the necessity behind space-time as it is and don't go getting all teleological on me. A lesser number of spatial dimensions, it just so happens, couldn't provide enough juxtapositions to get molecules of any complexity, let alone, say, brain cells. More than four, which is what you have with space-time, the complexity increases but not significantly: four is plenty, sufficient. O.K.?"

Dale nods, thinking of Esther and myself, himself and Verna. Juxtapositions.

"So," says Kriegman. "Imagine nothing, a total vacuum. But wait! There's something in it! Points, po*ten*tial geometry. A kind of dust of structureless points. Or, if that's too woolly for you, try 'a Borel set of points not yet assembled into a manifold of any particular dimensionality.' Think of this dust as swirling; since there's no dimension yet, no nearness or farness, it's not exactly swirling as you and I know swirling but, anyway, some of them blow into straight lines and then vanish, because there's nothing to hold the structure. Same thing if they happen, by chance—all this is chance, blind chance it has to be, Jesus"—Kriegman is shrinking, growing stooped; his chins are melting more solidly into his chest; he bobs like a man being given repeated blows on the back of his head—"if they configurate into two dimensions, into three, even into four where the fourth isn't time; they all vanish, just accidents in this dust of points, nothing could be said to exist, until—even the word 'until' is deceptive, implying duration, which doesn't exist yet—until bingo! Space-time. Three spatial dimensions, plus time. It knots. It freezes. The seed of the universe has come into being. Out of nothing. Out of nothing and brute geometry, laws that can't be otherwise, nobody handed them to Moses, nobody had to. Once you've got that seed, that little itty-bitty mustard seed—ka-*boom!* Big Bang is right around the corner."

"But—" Dale is awed not so much by what this man says as by his fervor, the light of faith in his little tripartite spectacles, the tan monotone of his face and its cascading folds, his receding springy hair, his thick eyebrows thrust outward and up like tiny rhinoceros horns. This man is living, he is on top of his life, life is no burden to him. Dale feels crushed beneath his beady, shuttling, joyful and unembarrassed gaze. "But," he weakly argues, " 'dust of points,' 'freezes,' 'seed'—this is all metaphor."

"What isn't?" Kriegman says. "Like Plato says, shadows at the back of the cave. Still, you can't quit on reason; next thing you'll get somebody like Hitler or Bonzo's pal running things. Look. You know computers. Think binary. When matter meets antimatter, both vanish, into pure energy. But both existed; I mean, there was a condition we'll call 'existence.' Think of one and minus one. Together they add up to zero, nothing, *nada, niente,* right? Picture them together, then picture them *separating*—peeling apart." He hands Dale his drink and demonstrates separating with his thick hairy hands palm to palm, then gliding upward and apart. "Get it?" He makes two fists at the level of his shoulders. "Now you have something, you have *two* some-things, where once you had nothing."

"But in the binary system," Dale points out, handing back the squeezable glass, "the alternative to one isn't minus one, it's zero. That's the beauty of it, mechanically."

"O.K. Gotcha. You're asking me, What's this minus one? I'll tell you. It's a *plus one moving backward in time.* This is all in the space-time foam, inside the Planck duration, don't forget. The dust of points gives birth to time, and time gives birth to the dust of points. Elegant, huh? It *has* to be. It's blind chance, plus pure math. They're proving it, every day. Astronomy, particle physics, it's all coming together. Relax into it, young fella. It feels great. Space-time foam."

Kriegman is joking; Dale prefers him zealous, evangelical on behalf of nonbelief. Esther has vanished from the arch-way. New guests keep arriving: Noreen Davis, the black receptionist who so smilingly gave him those forms seven months ago, with her bald co-worker in the Divinity School front office, and somebody who looks like Amy Eubank but can't be, his recognition apparatus must be out of whack. He masochistically asks Kriegman, "How about the origin of life? Those odds are pretty impossible, too. I mean, to get a self-replicating organism with its own energy system."

Kriegman snorts; he twists his face downward as if sud-denly very shy; his whole body beneath its garland, in its dirty corduroy jacket with patched elbows and loose but-tons, appears to melt and then to straighten again into a bearing almost military. "Now that just happens to be right up my alley," he tells Dale. "That other stuff was just glorified bullshit, way out of my field, I don't know what the hell a Borel set of points are. But I happen to know ex-*act*ly how life arose; it's brand-new news, at least to the average layman like yourself. Clay. Clay is the answer.

Crystal formation in fine clays provided the template, the scaffolding, for the organic compounds and the primitive forms of life. All life did, you see, was take over the pheno- type that crystalline clays had evolved on their own, the genetic pass-down factor being entirely controlled by the crystal growth and epitaxy, and the mutation factor deriv- ing from crystal defects, which supply, you don't need me to tell you, the stable alternative configurations you need for information storage. So, you're going to ask, where's the evolution? Picture the pore space of a sandstone, young fella. Every rainstorm, all sorts of mineral solutions are percolating through. Various types of replicating crystals are present, each reproducing its characteristic defects. Some fit together so tightly they form an impervious plug: this is no good. Others are so loose they're washed away when the rains come: this is no good either. But a third type both hangs in there and lets the geochemical solutions, let's even call them nutrients, wash through: this is good. This type of crystal multiplies and grows. It *grows.* Now in that sandstone pore you have a sticky, permeable paste that replicates itself. You have a prototype of life." Kriegman takes a long swallow of my Almaden and smacks his lips. A half-empty glass sits abandoned on the walnut end table beside the red settee, and my beloved neighbor deftly swaps it with his own, emptied glass.

"But—" Dale says, expecting to be interrupted.

"But, you're going to say, how about us? How were the organic molecules introduced? And why? Well, not to get too technical, some of the amino acids, di- and tricarboxylic acids, make some metal ions, like aluminum, more soluble. This gives us a proto-enzyme. Others, like the polyphos- phates, are especially adhesive, which, like I say, has sur- vival value in this prezoic world we're trying to picture.

Heterocyclic bases like adenine have a tendency to stick *between* the layers of clay; pretty soon, relatively speaking, you're going to get some RNA-like polymer, with its negatively charged backbone, interacting with the edges of clay particles, which tend to bear a positive charge. *Then*— listen, I know I'm boring the pants off you, I can see from your eyes you're dying to mix it up with somebody over my shoulder, maybe one of my girls. Miriam's the one you might take a shine to, if you don't mind a little Sufi propaganda; it's the no-alcohol part of it that I couldn't hack. Then, as I was saying, once you've got something like RNA in *not* the primordial soup this time—nobody in the know ever was too comfortable with that crackbrained theory: too —what's the word?—soupy—but a nice crisp paste of clay genes, organic replication is right around the corner, first as a subsystem, a kind of optional extra parallel with the crystal growth, and then taking over with that gene swap I mentioned earlier, and the clay genes falling away, since the organic molecules, mostly carbon, can do the job better, once they're established. Believe me, pal, it fills a lot of theoretical holes. Nothing to matter, dead matter to life, smooth as silk. God? Forget the old bluffer."

Esther has returned to the living room, far on the other side, and has taken up talking to a young man Dale doesn't know, a graduate student in some professor's entourage, a fair harem boy with messy lank hair that he keeps flicking back with his fingers; Esther's little head, its glowing wide brow and folded gingery-red wings, is tilted amusedly, as it was with Dale at Thanksgiving last year. "How about life to mind?" he asks Kriegman. His own voice in the bones of his head sounds far away.

Kriegman snorts. "Don't insult my intelligence," he says. His smile has dried up. His pants have suddenly been bored off. "Mind is just a manner of speaking. It's what the brain does. The brain is what's evolved to operate our hands, mostly. If what you've given me is all there is to your theories, young fella, you've got a long way to go."

"I know," Dale says, humbly. In his sick-Christian way he relishes the taste of ashes in his mouth, the sensation of having been intellectually flattened.

"You got a girl friend?"

The abrupt gruff question dumbfounds Dale.

"Better get one," Kriegman advises him. "It might clean out the cobwebs."

Seeing Kriegman turn his hunched corduroy shoulders and plough back into the thick of the party, Dale takes an instinctive step to follow up, to prolong the entanglement, to learn more. The older man lumbers drunkenly, like a Minotaur who has fed, his neckless head still bearing the wilting garland. Dale is alone. He sees all the others happily engaged with one another, a percolating gene paste. Even the youngest of the Kriegman girls, fifteen-year-old Cora, in braces and ponytail, is animatedly entertaining a circle of admirers—Jeremy Vanderluyten solemnly nodding in a three-piece suit, including watch fob; Mrs. Ellicott's feeble-minded son politely, dimly smiling; and Richie Lambert watching with a mixture of amazement and disgust Cora's fledgling yet confident effort of female display. Esther has vanished again. All that has preoccupied Dale through this winter and early spring, inflating his brain tenderly, has proved illusory. He misses Verna, another loser. He wonders why she isn't here. Here comes a man who would know: his host, gray-eyed, gray-haired, opaque as lime-stone. Humorously, I exude false solicitude.

"You poor devil," I say. "Did Kriegman put you through his wringer?"

"He has a lot to say."

"On any subject. Pay no attention to the old bluffer. You look stricken."

"I was wondering, where's Verna?"

"Esther and I thought she might not mix."

"How is she, anyway? I've lost touch lately."

"She's well. She's fighting the Department of Social Services' attempt to take Paula from her." I told Dale the story, leaving out the good part, our fornication. He seemed relieved to shift his attention to less than cosmic issues.

He said, "She needs help. I should get in touch with her."

I told him, "I think you should."

Esther came up to us. She ignored me. "Dale," she accused, "you're *not* having a good time. Come have some chili and talk to me." She tugged at his suit sleeve. Her upper lip was sweating, faintly furry. From my vantage beside and slightly above her face I could see this and also the bulge of her corneas with their pale-green irises; I could feel poor Dale believe that some intimate message was pressing toward him from behind that moist bulge, some final, cellular secret such as that she was dying of leukemia, or pregnant.

"He's been having a *very* good time," I objected. "He's been trying out his theology project on Kriegman."

"That was cruel of you," Esther said, for Dale to hear, "to sick super-boring Myron on him. It's Myron's girls he ought to be meeting."

"I did," Dale said. "Flopsy, Mopsy, and Cottontail."

We all three laughed, loving one another in our sorry way.

iii

Next day, as if in amends for not having her to our party, I phoned Verna and invited her out to lunch. I knew she was shy of getting trapped in her apartment again with me. An awkward ethics of lovemaking dictates to the woman that, once this ice has been broken, a refusal is too hurtful to the man; her maternal and protective feelings now compromise her own sexual wishes. I sensed that Verna no more wanted to be put to the trouble of accepting or rejecting me than I wanted to be put to the trouble—the *work,* as they used to say in high-school physics text, in reference to moving ideal cubes of weight up frictionless ramps—of posing the question. For if I failed to make a move on her, this, too, was hurtful. We had become obligations to each other.

I took her to the crassly swank restaurant called the 360 because, located on the top floor of the city's highest skyscraper, it slowly, with only the barest rumbling of gears, turns a complete revolution every hour and a half—which tactfully tells you how long they think a meal should take.

I read in that morning's newspaper—unsuspecting Esther's face looking puffy and vexed across the kitchen table, which Richie had also burdened with the little Sony and its yipping, concussive babble of rerun cartoons—that an estimated three hundred thousand American children are involved in the production of child pornography. The number seemed absurdly high, like the oddly similar statistic I had read some days before in the same newspaper (a pompous liberal sheet that tries to salt its bland elitism with crocodile tears over the "decline" of the "neighborhoods"): the estimate that three hundred *acres* of forest are consumed in the production of a single Sunday edition of a major metropolitan newspaper. Can these huge figures be right, or is some mad copy editor in love with the number 300? Most numbers, of course, seem much higher than they would strictly need to be, including three score and ten. As far as the gene pool goes, we deliver our mail much earlier in the day than we like to think.

Verna was sitting waiting in the almost summery sun on a bench of the project playground. The trees had suddenly come into leaf and the area seemed darker and compartmentalized, each zone demarcated by the walls of foliage, a poor version of the lavishly clipped "rooms" in the gardens of Versailles. Some such indoor-outdoor sensation must have been dancing in the mind of the Ellicott daughter's rapist as he had his way with her behind the rhododendrons and then strangled her as if crumpling a soiled napkin. When Verna stood up and walked toward my ambiguous-colored Audi, several loitering young blacks appreciatively hooted. High heels, off-white linen suit, unruly hair pinned back by tortoiseshell barrettes. Only the blond streaks growing up and out of her hair like shaggy rockets and an excess of rubber bracelets on her wrists remained of the rebel clad in overlapping rags.

My goodness, I loved her, not expecting to. Her stubborn wide face, her ample bosom under its linen lapels and severe beige blouse, her broad hips tapering to the ankles and calves shiny with nylon, and the spiky two-tone heels: a young woman. My noontime date. Paula was at the daycare center, and it had been arranged that today Esther would bring her straight to our home, where she spent more and more of her time. Verna, with her kicky high-heeled step, had slipped out of motherhood's harness.

"Every inch a lady," I said, as she sidled her bottom onto the velour seat beside me.

"Every inch a prick," she said in turn.

I was truly hurt. "Why did you say that?"

"No reason, Nunc. It just kind of rhymed. Assonance, or that other thing." She stared ahead through the windshield, postponing our inevitable quarrel. Her nose, perhaps I have already explained, looks not quite formed, a bit lumpy and coarse; but in profile straight enough. A straight nose is God's gift to a woman; most of the rest can be faked.

We drove to the center of the city. Over the river on the old brownstone bridge. Through the older brick sections, where a perpetual traffic jam and its fumes tint with haze the once-gracious rows, four-story townhouses long ago recycled as student apartments and now being ruthlessly condominiumized. Upper windows spilled the old plaster and panelling down through wooden chutes into rusty dumpsters that added to the traffic squeeze. Perhaps the haze also arose from the curbside trees—sycamores, horse chestnuts, elms bearing green transfusion boxes on their trunks like heart-transplant patients toddling toward death —as well as the stalled cars; in May a fearful seethe of pollenization, of stringy shed catkins and floating fertilizing fluff, overtakes the arboreal world. As our transcendent President was once unjustly criticized for pointing out, Nature is its own worst polluter. Creeds replace creeds; our Godless liberals will not have Nature blasphemed and mount petitions and topple senators to save the scummiest swamp in Christendom.

Out of this ruddy, once-rich neighborhood we jerked and crawled, through carbon monoxide and the optical torture of bright sun hitting curved metal, into the downtown proper, where a plague of insolent double-parking reduces the streets to single-lane alleyways. In an attempt to cope with the constant jam, the police department has taken to riding horses—incongruous, archaic great animals tiptoeing amid the paralyzed metal while blue-uniformed riders, both male and female and often blacker than their mounts, and as nervous, gaze down with an imperious uselessness. Towering glass buildings, acres of reflection and transparency, float above shops offering oddly humble wares—doughnuts, art supplies, greeting cards, phonograph records (the double-parking here was especially insolent)—as if all this architectural and economic grandeur rests upon our willingness to buy one another droll, semi-lewd birthday cards.

Verna and I in our vehicle drove down a curved ramp (work achieved in reverse; but the ramps in physics books were never curved) and parked in the skyscraper's underground garage, which bore a faint damp smell reminiscent of a springhouse my father and Veronica and Edna and I used to visit not far from Chagrin Falls. The farmer sold fresh brown eggs and sweet corn in season and always invited us, like a whiskery wine steward urging a rare vintage upon connoisseurs, to have a swallow of his spring water, taken from a battered tin ladle whose fragile aroma, of chilled tin, was also present here in this underground repository of cars, big hollow tinted shells shed for the moment like so many cumbersome overcoats. There were many levels to this garage, numbered and color-coded, each supported by concrete pillars conically swelling at the top. At a dank corner, adorned with urine puddles and discarded pint bottles, an unpromising door opened to reveal a vinyl-lined elevator that shot us smoothly upward. A disembodied orchestra picked its way pizzicato through an old Beatles tune. The elevator swooped to a stop to collect other passengers on the ground floor—tourists clutching guidebooks and cameras and wearing running shoes, heading for the viewing platform; businessmen already clothed in summer suits of gray and putty, heading for an expense-account lunch—and then ascended with such vehemence that our fingertips filled with blood and our knees threatened to buckle. The floor numbers flickered overhead in those electronic digits composed of tiny bulbs like rod-shaped bacilli, faster and faster, and then slow again, and then out we stepped, the tourists one way to the Sky View and its souvenir shops and constantly replayed tape of the city's history as intoned by some funeral director, and we onto the hushing steel-blue carpeting of Restaurant 360, its velvet ropes, its jungle ferns, its muffled tinkle of cutlery, its floor-to-ceiling windows overlooking the blocks and parks sixty stories below. Our old city from above is predominantly red, and the view is shocking, a vast surgery or flaying.

As we were led to our table by the lantern-jawed maître d', we walked on cloudy carpet through dizzying bright volumes of upper atmosphere, and I felt myself exposed with Verna as sharply as in a photograph. Eyes flickered across us; some lingered. Years ago we could have been assumed to be a man and his daughter or, as was the case, his niece; now the glances would register a young thing and her grizzled, aging lover, which was also, in a sense, the case. By contrast with Verna's smooth, shimmery, piscine youth I must have loomed in the raking light as a craggy old fisherman indeed, with every pinch that lust and spite had delivered in a half-century of egoism somewhere remembered in the slack and creviced texture of my cunning, cautious face; yet I was oddly unembarrassed to be seen with Verna. No one I knew, from the Divinity School or its neighborhood, was apt to have found his or her way into this celestial tourist trap; modest but precious restaurants—seven tables and a sooty patio tucked between a laundromat and a health-food store, the chef a former student and the menu a simple blackboard—were our academic style. Verna moved easily among the glancing tables with a nice fuck-you poise (her young life, so impoverished in many respects, has been rich in public dining), and, except for the rubber bracelets and rather clunky earrings, she was dressed not inappropriately. She was not, it occurred to me for the first time, a disgrace to her/our family, but one more member of it, with that same rounded, almost hunched, patient back that Edna had had, and Veronica before her, once the vixen had put on weight. Each generation is a stick poked into the water of time and only apparently crooked.

Our table was on the moving circumference, with the view. As we sat, I could feel the floor tug us softly along, from one steel rib of the tall viewing windows to the next, as angled rooftops and receding vistas melted one into the other, our city displayed to the hazed, indecipherable horizon.

She must have sensed what I had brought her up here to negotiate, for she went quickly on the attack. "What have you done to Dale, Nunc?" she asked, leaning forward above her empty plate, the brimming water glass, the folded napkin, and the knives and forks with their minute glittering scratches. "He's in terrible shape." I noticed in this high light a few freckles that had appeared on her brow and nose; Edna, I remembered, would grow a crop of freckles, playing tennis and swimming and lounging at the club all those monotonous, priceless summers.

"How so?"

"He says he's lost his faith. Some guy he met at that party you didn't invite me to made him see how silly it all was. Also, I don't think his computer stuff is working out too well. It's like he expected some miracle that didn't happen."

"You wouldn't have had a good time at the party. It's just something we have every year to clean up our social debts. The computer stuff, as you call it, was to have been a proof of God's existence. If he had brought it off the world would have had no choice but to end. The bastard was trying to end the world for us. He better have something to submit by June first or his grant won't be renewed."

"I don't think he wants it renewed. The way he talks, he wants to get out of this area and go back home. He says some people can't hack the East and he thinks he's one of them. He thinks I'm another."

Our view at the moment was east, toward the harbor: the ins and outs of the old wharves, the long granite warehouses with their dormered roofs of heavy slate outlined in pale-green copper flashing, some tall harborside apartment buildings with rounded corners like playing cards, and at their feet decaying old commercial buildings of brick and tar and a battered expressway in the throes of being widened. The new lanes were a margin, churning with tiny men and machines, of scraped orange earth. Who can believe, about any city, how thinly it overlies earth and rock? Beyond the wharves there was water, striped blue and gray, with a few toy ships and some shabby harbor islands, sandbars shaped like brush daubs, one of which held a reformatory and the other a fertilizer plant. The long blue low cloud of a peninsula, paler and paler into the distance, was tipped by a lighthouse. The southern edge of our view held a flat piece of airport, with a foreshortened runway and on two white stilts the control tower, its green windows like tiny emeralds. Above all, higher than we usually see it, the serene kiss-off of the horizon, flat as the oscillograph of brain death. The waiter in his tuxedo came, and I ordered a martini and Verna a Black Russian.

"How else does it affect him," I asked, "this alleged loss of faith?"

"Don't say 'alleged.' He's really having some kind of break-down."

This was womanly, as distinct from girlish, exaggeration. "Men are great sympathy seekers," I pointed out to her.

"He says he can't sleep now, because he always used to pray and that would put him to sleep. He says he goes to work on these fancy cartoons he does and it makes him sick, it's all so stupid. He says"—her voice took on that reediness, that timbre of a small rigid instrument ill-adapted for speech—"at times at work in front of the screen this actual wave of nausea comes over him and he thinks he has to throw up."

"And does he?"

"Well, not that he told me."

"Well, then. There you have it. He'll live. There's faith and there's faith, and what we think we believe is really a very minor part of what we do believe."

"You seem so pleased. What did Dale ever do to you?"

I answered promptly, from the heart. "He annoyed me. He came into my office clamoring about nailing God down and he wasted my time. When you get to my age, Verna, time is what you can least afford to waste. Not only did he bully me, he was trying, I thought, to bully God. Most 'good' people, in my limited experience, are bullies."

The martini was working on me; everything looked slightly polished. The circular floor tugged us and our table along. Verna's smooth cheek showed her dimple. "That must be why you like me. I'm bad."

"Bad only in the black sense." I clarified: "*Baad.* That is, good." I dared tell her, "I love you in that nice conservative linen; you blend right in up here."

"I try to do what other people want me to do, Nunc," she said. "But—"

"But girls they want to have fun," I supplied.

A young assistant waiter in a white dinner jacket brought us our first course: beef consommé for me, a shrimp cocktail for Verna, in cracked ice. The shrimp were hooked over the edge of a sherbet glass like faceless living creatures that had climbed up there hoping to drink at the pool of scarlet cocktail sauce. My consommé was too hot for the moment; as my companion bent her broad face to her food, I turned to the view again. It had become southerly. A neighboring skyscraper, a glass grid filled like a crossword puzzle with office workers in an alphabet of sitting, standing, and stooping positions, hung close; past its shoulder a low brick neighborhood, prettily laid out long ago with oval parks and crescent streets and a white-spired church or two, was struggling back into fashionability again, after a century in exile. Beyond it, neighborhoods too far out from the central city to be yet thus gentrified diminished in smoky tones of rose and gray and green toward a white smear of gas tanks, beside the rust of a high-arching iron railroad bridge. Like outsize tree stumps, the cluster of a large housing complex stuck up from the denuded hills that marked, on maps, the limits of the city; but in fact the city went on and on, following the expressway and the shoreline south, sucking village and farmland into its orbit until you could say it ended only where the far suburban edge of the next coastal city began.

"She's passé, Nunc," Verna responded, the last lick of cocktail sauce wiped with a childish, stub-nailed fingertip from one corner of her mouth. "Cyndi Lauper."

"So soon?"

"All the girls now are dressing like Madonna. Look." She reached out and rattled her bracelets at me. "That's Madonna. And these." She leaned her face forward and with an index finger beneath each lobe pushed into better view the mock-gold crosses dangling from her ears. "A lot of these girls are furious they got the sides of their heads shaved when Cyndi was in," she explained to me. "And purple streaks and all that weird stuff that's really self-mutilation. I was talking to my counsellor about it. Cyndi, you see, is a victim type. Did you see her not get all those awards she should have had at the Grammys, smiling right through it when it had really been her year? Whereas Madonna's tough. She knows what she wants and goes for it."

"And you? Do you know what you want now?" There was a direction I wanted this conversation to take, but it was perhaps too early for a nudge.

"My counsellor says I just want to be normal," Verna said. "That's why I had it in so for Poopsie: just to look at her kept reminding me I wasn't. I mean, all this stuff with blacks, just to annoy my father probably . . . "

"What's normal?" I remembered her saying, and echoed, "Wiggling your ass at Shaker Heights cocktail parties?"

"That might be part of it. But only part. I want *struc*ture, Nunc."

The Barthian in me protested: what right have we fallen creatures, given of our own free wills into chaos, to demand structure? Who is the guarantor of all this merely human order? I said, "Tell me about your counsellor."

"She's neat. I love her."

I felt a jealous flash. "A young woman?"

"Old. Older than you even. I don't think I'm supposed to talk too much about it." She cast her eyes down into her empty shrimp-cocktail glass, in its socket of cracked ice melting in a silver bowl. The waiter came and cleared her place; but I felt she would have fallen silent anyway. Out of her own associations she began a new topic, or one that would appear new. "Another thing bugging Dale," she told me, "speaking of wiggling your ass, is he's been having an affair with some older woman, somebody married who I guess is a pretty hot ticket."

"Oh?" I said, feeling the floor tug us clockwise.

"Yeah, it's really eating him up, for one thing because he knows they shouldn't be doing it, and yet he keeps doing it anyways, and for another because he doesn't want it to end and it is."

"How does he know it is?"

"I guess the lady's been giving him signals. That's another reason he wants to go back to Ohio, to get away from her. One night he and I split a six at my place—he's not so uptight about booze and what-all as he was—and he got into the sort of stuff they used to do, and I must say she sounds like she went all out. Up the ass and everything. Like she *wanted* to drive him crazy. She lives in this really big expensive house, Dale said. Somewhere in your neighborhood, I got the impression."

"It's a big neighborhood," I told her. "And by the time you get to this lady's age, there's very little reason left not to go all out. At *your* age," I advised, competing against my unseen rival counsellor, "you have to be careful how you distribute yourself."

"How old do you think I am?"

"Nineteen?"

343

"I have news for you, Nunc. I turned twenty last week." From her tone, this news was a defeat for me. Instead I felt the floor tug, and a tug of relief: she seemed somewhat less on my hands, on all our hands, at that age.

"Happy Birthday, dear Verna."

The waiter brought me my fillet of sole, her her lamb chop. He did not seem surprised when I ordered a bottle of champagne. He had a close, tidy haircut of the sort everyone wore when I was young but that now exclusively signifies homosexuals and—another marginal caste, viewed with distrust, as potential avenues of disaster—servicemen.

The view, westward, showed how the city had expanded, early in the century, when land was cheap. It had acquired its civic establishments: the public library and the fine-arts museum, both Italianate, courtyarded, and red-tile-roofed; the irregular deep-lipped green bowl that contained our major-league ballpark, rimmed with banks of lights like giant flyswatters and lined with seats that came in two flavors, cherry and blueberry; the long reflecting pool and marzipan dome of the Christian Science cathedral (Christian Science! as if there could be such a thing!). Many of the older mansions in their iron-fenced grounds had fallen lately to new construction—parking garages whose roofs bore playful patterns of arrows, and a combination hotel and vertical shopping mall whose irregular geometrical forms, seen from above, suggested Lego. The perspectives of this brand-new structure led erratically down to entrances whose bright-blue canopies stuck out no bigger than coding tabs in a filing cabinet. There arose to us at this altitude, through the thick glass, the anesthetized city's only voice, the urgent hiccup of a police siren.

The champagne came, and with its sparkling sourness I toasted my companion. "How's your lamb?" I asked her.

"O.K. I mean it's great. This is really a nice expensive lunch. Nunc?"

"Yes, Verna?"

"Are you sorry you fucked me, is that what you're trying to say?"

"My goodness, you dear child, no. I'm ever so glad, it was lovely. As you said it would, it relieved something. It's helped me get ready for death." The moment had come; she had led me here. "But it needn't be repeated, perhaps, and something I'm *not* grateful for—"

"Is Paula."

"No, Paula's no great problem, once she gets the cast off her leg and stops scratching up all the floors. What I'm *not* grateful for is all these attentions from the Department of Social Services: is getting my name involved with their miserable records. In my position at the Divinity School—"

"You got to keep your nose clean."

"Clean in a certain way, or, rather, not dirty in a way that looks absurd to my colleagues. We can tolerate dirt over there, 'fallible human nature' we call it, but it must take certain traditional forms. This thing with Paula's injury and so on is worse than bad, it's *gauche.*"

She abruptly volunteered, "Dale wants me to go back to Cleveland with him; maybe I said that."

"Why, no. I don't think you did. When was this—after the sixpack?"

"You keep getting the wrong idea about him and me. He just thinks I should try to make up with Mom at least. And he says if I'd just get my certificate they have these great night courses at Case Western."

"Don't go back, Verna," I said, against all my own interests. "They're such awful people back there."

"My counsellor says they're the only people I really care about."

"Well, I suppose that's safe enough Freud." I sighed in grateful surrender. "Would you like me to buy your ticket?"

"Hey, sure, if you'd like to, that'd be super." Her eyes, often rather dead in their slightly slanted envelopes of lid, were shining: perhaps it was the champagne, or the brightness up here, which made even the smallest scratches in the silver gleam. When she smiled, her teeth were as little and round as pearls. "There was another favor I was going to ask."

"Yes, dear?" I was trying to decide why I found the crosses in her ears repulsive: because of the barbaric religion of blood atonement they symbolized, or some atavistic superstitious scruple of mine about their being worn so frivolously? Yet for centuries crosses have been bouncing in that sweaty cleft between women's breasts. Who made a woman's body? God, we must keep reminding ourselves.

"It'd be neat if you'd call my mom and see how she feels about my coming home. I don't have the nerve."

"I don't either."

"Why not, Nunc? She's your sister. Your half-sister. Oh. I know what it is." She dimpled. "You're afraid she'd hear it somehow in your voice."

My sole was slightly dry, and slow to leave the mouth. I swallowed with a little haste, and it hurt. "Hear what?"

"That you've fucked me," she said distinctly, having cleared her throat.

Several sleek, blow-dried heads at nearby tables turned our way.

"Don't shout," I pleaded.

Her eyes, their amber full of gold dust in the high light, narrowed with the delight of an imagined perception.

"That's why you want to be rid of me, you old prick. I'm walking evidence. I might start getting grabby and upset your applecart, not only with your job but with that hot-shit little wife of yours. She's the one with the money, isn't she, for all that nice stuff in your house? You didn't get all that on a professor's salary. Dale told me how her father's some kind of big shot."

I explained to my accuser truthfully, calmly, "Esther is part of my life. I once went to a great deal of trouble to make her part of it and I'm too old to do any more rearranging."

For dessert, Verna had *baba au rhum* with Irish coffee and I, feeling fat on the champagne, simply a tarry cup of espresso; a stack of heretical examination booklets waited for me back in the office.

Now our view was north. From on high the river looked much broader—grander, more primeval—than it felt as you nipped across one of the bridges in a car. The university, which loomed so large in my mind and life, almost vanished in the overview of this part of the metropolis; the domed science buildings and the Cube and the several spired campuses devoted to the humanities and student housing were less conspicuous than a number of riverside factories I had never noticed before, with their acres of flat gravel roof and their admonitory smokestacks. There was upon this face of the city, as upon a pond at dawn, a clinging haze, a haze in which I could not locate the limestone buildings of the Divinity School. But I could trace with my eye Sumner Boulevard's straight line back from the river and found the intensified green, the leafed-out beeches and oaks, of my neighborhood; I thought I could even make out the verdant dab of Dorothea Ellicott Memorial Park, and the roof of my own house, its third-floor windows. There, in that dim patch of scum on the hazy pond, I had my life; up here I had fought for that life, successfully. Getting Verna out of town would give me space and the deeds in the dark an interval in which to erase themselves. Yet depression dragged my heart down as I pictured her heading into that heartland muddle, that tangle of body smells and stale pieties, of parental curses and complacent mediocrity; her life, so vivid before me in its moment of bloom and sass, seemed a waste whether spent back in Cleveland with Edna and Paul, who would try again to tie her to the rotten wood of the old prohibitions, or here with us, in our Godless freedoms that become, with daily use, so oddly trivial. I could not stop my mood from sinking, as if it were I who had condemned this child to life. "No matter what you do," I said, pleading again, "you must finish up your certificate."

"That's what she says, too. My counsellor. But why? So I can become like the rest of you boobs?"

At the farthest, looking north, the city, its pointed roofs picked out in asphalt and copper, melted into a kind of forest, green ridges speckled more and more sparsely with brick and rising into blue hills, ridge after ridge, green to blue to a gray insubstantial as fog. This city spread so wide and multiform around and beneath us: it was more than the mind could encompass, it overbrimmed the eye; but was it all? Was it enough? It did not appear to be.

Downstairs, in the great fake-onyx, neo–Art Deco lobby, we tried to estimate how much a one-way ticket would cost. "Also," she said slyly, "there are travel expenses."

"Why am I always having to bribe you to do what's best for you anyway?"

"Because you think I'm nifty, remember?"

I had paid her three hundred for the abortion; this was surely worth less. She thought it was worth more, since it was longer-range in a way and involved her directly instead of some little unborn thing like a sardine. Happily, my statewide bank had installed an automatic teller in the lobby of the skyscraper, and its limit of cash payout was three hundred dollars. We settled for that. The machine, with a hum and some clicking, accepted my card, recognized my code word (AGNUS), and counted out with a rhythmic internal rumbling the necessary bills. DO YOU WISH ANY MORE TRANSACTIONS? I punched the NO button.

"Some day," I told Verna as I handed over the cash (bills so new they felt abrasive, like very fine sandpaper), "you may have to do without a nice uncle who gives you presents."

As she took the money I could see her wanting to laugh with the gaiety of it—of the fresh clean machine-fed bills, manna in their freedom hitherto from human touch—but then pulling herself back from a reaction so elemental, so immature. She teased me: "You seem down, Nunc. What's the matter? Isn't everything coming out just the way you wanted?"

"Promise me one thing," I blurted helplessly. "You won't sleep with Dale."

"With Bozo?" Now she did let herself laugh. The onyx walls echoed, her broad face between the crosses shimmered with mischief. "You have too many fantasies," she told me. "You know the kind of dude that turns me on. Dale's a non-turnon. He's not even evil, like you." In spontaneous mercy Verna gave me a kiss on the cheek; it felt like a drop of rain in the desert.

iv

For nearly four weeks I have been waking in my house to the clatter of little Paula's plaster cast scraping and bumping across our floors as she dauntlessly crawled here and there. Many times, as I sat in my study trying to force my mind through the prevarications and self-satisfying loops of theology, our little guest has sounded like a boulder being tumbled downstairs, only her accompanying prattle indicating that no catastrophe was, so to speak, afoot. Now, her cast has been removed, at the hospital—cool and proper Esther my companion instead of frantic, disreputable Verna, and none of the emergency staff the same—and the innocent child goes about whimpering, feeling she has lost part of herself.

This morning she was whimpering beside me in bed, where Esther had placed her as if ironically, in lieu of her own body. Paula, her irises inky and shiny and the whites of her eyes distinctly blue, was inspecting my bristly face with her little slobbered fingers and sharp miniature fingernails. "Da?" In the perfect convex surfaces of her corneas there were tiny squared images of the window beside my bed, with its stained-glass fanlight. "Da widey wake?"

It was Sunday; Sunday-morning light has a baleful quality, and there is an accusatory silence, with the lack of usual traffic. Coded birdsong can be heard in the trees. Church bells pathetically call. "Da up-up," Paula commanded.

A sweetish ache traversed the frontal lobes of my brain; we had been late at a little party last night. Ed Snea, in his bachelor digs, was celebrating his wife's willingness, at last, to give him a divorce. The hipless girl with Rapunzel hair whom he had brought to our party was present, as a kind of informal fiancée. Who would marry them? I had drunk too much and got into ugly arguments with Ed over demythologization and with a Nigerian M. Div. candidate over the efficacy of South African divestiture. All protest movements in America, I remembered shouting through the chemical tumult of alcohol being assimilated into my bloodstream, are nothing more than excuses for middle-class young white people to get together and smoke dope and feel morally superior to their parents. These rabid views of mine—where do they come from? They seem quite sincere as I spout them.

Paula gave off a delicate, powdery aroma as she warmed the bed beside me. I reached over to the leg, so touchingly flexible and small, that was now wrapped in a (pink) flesh-colored bandage, and lightly gave it a squeeze, to remind her of the missing cast. Her face underwent an anxious convulsion, her mouth pulling down and the lower lip protruding, showing its violet inner side. Satisfyingly, she began to whimper. I got out of bed; my gray pajamas were twisted into ropey creases by the night's restless sleep. It was time to switch to summer covers. I lifted the anxious child into my arms and carried her into the spare room, once a maid's room, that we had made into her room. I changed her diaper; her skin was delicious to touch, fine-grained and blemishless, like silk without the worminess. I had never before seen female genitals in so new a condition. They were sweet—two little lightly browned breakfast rolls fresh and puffy from the oven. I dressed her in corduroy overalls, with a bunny face sewn on the bib. Esther had found boxes of Richie's old baby clothes up on the third floor, behind her neglected paintings.

Where was Esther? Her absence felt like a presence, an electrical charge of silence in the house.

The shower was running behind the bathroom door. I went downstairs and used the toilet beneath the stairs. I sat Paula in a corner, where she deftly unrolled all the toilet paper. Richie was watching cartoons in the kitchen, his rapt face moronic in the flickering glow. I sat Paula in his lap and put half a sugar doughnut in her hand; instantly the lower half of her face was bleached and powdered sugar had drenched the corduroy.

Richie accepted her on his lap without complaint. Since her arrival he has grown more manly, protective, and tutorial; he is no longer the baby of the house. Their two faces turned to the television screen like flowers to the sun. Three faces, counting the one on her bib.

Through the kitchen window I could see the Kriegmans doing aerobics on their redwood deck. Myron was leading the rite, in what seemed his underwear; Sue and their daughters wore clownish outfits of luridly colored leg-warmers and leotards. They were performing disco steps, and pelvic rotations, in the dappled spring shade, to one of Bach's more upbeat fugues. So this was civilization and health. Nevertheless, Kriegman's belly and pseudo-mammae jiggled conspicuously. He did not look well. I think he has curvature of the spine, from bending over the microscope. He saw me spying and gave a hasty wave, out of rhythm.

What did Esther feel, pulling baby clothes from the third floor? When did she and Dale make love for the last time, and what did they say upon parting? She would take it upon herself to lighten the occasion, she being older and more familiar with finitude, trying to tease him up from his terrible heaviness of defeat into erectitude. Her naked body gleams at those points where bone presses flesh from within; her tongue and hands seek the light touch within the awful claustral ardor of his despairing embrace. He does not want to let go. She catches sight of her feet bare on the dirty mattress, their veins more conspicuous, more yellow and blue, than one of the Kriegman girls' (or Amy Eubank's) would have been; she then cannot stop being aware of her own body, a complex fragile costume to be some day painfully cast aside, while she caters to his, its raw boniness, its waxy skin, the fur of his buttocks and thighs and lower back defenseless as a puppy's belly, the touching tendony interlock where his arms and shoulders hinge and stretch, the acne along his jaw like a half-healed wound, his head on its long neck bowed in submission to this decree. She caresses with her right hand the long straight line of his neck and with her left the beautiful perishable hardness and length below, while her face behind its scrim of tears smiles, some impossible promise implied in her smile. . . . I could not picture it, quite.

It depressed me, trying to picture it.

One of these days, Edna must call, to discuss things. Her child, her grandchild. I have sent Verna to her as a message she must answer. Her voice will be roughened by all these years, but not in essence changed: vulgar, self-satisfied, platitudinous, sexy. Pleasantly pungent, like the smell of one's own body. Flat-tasting but oddly delicious, like the meals served up to me in our solitude by my mother, love-miserly Alma. The certainty of this contact, between now and death's certainty, felt to me like money in the bank, earning interest. Edna must call, and Paula would be taken away. Things had indeed worked out very well. Somebody had said that to me, recently. Who?

I poured a second orange juice and tried to decide, looking ahead, between Total and an egg. The Kriegmans were retiring from their deck, in single file, the females in their patchy garb gaudy as parrots. In Esther's garden the azaleas were mostly by, their shed hot-pink petals dissolving in the lawn, and the irises were coming on. She has been irritable and abstracted these recent days, and eats late at night, and sleeps more than usual. Most strangely, she has stopped watching her weight; I am sure she weighs more now than a hundred pounds. She came into the kitchen dressed in a crisp dark suit, with lace at her throat. Her hair was done up in a somehow triumphant sweep.

"Where on earth are you going?" I asked her.

"Obviously," she said, "to church."

"Why would you do a ridiculous thing like that?"

"Oh—" She appraised me with her pale green eyes. Whatever emotions had washed through her had left an amused glint, a hint or seed. In her gorgeous rounded woman's voice she pronounced smilingly, "To annoy you."

A Note About the Author

John Updike was born in 1932, in Shillington, Pennsylvania. He graduated from Harvard College in 1954, and spent a year as a Knox Fellow at the Ruskin School of Drawing and Fine Art in Oxford, England. From 1955 to 1957 he was a staff member of *The New Yorker*, to which he has contributed short stories, poems, and book reviews. He is the author of eleven novels and sixteen other books, including five collections of verse. Since 1957 he has lived in Massachusetts.

"Indisputably at the top of his craft" TIME

JOHN UPDIKE